WHERE THE CORN GROWS TALLEST

WHERE THE CORN GROWS TALLEST

A Tale of Mystery and Murder in America's Heartland

A Novel

SCOTT DOUGLAS PRILL

ISBN: 978-0-9908604-6-4

U.S. Copyright Certificate of Registration Number: Application submitted.

FOREWORD

When I finished the second editions of *Into the Realm of Time* and *From the Realm of Time,* I realized I had reached a proverbial crossroads in my writing. I could write another historical fiction novel centered during the Roman Empire, or I could switch things up and write a more modern novel. I chose to write a murder/mystery that takes place primarily in the fall of 1970.

The idea for this novel was inspired by the disappearance of a distant relative in the 1930s in a small town in Iowa. This relative's body has never been found. During the past decade, a situation developed in which there was the possibility that his remains were found in a footlocker in Wyoming. After DNA testing, though, it was determined the remains were not related to my family. The correct family was eventually identified. My relative's remains are still missing.

Where the Corn Grows Tallest is a work of fiction. The characters, events, agencies, and places are fictional; although, my memories of growing up in Iowa played a part in the story. There are references to major cities, such as Des Moines, Iowa, and significant events (e.g., the Vietnam War) that are real. After this Foreword is a Cast of Characters to assist you, reader, with the story.

Since I turned sixty, I have written three novels, including two editions of the Roman books, and several short stories. I will leave it up to the individual reader to decide whether they like the books and stories.

My point, though, is you are never too old to start something new or do something different. So, give whatever you're waiting for a try today.

A theme carried throughout my Roman books is how fleeting time is. And it seems the older one gets, the faster time goes. Experience something new; enjoy life and what it brings.

Scott Douglas Prill
May 2023

Cast of Characters[*]

Richard Franklin Frost: Brinson businessman, 1940

Ethel Frost: Richard Franklin Frost's wife, 1940

Wilber Roberts: Brinson constable, 1940

Suzi Thornton: Café owner in Brinson, 1940

Brent Theodore Frost: Fourteen-year-old freshman in Brinson

Tim Frost: Brent's father

Angela Frost: Brent's mother

Tom Woodhouse: Brent's friend

Ron Sands: Brent's friend

Billy Bridges: Brent's friend

Jack Osterman: Brent's friend

Ward Jenkins: Brinson native; killed in Vietnam

Bert Jenkins: Ward's father

Lola Jenkins: Ward's mother

Dale Jenkins: Ward's younger brother; Brent's friend

Reverend Graham McFadden: Presbyterian minister in Brinson

Janice Hinton: Owner of the Hinton General Store in Brinson

Bud Nichols: Employee of the Hinton General Store

Alice Nichols: Bud's wife

Lily Nichols: Bud's daughter

---

* Characters are listed by general order of appearance. Unless indicated otherwise, all characters appear in 1970.

Gary Knowles: Ward's friend; Vietnam War veteran

Carl Dinkins: Brinson resident

Chief Ellis Thompkins: Brinson policeman

Harry "Civil War" Templeton: Mayor of Brinson

Fred Barnes: Detective with the Iowa Crimes Commission ("ICC") in Des Moines

Clara Barnes: Fred's deceased wife

Delvin "Del" Robinson: Fred's partner at the ICC

Marge: ICC administrator

The Captain: Fred and Del's supervisor at the ICC

Robert (Rob) Franklin Frost: Richard and Ethel's son

Officer Peterson: Town of Manlo policeman

Shirley: Server at the D&R Drive-In restaurant

Gil: Bartender at the Thirsty Bull

Maxwell Sturgess: Owner and publisher of the *Brinson Bee* newspaper

Mabel Knuth: Employee of the *Brinson Bee*

Brenda: Employee of the *Brinson Bee*

Elmer Juntlo: Brinson town curmudgeon

Eldon Juntlo: Elmer's older brother; Brinson farmer

Wally Nelson: Reed County Deputy Sheriff

Dr. Henry C. Deisman: Reed County Medical Examiner

Cindy Williams: Freshman in Brinson; daughter of the town banker

Bea and Herbert Waller: Minnesota residents; relatives of Gary Knowles

Rose and Gene Hancock: Brinson farmers

Kevin Hogan: Environmental scientist with the Iowa Department of Environmental Quality

Cory Poleczyk: Hydrogeologist with the Iowa Geological Survey

Vince Riggins: Iowa Highway Patrolman

Deputy Yoder: Reed County Deputy Sheriff

Donald Reiss: Local fisherman

Harold Larken: Reed County Sheriff

Brinson, Iowa
1940

Chapter 1

Thursday, November 7

A rich darkness blanketed Brinson, Iowa, as the clock heralded dawn's emergence. The thick moisture that hovered in the air could not decide whether to be rain or snow, or even worse—freezing rain. The land felt cold as the last vestiges of autumn were about to be touched by the icy fingers of winter. Still, the ghosts of All Hallows' Eve lingered.

None of that mattered to Richard Franklin Frost. He was focused on finishing his shaving routine. When completed, he wiped the straight razor with a white cotton towel and dried his face. He cleaned his razor and placed his shaving kit back in the drawer and looked in the mirror.

Richard had a full head of white hair that he combed back. His forehead wore wrinkles he wished were not there. He reached for a small pair of scissors and trimmed a few errant moustache hairs. He was about to put the scissors away when he noticed a single nose hair that needed a quick trim. With that done, he put on his white button-down shirt and carefully slid each button into place. He checked to make sure his gold cuff links were positioned correctly. Richard finally tied his navy-blue tie in a double Windsor knot. He smiled at his image in the mirror.

I certainly don't look fifty-one, he told himself.

Ethel Frost stood in the kitchen over a new stove and oven. Today would be two eggs over easy, two pieces of bacon, a slice of white toast with butter, and a hot cup of coffee. Ethel made this breakfast for

Richard every morning—except Sundays when she substituted sausage for bacon.

"Good morning, Richard," Ethel said as her husband methodically walked into the kitchen.

"Morning," he replied. He reached for the daily newspaper and read the headlines before turning to the business page.

"Hitler is really stirring the pot over in Europe, don't you think?"

"I don't want another war. The Great War was bad enough. I'm sure our friends in Europe can contain Hitler. Is breakfast ready? I have a couple meetings this morning."

Ethel gently placed Richard's breakfast and a steaming cup of coffee in front of him. "With whom?"

"You know I can't tell you that. It's private."

"Everyone in town knows who your clients are. People sit outside the library and watch everything that happens on Main Street, including who goes in and out of your office."

"Yeah, I suppose … but you and all the other busybodies don't know what we talk about."

Richard turned to the sports page and appeared to read something interesting—or perhaps he didn't want to converse with Ethel anymore. Ethel sighed and made herself two pieces of toast, which she would eat after Richard left.

After fifteen minutes, Richard got up from his chair and went into the bathroom. He gargled, donned his suit coat that was hanging on the back of the bathroom door, and took one final glance in the mirror. He walked back to the kitchen table where Ethel waited for him. She held out a bag.

"Here's your lunch—a ham sandwich with a light spread of butter, Kitty Clover potato chips, a carrot, an apple, and a cookie."

"You'll be at Dorothy's this noon?" He already knew the answer.

"Yes, and remember, we play bridge afterward until four o'clock. For dinner tonight we're having roast beef with potatoes, gravy, and carrots. Don't worry—all will be ready so you can be on time for the poker game."

Richard smiled. Thursday was his favorite night of the week: Ethel's roast beef and poker in nearby Carlson, the county seat.

"Good. I'll be home at five-thirty sharp, and I need to leave at six-thirty. The boys want to start at seven, and I'd like to be there early."

Ethel had heard those same words before—so many times.

Richard put on rubber shoe covers, a Fedora, and a heavy black top-coat and pulled an umbrella from the stand. He strode over to Ethel, took the lunch bag and gave her a peck on the cheek. Impeccably dressed, he left for his office.

Ethel still wore her nightgown covered by a wool bathrobe. She would take a bath and do some minor house cleaning before heading to Dorothy O'Brien's. She looked forward to Thursdays as much as her husband did.

Richard and Ethel married in 1912 when Ethel was twenty and Richard was twenty-three. They had one son, Robert, who moved to Colorado immediately after he graduated from high school in 1935. Over the past twenty-eight years, the love Richard and Ethel once had for each other had turned into a marriage of convenience. Their lives became a settled matter; he lived for his work and poker, and she for her social life. Breakfast and dinner were about the only times their lives intersected.

Richard's insurance office was three and a half blocks from their house. Suzi's Café stood across Main Street from his office. Richard stepped inside the café, closed his umbrella, and left it by the door. Suzi, attractive in her white uniform, stood behind the counter.

Early risers in the café included a table of older farmers wearing overalls and a booth with two young businessmen in suits. They were at the café to appreciate more than the food.

"Hey, Richard," Suzi called out. "Nasty day out there. Is it slick out yet?"

"Yep. You, though, are looking fine today, despite the weather."

"Do you think it will snow?" she asked, ignoring his comment.

"Hope not. Did you find someone to shovel your sidewalk?"

"Not yet." Suzi Thornton was forty years old and recently divorced. Her ex-husband had moved to Des Moines with a schoolteacher from Carlson one year before.

"I'll take my usual black coffee and a Danish for Arleen."

"I'm sure your secretary appreciates your thoughtfulness."

"She always does." Richard winked at Suzi.

Suzi already had the coffee poured and the Danish in a bag. Richard ordered it every Thursday. Richard paid Suzi and smiled. "Have a nice day, if you can."

He reached for his umbrella and opened it once he was outside. It was a little brighter out now even with the heavy drizzle; perhaps the entire day would be dreary. *A good day for work,* he thought with a smile.

◢

Ethel returned from her bridge outing at about four o'clock. It had been a festive afternoon with the ladies, especially when Dorothy put brandy in the coffee.

She had dinner on the table at five-thirty sharp. On Thursdays, Richard would arrive home directly from his office and change into more casual attire. They would make small talk as they ate dinner together. At six o'clock, Richard would address a few housekeeping matters, such as reviewing the mail, checking his schedule for the next day, and using the bathroom. At six-thirty, he would leave for Carlson and his card game.

Tonight was different—very different. Richard never arrived home from work. Five forty-five, six o'clock, six-fifteen, and then six-thirty came and went—no Richard. Ethel's worry grew exponentially with each passing minute. *This has never happened before,* she quivered. If there was ever a man who followed a strict routine, it was Richard.

Ethel called Dorothy, followed by several frantic calls to other friends. Nothing—no one had seen Richard or heard anything about him today.

◢

Wilber Roberts sat at his dining room table with his dinner in front of him. The radio had just started broadcasting his favorite show, *The Adventures of Ellery Queen*. Roberts had been the Brinson town constable for thirteen years. Since his wife's death nine months earlier, the women of Brinson had steadily provided him with regular meals. Tonight's dinner had been prepared by Ethel. Her cooking was his favorite, and he couldn't wait to begin eating, but the abrupt ring of the telephone shook him.

"Constable Roberts—may I help you?" he said, annoyed that *his* time had been disturbed.

The voice on the other end combined panic and desperation. "He's gone!"

Roberts recognized the voice. "Ethel?" He had always had a bit of a crush on her.

"Wilber, do something. He's gone!"

"Who? Are you talking about Richard?"

"Who else would I be talking about? He didn't come home for supper tonight before his card game at the Elks like he always does! Something's wrong. I know it."

"Maybe he decided to go play cards directly after work. Maybe he didn't have time to stop by before he went to—"

"Wilber! You're not listening!" Ethel's tone was harsher than he'd ever heard it before.

"OK, I'll call the Elks in Carlson and see if he arrived yet. They should have started by now." Roberts gazed at his watch. *Seven-fifteen; yep, they'll have started.*

At nine o'clock, Constable Roberts knocked on the Frosts' front door. He had to park down the road because the street in front of the house was lined with automobiles. Dorothy opened the door and motioned for Roberts to come inside. He saw Ethel sitting in the middle of the living room sofa, a tissue in her hand. Louise Brickman and Ruth Aden sat next to her, and he heard the voices of several other women in the kitchen.

"What have you found out?" Dorothy spoke for the group.

"I called the Elks twice, once after I talked to Ethel and again just before I came here. No one there has seen him. They thought he was sick. I stopped by his office, and it was dark. I used my flashlight but couldn't see anyone inside. I called Arleen, and she said she didn't go into work today because she was ill. No one I've talked to has seen him, except for Suzi at the restaurant. She saw him first thing this morning. I have no idea where he is."

"What are you going to do?" Dorothy spoke again for Ethel.

"I called the county sheriff."

During the next two weeks, activity regarding Richard's disappearance picked up steam and reached a crescendo. The authorities interviewed every resident in town and followed every lead. No one had any idea what happened to the man. Ethel never spent a minute alone as her friends and pastor kept vigil with her.

As time passed and with no new information, the energy to find the missing man waned. Winter and the Christmas season arrived, and the town folk and authorities gradually lost interest. People moved their focus to farm prices and the specter of joining the war in Europe. By the fall of 1941, Richard's disappearance was given cold case status in Des Moines. Ethel had also moved on. Several men in the town started jockeying for her attention. After all, she was a great cook.

The case of Richard Franklin Frost was never solved. Several investigations could not uncover a shred of evidence pertaining to his disappearance. Multiple theories were expounded, ranging from running away to another life with a new wife to being a victim of foul play to being kidnapped by aliens. One thing was certain: he was never seen again. Richard Franklin Frost simply vanished into the gloom of that cold November day.

DES MOINES, IOWA
2020

Chapter 2

Monday, September 21

The front doorbell rang and the dog yelped, both of which woke the man. He was in his mid-sixties and the commotion had awakened him from a restless nap. He opened the door with one hand as he kept the other hand on the dog's collar while it voiced displeasure with a rousing chorus of barks and growls.

"Don't mind her," the man said as he looked at the unsmiling UPS deliveryman.

The stranger motioned to the package and to the signature line without saying a word. The man signed it and was handed the package.

"Thank you. Have a nice day," he said as he closed the door. "I've been waiting for this."

He eagerly opened the package and looked with pleasure at the bound manuscript as if he had found the Holy Grail. It was three hundred and fifty-five typed pages. The man walked to a large kitchen table and moved aside a newspaper screaming about the coronavirus pandemic. He set the manuscript on the table and poured himself a cup of coffee. He added a shot of whiskey to the cup, returned to the table, and adjusted a lamp.

"It's going to be a long night, Barkley," he said to the dog. "I should have named you Barks-A-Lot."

The light from the lamp reflected off his glasses. He opened to the first page of the manuscript and began reading the short prologue:

What shapes a person's life is different for each of us. For most people, it is many things, including the people we meet, the events we experience, and timing. For me, however, it was one brief period that set everything in motion and created the man I am today.

I had to write this book because the story must be told for the people who were there. I have waited so long to write and publish this book because I personally needed to face the demons that have haunted me for decades, and I have done so. I also wanted time to pass until the people involved in this story were deceased or would not be offended by or object to the story. My attorney gave me that advice.

And here it is. Everything in this book is true. It's not historical fiction. It's not based on enhanced memories—it is the truth. So help me God.

Barkley jumped up on her chair and stretched out, assuming a potential sleep position.

The man took a drink of his spiked coffee and continued reading.

IOWA

1970

Chapter 3

Brent Theodore Frost was born in Brinson, Iowa, on April 2, 1956. His parents were also born in Brinson, as well as three of his grandparents. The Brinson cemetery is littered with headstones carrying the Frost name. Suffice to say, Brinson has been home to the Frosts since it was incorporated in 1860.

In September 1970, Brent was a freshman at the Brinson Municipal High School. His class consisted of seventy-nine students. Brent was average in every way. He had a nice head of sandy brown hair. He tried to let it grow out, but at a certain length, he had a parental-forced session with the town barber.

By most accounts, he was a boy naïve about everything except sports. He viewed the senior boys as huge and the senior girls as advanced. He was invisible to the upper-class students, which was good because he avoided being the target of their pranks and teasing. Many of his fellow freshman boys weren't so lucky.

Brent wasn't particularly popular among his classmates, but he wasn't unpopular either. He had a core group of friends, including Tom Woodhouse, Ron Sands, Billy Bridges, and Jack Osterman, who shared a passion for all things sports. In summer it was baseball, in fall it was football, and in winter, basketball. Spring was a time of impatience, waiting for summer and baseball. Their idols were professional athletes. None of the boys had a girlfriend or had been on a solo date.

Brinson's population of just under two thousand people had changed little over the decades. There was a movie theater, bowling alley, grocery store, bank, library, newspaper, hardware store, café, gasoline service station, lumber yard, drug store, drive-in restaurant, barbershop, two taverns, several churches, and a K-12 school system. In other words, it had about everything you needed to survive—but it did not have what you needed to thrive.

You had to go to Carlson for a car dealer, swimming pool, fancy restaurant, real supermarket, or clothing store. Carlson was almost nine miles east of Brinson on Highway 40. Des Moines, the metropolis, was a little over an hour's drive from Brinson. A lot of trips were made by Brinsonites to Des Moines. After all, Des Moines was the state capital, and the buildings were more than three stories tall.

Life was good in Brinson. The full effect of the fallout from the Vietnam War had not been directly felt yet. The counterculture movement in California seemed like a universe away. There wasn't a drug issue, and the worst school violation was boys smoking in the restroom.

It was a time of innocence in Brinson. Brent was a part of that innocence—an innocence about to be lost.

Chapter 4

Tuesday, September 22

"You should've seen what I saw," Jack exclaimed breathlessly. Jack was the most physically developed of Brent's friends, and he started as a safety on the junior varsity football team.

"What are you talking about?" Ron demanded.

School had let out early for a teacher workshop, so Brent, Jack, Ron, and Tom had ridden their bikes to a grove of oak trees about a half mile south of Brinson, just off County Highway H. The road had recently been paved, which allowed the boys to race the half mile on the blacktop to the trees. There usually was little traffic on the road, particularly in the middle of the day.

The leaves on the old oaks were green on that late September day, but evidence of fall penetrated the leaf edges with brown and a tinge of orange. The boys brought a football to play catch with under the oaks. Jack also brought cigarettes to try. He offered them to the other boys, who all declined. After lighting up and taking a few puffs, Jack choked and threw his cigarette on the ground.

"That sucks," he said through a coughing fit.

He kicked the cigarette under some fallen leaves, igniting a small fire.

"Shit!" Jack yelled and stomped out the little flames.

"My mom and dad would kill me if I smoked," Brent said as he watched Jack finish swearing at the pile of burnt leaves.

Neither Brent's mom nor dad had taken up the habit, which was unusual in 1970 Brinson, when most adults smoked. Many of their offspring also smoked, although secretly.

"Geez, Jack. What's so interesting?" Ron returned to Jack's original comment.

"Last Tuesday, right before supper," Jack dropped his voice so low that even the oaks could not hear him, "I was riding in the alley by Hinton's house."

"Yeah, so what?" Ron rolled his eyes. Ron was the skeptic of the group. His parents forced him to play trumpet in the school band, but he had a growing fascination with the electric guitar.

"Mr. Bridges' car was parked on the side of the street where the alley comes out."

"He lives on the other side of town," Tom joined in.

"That's not the worst of it. I saw Mr. Bridges kissing Mrs. Hinton on her back porch. I then watched them go into the house and the curtains closed in a room upstairs."

"What were they doing upstairs?" Brent asked, not having a clue what this meant.

"If your mom kissed Mr. Bridges and took him inside your house, what do you think?" Jack looked oddly at Brent.

"God, that's Billy's Dad." Brent's eyes showed confusion.

"No shit! He's screwing around on Mrs. Bridges. And this ain't the first time I've seen his car around Hinton's house, either."

"It's cheating," Ron added. "I saw a movie about cheating—it's called adultery."

"That's one of the Ten Commandments," Jack nodded seriously. "We talked about it in church last week during the boring sermon."

"Where was Billy during this?" Tom asked.

All the boys knew the answer.

"He was at the 4-H meeting in Carlson. His mom drives him there every Tuesday night. They don't come back until nine o'clock," Jack added.

"I don't believe this could happen. Mr. Bridges has always been so nice to us. Billy seems happy." Brent kicked some leaves while hanging his head.

"It's for show," Jack said. "Mrs. Bridges can be mean. I've seen her yell at Billy and Mr. Bridges. She doesn't want Billy to hang around us so much anymore. We're bad influences. That's why he does 4-H, and she makes him practice the piano all the time."

"We are *such* troublemakers," Ron said sarcastically.

"I don't know about this." Brent was still skeptical.

"Grow up, Brent," Jack smirked. "This isn't middle school. Bridges and Hinton are screwing. It happens."

Silence fell over the group of four as they became lost in their thoughts about the Bridges and their own families. Brent was convinced his dad wouldn't cheat on his mom.

Jack broke the silence. "It's Tuesday. Meet at the alley by Hinton's house at eight-thirty tonight and let's see what happens."

Brent and Ron agreed, but Tom begged off—he had to write an essay on *Huckleberry Finn* that was due the next day.

Just before eight-thirty, the three boys assembled in the alley outside Janice Hinton's back door. It was dark, but the boys still hid behind a clump of honeysuckle bushes. The porch light came on, illuminating the area around the back door.

Art Bridges came out of the house and gazed into the darkness toward where Brent, Jack, and Ron were hiding. Even though Bridges could not see them, the three boys crouched even tighter in the bushes.

Bridges stepped back into the doorway and two arms fell around his shoulders, then he and Mrs. Hinton shared a lingering kiss. Without saying a word, Bridges disappeared into the dark.

The boys froze. *Did he see us? Is he coming after us in the dark?* Brent thought. After a few tense moments during which the boys barely breathed, they heard a car door shut. The motor started and the sound of the engine soon merged with other noises of the town.

The boys quickly clambered onto their bikes and vanished into the night.

Wednesday, September 23

No one really knew who leaked the details of the previous evening. It could have been Jack, Ron, or Brent, or a combination of the three. Sometimes a secret is too hard to keep. Word spread through the school like smoke from a fire fueled by wet wood—Mr. Bridges and Mrs. Hinton were seeing each other on the sly.

For Brent, Jack, and Ron, knowing something that no one else knew and sharing that with others to raise their status was exhilarating initially. But that feeling soon gave way to regret. Billy found out as the whispering and smirking continued behind his back. He was crushed and, to his dismay, found his friends avoiding him.

Thursday, September 24

Billy left school at lunchtime the next day and never returned. In the middle of the night, Mrs. Bridges took Billy and moved to Peoria, Illinois, where her parents lived. The storm had been brewing in the Bridges' household for years, and the public airing of the affair drove Mrs. Bridges to act irreversibly by moving out of town.

Art Bridges was an International Harvester representative based out of Carlson. He remained in Brinson for a week until he transferred to the Des Moines office.

Janice decided to remain in Brinson. She had roots there and needed to run her deceased husband's business, the small grocery store on the northwest corner of First Avenue and Main Street.

A letter without a stamp appeared in Brent's mailbox the day Billy moved. Inside was a handwritten note in red ink. The letters were thick and dark—the pen had been pressed hard into the paper while it was being written.

Brent—I know it was you who turned my life into Hell. Mom and Dad are divorcing, and I will get split between the two of them. I don't like Peoria or Des Moines. My life was good and now it's shit. If you hadn't snooped around, things would be fine. Now they aren't and you're to blame. I hate you and hope you have a crappy life.
William Bridges

Brent hid the letter and cried into his pillow that night for his lost friend and for himself.

⚜

Friday, September 25
On Friday, Brent sat quietly at a lunch table at school. Jack and Ron approached him.

"Brent, d'you see a ghost, or are you sick?" Jack asked.

Brent shrugged and hung his head.

"Did you get one?" Ron asked quietly.

"What?" Brent knew the answer.

"A letter." Ron continued, his voice more hushed.

Brent gazed up into a face that looked like his own.

"Yes."

"What do you think this means?" Ron's voice shook.

"Nothing," Jack interjected. "It means nothing. Billy is gone and we won't see him again. Forget it. Life sucks for some people. Be glad it's not us."

Chapter 5

Friday, October 2

"Barnes, don't forget it's your turn to get the coffee." The man's deep voice resonated down the hallway. "Don't screw it up."

"Crap," Detective Fred Barnes said to himself. *I forgot it's my turn to get the coffee and rolls. Damn!* "Yeah, Captain, I'm on my way."

Barnes grabbed his coat and checked his wallet for cash. Satisfied he had enough, Barnes left his office at the Iowa Crimes Commission in downtown Des Moines and walked down the hallway to the building entrance. Outside, he took a right turn and then another into the Made-Right Café.

"You're late, Fred. I didn't think you'd make it today." A gray-haired woman wearing a hairnet stood with her elbows on the white Formica counter holding a cigarette in her right hand. A large thermos and a paper bag sat to her left.

"Time got away from me, which seems par for the course these days."

"You doing OK?" The woman's husky voice hung in the air.

"Yeah, Hazel, I'm fine. I wish you wouldn't smoke, though. I quit and don't miss it."

Hazel brusquely smashed the cigarette into a round glass ash tray.

"Is it the usual amount for the coffee and rolls, Hazel? Three dollars?"

"Yep."

Barnes already had the money out and placed it on the counter. "There's an extra dollar for you. Have a good day."

"Thanks. You, too. Oh, and your tie isn't on straight."

Barnes looked down and saw she was right. The knot he had tied had drooped between the first and second buttons of his shirt and angled to the left. *I hate ties. I'm glad Hazel noticed this and not the captain,* he thought.

Hazel motioned without expression to a small mirror at the far end of the counter where no one was sitting.

"Thanks," Barnes muttered as he moved to the mirror.

Barnes strolled briskly out of the café, his tie in the appropriate position, and returned to the office building. In the breakroom, he placed the tall, coffee-filled thermos and bag of rolls on the round table. He unscrewed the thermos top and poured a small amount of coffee into a Styrofoam cup. He poked his head out of the lunchroom and called out, "Coffee and rolls are here."

"'Bout time," a voice answered back.

"You're getting slower, like an old man," another man said.

"I'll time *you* next week," Barnes laughed.

The sound of chairs scraping against the floor echoed in the hallway. Soon five men and two women entered the lunchroom.

Detective Delvin "Del" Robinson placed his hand on Barnes' shoulder. "Thanks, partner," he said as he headed to the pastry bag. Robinson was a slender Black man who never seemed to part from his three-piece suits. He was around fifty years old, although he would not disclose his exact age to anyone.

Barnes smiled and glanced at the wall in front of him. A bevy of wanted posters featuring men—and even a woman—stared at him. He stared back. *I would like to get you all, you pieces of shit.*

Barnes decided a pastry was not in his short-term future. He had a trim profile, but lately he had let his conditioning slide. As he approached forty-two, he was finding that he had to put more work into staying fit, so today he vowed to do better. He picked up his cup of coffee and ambled slowly to his office. He sat down at his desk and peered at several files scattered across it. He sighed and picked one up.

"Bradley Karl Garrett" was typed on the cover. Fred opened the file and read the first page. "Wanted for suspicion of spousal murder" was in bold letters. He sighed again and turned to look out the window. Cars were streaming by to unknown destinations. *Clara and I were going to take a road trip to California this summer. She wanted to see Big Sur, Muir Woods, and Yosemite.*

Barnes was picturing that heavenly vacation when a voice jolted him back to reality.

"Fred, are you all right?" Marge's coal black hair bounced off her shoulders as she talked. The piercing green eyes of the office administrator were soft and concerned, yet she spoke with her accustomed directness.

"Fine," Barnes said, unconvincingly.

"I see you are. So, I'm inviting you to our house for supper tonight. Herb is going to barbecue some T-bones, and I know he'll need your help. You have a reputation as the best griller in the city—isn't that right?"

"Maybe in the neighborhood." He flashed a forced smile.

"Six o'clock sharp, and you don't need to bring anything—just yourself and your talents on the grill."

"What about …?"

"I said you don't need to bring anything. Herb has Hamm's in the fridge. Steak and Hamm's—that's a good start." She grinned. "Yeah, I know what you can bring—a smile."

"I'll be there. And thank you."

Marge turned and left his office. The heels of her shoes clunked on the wood floor as she walked down the hallway to her desk.

A

After supper, Barnes helped Marge with the dishes while Herb cleaned the grill and ran an errand.

"You've gotta let things go, Fred. Clara was a wonderful person and wife, but she has moved on to a better place. You need to move on, too. Don't forget her, but move on. I hate to see you struggle like this."

"I know what you're saying. I think about that a lot. There are days when I just can't, though. I know she loved me, even if her family didn't think much of me. They thought I loved my job more than her, and that the stress of her worrying about me working at the ICC caused her cancer. They're wrong. I loved Clara more than anything. Yes, looking back, I wish I'd worked less and spent more time with her. That does pound my soul."

Barnes stopped drying the dishes, his brown eyes staring blankly out the window in front of him. "Her family would not speak to me at the funeral and hasn't since. I don't think they ever accepted me or my job, or maybe both. That makes me feel so inadequate as her husband."

"Yes, I remember. Listen to me, that's all crap. You two were the best couple I know, except of course for Herb and me." Marge smiled as she handed Barnes a pan to dry.

"If you look inside your heart, you'll feel the love that you and Clara had for each other. That's what's important, and it's that simple. You're a good man. Now, get busy here. You're falling behind." Marge waved her hand at a stack of freshly washed, wet dishes.

When Barnes returned home, he felt Clara's presence beside him and crumbled into bed. The pain of losing her was still almost too much to bear.

Chapter 6

Friday, October 2

Friday, October 2, 1970 will be remembered for a long time in Brinson. It was the day when the reality of war hit home. Private First-Class Ward Jenkins had been killed in Vietnam.

After a battle in March 1970, Ward disappeared and was designated as "missing in action." Recently, human remains were found by a South Vietnamese villager and turned over to the U.S. Army. The Army determined the remains were Ward's, and changed his designation to "killed in action."

Bert and Lola Jenkins, Ward's parents, had endured the anguish of several months of their son's MIA status hoping and praying he somehow was alive. They knew that possibility was highly unlikely.

Bert was home on that Friday morning. He had decided to start work later than usual. He owned the lumberyard in town and was confident his second-in-charge could manage opening the yard for business. Bert wanted to enjoy the sports pages and take his mind off Ward.

Lola was in the basement beginning the laundry for the week. There were several loads to do as their family could create piles in what seemed like a matter of hours. Their younger son, Dale, was in Brent's class.

The notice came quietly as two smartly dressed servicemen knocked on the Jenkins' front door. "Mr. Bert Jenkins?" the taller officer began when Bert answered the door.

"Yes," Bert answered.

"Is your wife home, sir?"

Bert felt a dry knot forming in his throat. "Yes. What's this about, officers?" he sputtered, knowing the reason for their presence.

"We would like to speak to you and your wife, sir."

"Lola!" Bert's voice trembled. "Please come here, now. Some army officers are at the door."

Footsteps could be heard coming up the stairs from the basement. "Army people? Why?"

Lola stopped in the dining room when she saw the somber, rigid posture of the uniformed officers in front of her and collapsed on the floor.

◢

It was difficult to tell who desired Fridays more—the teachers, the students, or the staff. It is fair to say it was a tie.

At nine-thirty in the morning, Brent Frost sat in first-year Spanish class. He was daydreaming as Mr. Leon droned on about verb conjugations. A knock on the classroom door shifted Brent out of his doldrums. Principal Harris walked in and bent over to whisper in the teacher's ear. Mr. Leon looked at his desk as Mr. Harris spoke. Mr. Harris finished whispering and straightened up while Mr. Leon continued to stare downward. Finally, the Spanish teacher tapped his desk with his fist and looked up.

"Dale, you are excused to go with Mr. Harris—now. Take your books."

The eyes of every student in the room followed Dale as he walked out, and Mr. Harris followed him. They all knew the story of Ward missing in Vietnam, and after Dale left, the tone of the class changed dramatically.

"Please spend the rest of the period on the worksheet in chapter five. The answers are in the back of the book."

Mr. Leon took off his glasses and his eyes were moist. The students sensed something was wrong and were as quiet as they ever had been.

After school, Brent met up with Jack and Tom in the hallway. "Dale was pulled from class early today," he announced.

"Why?" both boys asked simultaneously.

"I don't know. Mr. Harris came and got him, and Mr. Leon got very quiet. Something bad happened with Ward, I just know it."

†

Saturday, October 10

The funeral for Ward Jenkins was held eight days later. It was a big affair for Brinson. The lieutenant governor came with other dignitaries and an army colonel. Brinson's mayor, Harry Templeton, also attended, as well as all the town's councilmen. Reverend Graham McFadden gave a eulogy full of heartwarming stories of Ward's life that were a combination of the Reverend's memories and those of Ward's family members. At the end, he prayed the Jenkins family and the town could find solace and peace in Ward's return home, for the final time.

The Presbyterian Church overflowed during the service, and some had to listen through a squawky speaker in the basement. Others had to wait outside in the mild fall sunshine.

"I'm glad I didn't have to go in—too many people," Brent said to Jack and Ron outside the church. "Mom and Dad are in there, though."

Brent and Dale were more acquaintances than friends. Only Dale's closest friends attended the service, who told Brent afterward that there were a lot of tears and sad speeches. The speech by the lieutenant governor stood out, the boys said.

"He gave his life for his country. His ultimate sacrifice cannot be forgotten," the lieutenant governor had intoned. Brent felt a strong pull of sympathy for Dale.

After the funeral, the entire town and dignitaries moved to the cemetery. The procession was led by an Iowa Highway Patrol car followed by the hearse containing Ward's casket. The lieutenant governor's limousine with Ward's parents was next in line. Three army vehicles followed and, finally, well over one hundred automobiles.

The cemetery was located north of the town and across Highway 40. The Iowa Highway Patrol and Reed County deputies closed the highway and rerouted traffic so that the long funeral procession could cross the highway to the cemetery without interruption. Once everyone had found a place, more speeches were given and Reverend McFadden said a heartfelt prayer.

When he finished, seven army soldiers with rifles stepped forward in a straight line. Their commander gave an order, and they fired three rounds into the air and then stood at strict attention. Brent was frightened and enthralled at the shots. He had seen a gun before, but never heard one being fired except in the movies or on television.

The burial concluded with the solemn playing of *Taps*, and the participants and observers slowly left the cemetery. There was no rush as they wanted to pay their respects to a popular young man whose life was cut short by a strange war in a far-away land. It was a day to linger and ponder.

Brent got in his parent's car and looked back to the gravesite as they drove out of the cemetery gates. A shaggy looking man stood near the pile of soil by the grave. He had long hair and a brown wiry beard, and wore an army jacket, but it was rumpled and dirty. His disheveled presence was out of place in the immaculate cemetery surrounded by American flags.

Chapter 7

Monday, October 12

Brent wrestled with bad dreams most of the night. Thoughts of Billy Bridges and Ward Jenkins crept into his mind and hunkered down there. He also had a history paper due by Friday that he hadn't started yet. When he awoke in the morning, he did not look well.

"Are you feeling all right, honey?" his mother, Angela, asked.

Brent sat down at the kitchen table. "Yeah, just tired, Mom, but I can go to school."

"That's good." Angela's mind was elsewhere as she plopped a giant, gooey spoonful of oatmeal into a bowl and set it in front of him.

Brent took the carton of milk and poured a small amount into the bowl and stirred the mixture. When he was satisfied, he added a scoop of brown sugar on top. Angela placed a piece of buttered toast on a plate next to the bowl and went to the counter to fix Brent's lunch.

When finished, she handed Brent the paper bag. "I have to leave early today. I'm going to church to work on the fundraiser. I'll see you tonight, sweetie."

Angela hustled upstairs to get ready. When she returned, Brent had left for school.

The school day was uneventful, which was fine with Brent. His math teacher was out sick, and the substitute was clearly in over his head regarding the subject, so it ended up being a workbook day. Brent already knew the vocabulary covered in Spanish class. English, as usual, was a snooze fest. And in history, the teacher showed a film of some inane ancient Egyptian topic. In PE, he played flag football and scored a touchdown, along with most of the other boys.

Before dinner, Brent's attitude improved and he appeared in the kitchen, hungry. Angela, as usual, was a whirlwind of energy, doing several things at once. She tended to the meatloaf baking in the oven, mashed the potatoes, and stirred the corn seemingly at the same time—all while taking a telephone call from a friend. Angela was the prototype of a multitasker, whose curly, strawberry blond hair never seemed out of place.

Angela cheerfully hung up the phone and turned to Brent. "We'll have dinner in half an hour."

"Smells good, Mom." Brent's hunger dominated all other feelings.

"I'm glad to hear you're hungry, honey." Angela peered at the meatloaf in the hot oven.

A man's voice called out, "Brent, come here. I've got something for you to do before dinner."

Brent followed his dad's voice into the den. Tim Frost was a youthful-appearing forty-year-old who favored blue button-down shirts and a crewcut. Recently, though, he had begun to let his light brown hair grow out.

"I need you to go to Hinton's and get me a box of those cinnamon cookies I like. And get your mother a carton of milk. Here's five dollars. Bring back the change."

"OK," Brent answered like a robot, thinking of dinner. He took the money, went outside to his bike, and rode the four blocks to the store. He dreaded going inside in case Mrs. Hinton was there. *I know she saw us watching her and Mr. Bridges,* he thought.

As he wavered on his task, Brent heard a commotion coming from inside the Thirsty Bull Tavern across the street from Hinton's General Store.

"Get the hell out of here, you piece of scum," a voice yelled from inside the bar.

The door flew open and a large man with a butch haircut came out dragging something that was resisting leaving the tavern. A second man brushed against the doorframe and then another. Finally, the group yanked out a body. The large man plowed his fist hard into the crumpled figure's stomach.

"You're trash. You're a veteran, for God's sake, and you mock our great country," he bellowed. "Saying the war is wrong and Nixon is a killer are lies, asshole. You've insulted Ward Jenkins' memory and all the others who fought in Vietnam and for this country, including my cousin. You worthless disgrace."

Two other men kicked the fallen figure.

"Come in here again and we won't be so gentle." The large man pointed his middle finger forcefully at the body, and he and the others returned to the bar.

Brent, still on his bike, couldn't move as he watched the scene before him. He felt a light push on his left shoulder, which made him jump. Janice Hinton stood beside him and stared across the street at the beaten body.

"Bud, get out here, now!" she yelled back into the store.

She looked at Brent. "Help Bud and me carry him over here … please."

Bud Nichols emerged through the store entrance. "Over there, Bud," Janice shouted to him.

The two started across the street when Janice cried out to Brent. "Now!"

Brent quickly jumped off his bike, laid it on the ground, and ran with Janice and Bud to the battered figure. Janice raised the man's head gently, and Brent recognized him immediately. It was the bum who was standing in the background at Ward Jenkins' funeral.

"How are you? Where does it hurt?" Janice asked the figure.

He managed to say, "My gut and arm. They twisted it pretty bad."

"We're going to get you out of here and take you back to my store."

They started to lift him up when Bud noticed the army tattoo on the man's forearm.

The big man from the bar appeared in the doorway again. "Well, if it isn't the marriage killer helping a traitor. That's about right, ain't it, boys."

The man turned back to the bar door to shout something. When he spun back, he was face to face with Bud. Brent knew there would be a fight—a real fight this time.

"You don't talk to Mrs. Hinton that way," Bud snapped at the man. Bud's hands were closed into fists and veins stood out on his neck. "I served and so did he." Bud gestured to the beaten man. "Where were you, Carl? Oh, I know, sitting in this bar, drinking beer."

Bud was becoming angrier while Carl Dinkins stood his ground. No one spoke as the two men glared at each other.

Bud had spent two tours in Vietnam and suffered a wound to the head that affected him more mentally than physically. When Bud returned home, Janice gave him a job at her store. She needed help after her husband died. While a little limited in the mind from his wound, Bud was an excellent worker. And he was a physically dominating man. There was a saying in Brinson: You do not want to make Bud mad.

Gradually, Bud's intimidating anger deflated Dinkins' beer-fueled bravado. The thought of Bud's massive fist in his face made Dinkins wish for a way out.

"Bud, stand down." The voice came off to his side.

Bud reflexively stepped back and relaxed slightly. "Yes, sir."

Police Chief Ellis Thompkins surveyed the situation and came to a fast conclusion. "Carl, get the hell home right now and I won't press charges. Spend more time with ya family and less time here."

Although Thompkins' official title was Brinson Town Constable, he preferred to be called Chief. No one argued with him even though he was the sole policeman in town.

Dinkins pivoted and disappeared down the street without saying a word.

The battered man who was the subject of the incident sat up. Chief Thompkins bent down to him.

"Who are ya? I'm Chief Ellis Thompkins, the police here in Brinson."

"Gary Knowles," was the answer in a hoarse voice.

"I assume ya served in Nam?" Tattoos of the 101st Airborne adorned both of Gary's forearms.

"Yes, spent most of my time in Da Nang, some in Hue—all over. I hated it. Saw lots of brothers die. The war is a shit mess. Good for dying."

"How old are ya, son?"

"Twenty-two."

"I was in the military, too, Gary," Thompkins said, "but not in a war zone—too young for Korea, too old for Vietnam. Ya need to be careful around here. The Jenkins lost their son recently. They're popular here in Brinson. I hear ya been spouting anti-war crap. That's going to get ya in real trouble, worse than this. Why are ya here, anyway?"

"Ward was a good friend. We served together like brothers. I came for his funeral. I was there when he got killed in Nam. Us soldiers don't know if it was the VC, NVA, or our own people who killed him."

"What?" Thompkins asked, creasing his brow. He looked over his shoulder to the bar and quietly said to the group, "Let's get him over to the other side of the street—to the store. It'll be better there."

Thompkins and Bud helped Gary to his feet and slowly walked across the street. Janice led and Brent followed behind. They sat Gary gently on a flimsy aluminum chair outside the grocery store. Janice whispered to Bud, and he went into the store and returned with a bottle of Orange Crush.

Thompkins wasted no time questioning Gary after he took a sip. "What do ya mean you don't know how Ward died? We heard he went MIA and that communists killed him."

Gary hesitated, took another sip, and closed his eyes to relive the scene. "No, I know how he was killed. We were on patrol along a ridge at a point the locals call the Tiger's Lair on a warm humid day in March. We spotted Charley up ahead. You have to be careful, though. You think you have them and then BAM!" Gary slapped his palm onto his knee. "We were in a hell zone. Fire was coming ahead of us. It came in waves. Then everything flashed.

"The sound of the blast knocked me to the ground. I was out. When my senses returned, I looked around in the haze. Most of my patrol had been killed or injured by the blast or bullets. I crawled over to Ward. He was badly hurt. I called for the medic, but Ward died before the medic got to us.

"I passed out and woke up in a crowded hospital. I asked about Ward, but no one knew what had happened to him. I knew he was dead, though. I saw it. MIA was just a tag they put on him. I am grateful they found what was left of him.

"Why I lived and he died eats at me every day."

Gary fell silent, took a deep gulp of the pop and looked straight ahead at something no one else could see.

"Nope, sounds to me like the enemy got Ward." Thompkins' tone confirmed that he believed his own statement.

"Don't agree, Chief. The blast that blew a hole in him came from behind, where our artillery was. It was friendly fire."

"I don't believe ya," Thompkins said dismissively as he adjusted his hat on his bald head. "We're winning this war and I doubt shit like that actually happens. Ward was killed by the enemy and he's an American hero. Watch the news reports, damn it. There's nothing about friendly fire in those reports. We're killing thousands of those Viet Cong and the aggressors from the north daily. They're going to run out of men soon, and we'll win. Just ya watch!"

Gary sat up in his chair and bristled. "I was there, in person, sir. The government lies, Nixon lies. We're not winning the war and Ward was killed by our own military."

⋏

Chief Thompkins arrived home at seven o'clock on that Monday evening. The phone rang.

"Hello?"

"Good evening, Chief Thompkins."

Thompkins immediately recognized the raspy voice. "Yes, Mayor."

Harry Templeton was in his eighties and had been mayor of Brinson for more than forty years. The kids, and some adults, jokingly called him "Civil War" Harry because he was so old, though he was not a lightweight in Brinson's affairs.

"I heard there was a ruckus today at the Thirsty Bull."

"Yes, there was, but I handled it."

"I hear we have a drug-using hippie communist in town and he instigated the whole thing."

"Yes, but Carl Dinkins and some of his buddies were also involved."

"They're Brinsonites—good, tax paying folks. That Knowles character is a vagabond rabble rouser. Where's he now?"

Thompkins was embarrassed. "Not sure. He was with Janice Hinton last time I saw him."

"Christ, a vagabond and a tramp—both hate our great country. Clean this mess up, Chief, or I'll have to. Good night!"

Thompkins cursed when he heard the phone slam on the other end. "Ya conniving son of a bitch," he growled to himself. "The only reason ya're mayor is because no one else wants the job."

Chapter 8

Monday, October 12

Brent arrived home, shaken from his experience outside the Thirsty Bull.

His father frowned as Brent walked empty handed through the front door into the living room. "Where's the cookies and milk?"

After a pause, Brent shook his head. "I'm sorry, I forgot." He looked downward as he mumbled his response.

"How could you forget?" Tim asked, disappointed. "Do you still have my five dollars?"

"There was a fight at the Thirsty Bull. I saw it."

Angela hurried into the living room from the kitchen. "What? A fight?" she asked, worried. "Tell us."

"Carl Dinkins and some other guys beat up a man and threw him out of the bar. They were going to beat him some more, but Mrs. Hinton and Bud stopped them."

"Did someone call the police?" Tim asked.

"I don't know, but Chief Thompkins showed up pretty fast." Brent slid his hands into his pockets.

Angela moved close to Brent. "Who were they beating?"

"He's an army guy. He said he and Ward were friends."

"Was he the guy at the cemetery during Ward's funeral? Way in the back? Kind of outta sight?" Tim looked at Angela and Brent. "Yeah, he didn't look like a soldier. More like a hippie you would see in San Francisco."

"He said Ward was killed by our own troops and that President Nixon is a liar." Brent wasn't sure what those words meant.

"He said that?" Tim paced on the living room carpet. He stopped and stared out the window. After a minute, he turned around and said, "Brent, we're going back to the store. I want to talk to this man. Do you know his name?"

"I think he said his name was Gary something."

Tim and Brent drove to the Hinton General Store in the family's Plymouth Satellite. Tim entered the store first, followed by a reluctant Brent. Janice stood at the checkout counter. She had tied her straight dark hair behind her neck.

"Hi Janice," Tim began.

"Hi, Tim, Brent."

Brent's eyes focused on Bud behind the meat counter. Bud held a large shiny cleaver while he whistled a tune. *God, he's a scary guy*, Brent thought. *He could cut off Carl Dinkins' head with that thing.*

"Brent told me there was a problem at the Thirsty Bull today." Tim jerked his thumb in the direction of the bar.

Janice briefly summarized what had happened while Brent watched Bud aggressively trim several kinds of meat.

"What about the young man? Gary, I think that's his name." Tim glanced at Brent.

"Yeah, Gary Knowles. He learned that you don't say certain things to certain people, particularly rednecks in a bar." Janice's eyes sparked anger.

"Did he actually say that Ward was killed by friendly fire and the government is lying about the war?"

"Yeah. He was there. You and I and Carl were not, so I believe him. We shouldn't be over there. I've been telling people that for years, but most don't listen or want to listen."

"Where is Gary now?"

"Bud dropped him off at my house." Janice lived in a well-kept white, two-story, three-bedroom, two-bathroom house located in the south-eastern part of Brinson, about eight blocks from the store.

"I have a basement apartment that I rent out from time to time. It has a separate entrance, and he can't enter the house through the basement unless I unlock the door. He can stay there for a couple of days until he recovers from his beating. He doesn't want to see a doctor. He's afraid they will do something to him."

"Like make him better?" Tim noted sarcastically.

Janice frowned and Tim put his palms up in a gesture of peace.

"Is that wise? Letting him stay at your house? You know nothing about him."

"Why not? I'm already ostracized here in Brinson. Another layer won't hurt me."

"Be careful, though. See that Bud walks you home. I don't know what the Jenkins' will think of Gary's presence in Brinson. We do know what Carl and his group think. I'll have Angela call you tonight."

"Thanks. You and Angela are good friends."

Tim started to walk out of the store, preoccupied. He suddenly turned around and blurted out, "Brent, we forgot again. Get the cookies and milk, and add a box of Frosted Flakes."

Brent dutifully complied. On their way home, Brent asked his father, "Is Mrs. Hinton going to be OK?"

"Yes, she will be. She's taking a stand on something that's unpopular—she believes that the Vietnam War is being fought on a bed of lies."

"What do you believe, Dad? Do you agree with Mrs. Hinton or Carl Dinkins?"

"I used to think the war was justified. Now, I don't know. I have my doubts."

"What about Mrs. Hinton and Mr. Bridges?"

"That's all in the past. It doesn't involve us—move on."

Angela met Tim and Brent at the door when they arrived home.

"How is everything? How's Janice?"

"She's fine for now. It seems our stranger is a Vietnam veteran and a friend of Ward's. His name is Gary Knowles, and he is vocally anti-war. That set Carl and his bar buddies off on him."

"Oh dear. Janice is no supporter of the war, either."

Tim shot a glance at Brent. "Shouldn't you wash up for dinner?"

Brent took the hint and left his parents alone.

When Brent was out of sight, Tim said, "Gary is staying at Janice's until he gets better. She has that vacant apartment in her basement. She'll be fine as long she uses her head."

"That's one worry. The other is the whole town will find out soon enough that Gary is staying at her house. You know town gossip. And that won't be good for Janice or Gary. She has enough problems already."

"Yeah," Tim shrugged, "and I'm thinking more people will boycott her store. Throw in Dinkins and his buddies, friends of the Bridges family, and we're not sure where the Jenkins stand."

"Add in Mayor Templeton. Janice told me that he has called her out several times as a trollop and traitor to our country. He says loudly that he only shops in Carlson." Angela rested her clenched fists on her hips. "But Janice is my friend, and I—we—will support her."

"I said you would call her tonight." Tim sucked in a deep breath. "Our quiet little town is going through some troubles."

Chapter 9

Tuesday, October 13

The following morning, Brent was riding his bike past Janice's house on his way to school when he spotted Gary sitting on the stairs. He was smoking and had a paper bag by his side. Something compelled Brent to ride over to the veteran.

Gary squashed the cigarette under his worn sandal as Brent rode up. The dissipating smoke did not smell like any cigarette Brent could recall. "Morning, kid."

Brent crinkled his nose at the weird odor.

"It's a medicinal cigarette. I need it to help me." Gary changed the subject, "What's your name, kid? I don't think I caught it yesterday."

Brent hesitated then told him. "Brent."

Gary reached for whatever was in the bag and pulled back sharply as if a wasp was inside. Instead, it was a partially drunk bottle of Jack Daniels.

"What's in there?" Brent pointed at the bag.

"Nothin', kid. Just a bottle of pop from Hinton's store."

"If it's pop, why is it still in the bag?"

"To keep it colder. I like it that way. Maybe I could give you some money to buy me another bottle. I've been advised by your town cop not to venture downtown. By the way, thanks for being there yesterday. You helped."

"I did?"

"Sure, kid."

"Aren't you afraid you'll run into Carl again?"

"Nope, I'm not afraid of him or anyone else in your town. Now over there," Gary pointed to the east, "that is something to be afraid of."

Brent shook his head, confused. "Who's over there?"

"In Nam you can't trust anyone—the Cong, our allies, us."

"That doesn't make sense. Not even our own soldiers?"

"Seems that way, kid. If I were you, I would do whatever it takes to avoid joining the Army and, for God's sake, ever going to Nam."

"You knew Ward pretty well?"

"Yep, we were blood brothers. Many of us were. That's what gets you through the shit—until it doesn't. Sorry, wrong word."

"Did you ever kill anybody over there, Mr. Knowles?"

Gary stared hard at Brent for several seconds. "That's between me and whatever god is out there, assuming there is one. I don't like to talk about the war, kid."

"You don't believe in God?"

"Nah. I did once, a long time ago, but not anymore."

"That's sad." Brent noticed Gary was fidgeting back and forth, rocking.

"You believe in what you want, kid, and so will I. I need to go inside now. You've tired me out with all your questions." Gary flashed Brent a slight smile.

Gary stood up and his eyes appeared glazed over. "Remember what I told you, kid. You'll be better off if you do. Thanks for coming by." Gary retreated into Janice's basement apartment.

Brent reached school and couldn't wait to tell Jack during first-period P.E. about his talk with the strange man.

"You'll never guess who I just talked to."

"Hopefully, no one to do with Billy." Jack's face was screwed up in puzzlement as he flung a worn football to Brent.

"No, no, nothing to do with him." Brent had forgotten about Billy since the fight at the Thirsty Bull.

"Well, come on, then." Jack gestured for Brent to toss the football back.

"That man who was at Ward's funeral. His name is Gary Knowles, and Carl Dinkins beat him up at the Thirsty Bull yesterday."

"Dinkins is an ass and a drunk." Jack flipped the football between his hands.

"Mrs. Hinton, Bud, and Chief Thompkins broke it up. Gary is staying at Janice Hinton's." Brent wanted to get to the point of his story.

"Wonder if he's picked up where old man Bridges left off." Jack stopped tossing the football and grinned at Brent.

"No. He's staying in her basement until he moves on."

"Yeah, when he moves on up to her room. We all know what kind of woman she is."

"Shut up, Jack, and listen. Gary is a Vietnam veteran. He fought side by side with Ward. He said he saw Ward get killed by our own men."

"What? You're kidding." Jack focused on Brent's face.

"That's what he said—American soldiers."

"Jesus, I don't believe it."

"Well, you can ask him yourself. We can ride by Janice's after school and see if he's out. He is not a bad guy. He looks rough and smokes weird smelling cigarettes."

"Gee, I don't know," Jack said diffidently, his bravado waning.

"He's not going to hurt you. Look at me, I'm fine."

"Let's get Tom and Ron. Strength in numbers, and all that."

⋏

Curiosity is a powerful persuader, and after school the boys rode to Janice's house.

As expected, Gary was outside. He was raking a pile of leaves from the dying elm tree on the west side of the property.

"I see you've multiplied," Gary quipped to Brent as the four boys rode up. Jack, Ron, and Tom straddled their bikes, unsure whether they might have to flee in case Gary turned into a daytime werewolf.

"You here to see the mad soldier?" Gary stared directly at Brent.

Brent felt no fear, unlike his three comrades. "I brought my friends over to meet you, Mr. Knowles."

"Yeah, I'm Gary Knowles." He looked at the other three boys one at a time from right to left like an officer inspecting his men. "And you are?"

Brent pointed to each of them, "That's Jack, Ron, and Tom."

"You don't look like an army guy," Jack blurted out.

"You don't know squat, kid," Gary said sharply. "How am I supposed to look?"

Gary wore faded jeans and a flannel shirt. A worn Chicago Cubs baseball cap was tilted backwards on his head. Scuffed combat boots peaked above the small pile of leaves. He had a straggly beard that covered most of his face. It hadn't been trimmed in weeks. Gary's eyes were bloodshot without any evidence of tears. He was an oddity to the boys.

"I told the guys you fought in Vietnam. You were with Ward." Brent wanted to get to the reason they were there.

"Yeah, that's true. Ward and I and lots of other men served this country with blind eyes."

"My dad says it's a righteous war," Jack retorted. "We have to stop the communists from taking over Vietnam and the rest of Southeast Asia."

"Bullshit!" Gary hawked a loogie into the leaf pile. It turned into a bout of coughing. At the end, Gary reached into his shirt pocket, plucked out a tissue and blew his nose. As he did, the shirt lifted, revealing the hilt of a knife poking out of a large, worn leather sheath attached to his belt.

Gary saw the surprise on the boys' faces and quickly pulled his shirt back over the sheath. "I always keep my friend with me. I can't have a gun, so I have my knife. It's for protection and skinning squirrels and other varmints." Gary laughed as the boys edged their bikes back a foot.

"Did you kill anyone with that in the war?" Ron pointed to the knife.

"As I told your friend," Gary glanced at Brent, "I don't talk about the war."

"Why?" Jack asked. "I would think people would want to hear your story."

"Some would, most wouldn't. In this town, with Ward's memory still strong, they wouldn't. They want to think Ward was a valiant soldier fighting against the godless communist devils."

"Was Ward a good soldier?" Tom edged his bike forward slightly.

Gary relaxed. "Yes, yes, he was. He was a credit to the Army. It's too bad the Army didn't return the favor. If we hadn't gotten involved in that war, Ward would still be alive, and I wouldn't be here."

"Were you a good soldier?" Ron asked hesitantly.

"Of course, he was," Brent interjected. "He went when others didn't."

"Thanks, kid," Gary smiled, "but you don't know that any more than your friends." He paused. "Yeah, I was a good soldier. I trusted my government and then they lied and lots and lots of brothers died, or should have when they were horribly wounded."

"What was it like over there?" Visions of John Wayne's idyllic Green Beret movie filled Jack's head.

"It was hell, kid. Not like the hell your minister preaches about, but real hell—blood-and-guts hell. There were so many times we didn't know if we would be alive in the next minute or have some damned booby trap wedged in our chests or step on a mine and, if lucky, lose just a leg or get shot in the head. Shit! I wouldn't wish it on anyone."

Jack's vision faded.

Gary was tiring and the boys needed to go.

"Thank you, Mr. Knowles," Brent said as they turned their bikes around.

"Listen to *Fortunate Son* by Creedence Clearwater Revival. It may give you a perspective of things." Gary slung the rake over his shoulder like a rifle.

Brent and his friends rolled off down the street, talking.

The boys did not realize it, but the fabric of normally quiet Brinson had been torn. The affair involving two of its more prominent citizens, Janice Hinton and Art Bridges, shook the town's morals. Then, against hope, Ward's death shocked it. There had not been a war casualty in Brinson since World War I. A final blow was Gary's appearance, a veteran soldier who, to many, should have been a patriot, but instead gave the strong impression of being un-American.

The tight-knit community was about to undergo further rupture.

Chapter 10

Tuesday, October 13

Fred Barnes' night was disrupted by a cascade of weird, bad dreams. He awoke after each one and couldn't fall immediately back to sleep. So, he would pace around the house sipping water from a cup crusted with toothpaste residue and then visit the bathroom. Finally, he would tire and fall back asleep, only to have the night visions reappear.

In the most traumatic dream, a faceless man wearing a dark striped suit kidnapped Clara and took her to a large cavern with infinite passageways. Barnes could hear her cries for help, but could not find her. "CLARA! CLARA!" he called out in his sleep.

Barnes woke up in his bed in a full sweat. When he finally fell asleep near dawn, he had pulled the covers over his head and overheated. He sat up, holding his moist head in his hands for several minutes, muttering, "Oh God, oh God." He said a quick silent prayer to God to look after Clara. *God, I hope Clara is in Heaven and not …*" He couldn't bear to think of the alternative.

Barnes left his bed and escaped to a pleasantly cool shower, which made him feel better. He pondered the dream while he showered and realized what it was—a cry for help. He knew Clara was not coming back. She was in Heaven with all the other angels. She would be all right and so would he, in time. He smiled slightly and brushed his thick wavy brown hair away from his eyes. After two strong cups of Folger's coffee and a tie correctly in place, he was ready for the day.

Barnes arrived to work at the Iowa Crimes Commission and thought he felt fine. His face revealed a different story.

"Morning, Marge."

"Good morning to you, too." Marge squinted at him.

Barnes didn't pick up on the cue and walked to his office. He set his coat and briefcase down on his desk and ventured to the kitchen for another cup of strong coffee.

"Jesus, Fred. Did you wrestle a bear last night?" Robinson opened his eyes wide at Barnes and smiled.

"What? Why do you say that?"

"Look in a mirror, man." Robinson pointed to a small mirror splattered with food hanging by the counter in the kitchen.

"I slept poorly last night. I'll be fine—especially with some more coffee. Did you make this pot?"

"No, sir, Marge did. She doesn't like my coffee. She says it tastes like something drained through a pond. I disagree, of course. My coffee gives you a jolt to get going in the morning. I feel good, man."

"What about Celia?"

"My wife makes her own coffee. She says mine is too strong and gives her the jolt in the john. So, we have two coffee pots—mine and hers. It works."

"What are you working on, Del?"

"Remember that Washburn kidnapping in Lewisburg?"

"Sure. Happened a couple weeks ago."

"We haven't located the victim or the perpetrators yet, but we have some solid leads." Robinson stirred a couple sugar cubes into his coffee and took a slow sip. "Needs more, man." He shook three more cubes from the box into the cup.

"Jesus. And you're so slim." Barnes shook his head and poured his own cup. "No sugar for me. If you need some help with your kidnapping case, let me know. I'm kind of in a lull. The captain seems to be leaving me out. You know, by now the kidnapper usually would have killed the victim."

"You're right. The keyword is 'usually.' This time, though, I'm hopeful she may be alive. Being eighteen and attractive, she may have more long-term value to the son-of-a bitch who took her. I haven't given up yet, man." Del took another sip of his coffee and grimaced.

Barnes grinned as he grabbed his cup and returned to his office. The two were partners who complemented each other. Robinson was thoughtful and effective in his approach to cases, which served to temper the more impulsive actions of the younger, energetic Barnes. He knew Robinson was a bulldog who would not give up easily.

Barnes sat at his desk peering at Garrett's file and thinking about last night's nightmare. He pivoted his chair to scan the surroundings outside the window.

Marge came into the breakroom after Barnes left and stared at Robinson holding the box of sugar cubes and sighed. She pointed toward Barnes' office. "How's he doing?"

"It's been well over a year, and he still looks lost. The captain won't give him any challenging work because he doesn't trust that Fred can handle it."

"He's a good detective. He just needs a case to take his mind off things."

"Yeah, I know. He should see that state psychologist over at the Wells building. But he won't." Robinson shrugged. "Can't force him to go, man."

Robinson started to leave for his office when a young man wearing a black tie ran up to him.

"Detective Robinson—a call came in about the Washburn kidnapping. You'll want to take it."

Chapter 11

Tuesday, October 13

Brent said goodbye to his friends and returned home after his visit with Gary. His dad was in the garage sorting through a box of junk waiting for a late supper.

"Dad, can you play the song *Fortunate Son* by Creedence Clearwater Revival for me?"

"What?" Tim was surprised by his son's request.

"I know you have the record. I've seen you listening to it. I think I've heard it."

"Yes, I have it. Why do you want to listen to it? Ah, I didn't think you had any interest in the music your mom and I like."

"Mr. Knowles said I should hear it to understand the Vietnam War."

"When were you talking to him?" Tim's eyebrows rose.

"Just now, and he said the war was bull ..." Brent caught himself before uttering the last part of that word.

Tim frowned. "Don't swear. It's unseemly, especially for a young man."

"OK, fine. But can I hear it now?"

"Let me finish going through this box. Your mother wants it out of here." Tim winked at his son.

Brent's interruption gave Tim a wanted break, and he wandered into the house and headed straight to the stereo system in the family room. He sorted through his record collection and found the requested album. He placed it on the turntable and called out, "Brent, come in here if you want to hear that song."

In seconds, Brent scooted into the room and stood in front of the speakers. His dad took the arm and gently placed the needle on the record at the right place for the song. After a few crackles, the music began. It was three simple verses with a powerful refrain.

"Play it again," Brent said as the song finished.

"Please!" Tim said as he focused on placing the needle back on the desired spot.

"Yes, please. Thanks."

The song played again. When it ended, Tim put the arm back in place and turned to Brent.

"Do you understand what the song is saying?"

"No, not really."

"When you have a war, like Vietnam, some people want the war and reap the benefits. Others aren't so lucky and pay the price."

Brent stared at the floor for a minute and looked up at his dad. "Who benefits?"

"The people who make the guns and bombs and say the cause is worth it," Tim said with a hint of bitterness.

"And who pays the price?"

"The unlucky ones who fight and are wounded or killed, and their families."

"Like Ward Jenkins?"

"Yes, like Ward and, I suppose, Gary and Bud."

"But Mr. Knowles and Bud are still alive."

"We don't know what happened to Gary over there. We do know Bud's mind was injured." Tim tapped the side of his head.

"Did Ward want to fight in Vietnam, Dad?"

"I don't have the answer to that. He went over there without question and served his country well."

"Is he a hero?"

"Yes, he and Gary and Bud are all heroes in my mind."

Brent thanked his dad and went to his room after supper. He tried to do his algebra homework, but instead read comic books and fell asleep.

Wednesday, October 14

In the morning, Brent again rode his bike past Janice's house. To his dismay, Gary was not outside. After school, he stopped by again and spotted Gary sitting on the stairs smoking.

"Well, kid, you're back," Gary said, mashing an odd cigarette into the ground with his hand. "Glad to see I didn't scare you away."

"Nah. What's that cigarette, Mr. Knowles?" Brent pointed to the ground.

"What the hell, I'll tell you. It's marijuana, and it's medicinal for me. Not for you, though. I advise you to stay away from it and any other drugs." Gary's eyes were glassy.

Brent squinted in confusion. "If it's bad for you, why do you smoke it?"

"It helps me forget stuff that I want to forget."

"War stuff?"

"Yeah, that's it, war stuff."

"Can you buy marijuana at the drug store?"

"Nope, you can't get it a drug store. I get it through personal means. Don't tell anyone about this. They wouldn't approve, and neither would your town cop. It'll be our secret. OK?"

"Yeah, sure."

"Did you listen to *Fortunate Son*?"

"Yeah, my dad and I played it a couple of times. I like it. It's kind of sad, though. My dad said the ones who start the war get rich from it, and they aren't the ones who fight."

"Or die," Gary added. "Or carry the scars."

"You weren't fortunate, were you, Mr. Knowles?"

"No, I was drafted into the war, like Ward. Ask your dad about the draft, and now there's a lottery draft. It's all shit." Gary stopped. "Sorry."

Brent sat on the ground opposite from Gary, silent, rubbing his hands.

"I can tell something is eating at you, kid. Want to get it off your chest?"

Brent paused and took in a deep breath. "My folks don't even know— a few of my friends do, though." Brent debated his next words carefully. "But this is our secret—like your marijuana." Brent looked to Gary for confirmation.

Gary nodded, "Relax. Go ahead."

Brent launched into the Billy Bridges saga. The more he talked, the more it became a confessional. At the end of his monolog, Brent looked to Gary as a spiritual leader.

"We all make mistakes—if you call that deal with the Bridges boy a mistake."

Brent looked puzzled.

"The way I see it is the Bridges family was at its end anyway. You just sped up the inevitable."

Brent hadn't thought of it that way. "I still feel bad for Billy. He didn't deserve what happened to him."

"It's called collateral damage, kid. Sometimes innocents are hurt when targets are hit. Happens in war all the time. You don't hear much about civilian casualties, but they happen a lot. That's what happened to your friend—collateral damage. He'll get over it and so will you."

"But aren't you still getting over the war?"

"Yes, but war is a lot different than your dust-up with your friend. It may not seem like it to you now, but it is."

Gary slouched back and eased his head onto a stair and closed his eyes.

"I'm tired. I need to sleep. Stop again soon. And remember our secrets."

"Yes, sir." Brent rode his bike home.

There, he waited until his father came home from work and said, "Dad, I saw Mr. Knowles again today. He said he and Ward were drafted into the war. Can you explain that? Mr. Knowles was too tired."

At supper, Brent and his parents discussed the war in general and Brent's conversation with Gary in particular. As promised, Brent did not mention Gary's marijuana use.

Afterward, Brent was conflicted. His thoughts about the glory of war and readily defeating enemies that he had seen depicted in movies and on television were in stark contrast with what he had heard from his parents and Gary. His mom and dad also appeared ambivalent about his contact with Gary, a stranger, which seemed unusual. He was developing sympathy and affinity toward the veteran.

⅄

At dinner time, Janice brought a plate of pork chops, mashed potatoes, and peas down to Gary. When he answered the door, the odor of marijuana competed against the fragrance of a delicious dinner. To Gary, the look and aroma of the food was irresistible. To Janice, the marijuana odor was overpowering.

"I had some leftovers and thought you might want them." Janice coughed.

"Sure, thank you. I'm not much of a cook. I tend to open cans and eat what's inside. I did a lot of that in the Army." He ignored Janice's cough and look of disapproval.

Janice pushed ahead. "I would like to talk more with you about the war and your experiences sometime. I would like Bud to listen, too. I think it would do you both some good. Bud has nightmares and it scares his wife and daughter."

"I don't like to talk about the war. Most of my experiences were bad. But I will, for a fellow vet." Gary eagerly took the plate of food.

"Good. We can meet in the back room at the store. I'll close for a bit. And I don't need to be with you the entire time."

"When? A lot of your townsfolk don't like me much."

"How about one-thirty tomorrow, after lunch? We aren't usually busy then. And I'm not concerned about what some townspeople think."

Gary nodded. He couldn't wait to get started on the food in front of him.

"Please make sure what you're smoking is put out completely. I don't want the house to burn down on account of you leaving a blunt burning, should you pass out."

Gary smiled. "You smoked joints before?"

"Yes. Good night." Janice turned to leave.

"One question. What happened to Mr. Hinton?"

"He died in a hunting accident a couple years ago. He tripped on a log and his gun went off into his chest. It's important to keep the safety on."

"I'm sorry. Sounds like another version of death by friendly fire."

"Yes, I suppose so." Janice started up the stairs and turned back as Gary cleared his throat.

"Be sure you keep the door locked between the apartment and the house." Gary looked straight into her eyes.

A shiver swept through her.

"Why?" she asked hesitantly. "Should I be worried?"

"I like locked doors," he answered and began eating.

At three o'clock in the morning, Gary woke from a fitful sleep. He peered over at the staircase leading up to the main house. In one flowing movement, he sat up and got out of bed. Silent as a cat following the trail of a mouse in the dark, he climbed the stairs to the door. He reached for the door handle and tried it. The handle would not turn. Gary gave the door a light push, but it did not move.

"She did lock it. Good girl, good girl," he said to himself.

Gary went back down the stairs to a cloth-backed chair. He sat there naked, staring into space, until morning.

Chapter 12

Thursday, October 15

The next day at one-thirty sharp, Gary walked into the Hinton General Store. A brief October rainstorm had shot through the town and soaked everyone who wasn't under cover. Gary didn't mind being wet and shook the rain off his poncho.

"I learned to not mind the rain from my time in Nam," he told Janice as he flipped the poncho over his head. A small puddle accumulated at his feet. "Sorry," he grunted.

"Go to the room on the left, down the hallway." Janice pointed at the short hallway. She grabbed a towel and wiped up the floor where Gary had stood.

Gary did as he was told and sauntered down the hallway to the room and went inside. The walls were ringed with shelves where the overflow inventory of dry goods was stored. The center of the room contained a card table with four chairs. The table was stained with an unknown substance that looked as if it could not be completely removed.

Gary heard Janice's voice. "Bud, close the store and come on down to the stock room."

Within a minute, Bud entered the room, unsmiling. He wore a butcher's apron blotched with blood stains.

Janice followed him and closed the door. She motioned for the two men to sit. Janice was carrying three bottles of Orange Crush and placed one in front of each man. She then took a seat.

The contrast in appearances among the three could not be more striking. Bud, clean shaven with a short crew cut, was naturally strong. The tan long-sleeve shirt underneath his apron could not hide his bulging biceps. Gary's thin, wiry shape was covered by jeans and a rumpled sweatshirt. His brown bushy hair blanketed his head and his beard masked much of his face. To Janice, it appeared he had taken a shower and lightly trimmed his beard for their meeting.

Janice wore a bright white button-down blouse. Her pale complexion set off her straight, shoulder length hair that shifted between hues of deep brown and black depending on the lighting. She had green eyes that glistened when there was a subject that interested her, and she favored shades of reddish-orange lipstick.

"That's the strongest drink we have here, Mr. Knowles." She pointed at the pop.

"Fine with me, ma'am," Gary took a pull from the bottle.

"Bud, here, would like to talk about your time in Vietnam. We believe it will do him some good. I'd like to listen, too."

"Sure, Bud. What do you want to talk about?" Gary looked directly at Bud. "First, though, call me Gary."

"Where'd you serve, Gary?" Bud asked hesitantly.

"I was drafted, then I volunteered and qualified for the 101st Airborne. We went to lots of provinces, hamlets, and such. I don't recall the names of most of them. They all sounded similar. For part of the time, we were based out of Da Nang."

"I enlisted. I was in an artillery unit. I don't remember where, except one time we were near a trail." Bud scratched his head trying to remember.

"What trail?" Janice asked.

Bud continued to rub his head, becoming frustrated. "I don't remember things sometimes."

"Ho Chi Minh Trail?" Gary reached over and put his hand on Bud's forearm.

"Yeah, that sounds right." Bud nodded slowly.

"What happened on the trail?"

Bud took a drink of pop. He clenched the bottle so tightly Gary thought he might crush it.

"It was hot and humid. Our clothes were so soaked with sweat. The smell of the jungle—once you smell it, you never forget it. I remember that. We were firing artillery across the valley and a shell misfired and a piece of it glanced off my head. My sergeant said I was lucky to be alive. That was my last action—at least, what I remember."

"You *are* lucky to be alive." Gary smiled at Bud. "Those malfunctions can kill a man."

Bud looked at Gary like a man in pain. "I try to think about everything, but I just can't remember. It's hard. It hurts. Thank God my wife hasn't left me. It's so tough on her and my daughter."

"I know, partner." Gary's eyes and voice flashed sympathy.

"Did you ever kill anyone?" Bud's eyes fastened on Gary.

"Yes, I did, but I don't talk about that—not even with other vets. That stays here." Gary tapped his head. "Taking another's life—I never got used to it. After a while, the deaths pile up on you."

"I know our artillery killed lots of them. It had to—it was so powerful. I know we never fired on our own men, though, like what happened to you and Private Jenkins." Bud straightened his shoulders in an act of pride.

"I know." Gary gave Bud a slight smile.

Janice rubbed Bud's shoulder. "We're here for you."

"Thanks, Mrs. Hinton." Bud glanced warmly at her.

"At first, I had a good go-get-'em attitude." Gary stared upward. "I did what they told me to do, did it well. Even got promoted to E4. Then I figured out what was going on over there—we were just expendable fodder for the brass. I survived, but I had to get the hell out or lose what was left of my sanity. And I did in May, when my time was up."

"Did you get any medals, Gary? I got one," Bud said proudly.

"That's because you deserved it."

Bud stared at Gary for a long time wanting to hear from him.

"Yeah, they gave me a Purple Heart and a medal for distinguished service." Gary did not disclose what he did to earn the medals or that he wanted to give both away. "Do you know what really hurts?"

Bud knew what Gary was going to say.

"That I made it back here when so many others didn't—like Ward." Gary stared at the boxes of cereal on the shelf in front of him and winced at the smiling faces of the cartoon animals.

Bud nodded and the trio entered a period of silence as they massaged their own thoughts.

A hoarse shout came from outside the store.

"What are you commies planning in there?" Carl Dinkins stood brazenly on the sidewalk outside the store. "Come on out here so we can see you cowards."

Janice heard Dinkins' grating voice and cringed. "Excuse me," she said to Gary and Bud. She headed for the front door.

She stepped outside and saw Dinkins, Eddie Horst, and three others standing in the street.

"Isn't it a little too early to be drinking, Mr. Dinkins? Shouldn't you be at work?"

"I took the day off, lady. I can do what I want." Dinkins' speech was slurred, but he was standing rock solid. "What's ya doing in there anyway? We're concerned citizens and want to know." He pointed to the men behind him.

"Well, that's none of your business." Janice stood defiant. "Just like I don't care to know what you and your friends are discussing in the bar. That's not my business."

"It's our business if you're plotting against our country, the good ol' USA." Dinkins smirked.

"We're Americans like you, Mr. Dinkins. We're not plotting anything. We were talking about the war. I thought it would be good if Bud talked to another vet, like Mr. Knowles. Bud can't talk to you because you weren't in the service, were you?"

"Bullshit!" he shouted. "I was wondering which of them two you're screwing. You've gotta be lonely now that Bridges left town."

The men behind Dinkins chuckled nervously. The situation was going beyond where they thought it would. Besides, their beers weren't getting any colder in the tavern.

"Tell that punk-ass traitor to come out here," Dinkins shouted.

Instead, Bud charged out of the store wearing his blood-stained butcher's apron, his face beet red. In his right hand, he carried a thirty-six-inch Louisville Slugger. He posed a menacing sight, and the men behind Dinkins shrunk back. Gary followed Bud out of the store.

"You don't speak to Mrs. Hinton like that, Dinkins. If you want a war, I'll give you one, right here, right now!"

That goddamned Bud again, Dinkins thought.

A siren blast from a police car startled everyone. The four men behind Dinkins fled back to the Thirsty Bull faster than Olympic sprinters.

Chief Thompkins got out of the vehicle and put on his hat.

"This again." Thompkins surveyed the scene in front of him. It didn't take Sherlock Holmes to reach a conclusion as to what was happening. "Dinkins, get the hell out of here or by God, I will arrest ya for creating a disturbance. Ya've pissed me off for the last time. Get out of here! Now!"

Dinkins turned and slipped. He caught himself before hitting the ground and pulled himself up. He started to return to the Thirsty Bull and Thompkins' angry voice caught him like a punch to the gut.

"Not in there, ya ass—go home!" Thompkins shouted.

Dinkins steered left and stumbled down the street, made a right turn and disappeared.

Thompkins adjusted his hat and turned to Janice, Bud, and Gary.

"I'm sorry, Janice, Bud." He just nodded at Gary. "I received three emergency calls about what was happening here, so I came as fast as I could. One came from the bar."

"Carl Dinkins is a problem, Chief," Janice sighed.

"He was about to get a beating." Bud smacked the bat into his left hand.

"Easy, Bud." Thompkins smiled. "I want ya to avoid trouble. Remember, ya've a wife and kid. I'll take it from here."

Thompkins walked up to Gary. "Ya're proving to be a problem. People don't want ya here—they don't share yar views. They say ya're using drugs and are a bad influence on the children."

"That's not true," Janice interrupted. "I've had no trouble with him and it's a free country. I thought that's what he fought for—to keep us free."

"Not now, Janice," Thompkins barked. He kept staring at Gary. "When are ya leaving here? The sooner ya do the better it will be for everyone."

Gary shook his head and his long brown hair flowed with his head. "I don't know, sir. Maybe tomorrow, maybe next week, or maybe I'll buy a house and settle down here. I can do whatever I want."

Thompkins moved close to Gary so that their faces were less than a foot apart.

"You're not going to intimidate me. I've had closer encounters with the Cong. You're just a small-town cop."

"Ya're a smart ass, Knowles, aren't ya?" Thompkins snarled. "I want ya out of here soon. Maybe I'll deputize Dinkins. He won't be as patient as me."

"He can try." Gary said, "But I have the right to protect myself." He pulled up his sweatshirt, exposing the knife sheath.

"What the hell. I don't like that, Knowles. Why don't ya give me that knife."

"I can carry my blade with me just as long as I don't pull it out in public. I have no intention of doing so—unless I'm threatened." Gary put his shirt back, covering the knife.

"Do ya feel threatened now?" Thompkins moved away from the vet.

"No, that's why she's staying in her sheath. I've had real-world experience with my friend." Gary patted the top of the knife handle. "Now Dinkins is a threat."

"Be on ya're best behavior, Knowles. I'll put ya in jail for anything improper that I see ya do. The legal system can take it from there. Be warned: we take a harsh view on turncoats."

"Leave him be, Chief. He's got medals, like me. He's my brother. You don't agree with him, but he fought just like me." Bud had become more agitated during the exchange between the chief and Knowles.

"Bud, ya're right." Thompkins softened. "I apologize, Mr. Knowles. The subject of Vietnam gets people overheated around here."

Thompkins shot a look at Janice. "Can I trust ya to make sure he returns to the apartment and stays out of trouble? I can't protect him if he's out and about. Lots of folks don't like him."

He strode to his car and drove away.

Gary stared at the car until it was several blocks down the road.

"I don't want to get either of you in any more trouble than I already have." Gary's tone softened. "I'll be leaving in a couple days. I've got people in California and Minnesota I can stay with. You two and that kid have been a comfort to me."

CHAPTER 13

Thursday, October 15

Del Robinson hustled into the captain's office.

"Captain, we just got a tip on the Washburn kidnapping. The suspect, Derrick Vincent, has been spotted in Manlo. We don't know if the victim, Charlotte Washburn, is alive or dead, though."

"I know," the captain said, drumming his fingers on the desk. "Take Barnes with you. I'm tired of seeing his sorry ass around here. His moping is a distraction to my other detectives. Getting him out in the field again would be good for him and us. Oh, and Del, he's running out of chances."

"Yes, sir." Robinson left the captain's office.

Robinson found Barnes in his office with his feet propped up on the radiator next to the window. He was staring outside. In his right hand he held an unopened *Time* magazine.

"Captain wants us to head up to Manlo. It's the Washburn kidnapping tied in with a drug house."

"What?" Barnes answered as if he had just awoken from a trance.

"Get what you need, man." Robinson waved his hand, indicating the handgun on Barnes' desk and the jacket wrapped around his chair. "I've got an extra set of clothes for you. I'll bring the car around front and pick you up in two minutes. I'll fill you in on the way."

Barnes got in the unmarked white Ford LTD Robinson had parked outside the ICC building. Without wasting a second, Robinson drove to the interstate, speaking rapid-fire.

"Charlotte Washburn was Derrick Vincent's ex-girlfriend. He was abusive and she reported him to the Des Moines police. She had a restraining order, but those are worthless. Vincent kidnapped her last week and they disappeared. Yesterday, the Manlo police saw a man fitting Vincent's description go into a rundown one-story house on the northeast part of town. We think Vincent is at the house along with a friend, the owner of the house, a man named Emory Willus. Whether Charlotte Washburn is there, too—we don't know. There's a lot of guessing here. The Manlo police aren't equipped to take the lead. Manlo only has two cops, an old man and his inexperienced son. They want the Clark County sheriff to be in charge and for us to assist them. We're only to do reconnaissance and report back to the captain. He'll coordinate the next move with the sheriff."

"I presume both Vincent and Willus are armed?" Barnes broke into Robinson's monologue.

"Yeah, assume so," Robinson said. "These are bad men. They served time together at the House of Corrections for armed robbery. And Willus is a known drug dealer." He spat out the car window.

After an hour drive from Des Moines, the LTD pulled up to a Manlo police car stationed outside the tiny Manlo police station. Evening had arrived with a clear sky. Stars peppered the sky with spotty brightness. Far down on the eastern horizon, the moon crawled up through the skeleton-like tree line.

Robinson and Barnes exited their car and approached the Manlo police car.

"I'm Officer Peterson," an ancient-looking uniformed man said, not bothering to get out of his cruiser.

"I'm Detective Robinson and this is Detective Barnes of the ICC."

"Good," Peterson said. His eyes locked on Robinson as if he were a mythical beast. "We don't get many negroes up here."

"And a detective at that." Barnes intervened before Robinson or Peterson could speak. "Rest assured, Officer Peterson, Detective Robinson has more experience and is better qualified than most cops in this state."

"Better than you, Detective Barnes?" Peterson raised his eyebrows.

"Yup, that's true." Barnes added, "Except in poker."

The slight chuckle shared among the men eased the tension.

"All right then, detectives. I'm glad you're here. My son is ah, ah, ah at night class and can't be here. But I know the lay of the land. Follow me."

Barnes and Robinson returned to their car and followed Peterson to an alley on the north side of town, where they parked. The detectives left their car and angled their way to the trunk to grab their gear.

"You're aware that he doesn't want his son hurt or killed and that's why he isn't here," Robinson said to Barnes, his voice low.

Barnes and Robinson changed clothing and dressed head to toe in black—pants, jackets, baseball caps, and tennis shoes.

"Are you missing your suit yet?" Barnes asked as Robinson neatly folded his suit coat, vest, and slacks.

"Always, man. I can give you fashion tips any time. You need 'em."

Barnes scoffed lightheartedly.

When finished, they walked quietly to Officer Peterson, who was leaning against his car. He had not changed clothing.

"Where's your gear? Aren't you coming?" Robinson asked.

"I figured I'm more useful out here. I can coordinate from here."

"Where's the Clark County sheriff?" Robinson tried not to sound too critical.

"They'll be here soon enough, detectives. They're dealing with a vehicle-related fatality several miles south of here. I'll be right here waiting for them."

"Well, all we're supposed to do is conduct surveillance until the sheriff gets here. He'll take command then. So, Officer Peterson, show us the way to Willus' house.

Peterson nodded. "Follow me."

The three men moved cautiously down the alleyway. Shadows from the rising October moon covered most of the alley. It was a cold night. After walking and crouching for one hundred feet, Barnes felt a tap on his left shoulder.

"Willus and Vincent are in the house two houses down and to the right. We hope Miss Washburn is all right if she's there. I'll meet you back over here," Peterson said as he pointed back in the direction from which the threesome had come.

Barnes and Robinson nodded, but Peterson had already turned back.

"Geez, OK. I'll take the front, you take the back," Robinson whispered. "Remember—recon only, man. We'll meet back here in thirty minutes, sharp. The sheriff should be here by then. Set your watch."

"10-4, Detective Robinson."

The two men split up and took their positions around the suspects' house. Ten minutes into the surveillance, Robinson observed a light-colored Oldsmobile drive up to the house. A man with exceptionally long hair got out of the car and pulled what appeared to be a blanket from the trunk. He knocked three times on the door of the house and was let inside. The curtains on the street-facing side of the house were closed tightly.

Barnes only knew a car had stopped outside the house. The car door had opened and closed. *Who's that?* he thought. The windows in the back were also covered—except one mostly shuttered window on the south-eastern corner.

Barnes watched images of two men go back and forth in that room through the viewable part of the window. *I'm assuming there's a third man from the car. Where is he?* Barnes thought. The room went dark, forcing Barnes to move closer to the house while trying to stay behind some sort of cover. The bright full moon was now over the tree line, illuminating the ground. Barnes knew he had to be careful to avoid being seen.

He noticed a light come on through the basement window well. He thought he heard a cry. *I've got to get closer,* he thought as he stealthily moved up to the back of the house. He barely avoided becoming entangled in an unwrapped garden hose and crawled to the window well. Barnes heard another muffled cry. He peered through what he could of the window. He saw three pairs of shoes moving around as a blanket was unfolded. The cry became a whimper between the mumbling of the others.

Good God, they're going to kill her and take away her body in the blanket. There's no time to wait for the sheriff, he thought. *And if I try and meet up with Del, they'll have killed her already. And Peterson is next to worthless. Shit. God, if you're up there, look after me.*

Barnes pushed himself up into a crouch. He duckwalked his way over to the partially draped window. With his pocketknife, he gently cut away the screen. He pushed up on the sill and was surprised when it gave way and opened for him.

So far, so good.

Gripping the windowsill, Barnes hoisted himself up and eased his way through the open window as quietly as possible. He followed the light from the darkened room to the hallway, listening for sounds. He could hear voices coming from the basement. Barnes pulled his department-issued Smith & Wesson .38 Special revolver from its holster and moved to the basement door.

He bent over as much as he could to view the basement without being seen. Keeping that posture, he silently moved down the stairway, one slow step at a time, eyes forward. He listened for anyone behind him. To his relief, no one was in the room at the bottom of the stairs. Sounds came from the walled-off room straight ahead.

"We'll roll the body in the blanket and haul it to the car," a gravelly voice said.

A second, smoother voice added, "Yeah, no one should see us. Then we can run things how we want to."

A whine came from the room. *Her mouth is taped shut, but she's alive—there's still time,* Barnes thought.

"Use the rope—no blood," the gravelly voice said roughly.

Barnes heard a series of moans; a foot slapped the floor, hard. *She's being strangled. Three against one, but I do have surprise on my side. I must move now.*

"Police!" Barnes shouted as he barged through the door to the room.

The long-haired man reached for a shotgun leaning against the wall next to him. Barnes fired, hitting the man in the chest, throwing him back into a wall-mounted shelf containing several jars. The jars shattered as they hit the floor, spilling liquid across the surface.

Barnes' eyes turned to the man hovering over the body sitting in a chair. He held a thin rope in his hands. Barnes glanced at the intended victim and his eyes widened with shock. The person in the chair was a man, not Charlotte Washburn.

For a second, Barnes froze. Two thoughts raced into his mind like flashes of air-to-ground lightning. *Who is the man in the chair? Where is Charlotte Washburn?*

Thunk! Barnes felt something hard strike his head. His last remembrance was the man with the rope running over to him and reaching for his gun. At the same time, a woman shouted, "Kill him! Kill the bastard!"

What Barnes didn't see was Robinson hurtling into the room. In two almost simultaneous moves, he kicked the woman in the chest, sending her tumbling onto the floor as she groaned.

Robinson yelled "Stop!" to the man who had grabbed Barnes' gun.

The man did not heed Robinson's warning and started to aim. Robinson fired into the man's left shoulder, causing Barnes' gun to flip out of the man's hand and fall to the ground.

Robinson ran over and kicked the gun away from the wounded attacker. He glanced at the long-haired man, who lay motionless in a growing pool of blood. He turned and saw the woman crawling to the stairs. "Not so fast!" he shouted at her.

Robinson reached up and took ahold of her right arm, pinched a handcuff around her wrist and clasped the open handcuff around her other wrist. He led her to a chair and pushed her into it.

"Move and I'll shackle you to that pipe." Robinson nodded at an overhead water pipe.

Outside, sirens wailed as police cars rolled up to the house. Several Clark County deputies entered the house with their weapons drawn, followed by Officer Peterson.

Robinson knelt by Barnes. He saw a scrap piece from a two-by-four on the floor next to his partner. He brushed back Barnes' hair and saw a large welt forming at the back of his skull.

"Jesus, Fred."

Chapter 14

Friday, October 16

At four thirty in the morning, Gary drifted off to sleep. Slamming car doors, yelling, and squealing tires jolted him awake. He threw on his jeans and a sweatshirt and ran outside. Two fires burned six feet apart on the lawn in front of the apartment. Between the fires was a large dead raccoon. Its legs were splayed apart and nailed into the ground. The animal's insides were gutted and laid in a semicircle on the ground next to it.

By the time Gary had taken in the scene, Janice had flicked on the outside lights and hurried down the porch steps to the gross display. The two did not flinch from the massacre and watched the twin fires dance into the night air as if in a pre-Halloween ritual. Like a solider, Gary maintained a calm demeanor, while Janice seethed.

"What the hell!" she yelled.

"Your bar boys are making another statement."

"Well, I'm not going to put up with this shit! I'm calling Chief Thompkins right now." She stormed into the house and returned a minute later.

Gary reached down and picked up a crudely written note set by the raccoon. He read it to Janice.

THIS IS WHAT HAPPENS TO COWARDS AND TRAITORS
YOU'RE NEXT

"I'll find out who did this. Then I'm going to press charges," Janice fumed. "I'm so mad!"

Five minutes later, Chief Thompkins drove up without lights and sirens, wearing civilian clothes. The fires were petering out.

"What do we have here?" he asked looking at the sight. "Mr. Knowles, trouble doesn't want to leave ya alone. As I said, ya presence in our town is a problem."

"How about you do your job and find out who did this?" Janice glared at Thompkins.

Thompkins questioned Gary and Janice. "Did ya see the cars? Can ya identify the voices? How many cars and people were there?"

Neither could provide any details.

"Well, we have nothing then. I'll poke around and see if I can find out something. I'll find out where Dinkins and his yahoos were just now. I'll let ya know if I uncover anything."

Thompkins headed back to his car. As he did, he said, "Knowles, I'd say it's time for ya to be moving on."

Janice shot back, "Do your damn job, Chief."

As Thompkins left, she turned to Gary. "Are you all right?"

"Yes, ma'am—these country hillbillies don't scare me. I faced much worse in Nam. I'm more worried about you. I can move on outta here, but you'll stay here like that tree. A lot of people in your fine town don't like either of us. Oh, and I think it best we don't mention this to anyone." Gary pointed at the dead animal. "The town's stirred up as it is. And I doubt the chief will do anything."

"I don't give up easily."

⟁

After school, Brent cruised by Janice's house on his bicycle. He had put his football in a bag and hung it on the handlebars. Brent saw Gary working in the yard and rode up to him. There was no trace of the early morning vandalism.

"Hey, kid. What's going on?" Gary seemed more alert than normal.

"Just going home after playing a game with some friends. You've met most of them."

"Yeah, they seemed like good guys—a little skittish, though. What's in the bag?"

"My football."

"Yeah, I had a hunch. Wanna play some catch?"

"Sure," Brent nodded and eagerly pulled the football from the bag. He had his doubts that Gary could throw a football.

"Down and out, start here." Gary pointed to his left side.

Brent ran the play and was surprised to get a football fastball in his chest. After a few more perfect passes, Gary said, "Go long, angle right."

Brent ran the pattern and Gary waved him to go farther. When Brent reached a spot he was certain Gary would underthrow to, Gary launched a spiral that landed softly in Brent's arms.

Brent ran in and tossed the football to Gary. "Where did you learn to throw like that?"

"I played high school football—seems like a long time ago. I was the quarterback."

"Were you good?"

"I guess so. A couple of colleges offered me scholarships, but I decided to take a year off and get my head on straight. Bad decision."

"Why?"

"Uncle Sam drafted me into that damned war, that's why." Gary paused. "Do you have dreams, kid? Not night dreams, but dreams about what you want to do with your life?"

"Kind of. I want to be a major league baseball player. I'd like to play second base."

"That's good thinking, kid."

"Maybe a forest ranger after baseball. That would be great." Looking at Gary, Brent asked, "Do you have dreams about what you want to do?"

"I used to. I wanted to play pro football for the Green Bay Packers. That's over now. I don't have dreams anymore, except the scary kind.

Most of my dreams dissipated in Nam." Gary looked at the ground. Changing the subject, he called for Brent to run several more pass patterns. Brent eagerly obliged. He had never played with anyone who could throw as well as Gary.

After a final down and out pattern, Gary said, "You wore me out kid. I need to rest a bit."

"You're the best! Can I bring the guys by sometime so you can give us pointers?"

"Sure, kid. Do it soon, though. I'm leaving Brinson. I've somewhere I need to go." It was the first time Brent had seen Gary smile a genuine smile.

Chapter 15

Saturday, October 17

Brent's interactions with Gary had opened a world he had not experienced. Gary went against what Brent was familiar with, and that excited him. Brent couldn't wait to learn more from this intriguing man. *Before he goes, I want to see him as much as I can.*

Brent's wish was soon granted. On Saturday morning, Lola Jenkins called Angela and asked if Brent could introduce Dale to Gary so Dale could give Gary a note. Brent eagerly agreed.

Brent biked to the Jenkins' house and waited in the driveway. Within a minute, Dale appeared and the two boys rode to Janice's house. Dale was a slightly smaller, quieter version of Brent, although Dale had a big brother war hero to live up to. Brent was an only child.

When they pulled up to the basement apartment, they saw Gary propped against the trunk of a nearby maple tree, resting. He looked up as the boys approached.

"Hi, kid. Who's your friend? I haven't seen him before."

"This is Dale, Ward's brother," Brent said.

Gary perked up at the name. "Hey, Dale. It's nice to meet another Jenkins."

"Sir, Brent says you knew my brother. You were friends. Is that true?" Dale asked cautiously.

"No need to call me sir, Dale. I can't be *that* much older than you. Yeah, we were real good friends. War has a way of creating unlikely friendships."

Dale and Brent shot puzzled looks at Gary.

"We never would have met and become friends if we hadn't gone to Nam together," Gary clarified.

"Was my brother a good soldier?"

"The best. It was an honor to serve with him."

"Some people in town say you're a traitor because you don't support the war."

"He's not a traitor," Brent interjected. "He's got medals."

"Where did you hear that, kid?"

"Bud said so at the store. And Bud doesn't lie—everyone knows that."

"Yeah, sure, it's true. Forget that. I want to say, Dale, your brother was the bravest soldier I knew. He could also do magic tricks and tell funny stories about life in Brinson at the same time. His lame jokes covered up his lack of skill at being a good magician." Gary chuckled recalling a funny memory that would be inappropriate to tell the boys.

Gary became serious. "I don't like talking about the war, about what I did or about what Ward did. You boys should know—and I want you to remember—that war is not like anything on television, in the movies, or in comic books. I hope to God that if there is another one, you don't ever have to fight unless you choose to. I mean that."

Brent and Dale nodded, not entirely sure what Gary meant.

"Mr. Knowles, I have a favor to ask you." Dale handed him a piece of paper. "This is from my parents."

Gary took the letter and read it. He then carefully folded the letter, gently slapping it on his knee. After a few moments of peering out at nothing, he unfolded the note and read it again.

Mr. Knowles,

Our hearts were shattered when Ward went missing, and crushed when we received official news of his death. He was our son, and we know he was a fine soldier. He told us you were his best friend in Vietnam. You both saw more death and violence over there than we can imagine. He wrote that you showed exemplary bravery in the war, and how he and the others looked up to you.

Ward was in Vietnam less than a year. At first, we were so proud that he was fighting for a just cause. In time, we questioned why we were in this war and why so many of our soldiers were being killed and wounded. Then Ward was killed and, from what we have heard, it was by our own forces. We know that can happen, but why Ward? It breaks our hearts.

We were initially angry when you showed up here in Brinson speaking out against the war—the war that cost Ward his life. That anger was misplaced, and we feel badly about that. Ward would be unhappy with us for thinking of you that way. For that, we are sorry.

We would like to invite you to dinner tomorrow night, Sunday, and talk with you about Ward and the war. It will help us find a way through this. We promise this is not an ambush, so please remove any suspicion that we have other motives. We don't; we just want to talk.

Brent and his folks are invited, too. We know their feelings about the war are like yours. They will want to hear what you have to say.

Gary, please come.
—Bert and Lola Jenkins

Gary hesitated before taking a worn pencil from an inside shirt pocket. He wrote on the Jenkins' letter.

For Ward, I accept your offer, with one condition—I will not discuss what I did in the war. Anything else is on the table.
Gary Knowles

Gary folded the letter again and handed it to Dale. A smile creased Gary's face. "Your folks seem like good people. It took them a lot to write this. I know they and you are grieving. I am, too. I see where Ward got his spirit. Do you have the same spirit, kid?"

"Yes, sir." Dale nodded and gazed downward.

Gary felt Dale's grief. "Ward was proud to be your big brother. He told me that you're smarter as a freshman than he was as a senior. Yeah, and he wanted me to tell you that if you smell smoke coming from the boy's restroom—run. Don't let Principal Harris catch you in there—that's based on his personal experience."

Gary laughed heartily and Dale raised his head with a slight grin. "Ward loved washing his car. He'd say, 'I never took a date in a dirty car.' Now kid, you've got a tradition to live up to."

"I see Brent and his parents are invited, too." Gary changed the subject. "Good. What time tomorrow night?"

"Six o'clock, sir."

"It's settled then, boys. See you tomorrow night at eighteen hundred hours."

Brent and Dale looked confused.

"That's six o'clock p.m. for you two. Now, scoot." He extended the peace sign to the boys.

"Mr. Knowles, when can I bring my friends over to play football with you?" Brent hoped the answer would be soon.

"How about the day after tomorrow? But I'll be the quarterback. I don't want to run much."

⅄

Sunday, October 18

Sunday trolled by slowly as Brent couldn't wait for dinner at the Jenkins. At six o'clock, Brent and his parents gathered at the Jenkins house. By six-thirty, there was no sign of Gary.

"He said he would come, Mom," Dale said. "And he wrote yes to your letter."

"I heard him, too," Brent seconded.

"You two," Bert pointed after receiving a nod from Tim, "go over to Mrs. Hinton's house and see if Gary is there. Have Mrs. Hinton check. Got it?"

When the boys arrived at Janice's house, they saw a light on in Janice's kitchen.

Janice answered the door and said she hadn't seen Gary the entire day.

"I'll go check the apartment."

With the boys in tow, she went outside and knocked on the apartment door. There was no answer. She knocked again, this time more forcefully. Still, there was no answer. She got out her key and unlocked the door. It was dark inside, which was unusual. Gary kept a light on in the apartment late into the evening.

"Gary, are you in here?" After a pause, she called out again with more emphasis, "Gary? You two stay here," Janice said to the boys as she entered the apartment.

A minute later, she came out. Her face was ashen and her body shook, frightening the two boys.

"We need to call the police—NOW!" she screamed.

Chapter 16

Friday, October 16 to Monday, October 19

Barnes flirted with consciousness. He could barely make out his surroundings before the urge to surrender to overwhelming fatigue led him into a bout of sleep. In a dream, he saw Clara. She had a glowing presence. Smiling, she waved to him and disappeared into a lighted background.

Finally, his eyes opened and fixed on a painting in front of him, a pastoral scene featuring a flock of sheep. *What was Clara telling me?* he thought, gazing at the painting.

"Well, look who's finally awake," a voice spoke off to his side.

Barnes could not see the speaker, but he knew the voice.

"Glad you're back with the living," the voice continued warmly.

"How long have I been here, Del?" Barnes started coughing, tried to sit up, and groaned.

Robinson moved over and put an extra pillow behind Barnes' back to provide support for a more upright position. "Comfortable now? You got a nasty bump on the back of your head. Charlotte Washburn hit you square on with the flat side of a chunk of wood. Fortunately, it wasn't something sharp, like either end of a hammer or a pipe wrench. It could have been much worse, man."

The door opened and a nurse entered, followed by a doctor. Del stood, feeling a little uncomfortable.

"It's time for my afternoon coffee, partner. I'll leave the doctors to it." Robinson turned to leave. He pivoted back and faced Barnes. "For what it's worth, we got 'em. I'll let the captain know you're awake."

The day after the incident in Manlo was a blur to Barnes. Initially, he vaguely remembered going into the house's basement and shooting the long-haired man. On the second day, the memory fog began to clear.

The doctor told Barnes, "You should regain your memory in time, just not all at once. You took a significant blow to your head, but fortunately we found no indication of a skull fracture. It appears to be a concussion. You'll continue to have those headaches and bouts of memory loss a little longer. To be safe, we want to keep you at the hospital for another day and monitor your progress."

"When will I be able to return to work, Doctor?" Barnes pestered the doctor with that question during each visit.

"Let's give it a few more days, just to be sure," was always the doctor's response. "We want you clear-headed with no headaches."

Barnes wasn't lonely during his hospital stay. His fellow detectives, the captain, Marge, and other ICC staff members stopped by to see how he was progressing. Marge told him that he and Robinson were heroes. The captain offered less effusive praise, which Barnes took as a sign there was a problem.

Barnes returned home Sunday after the incident. His memory had fully returned, and any headaches were vanquished by a couple of Bufferin tablets. His cat, Fluffy, was particularly pleased to see him. Marge and kind neighbors helped him settle back in. Surprisingly, he felt more at peace with himself than before the Manlo incident. His dream with Clara brought him a contented feeling of closure.

⚊

Barnes was sifting through a large pile of mostly junk mail on Monday afternoon on October 19 when his doorbell rang. He hustled to the door thinking Marge was bringing more of her delicious cookies. He was, therefore, surprised to see the captain standing on the threshold.

"Captain, I wasn't expecting you. I appreciated your visit at the hospital. Thank you. Please, come inside."

"Good afternoon, Detective Barnes—Fred." The captain slid past Barnes into the living room. He wore civilian clothes.

Barnes frowned to himself. "Can I get you a cup of coffee or something else to drink? I have lemonade and cookies. Marge brought them over."

"Yeah, some lemonade would be fine. There's something about Marge's lemonade. She really makes it good. Maybe it's the extra sugar."

"Have a seat, Captain, and I'll get us each a glass and Marge's chocolate chip cookies. I try to ration them, but they're irresistible."

"She's a woman of many talents." The captain sat.

Barnes got the lemonade and cookies, and moved to sit to the captain's left.

"I'm here unofficially. We need to discuss something away from the office. I know you're well on your way to a full recovery."

Barnes felt cold nerves flutter through him. He started to squeeze his right hand into a ball and his head began to pound.

"You did a courageous thing in Manlo. I believe your actions saved someone's life. That's fine."

That sounded more positive than expected but, in the back of Barnes' mind, he sensed what was coming.

"However, first, you disobeyed my orders to not enter the house. You and Robinson were to conduct reconnaissance *only* and report back to our partners at the sheriff's office on what you saw. Only then would the appropriate coordinated actions be implemented. Orders are issued for a reason. I do not like having my authority disregarded.

"Second, you put Robinson's life in danger. It would look bad if our only Black detective was hurt—or worse. For God's sake, Barnes, he has a family.

"Third, the person you saved was a drug dealer. If you would have done the proper reconnaissance, you would have known that."

"I thought it was Charlotte Washburn."

"Wrong. We now have a pretty accurate account of what happened. Emory Willus, who owns the house, ran a drug distribution center in Des Moines for his partners based in Chicago. He used the house in Manlo as a staging area to store drugs before they were shipped to Minneapolis. His stash ran the gamut—from marijuana to amphetamines, LSD to heroin.

"He needed help, so he recruited Derrick Vincent. Vincent had bigger balls than brains so he cooked up a scheme with Washburn whereby she would pretend to betray him, and so she had to die. Vincent brought her to Willus' house to kill her and dispose of her body, but it was just a ploy. Willus was Vincent's target because Vincent wanted to take over Willus' operation. Vincent hired a goon from Illinois to help him with his plan, and that's the guy you shot.

"Vincent, Washburn, and Willus all survived and are going to spend quite a bit of time in prison. So, there you have it. You and Robinson are going to receive commendations for your bravery. Hell, maybe Manlo will name a park after you two. It doesn't matter who you saved—but you stopped a drug operation from continuing in a small town. The public loves that.

"But what I know will remain between us. I won't put your failure to follow orders in the report. Keep in mind, you haven't been the lead on a case in some time. I don't know if I can trust you again. This is not a business of third and fourth chances. Take under advisement that I will dole out future assignments accordingly."

The captain practically inhaled the rest of his lemonade, grabbed a cookie, and headed for the door. He turned to Barnes and said, "Thank you for the refreshments. Like the doctor said, barring any more headaches or memory problems, I'll see you at the office next Monday, the 26. I'll come up with something appropriate for you."

Chapter 17

Sunday, October 18

Sirens from emergency vehicles settled in around Janice's house, which was just two blocks from the Jenkins. Tim became worried. His son and Dale were still out there.

Tim avoided the vehicles, which were also driving to the house, and parked in the adjacent alleyway. Judging by all the emergency personnel coming in and out of Janice's basement, something was terribly wrong. He glanced to his left and saw the two boys standing off to the side. He yelled to them and they ran over.

The scene before them was something new. Tim placed his arm around his son and put his other hand on Dale's shoulder.

"What happened?"

Brent looked at his dad, dazed; Dale stared straight ahead.

"We don't know, but something bad happened to Mr. Knowles."

A voice from behind surprised them. A Reed County deputy sheriff tapped Tim on the shoulder.

"Sir, please take your boys away from here. They don't belong here."

"Can I ask …" Tim asked.

"Chief Thompkins will issue a report and you'll know then," the deputy interrupted.

"OK, thanks. Let's go, boys." Tim picked up the boys' bikes and they walked to his car.

After loading the bikes and the stone-faced boys into the Plymouth, Tim drove to the Jenkins' house and dropped off Dale.

"What's going on?" Lola's voice aired concern.

"I don't know anything right now except I think Gary is in some sort of trouble. We can talk tomorrow. We should know more then."

Silence marked the rest of Tim and Brent's trip home. Angela met them at the door. She had walked apprehensively back home from the Jenkins'.

She looked into Tim's eyes to try and get a read on the situation.

"Let's talk later, honey." He glanced at Brent.

"I want to hear, too. He was my friend."

"OK. But we don't know much." Tim rubbed his son's shoulder. "Yes, it appears to have involved Gary and looks serious."

"Did someone hurt him?" Angela asked. "That nasty Carl Dinkins and those others could have done something."

"I don't know. Chief Thompkins will give a report when they know something more. Now Brent, it's time for you to finish your reading for school."

Brent tried to read *Huckleberry Finn*, but in his state of mind, it was fruitless.

⅄

Janice sat stunned at her kitchen table sipping a cup of hot tea. She brushed her dark bangs away from her swollen eyes. Chief Thompkins was talking to her and the men who appeared and disappeared into the October night.

"I know it's hard to believe, but Gary took his own life. We have the bottles of whiskey, the sleeping pills, and the heroin. It's a no-brainer."

"He didn't do that, Ellis. I know it."

"The evidence is clear. But we'll take the body to Carlson and Doc Deisman will issue his official report. Then we can put this matter to bed. By the way, where's Bud? I'd have expected him to be here by the first siren."

"He, Alice, and Lily are visiting Alice's father in Des Moines. He's ill."

"Good—Bud won't like this. I expect I'll need to keep him away from Carl. This town has enough problems, and I don't need any more."

Thompkins rose from his chair, adjusted his hat, and left the house. Soon the ambulance, firetruck, and police cars were gone.

Janice continued to sit and covered her eyes with her hands.

Chapter 18

Monday, October 19

After a restless night of sleep, Brent decided to walk to school, his thoughts focused on what had happened to Gary. In P.E., he met up with Jack and Tom.

"Did you hear about what happened over at Hinton's house?" Jack tossed a football to Tom.

"I was there."

"What?" Jack caught the football back from Tom and both boys jogged over to Brent.

"Last night, Dale and I went over to where Gary was staying. He was supposed to have supper at the Jenkins, but he didn't show up. We asked Mrs. Hinton to see if he was there. She went inside his place and came out white as a ghost. She yelled for a neighbor, and they called the police. That's all I know."

"Wow," Jack said. "Did you see him?"

"No. There was an ambulance, a fire truck, county cop cars, and Chief Thompkins."

"He's probably dead, from the sound of things." Jack lobbed the football back to Tom. "A lot of people in town didn't think much of him, including my dad."

"I hope he's not dead. He wasn't a bad man, and he was my friend."

Brent decided to head in from class early and shower. He did not want to hear any more unkind things about Gary.

Brent arrived home after school and found his mom, Mrs. Jenkins, and Mrs. Hinton having coffee. Janice had a quiet presence as the other women talked, but none of the women were smiling. Brent stood in the doorway and listened.

"He said he was coming to supper." Lola held up the note she had written, which was underscored by Gary's handwriting.

"May I see the note?" Angela asked.

Lola handed Angela the note. When Angela finished reading it, she said, "I agree with you, Lola. Unfortunately, we don't know if he was masking his feelings and had no intention of going to your house. We don't know what was going on in his head."

"He showed no signs that he was thinking about doing such a thing." Janice used both hands to guide the coffee cup to her mouth. "I know he was unhappy with life and how things turned out, but was he unhappy enough to …?" She glanced at Brent and stopped speaking.

"Brent," Angela asked, "when you talked with Mr. Knowles, how did he seem to you?"

"Fine, like usual—only even better," Brent replied. Replays of his last memories of Gary worked through his mind. He wasn't paying attention to the three women in front of him.

"Thanks." Angela sensed it wasn't the right time to discuss Gary in front of him. "That garage needs cleaning. It needs to be done by the time your father gets home."

"Yes, Mom." Brent shrugged and turned to leave. He turned back and asked no one specifically, "Any report from Chief Thompkins?"

"No," Janice added. "We probably won't hear anything more until later in the week."

"Is he dead?" Brent already knew the answer.

"Yes, honey, he is. It was suicide." She paused. "He killed himself. This is a sad day." Angela moved to hug her son.

Brent walked to the garage dejectedly where he found an old box containing comic books. Forgetting about cleaning, he settled in to read. He rediscovered stories that didn't involve Gary or cleaning the garage.

⅄

Thursday, October 22

The following Thursday, the medical examiner issued his report. Janice obtained it from Chief Thompkins. After reading it herself, she called Lola and Angela to come to her house. There, Janice read out loud the summary findings verbatim.

The results of the autopsy showed Mr. Gary Knowles died of an overdose of a combination of sleeping pills, alcohol, and heroin. He died at approximately 0200 hours on Sunday, October 18, 1970. Signed Dr. Henry C. Deisman, Medical Examiner, Reed County, dated Wednesday, October 21, 1970.

"Heroin, my goodness," exclaimed Lola.

"The war really affected him, I guess," acknowledged Angela.

"That's bullshit," Janice snapped. "I know he smoked marijuana and did some drinking, but I never saw any sign of heroin."

"You know what they say, Janice, marijuana is a gateway drug. You didn't know him well enough to say he didn't do heroin," Lola argued.

"Good gracious," Angela said tightly. "Brent spent quite a bit of time with him. Even looked up to him."

"Again, ladies, this report is pure bullshit. I don't believe it. And didn't you say that Gary agreed to come over for dinner? Did your boys say he looked depressed when he said he would come?"

"No," Angela said. "Brent is broken up over this. I need to go."

Lola joined her as they left Janice's house.

◣

Janice's frustration boiled over. She walked briskly to her car and drove to the Brinson Police Station, which was an extension of the red brick Brinson Volunteer Fire Department. Brown weeds sprouted up from a crack in the sidewalk in front of the building.

The police station consisted of three rooms: the reception area, where Thompkins kept his large cherry desk, a small bathroom, and a holding cell. The cell had only been used a few times during Thompkins' tenure as chief—all for confining rowdy drunks.

Janice stomped into Thompkins' office. "Do you really believe this report, Ellis?"

"Sure, why wouldn't it be true?" Thompkins sat behind his desk holding a Brinson State Bank pen between his hands as he talked, not looking at Janice.

"Because I know it isn't. And Bud agrees with me."

Thompkins laughed, "Bud? How would he know?"

"Let me remind you that Bud is a decorated veteran and he spoke to Gary. Bud is adamant that Gary didn't do what this report says."

"Well then, did someone murder him? And if that's the case, then who did it?" Thompkins' voice rose with impatience at her questioning. "Who are your suspects?"

"There are plenty of suspects—Carl Dinkins, for one."

"Dinkins? How would he have anything to do with Knowles' suicide and drug use? Alcohol, maybe. Ha! But he has trouble finding the beer in front of his face. There is no case here."

"Do your job, Chief." Janice knew she had to leave or she would say something she'd later regret.

But before she did, Janice popped one final question. "Where's his body?"

"Knowles has no living parents. He has a cousin in California, so that's where he was shipped. Let it go, Janice. We need things to return to normal around here."

Chapter 19

Thursday, October 22

The Burt Westbrick Park outside Carlson was seldom used in the fall when the children were back in school. On this day, a couple of cars waited patiently in the park for their masters. One car, a Chrysler, had a tow hitch for a small trailer used to transport an aluminum rowboat. The owner had driven the trailer down to a dirt landing and carefully pushed the boat into the lake. He then relocated the car with trailer back in the parking area. Once that was done, he skillfully hopped into the boat and rowed out to the center of the lake, which typically hosted the largest smallmouth bass.

The second car was a black Cadillac owned by the man who sat at the wooden picnic table in the pavilion overlooking the lake. It was a sunny October day with a temperature that vacillated between mild and cool. The man's smartly folded black overcoat rested by his side on the bench. He did not taste the ham sandwich he was slowly eating; his senses were focused on the fisherman. Occasionally, he took a sip from a flask of rum. His Black Hawk Crushable Wool Stetson kept the sun off his face.

The fisherman's actions were deliberate and not in a hurry. He'd cast to his left and then his right. A second pole for still fishing with a night crawler sat near his left leg. Finally, after an hour, he reeled in a bullhead. The fisherman tossed it back into the lake and returned to his fishing routine. Another half hour passed and the fisherman caught another fish. This time the hooked fish was a nice bass. The fisherman showed no emotion as he added the bass to a stringer attached to the side of the boat.

The man at the pavilion smiled at the fisherman and neatly folded his lunch bag. "Patience is truly a virtue," he said to himself. He stood, put on his coat, and placed the lunch bag in a trash can. He gave a slight wave to the lake, got into his car, and drove to Carlson.

He stopped at the Best Western-Carlson located on Highway 40 on the southern outskirts of the city. He entered the motel and faced a short, balding man with wire-rimmed glasses wearing a manager's tag.

"I have a reservation." The man pointed to a name in the guest book.

"Yes, sir. You'll be staying for the week?" the bespectacled man asked.

"Yes, maybe longer. We'll see. Don't worry about costs." The man took out a stack of money and gave the clerk three one-hundred-dollar bills. "That should take care of things for now, don't you think?"

The manager quickly took the money and placed it into the register. "Oh, yes, sir."

As the manager scribbled out a receipt, the man with the Stetson asked, "Do kids still swim in Westbrick Lake?"

"Yes, but they shouldn't. It's dirty and filled with algae and those weedy plants. And the Turner's son drowned there about ten years ago. That was really sad."

"I'll bet." The man tipped his hat at the clerk and began to walk out of the office.

"Wait, sir. You need to sign the guest book."

"Sure," he said and returned to the counter. The manager offered him a pen, but the man waved him off. He pulled a gold-plated pen from his coat pocket and signed his name with a flourish: *Robert Franklin Frost.*

Chapter 20

Thursday, October 22

Brent sat quietly at the dining room table thinking about everything but the food in front of him. In the past month, he had witnessed the father of one of his best friends kiss someone other than his wife, and then his friend moved away. Another friend's brother was killed in Vietnam. And a veteran of that war, who he had befriended, was harassed by the town and took his own life. *Why are all these terrible things happening?* His quiet, peaceful world revolving around family, friends, and school had turned upside down.

"You're not eating your mashed potatoes. I thought you liked those." Angela looked at her son.

"Sorry, I'm just not hungry." Brent stirred his potatoes with his fork.

Angela glanced quickly at Tim. "I made pudding pie tonight. It has graham crackers on the bottom, then layers of vanilla pudding and chocolate pudding topped with whipped cream. I know that's your favorite."

"Not tonight, thank you. Can I be excused? I have homework."

"Sure. I'll cut a piece for you and put it in the refrigerator. You can have it later."

Brent left the table for his room. Angela stared at the stairway long after Brent had walked up it.

"I'm worried. He's really bothered."

"I believe it has to do with Gary's death," Tim said. "Brent spent quite a bit of time with him over the past several days. Perhaps something they talked about affected Brent."

"Do you think Gary offered Brent drugs? Who knows what he was using." Angela turned her attention from the stairway to her husband.

"God, I hope not." Tim shook his head. "Janice told me that he drank and smoked marijuana. But she never saw him offer the boys any drugs or alcohol, and they never went inside his apartment. What did she say to you?"

"The same thing—she said he acted appropriately around the boys. He was a good man and was even awarded medals in Vietnam. She firmly believes that Gary wouldn't hurt children, including our Brent." Angela peered back into the darkness of the stairway again.

She took Tim's hand. "Janice told me and Lola that Gary didn't kill himself. Something else happened, but she doesn't know what yet. She's going to try and get his record cleared."

"Janice is stepping on landmines," Tim warned. "A lot of people in this town blame her for the Bridges' breakup, even though Art was just as much to blame—if not more. Now, she's standing up for a man who many think was a traitor and drug user who killed himself."

⅄

Late Thursday afternoon, flyers began circulating around Brinson. They read:

> *Service to honor Gary Knowles, U.S. Army E4.*
> *To be held at the Brinson Presbyterian Church, Saturday, October 24 at 2:00, the Reverend Graham K. McFadden presiding.*
> *All are welcome.*

Bud personally delivered a flyer to the Thirsty Bull. He handed it to the bartender and stared at the small crowd inside the bar, his blood-stained butcher's apron intimidating the patrons.

"Hi, Bud, what's this?" The bartender took the paper and read it.

"Here's some more. Pass 'em around, won't you, Gil?"

"Sure, I can do that. Is Mrs. Hinton behind this service?" Gil raised his eyebrows.

"No, it's my idea. Us soldiers got to honor our fallen brothers." Bud stood upright as he spoke.

"OK, I'll pass them out."

"Thank you, sir." Bud left the tavern.

Carl Dinkins, sitting at the dark end of the bar, got up and walked over to Gil after Bud left and read the flyer. Knowing Carl's volatility about the subject, Gil expected a cursing fit followed by Carl ripping the flyers into small shreds. To his surprise, Carl laid the flyers on the bar intact and walked back to his seat, not saying a word.

⨉

Friday, October 23

The night before the service, a group of men gathered outside in the parking lot of the D&R Drive-In. These men, though, were not interested in eating.

"What the hell," a short man in a white long-sleeved shirt said. "They're going to honor that drug dealing traitor?"

"Yeah, and he ups and kills himself. That's a coward for you." A larger man wearing a faded John Deere hat spat on the ground.

"A traitor and a damned coward," a man with a dark beard chimed in.

"Well, what are we going to do about it?" the first man spoke. "That cheating Hinton woman and that retard Bud are behind this sacrilege to Ward Jenkins."

The men nodded and focused on their next steps. They didn't see a man approach from one of the carports.

"Good evening, men," the newcomer said. Those gathered instantly recognized him.

"Good evening, Father … Reverend," they answered.

The Reverend Graham McFadden had long given up on the proper way for people to address him. He preferred Reverend, but was more frequently called Father or Pastor or sir. McFadden was a large, stout man of Scottish heritage. He had long gray curly hair that fell over his collar and sideburns that flowed down and merged with it. His size was noticeable, and his eyes could bore a hole through anyone in his disfavor. He had a booming voice developed over years of delivering sermons.

Reverend McFadden's intimidating presence instantly caused the agitated men to shuffle their feet and stare at the ground.

"What are you men up to on this beautiful Friday night?" McFadden's voice carried across the parking lot and over to the carports.

"Nothing, sir. We were just talking about the football game. Brinson kicked Otherton's …" The short man caught himself before saying the next word.

"Yes, that was a good game. What else?" McFadden's eyes settled on the man with the John Deere hat, one of his parishioners.

After a moment's hesitation, the man said, "Father, why are you having that service for Gary Knowles? He's a traitor."

"No, he's not a traitor. Where did you hear that? He was a decorated veteran, for goodness sakes."

"Did you fight in a war, Father?" the short man spoke.

"I became a navy chaplain during the Korean War. People react to war differently. I found God in the Navy. I think Gary was looking for something but didn't find it before he died. It's too bad—for him and for all of us."

"Did Janice and Bud put you up to this service?" the short man asked.

"No one put me up to anything." McFadden's piercing blue eyes zeroed in on the short man. "Yes, Bud spoke to me. But actually, it was Bert and Lola Jenkins who asked for the service. They want closure for Gary, just like Ward."

Surprise and silence followed, broken by McFadden. "Good, I trust I will see you all at the service tomorrow."

Mumbling among the men followed, and Reverend McFadden walked into the restaurant with a smile.

Saturday, October 24

The next day brought a typical October day; a cold morning that morphed into a mild, comfortable afternoon. The Brinson Presbyterian Church could easily hold one hundred fifty congregants. Today, managing a large crowd was not an issue; only about fifty people attended the service for Gary. There were no politicians or military honor guard. Most of the attendees were members of the church.

Janice was there wearing a long black dress. Bud wore his military uniform. Both sat in the front row. Bud's wife, Alice, and daughter, Lily, flanked him, holding his hands. The Jenkins family was present, along with Tim, Angela, and Brent.

Brent had never attended a funeral before. He listened to every word that was spoken while thinking of his time with Gary.

Reverend McFadden kept the service short; there was little choice in the matter. Gary was not a resident of the town and had no relatives in attendance. Few people knew him, and those who did knew little about him. There was word of a military funeral to be held in California, where Gary's body had been sent.

"Even though Gary was not from here, he was one of us. He was a son of America," McFadden's eulogy concluded. "Like all of us, he was conflicted. He had his issues. But his life was too short. A lot of good potential was lost when he died.

"He fought for this country—our country—so that we can have our freedoms. And he certainly deserved to voice his opinions because he defended that right. He also would want us to voice our opinions when something isn't right, including the war in Vietnam. Whether you are for or against the war, Gary fought, so he was more than entitled to his beliefs.

"Make no mistake, Gary Knowles is a hero. He has my respect, and he should have your respect, too. God bless him."

As the parishioners filed from the church, Reverend McFadden shook everyone's hand. When he came to Brent, he said, "I heard you knew Gary about as well as anyone. Sometime I would like to hear your thoughts about him."

For the first time in weeks, Brent felt comfort.

⚔

Chief Thompkins checked his mailbox on Saturday afternoon. A thin envelope was mixed in with the mail. There was no stamp. The note was handwritten.

Chief, I see the radical troublemaker Knowles has passed on. Good. What we have left is the sinner and equally radical Hinton woman. She's been cooking up more trouble, and influencing people like the Jenkins and Frosts. That's no good. What we need in Brinson is God-fearing folks who stand up for this country. Janice Hinton needs to go. I pray she sees the light and does so.

Keep an eye on her and report to me—no more trouble!

The letter was unsigned, but Thompkins knew who it was from—Mayor Templeton.

Thompkins wadded up the letter into a small ball. *I think our asshole mayor needs to forget about Janice Hinton and work on getting the town's rusty water tower painted.*

Chapter 21

Saturday, October 24

After Gary's service, Brent went straight up to his room. He would never see his friend again, and neither would anyone else. A knock at the door disrupted his thoughts.

"Hi." Tim opened the door and walked in.

"Hi," Brent mumbled back, looking first at his dad then out the window.

"Reverend McFadden gave a nice service for Gary, don't you think?"

"Yeah."

"I know that was your first funeral. It's a way to say goodbye to those we love and respect. A funeral is more for the living than for the one who has passed."

"I guess we all have a funeral at some point," Brent sighed.

"True, we all pass away. But you have a long way to go. Hopefully, that's true for your mom and me, too."

"Not for Gary, though. He doesn't get to go to college and play football, get married, or anything. He's dead."

Tim paused and said, "Yes, it's very sad. From what I understand, Gary was a confused young man. I can't speak for the choices he made. Besides Janice, and perhaps Bud, you knew him better than anyone in town. I'm proud of you for taking time to get to know him."

"I just don't understand. He didn't seem unhappy enough to do that to himself. I know it, and he was going to go somewhere else. He was looking forward to dinner with us and the Jenkins."

"You will find, son, that sometimes things don't make sense. You just have to move past them."

Tim reached into his back pocket and pulled out his billfold. He took out a ten-dollar bill and gave it to Brent. "Here, take this and see if some of your friends want to go to Power's Theatre tonight. *Two Mules for Sister Sara* is showing. It has Clint Eastwood. We can all use a distraction from what's been going on."

⋏

Brent asked several friends, and Tom, Jack, and Dale (who was now included in Brents' friend group) agreed to go to the movie with him. Ron, to his dismay, had to practice his trumpet. After the movie, the four boys scooted over to the D&R Drive-In restaurant for soft drinks and a giant basket of french fries. For a Saturday night, the restaurant was quiet.

"I really liked the movie," Brent volunteered as they waited for their drinks and fries.

"My dad likes Clint Eastwood a lot," Tom offered. "He was Rowdy Yates on Rawhide. He's gone from TV to being a big movie star."

"My dad still talks about him in *The Good, the Bad, and the Ugly.* I didn't get to see that movie, but I heard it was good," Jack said.

Shirley, the rotund waitress with permed blond hair, brought a heaping basket of fries and a tray of drinks to the boys' table. They immediately began devouring the fries.

Between bites, Brent turned to Dale. "You've been quiet lately. Something wrong?"

"Yeah, kind of. I don't understand why everyone is calling Mrs. Hinton a hippie and a communist. She has always been nice to me and my family."

"I know why," Jack said as he gulped down a fry. "She doesn't support America against the damned communists. She might *be* one. She should move to California and sing about peace and love, like the hippies do."

"Why?" Tom snorted. "She's getting all the love she needs right here."

"Shut up, Tom," Jack said as he reached for his glass of pop. "You wouldn't even know what to do with a woman like that." He held up a small fry in Tom's direction that flopped over limply. He pointed at Tom's crotch and then at the limp fry.

The boys laughed at Jack's display, though Brent and Dale laughed out of nervousness. Tom was silent. He didn't like jokes at his expense.

"Yeah, like you would, Jack," Tom said as he reached his hand across the table to slap the fry out of Jack's hand. Instead, his sleeve caught Brent's pop and it spilled across the table.

"All right, is everything good here, boys?" Not so much a question as an admonishment from Shirley, who seemed to materialize out of nowhere.

"One of you boys has a red face." She looked at Tom and then frowned at the mess on the table. "Which one of you spilled this?"

"Everything's fine. It was just an accident," Brent looked down at the table when he spoke. He knew Shirley was the town crier and may tell his parents about any unruly behavior. "Sorry about the spill."

Shirley stood back, her hands resting on her wide hips. "OK, calm down boys. Here's the check. Pay before you leave—like, now." Shirley held up the check, waiting for someone to take it.

Brent grabbed it—$2.36. He reached into his pocket and pulled out three one-dollar bills.

"Here, Miss Shirley," he said. "You can keep the change."

"Hmmmm." She took the money and walked away, mumbling about wiping up the spill.

"I wish Bud would chop you up, Jack," Tom grumbled.

"He'd probably forget what he was doing before he even began. You'd have to write him a reminder note." Brent grinned.

The redness in Tom's face dissipated and he smiled.

Jack added, "Besides, Tom, you better save your sweet love for Shirley, so she won't be so cranky all the time."

The boys laughed as one as they left the restaurant. Once outside, Dale took a handful of cold fries from the to-go bag Shirley had given them. "Do you think she will tell our parents?"

"No, she was just playing with us," Jack intoned unconvincingly.

"I've got to get home by ten," Brent said. "Don't forget we have that dumb history test Monday."

"That won't be a problem," added Tom. "Old man Everest just uses the questions from the back of the textbook. Study those questions and the answers. Easy A."

"Glad it's not an algebra test." Dale shook his head.

"Algebra sucks. I'll worry about that later," Jack declared. "By the way, I want to tell you guy's something, but it has to be later."

Puzzled looks formed on the other's faces.

"I said later. See you tomorrow."

The group split up and went home, either walking or by a parental pickup.

Brent arrived home at ten o'clock as the cuckoo clock chirped from its basement perch. The clock used to be in the upstairs hallway next to the bedrooms, but the twice-hourly cuckooing prompted its quick exile to the basement.

"Hi," Tim said from the living room as he put the Saturday newspaper down. "Did you like the movie?"

"Yeah, it was good. Thanks for the money."

"Who did you go with?" Angela asked suddenly from the top of the stairs.

"The usual guys—Jack, Tom, and Dale. Ron couldn't make it. I like Clint Eastwood."

"Did you go anywhere after the show?" Angela asked casually.

Brent got a quick lump in his throat. He had visions of fat Shirley tattling on him and his friends. *Crap,* he thought. *I'd better say something.*

"We went to the D&R for drinks and fries. We weren't there long." Brent hoped for no follow-up questions.

"Glad you had a good night," Tim said. "Time for bed."

"Sounds good," Brent silently thanked his dad for ending the conversation and walked swiftly up the stairs.

Sunday, October 25

The next day, Brent's thoughts of Gary were replaced by an unfounded fear of what Shirley would say to his parents. His father craved the malts at the D&R Drive-In and was a frequent customer. Dale was equally apprehensive. But Jack seemed unfazed, per usual. Tom was just Tom. He had moved on. After their usual Sunday football game, the boys gathered with Ron at the park.

"Jack, what were you saying last night? About what you would tell us later?" Brent spoke up and Dale nodded.

Jack took a deep breath. "The other night I was riding my bike and I stopped by old man Juntlo's barn. Someone was unloading three large metal boxes. I couldn't see real well, but I think it was Elmer Juntlo. He kept turning his head, looking this way and that to see if anyone was watching him. He didn't see me, though. There was another creepy man with him, but I don't know who it was.

"That's not the first time I've seen stuff being moved in and out of that barn, either. He's got something in there. I don't know what, but old man Juntlo was being very protective of those boxes. We need to find out what's in them. It could be money, bodies, or take a guess."

"We could be rich, or solve a crime," Tom said.

"We'll have to see when he's in the barn and when he's not," Ron added, nodding.

"Who's in?" Jack glanced at each of the boys' faces. He saw nods from everyone except Dale, who was more hesitant. "Good, let's meet here after supper tomorrow and put together a plan."

CHAPTER 22

Monday, October 26

At noon on Monday, the black Cadillac cruised into Brinson. The driver drove through downtown, turned around at the tracks, and slowly maneuvered to a diagonal parking spot in front of the Thirsty Bull.

Several minutes passed before the man emerged from the car. He stood and surveyed the street and the tavern. He was tall with good posture, and had a head of thick silver hair that bounced down around his collar. He had long sideburns, a broad white moustache, and pock-marked cheeks. He wore black jeans and a button-down cream shirt. His tan leather vest looked like it had escaped from a rodeo. His feet were encased in dark brown cowboy boots with silver tips.

The man removed his sunglasses and placed them in a silver case. He reached into the car, dropping his sunglasses case on the seat and grabbing his black Stetson. He gently placed his hat on, careful not to ruffle his finely coiffed hair. When he was satisfied, the man opened the tavern door and stepped inside.

Six men in their sixties sat at the rectangular wooden bar. All sipped beers and talked among themselves with the even-older bartender, Gil. All seven gazed at the stranger like he was an alien.

"Howdy, men," the stranger said in a deep baritone.

A couple "Hellos" rang out as Gil eyed the stranger.

"Not a bad day out there, is it?" Getting no response he added, "How is harvesting going? I heard on the radio that corn and beans are down, but hogs and cattle are up."

"Damned government, screwing with us again," an old timer at the far end of the bar said to the room.

"We'll be lucky to break even this year," another added while taking a gulp from his glass.

"Shit," a third man joined in. "I know ten times as much as those damned government ag people, and they make more money than all of us combined. And what's worse, they take it off our backs."

"Yeah, I don't trust the government either," added the stranger as he sat on a duct tape-covered stool.

"What do you know about any of this, stranger?" A suspicious Gil walked over to the man. "Who are you, anyway? I don't recognize you."

"That's because I haven't been here in a long, long time. I recall the last time I was here this place was called the Stop-In Tavern."

All seven men eyed the stranger with curiosity.

"That was awhile back." Gil cocked his head.

The stranger reached into his wallet and pulled out a crisp twenty-dollar bill. "A round for everyone here, including you." The man nodded to Gil. "Keep the change."

The bartender gladly poured eight cold glasses of Hamm's from the tap and handed them out to his customers.

Several men tipped their glasses to the stranger in appreciation. *I'll drink free beer all day,* was their silent consensus.

Finally, Gil asked, "Who are you, then, if you're not really a stranger?"

"My name is Rob, Robert Frost."

"Robert Frost—like the poet?" Gil questioned.

"Didn't he write a poem about forks in the road or something?" the man at the end of the bar mumbled. "There should have been signs for them roads."

"Do you mean *The Road Not Taken*?" Rob asked. He continued in his western drawl, "No, not Robert Frost the poet. I'm Robert Franklin Frost from Colorado. My father was Richard Franklin Frost, and my mother was Ethel Frost. Did you know them?"

The gasps from the men were drowned out by the sound of beer glasses hitting the bar.

"Have a good day, fellas." Rob finished his drink in one gulp and left the tavern with a wave.

Chief Thompkins sat at his worn cherry desk watching the latest episode of *Dark Shadows* on his small black and white television. If he adjusted the rabbit ear antennae just right, the picture came in pretty clear. Thompkins' favorite character was the remorseful vampire, Barnabas Collins. In this episode, Collins was explaining an important observation to a headless warlock. Thompkins was so engrossed in the story that he didn't see a man enter the office until the man was standing right in front of him.

"Hello, Chief Thompkins," the man dressed in western attire said. "Nice day, don't you think?"

Thompkins fumbled with his coffee cup and glanced at the television, hoping for a quick resolution to the mystery in the story. He knew that was not going to happen; quick resolutions rarely happened on *Dark Shadows*. He reluctantly turned off the television and sat up straight in his chair.

"Hi, what can I do ya for?" Thompkins stared, trying to put a name to the face. Clearly, he was not from the area.

"I'm Rob Frost," the man said as he held out his hand.

"Well, ya know who I am already." Thompkins shook Rob's hand and noticed the firmness of his grip. "Where are ya from, and what brings ya to Brinson, Mr. Rob Frost?"

"Outside of Denver, in Colorado," Rob said, adding, "Did you know my parents, Richard and Ethel Frost?" Rob's blue eyes stared into Thompkins' eyes.

"No, why, should I?" Thompkins stared back. "I know a Tim and Angela Frost. Are ya related to them?"

"Perhaps. How long have you been the police chief here in Brinson?" Rob stood erect and tucked his arms behind his back like a soldier at ease.

"Just five years. I came over from a county in southern Illinois. I was a deputy sheriff there."

"My father disappeared in November 1940 right out there on Main Street." Rob pointed in the direction of the street. "He was never found. I thought maybe something new has turned up in the past dozen years or so."

"I've never heard anything about that disappearance that I can recall. I can look into it for ya, if ya want."

"That would be kind of you. I'm staying at the Best Western in Carlson if you need to reach me. Here's the number." Rob handed Thompkins a piece of paper with the motel's number. "I'll check in from time to time."

"How long are ya going to be here?"

"I don't have a time frame in mind. Now you know where to reach me—if I'm not in town." Rob showed no emotion as he spoke. "Good day, Chief." He turned his back on the chief and left.

Chief Thompkins stared at the closed door for several seconds before turning the television back on. A commercial break had just ended, and Barnabas Collins' vampirish face filled the screen.

Chapter 23

Monday, October 26

Monday morning came like cold syrup poured over ice-cold pancakes. When Barnes drove to the office, his nerves shivered through him. He drew up in his usual parking space, switched off the engine, and just sat. *What does Del really think of me after Manlo? What are the people in the office thinking? What kind of assignments will I get from the captain going forward? I don't want the commendation—it should all be Del's recognition.*

Barnes was jolted out of his introspection by a rapping on the window.

"You have to come inside sometime, Fred," a friendly voice shouted through the window.

"I'm coming, Marge." Barnes forced a smile. He grabbed his briefcase and locked his car.

Marge waited patiently for him. "We're all glad you're doing fine and back at work. We've been worried about you."

"Thanks again for looking after me—and for those cookies!"

After dropping off his briefcase in his office, Barnes made a beeline to the breakroom for some coffee. The first thing he saw was a banner that read:

WELCOME BACK, FRED

Barnes smiled nervously reading it. A hand fell on his shoulder. Barnes turned and saw Robinson standing behind him.

"You're here, my man!" Robinson shook Barnes' hand, a bright smile plastered across his face. It was infectious and coaxed a similar smile from Barnes.

"Glad to be back, Del."

Marge and several other people offered Barnes kind words. When everyone had gathered, Marge pointed to a large box.

"We all chipped in and bought these." Marge opened the box, revealing a couple dozen donuts, rolls, and Danish pastries. "They're from your favorite, the Made-Right Café. And Hazel sends her well wishes."

Barnes and his co-workers all laughed, and a free-for-all began as many hands pawed the box of treats. The captain appeared in the doorway.

"Detective Barnes, could you stop in my office? Oh, and bring me a Danish. I already have coffee."

The party broke up, and Barnes walked into the captain's office carrying the requested roll.

"Thank you. Please take a seat."

Barnes complied and looked at the captain, not sure what was to come next. The captain had a single sheet of paper in his hands, and he took his time focusing on it. Barnes became increasingly nervous as time passed. *Am I getting walking papers?* he wondered.

Finally, the captain reached over his desk and handed the sheet to Barnes, not taking his eyes off Barnes' face.

"Read it and tell me what you think," the captain said, not giving any indication what was written. Barnes read the first line and relaxed. *I'm not being fired.* He read the rest of the letter twice before looking at the captain.

To the Iowa Crimes Commission—

Private Gary Knowles, formerly of the 101st Airborne, Vietnam, recently died here in Brinson, Iowa. Most people, including the local authorities, are convinced *he took his own life, intentionally or unintentionally, because of his involvement in the Vietnam War. However, there are those of us who believe he was murdered. We are asking for your help. He was a decorated war hero. The local authorities are in on a cover-up. Please investigate.*

The letter was typed and signed by hand, *Janice D. Hinton and Bud R. Nichols.*

"What do you make of this?"

"I don't know. These are strange times."

"That's not the answer I expected from a detective."

"Captain, it seems like a goose chase. We've not heard of any corruption in Brinson. This is a local matter."

"Again, not the answer I expect from one of my detectives." The captain raised his voice. "Try again!"

"We should look into the matter and determine whether there is a case?"

"Precisely. I know the Reed County sheriff, Harold Larken, personally. He's an earnest man." The captain paused and sucked in a deep breath. "This is what I want you to do: Go to Brinson, do your detective work, and report back to me whether Knowles killed himself or was murdered.

"I don't care whether you or anyone else is for or against the war. Was a crime committed or not? It's that simple. I'll give you a week to sort this out. There is a Best Western in Carlson where you can stay. Command wants an answer. You are to leave today. Report back to me daily by telephone. Get going."

Barnes nodded, "Thank you, Captain."

After Barnes left the building, the captain's second in command poked his head into the captain's office.

"How did he take it?"

"Fine," the captain answered. "Barnes needs a change of scenery, and this should be an easy case. He'll conclude that Knowles committed suicide, and that's that. And it gets him out of my sight. Since his wife died, there has been a notable decrease in his competency as a detective. I can't rely on his judgment or actions anymore. I'm afraid it's sink or swim time for Detective Barnes."

Barnes scanned his house for what needed to be done. First, he placed fertilizer stakes in each of his five plants and gave them a good dousing of water.

"That should hold you until I return," he told the plants after he finished watering.

They had been Clara's plants. He hadn't cared about them until she died. Then it became his mission to keep them alive and healthy.

Next, he cleaned the cat's litter box. He poured the old water out of its bowl and replaced it with fresh tap water. He took dry cat food from the cupboard and mixed it with an open can of wet Friskies he kept in the refrigerator. Fluffy watched with eager anticipation as Barnes completed his task. Once Barnes stood up and moved away from the food bowl, the cat raced to it and pounced on his feast.

"God, I'm glad you aren't a picky eater," he said as the cat inhaled its food. Fluffy was another holdover of Clara's. Barnes put up with it when Clara was alive. Now, the cat had become his best friend.

Barnes picked up the phone and dialed Edna Colder.

"Hello," she answered in her friendly warbling voice.

"Hi, Edna, it's Fred. I'm going out of town for about five days or so. Can you look after Fluffy for me? It'll be the same thing as always, like when I was in the hospital. Just be sure he doesn't try to flee when you open the door. I don't want him to develop a harem." Barnes and Edna laughed. "You have the key."

"Sure thing, Fred. Are you doing OK?"

He wasn't sure if she was referring to his recent brush with death in Manlo or the lingering effects of Clara's death. He didn't ask for clarification. "I'm fine. I have an assignment I need to complete."

After he hung up the telephone, Barnes methodically untangled the knotted phone cord. He grabbed his suitcase, said good-bye to Fluffy, and left the house. He took a department-issued blue Ford LTD to Brinson.

The drive to Brinson was a blur. Barnes became lost in his thoughts about Clara, the cat, and Manlo as the radio played the top forty songs of the week. He was troubled mostly by his last interaction with the captain. He wasn't sure if he was going to be demoted and placed on desk duty, or fired. He gave little thought to Brinson until he was close to the town limits. At the last minute, he decided he wouldn't go into town yet; that could wait until tomorrow.

He passed along the north edge of Brinson on Highway 40 on his way to Carlson. He looked to his left as he drove by, observing the straight streets and the town's smallness. The fall season had dug in, giving the area a desolate appearance. Barnes frowned. *The captain set me up on this assignment. Anyone could do this job; he just wants me out of his hair. Maybe he wants me out of the ICC. I sure screwed up in Manlo.*

Barnes sat up in his seat and contradicted his previous thoughts. *I didn't do anything wrong; I'm a good detective.*

He drove into the parking lot of the Best Western-Carlson, tired from overthinking. He registered at the desk.

"What brings you to Carlson, Mr. Barnes?" the heavyset bespectacled manager inquired.

"Oh, I'm here for a business matter in Brinson." Barnes took the key to room 119 and turned to leave. As he did, he spotted a black Cadillac pull up. A man in jeans, flowing silver hair, and a black cowboy hat got out of the car and disappeared into one of the rooms. He clearly was not from Iowa.

"Who's that?" Barnes asked the manager. "Doesn't look like he's from around here."

The manager liked to talk and dismissed any privacy concerns. "Oh, that's Robert Frost, from Colorado."

The manager was expecting a quip about Robert Frost the poet, but Barnes simply smiled and turned to leave for his room. He found himself face to face with the Coloradan. A moment of silence hung in the air until the motel manager intervened.

"Mr. Fred Barnes, this is Mr. Rob Frost—from Colorado. Mr. Frost, Mr. Barnes."

The two men shook hands saying, "Good to meet you," simultaneously.

The office quickly filled with motel patrons as the manager added, "It's cookie time."

Rob explained in his thick western accent, "Everyday at five o'clock sharp our friend here provides chocolate chip cookies. I might add, they are delicious."

Barnes took a cookie from the manager's platter and bit into the soft warm treat. "I agree," Barnes said after finishing off the cookie. "These are delicious. Could I have another, please?"

Barnes received his second and nodded to Rob, "I think I'll like it here."

Chapter 24

Monday, October 26

Janice slowly exhaled smoke out of her nose as she stared at the wall. She crushed the Marlboro in an ashtray full of forgotten cigarette butts. She checked the pack, hoping there was one left. There wasn't. "Damn," she said to the empty room. "I've gone through a whole pack since this morning."

Janice had smoked for several years and proudly quit on January 1, 1970. Today, though, she needed the comfort of an old habit. She gazed at the envelope in front of her. She'd opened it and read the note inside several times. Each time its effect was equally chilling.

WE ARE WATCHING YOU

Bud found the envelope when he opened the store that morning. It was addressed simply to "Janice." She had received similar envelopes with the same message in the mailbox at her house for the past three days. *What should I do?* she thought. Being a strong woman, she didn't want to show any signs of weakness. She knew she had taken a stand on issues that weren't popular with many of the townspeople, so she wasn't surprised to receive the ominous and anonymous notes. Still, they unnerved her.

Several knocks rapped on the storage room door where Janice had isolated herself.

"Are you all right in there, Mrs. Hinton?" Bud's voice boomed.

"Sure, Bud, I'll be right out."

She knew he would stay until she appeared. She opened the door and a haze of cigarette smoke flooded into the hallway.

"I thought you stopped smoking. It's not good for you." Bud waved his hand in front of his face to ward away the smoke demons.

"I had a temporary relapse. I promise I won't smoke anymore." She knew that promise would be hard to keep.

Bud looked down and saw the envelope in her hands, which shook slightly. He reached for the envelope.

"Can I read what's in there?" His tone was a statement, not a question.

"It doesn't concern you," she said unconvincingly.

Bud grabbed the envelope. Since returning from the war, subtlety was not a trait he possessed.

A deep scowl crossed his face as he read the short note. "Who sent this?"

Janice shook her head. "I don't know."

"When I find out, I'll crush him like a bug," Bud glowered at the note, instantly protective.

"Bud, we don't even know if it's a him or a her."

"It's a man, I know it. You need to tell Chief Thompkins about this. He'll do something."

"I don't want to bother Ellis. I'll tell you what—if I get another note, I'll inform the chief."

"You tell him, or I'll tell him—today!"

Janice knew Bud would follow through.

"OK, I will. Today."

"Do it now, Mrs. Hinton. I'll mind the store."

Chief Thompkins was not at the police station when Janice stopped by, but the door was unlocked. She wrote him a message about the mystery notes she had received, and placed it on his chair. *I can tell Bud I did as he asked, and that is all I can do for now,* she thought as she walked back to the store, contemplating the meaning and seriousness of the notes.

Chapter 25

Monday, October 26

Halloween was closing in fast and thoughts of it permeated the air. Most kids at school were anticipating the big day. Younger children looked forward to the evening trick-or-treat candy grab. The older high schoolers thought about the school dance. The in between kids wondered if they could do both—grab some candy *and* go to the dance.

Brent was at an age where he still wanted to get a candy haul and perhaps venture to the dance. He knew it was the last year he would trick or treat. His friends were of like mind.

Brent met his friends at the D&R Drive-In to talk about their anticipated Halloween adventures.

"What are you going to be?" Dale asked Brent.

"Don't know yet." Brent thought of several potential ideas from scary to cool.

"I'm going as Clint Eastwood from *The Good, the Bad, and the Ugly,*" Jack said resolutely.

"Damn—that's who I was going to be," Tom pouted.

"Not no more, Tom. You can be a mule from the *Sister Sara* movie," Jack chuckled.

The boys laughed at Tom's expense. "Very funny, Jack." Tom kicked the ground. Tom was the best student of Brent's friends, but at times the most immature.

"Did you guys think any more about investigating those boxes in Juntlo's barn?" Jack changed the subject.

"I don't know. When do you want to do it?" Ron wondered.

"Tomorrow after school—three o'clock," Jack said knowingly. "Old man Juntlo is always at the Thirsty Bull then. He meets a bunch of old farmers and they drink all afternoon. He doesn't always lock the side door to the barn. I've watched him, so I know."

"I want to see what's in those boxes." Brent surprised himself with his willingness to volunteer. He did not know what compelled him to act out of character. Perhaps it was a seed of independence he had acquired from his time with Gary. To go into Juntlo's barn was the germination of that seed.

"Good. We have a brave soldier here," Jack pointed to Brent. "We'll meet tomorrow outside the barn. As soon as he leaves, Brent will go inside and check out the boxes. We'll wait outside until you come back."

Chapter 26

Tuesday, October 27

Barnes slept in on his first morning at the Best Western-Carlson. Usually, he was an early riser—around five-thirty—but for whatever reason he didn't get up until seven o'clock. He took a shower and shaved with his electric razor. *My beard grows faster every day.* After splashing on some after shave, he viewed the clothes he had brought. *This will be an easy assignment,* he thought. *Today, I'll skip my usual suit and that damned tie for slacks and a sweater. It's much more comfortable.* Barnes reconsidered and wore a subdued tie, which he tucked under his sweater so only the top of the knot was visible.

Once dressed, he decided to get the *Des Moines Register* newspaper from the motel office. He stepped inside and found no one there, so he rang the bell on the desk. The same round man Barnes had met the night before came scurrying out from a back room.

"Good morning," the man said smiling.

"Good morning. I'd like a paper, please." Barnes handed the man the exact change and received the paper. He glanced quickly at the headlines. "Is there much going on today?"

"No, it's pretty quiet here this time of year. Farmers are finishing their harvests. Winter is around the corner. You'll need that jacket today." The clerk pointed to the coat Barnes carried over his left arm.

"Thanks, I'll take your advice. Say, you have a nice motel here. Are you the owner?"

"Yes, and manager, thank you." The motel man began warming up to Barnes.

"I'm going into Brinson this morning. Are you familiar with the town?

"It's a nice little town." The clerk emphasized "little." "Brinson is a bedroom town. A lot of people who live there work in Carlson. I guess they feel less crowded in a small town," he said sarcastically.

"Probably lower taxes, too." Barnes chuckled and the clerk laughed. "I heard there was a suicide there recently."

"Yeah, it was big news for a couple days. He was an army vet who lost his mind." The manager pointed at his head. "Check with the local paper in Brinson—the *Bee*. It's a decent enough paper, for a small town, and the newspaper people there probably know more about what's going on in Brinson than anyone."

"War can do bad things to good people. Thanks for the advice. Have a good day," Barnes said and left for his car.

The man shouted after him, "Remember, be here by five for the chocolate chip cookies! They go quickly."

Barnes made the short trip down Highway 40 to Brinson. He first drove on the outskirts of town and several side streets around Main Street, trying to get a picture of the area. The houses were midsized to small, but well kept. *Nice middle-class community*, he thought.

Barnes ventured up Main Street, also called Elm Street. He thought the name was interesting because there were no elm trees left on the street. *Casualty of the Dutch Elm disease*, he thought to himself. *Too bad. Elms are magnificent trees. I had one in my front yard and had to cut it down. Clara cried when it happened.*

He parked out front of the *Brinson Bee* and walked inside. The newspaper office was divided into two primary sections by a two-foot-wide counter: the front area for customers and guests, and the larger back work area where the papers were prepared for off-site printing.

"Good morning," Barnes said to two women seated in the rear area. They were stuffing envelopes.

"Yes, it is. Good morning to you, as well, mister. How can I help you?"

A smartly dressed woman wearing a bright blue sweater left her chair and approached him at the counter. She had blue eyes that matched her sweater, and a generous mound of reddish permed hair covered the top and sides of her head.

"Hi, my name is Fred Barnes and I'm visiting. I noticed Brinson has its own paper. Is that unusual for such a small town?"

"Maybe so, but the *Brinson Bee* has been published for more than seventy years. I wasn't here when it started." She giggled.

Barnes smiled. "What do you publish and how often?"

"Well, first, my name is Mabel, Mabel Knuth. Over there is Brenda." Mabel pointed to the shorter woman standing off to her side. "We publish a weekly newspaper on Wednesdays. We also publish an advertising bulletin on Fridays because shoppers come out on the weekend, you know."

"If you have an extra copy of the newspaper from last week, I'd like to buy it." Barnes reached for his wallet.

Mabel went back to a desk and returned with the requested copy. "It's on the house, Mr. Barnes. Buy me a cup of coffee sometime."

"Thank you." Barnes opened the folded paper to a bold headline: *VET COMMITS SUICIDE IN HINTON HOUSE*. "That's quite a headline," Barnes said.

"He was doing drugs and overdosed," Mabel said matter-of-factly.

"That's too bad. Did you write the article, Mabel?"

"No, that was our publisher, editor, and manager, Max Sturgess. He's been with the paper since the thirties, I think. He knows everything that goes on around here—he's basically a walking history book of the town. He's playing golf right now, despite the cold. The suicide was quite the event. Everyone with a badge was there. Really added some spice to our usually quiet nights. Quite the reaction for a traitor."

"Why do you say that? Didn't he fight in Vietnam?" Wanting to change the subject, Barnes asked, "Say, is there someplace nearby where I can get a pop and an apple?"

Mabel paused and said coldly, "There's Hinton's General Store up the street, but I wouldn't go there. No one goes there anymore. She is betraying our country and housed that traitor, Gary Knowles." In a hushed voice, she added, "And she sleeps with married men."

"I see." Barnes ignored her last comment. "Thanks again for the paper."

After Barnes left, Mabel turned to Brenda. "I don't know what to make of that man. He's handsome, and that wavy brown hair."

"That's not the last we'll see of him, I'll say," Brenda said as she stuffed envelopes. "He's either a reporter or a cop."

Barnes strolled into the Hinton General Store and found himself alone initially. The bell that announced his entrance brought a large man with a crew cut from behind the meat counter off to the right of the main door.

"Mornin'. How can I help you? I'm Bud."

"Hi, I'm Fred. A couple of things, Bud," Barnes said as he scanned the store. "Where do you keep the pop and apples?"

"Over there, in the cooler." Bud pointed to a horizontal standing cooler stationed off to the left. "We have all the brands, Coke, Pepsi, Orange Crush, 7Up, even grape. The apples are over there." Bud looked right, where a case of apples had been placed.

"I'll take a look, thanks." Barnes walked to the cooler and selected a Pepsi Cola and took a shiny red apple from the case. He approached the cash register.

Bud rang up the items. "That'll be forty-five cents."

Barnes picked a quarter and two dimes from his pocket and gave them to Bud. "Say, is Mrs. Janice Hinton here?"

"No, she's out." Bud became defensive immediately. "Why do you want to know?"

"I just want to talk to her about this." Barnes opened the paper and pointed to the article about Gary.

"He didn't kill himself. I know that's the God's truth," Bud asserted.

"Why do you say that?" Starting to realize how sensitive the Knowles case was in Brinson, Barnes tried to lighten the mood. "Do you have a bottle opener? My teeth aren't strong enough."

"Sure, sir." Bud grabbed a well-used bottle opener kept by the cash register and handed it to Barnes. "I know what the truth is and isn't," Bud repeated with emphasis. "And that's the truth."

"I understand what you're saying." Barnes reached into his billfold and pulled out a card. "I'm a detective with the Iowa Crimes Commission in Des Moines. I'm here to investigate the Gary Knowles case. You and Mrs. Hinton sent a letter to our office."

"That's right, sir. He didn't kill himself."

"Please give this card to Mrs. Hinton. I'm staying at the Best Western-Carlson. I can be reached at the number on the back. I'm in room 119. We'll be in touch. Thanks, Bud."

Barnes left the store and drove on the gravel roads of Reed County. He stopped at the Westbrick Lake Pavilion outside of Carlson. There, he read the article about Gary, followed by the rest of the paper in detail. It was becoming cold, so he bundled himself back into his car and drove to the motel. Rob's black Cadillac was there as Barnes went to his room. He wrote a series of notes and called the captain with a brief update.

Just before three o'clock, he received a phone call. "Yes, Mrs. Hinton, tomorrow's fine."

He decided he had time to return to Brinson. He wanted to become more familiar with the town and vicinity, and be back in time for cookies.

Chapter 27

Tuesday, October 27

The next day, a dreary Tuesday, came too soon for Brent. *God, what did I agree to?* The bravado of the previous day had disappeared. *I can't back out now. My friends will think I'm chicken-shit.*

Juntlo's barn was in the far southwestern corner of Brinson. Directly north of the barn was Eighth Avenue, the southernmost east-west running road in Brinson. Eighth Avenue ran into the intersection of Tenth Street to the right and County Highway H to the left. An unharvested cornfield lay directly south of the barn, and then field after field.

Brent, Jack, Tom, Ron, and Dale gathered after school half a block north of the barn on Tenth Street. There, they attempted to appear busy and act like they were meant to be there while keeping an eye on the barn. At precisely three o'clock, Elmer Juntlo left the barn through the side door. He got in his 1955 red Ford pickup truck and headed to the Thirsty Bull.

"Great, he'll be at the bar for hours," Jack nodded to Brent. "Now's your chance. We'll keep an eye out here. If he comes back, I'll whistle and you can get out." Jack stuck two fingers in his mouth and started to whistle, and caught himself. "You know the sound."

"But if he comes and you whistle, he'll see me when I leave." Brent's face creased with concern as he pointed at the door.

"Make it fast and you don't have to worry. We'll distract him," Jack said, not sure what the distraction would be.

Brent looked at his friends. They were all grinning with excitement—and a hint of worry. Dale, particularly, hung back from the others.

"OK, but if I find gold or some other treasure, I get a larger share when we take it out. But I'm not taking anything now—this is just surveillance." Brent had learned that term from Gary.

"Yeah," Jack said as the other three nodded. "Do your surveillance."

When Brent was sure no one was driving on the nearby streets, he walked by the barn. He saw the lock on the door and felt a burst of relief. On closer inspection, he sighed. The lock hung open on the door latch—just as Jack said. He could access the barn.

Brent took a lingering glance behind him. His friends huddled by an old oak tree. *It's now or never,* he told himself. He opened the door quickly and slid inside, gently closing it behind him. As he did, the lock fell to the ground. *I'll put it back when I leave.* He turned on the pocket flashlight he had borrowed from his dad.

Brent's first thought was, *My folks would kill me if they knew what I was doing.* Then he thought, *God, what a pigsty.* Junk was strewn all around the barn. Several vehicles, including a van, pickup truck, and parts of several cars, had been dumped randomly. The place smelled of rusty metal and oil. There were old bed frames, barrels of scrap metal, and other barrels containing an oily substance.

He glanced left and froze. A deer hung by its hind legs in the corner shadows. A thick layer of blood had congealed in a pan underneath the deer's head. Antlers sprouted from the head. Its eyes were open and seemed to say, "Why me?"

Brent had never seen such a sight and stood mesmerized. *God, how could Juntlo do this?* He saw himself in the deer's place, should old man Juntlo find him in the barn. A gust of wind followed by a tree branch brushing against the barn's roof shook him from his trance, causing his already surging heart rate to spike.

He took a deep breath and switched his gaze to other areas of the barn.

Dozens of assorted, rusty paint cans lined part of the west wall. Along the north wall sat an old wooden workbench. Various tools were scattered across the top and nearby floor, intermixed with wrappers from the D&R Drive-In. *What a mess. What does he do here? Nothing good.*

A second story could be accessed by a rickety staircase. *No way I'm going up there.* Cracked concrete extended across most of the building's floor except for an area along the south wall that was a hard dirt surface. The wooden walls looked like they were last painted a hundred years ago. Brent spotted holes at the bottom of the wall where the floor was dirt. *I'll bet some type of animal crawls through here to get at old man Juntlo's food wrappers.*

Brent's left eye began twitching as he continued to survey the barn. *I've got to find those boxes.* He knew that the faster he searched, the sooner he could leave this junky, scary place. He weaved around the barn through narrow openings from one area to another. The light seeping in from outside was spotty depending on the size of the cracks in the walls. Brent saw only one lamp in the building, and it was attached to the workbench. He was thankful for his flashlight. Brent's growing anxiety was pleading for him to leave when the flashlight beam swept across a trunk near the south wall. He carefully navigated his way across the floor, trying to avoid the sharp metal ends of a bed frame.

Too intent on the bed, he didn't see the jar of hardware placed on the hood of a car. His elbow hit the jar. *CRASH.* It smashed onto a brick on the floor and shattered. Metal and glass flew everywhere.

"Shit!" Brent whispered to himself. *Juntlo will know someone was here,* he thought. Brent was instantly sweaty and desperately wanted to get out of the barn. *I was so stupid to do this. I'm taking all the risk while my friends stand by.*

As he shuffled around the debris to determine the best way out, his foot bumped the end of the trunk. *I'm here, so I might as well check it out. It'll just take a second,* he thought. With the flashlight in his left hand, he squatted beside the metal trunk, which was the size of a large suitcase. On one side was a latch without a lock.

Brent took a deep breath and, with visions of gold or money or something valuable in his head, he lifted the lid. The rays from the flashlight lit up the trunk's interior. His mind could not process what lay in front of him. Cold seeped through his body and he was petrified.

A human skull stared back at him and seemed to say, "You found me, now what?" Neatly arrayed around the skull were many bones—long, short, legs, arms, hands. He didn't want to imagine.

Brent sat still as a stone for several minutes, his brain working to understand who it was, how they died, why the bones were in the barn, and why Juntlo had them. Fresh waves of dread cascaded over Brent.

He didn't hear the whistles or the pickup's loud exhaust until the truck was just outside the barn. Then he did. For the third time in minutes, Brent was stunned. Elmer Juntlo had returned to the barn unexpectedly.

Brent had two choices: *I can try and find a way out now, or stay hidden until Juntlo leaves and then get out. Of course, Juntlo could lock the door this time.* Brent cringed as he remembered, *The lock is on the ground! Juntlo will know someone's here! God help me.*

The door opened and Juntlo wandered in. He was muttering to himself about the lock as he shuffled over to his workbench and picked up something. He walked back to the door and pushed on it to make sure it was shut. While Juntlo was distracted, Brent closed the trunk. The lid squeaked.

"What's that? Who's here?" Juntlo rasped. "I've got my shotgun and I shoot thieves!"

Brent felt faint with fear and then rallied when he remembered the holes at the base of the wall just a few short feet away. He bent low and scrambled as quietly as he could for the openings, tucking the flashlight into his pants pocket. He could hear Juntlo behind him, tossing junk aside searching for the intruder.

"I'm coming for you, asshole! Try to steal from me. I've got some lead for you!"

Brent found a hole that was about two and a half boards wide and a foot off the ground. He squeezed himself into the space, praying he would fit through. He pulled himself out until only his butt and legs were still in the barn. He stopped struggling for a moment, listening. *I don't hear anything inside the barn. That's not good.*

Brent willed his way through the opening and, once clear, crawled down into the cornfield. He rested on his back for a second, but heard Juntlo's howls coming from around the side of the barn.

"I'm coming for you, punk!"

Brent jumped to his feet and ran as fast as he could through the cornfield, grateful with every step that the corn had not yet been harvested.

CRACK. A shotgun blast filled the air. Brent dove into the dirt between the corn rows. *CRACK.* A second blast erupted from the shotgun. Brent crouched back up and ran like a hunchback to County Highway H and a culvert that ran under the road.

"You can't hide when there's nowhere to run! I'll find you, shithead."

As Brent raced to the culvert in terror, he didn't see the blue Ford LTD speeding up County Highway H to the barn.

Chapter 28

Tuesday, October 27

Barnes heard the gunshots as he toured the southern part of Brinson, listening to the newscast on the WHO radio station out of Des Moines. He enjoyed these drives in and outside the town. The idyllic small-town nature of the place was therapeutic.

The shotgun blasts jolted him back to reality. He had a fleeting vision of that night in Manlo, but as he drove north on County Highway H into town, Barnes focused on the figure leveling a gun at something just above the cornfield. The shooter noticed the blue car, turned, and abruptly headed for the north side of the barn.

Barnes maneuvered off the road and pulled up in front of the barn. *I need to look into this, although it's outside my jurisdiction.* He quickly attached his ICC badge to his belt and grabbed his government-issued revolver from the glove compartment. He checked the ammunition. *Good to go,* he said to himself. He clambered out of the car and wedged the gun in his waistband at his right hip. He threw on his jacket with the ICC insignia and knocked on the barn door.

There was no immediate answer. Barnes knocked again, more forcefully. "I know you're in there. Come out. I just want to talk."

"Yeah, give me a moment," a hoarse voice barked back.

After a few seconds, the door creaked open. Barnes stood off to the side and had his hand on his sidearm, ready for the worst.

"What's you want?" the voice crackled.

"Just to talk with you, that's all."

"Who the hell are you?"

"I'm Detective Fred Barnes with the Iowa Crimes Commission."

"What the hell are you doing here? Ain't you out of Des Moines?"

"That's right. I'm just visiting. Now, open the door. I want to talk to you face to face."

The brown scratched wooden door opened and Elmer Juntlo stood in the doorway. He was unshaven and wore a trucker's cap with an insignia Barnes could not make out. The bill of his cap shaded his eyes. Juntlo was not holding a gun, and Barnes relaxed slightly.

"I saw you fire your shotgun into the field just now. Isn't it against the law to discharge a firearm within town limits?"

"What the hell do you know about Brinson's laws and the town boundaries?" Juntlo snapped, agitated.

"It's my experience. Now, who are you?" Barnes retorted.

"I don't have to answer to you, you damned fed. You're out of your jurisdiction here, boy."

"First, I'm not a fed. I work for the state. Second, I'm going to get the town police down here for a visit. I'm sure they would like to know what you're up to."

"I was shooting varmints, coyotes. They're a real menace around here, and I'm protecting my property, cop," Juntlo snarled. His face became a deeper shade of red.

"Whoever you are, we'll see what you are and aren't allowed to do." Barnes sensed he would get no further with this recalcitrant man.

"Get the hell off my land. And don't come back. My shotgun is always loaded to get rid of *any* vermin that come on my property."

"We'll talk later, sir."

Barnes returned to his car while watching the odd man close the barn door. *There is something off about him*, he thought.

Barnes slowly drove up Tenth Street and noticed a group of boys standing just off the street. One was noticeably dirty, but what caught

Barnes' eye was a piece of corn leaf stuck to his hair and a rivulet of blood running down his left cheek.

Barnes' next stop was Chief Ellis Thompkins' office. The chief stood by the coffee maker when Barnes entered. Thompkins held an American Legion mug in his hands while a television blared in the background.

"Hi, Chief Thompkins?" Barnes began.

"Yes, and …"

"I'm Fred Barnes, detective with the Iowa Crimes Commission."

The two men shook hands, each watching the other's eyes.

"I heard ya're in the area. I've been expecting ya, Detective Barnes."

"I imagine a certain newspaper woman mentioned me?"

"I have my sources. Now, what can I help ya with?"

"It appears you have a cowboy in town, Chief."

"Do ya mean the Coloradoan?"

Barnes paused, trying to work out who Thompkins was referencing. He realized Thompkins meant Rob.

"Ah, no, not him. I meant the man who owns the barn on the southwest part of town by the highway. "

"Oh, Elmer Juntlo. Yeah, he keeps a junk collection in there. I'm just glad it's enclosed so people don't have to look at it. What did old Elmer do this time?"

"He discharged a shotgun into a field behind the barn. He said he was shooting at a coyote."

"He is a bit of an ogre, I'll give ya that. We've had a couple incidents like that, but it's all been harmless. Why does this concern ya?" Thompkins poured himself a cup of coffee; he did not offer Barnes a cup.

"I think he discharged his shotgun within Brinson's town limits. I imagine that's a violation of your ordinances. And," Barnes added more ominously, "he may have been firing at a person, not a coyote."

"Whoa there, detective. Did ya see who he shot at?"

"No, but I could tell he wasn't being truthful. It's just a gut instinct."

"I'll wager it was a coyote. He really guards his barn. But I'll speak to him. He's a difficult man to control."

"You're the chief of police. People should not be shooting guns like that in the town, and especially not at a person," Barnes said condescendingly.

"Ya're assuming that happened in the town and that there was a person. Moreover, ya're telling me that shit doesn't happen in Des Moines? I read stories all the time about those goings-on in yar city. Ya should take care of Des Moines before telling me how to do my job. Now, was there anything else ya wanted to talk about?"

"Not at this moment. I'll catch up with you later."

Both men stared warily at each other, and Barnes left the police station thinking, *This town isn't as friendly as I first thought. Another misjudgment on my part.*

Chapter 29

Tuesday, October 27

Brent was a hero to his friends, who were in awe of him and terrified of the situation. He had gone alone into the devil's lair, got shot at, and made it out alive. When Brent returned to Tenth Avenue, Jack, Tom, Dale, and Ron were speechless at first, then they pelted him with questions.

"What's in that barn? Did you see old man Juntlo, or just hear him? How close was he to shooting you? Did you find the boxes? Are there bodies in the barn? See any gold?"

Brent had been scared like never before, but the hero worship by his friends gave him much needed courage. He described the barn in as much detail as he could remember—the junk, the hanging deer, the old cars, the drums filled with crap—and yes, he found the boxes. He could only open one before Juntlo came in. The only detail Brent did not divulge was the bones he saw in the box. He told his friends the box held nothing but dirt.

The boys were disappointed; they were hoping the box contained gold, cash, or something more tantalizing than dirt.

Tom startled the group by suggesting, "Maybe the box and dirt are for a vampire. Remember that Dracula movie we saw last summer, where Dracula needed a coffin of dirt from his home country to rest in during the day?"

"No, dummy." Jack shook his head. "Brent was there during the day. Any vampire would have been in the box then. There's no such thing as vampires, anyway. Geez."

The boys nodded in agreement, but internally they all had doubts.

Jack continued, "So there weren't any bodies?"

Brent was conflicted. He didn't believe in vampires, but he was relieved there wasn't one inside the box. Yet, there were those bones. *Was old man Juntlo trying to bring a vampire back with that box of bones?* The thought chilled him to the core.

"No, no body or anything else in the box, just dirt." Brent lied and tried not to show the others he was shaking.

Thankfully, Jack changed the subject. "After we saw Juntlo run around the barn and we heard the shots, we were scared for you. Then we saw you on the other side of Tenth Avenue—you must have gone through the culvert on the highway."

Usually-quiet Dale jumped in. "After old man Juntlo went running back into his barn, a car drove up and a man got out carrying a gun."

"Yeah, and we could hear loud talking between the two," Jack continued. "Then the man with the gun got back in his car and left. He drove right by us. You were with us by then, Brent. I'll bet he was a cop. Juntlo is in big trouble."

"Juntlo is such a turd," Ron added. "Jesus, Brent."

"That took super balls," Jack said with a big smile as he patted Brent on the back. The other boys joined in another round of congratulations.

Brent felt good that he was being recognized for his bravery. However, he knew he was lucky. *My Dad would kill me for such behavior. I would be grounded for life.* Then his stomach churned as he considered two things: *Could old man Juntlo identify me?* and *Whose bones are in the box?*

"Guys, can we please not tell anyone else about this? I, we," Brent said in a shaky voice as he pointed to his friends, "could get in big trouble."

They nodded in agreement, more out of concern for themselves and their roles in the incident than for Brent. He hoped they wouldn't talk, but he knew from the Billy Bridges' experience that juicy secrets are not kept well.

⋏

Brent arrived at home and the first thing he heard was a sigh from his mom.

"My lord, what happened to you? How did you get those holes in your jeans? And that cut?"

"Jack and the guys, Mom—we were playing tackle football. It got a little rough. I think I got the worst of it."

"I don't want you playing so rough. No more tackling. You could break a bone or crack your head …"

"I'm fine. Can you fix my jeans? Sew up the holes?"

"I can try. Be more careful next time, please. Toss those filthy clothes in the hamper and I'll wash them. You need a shower, too. Go!"

Brent did as his mother asked and climbed into the shower. The soothing warm water sluiced over his body and washed thoughts of his encounter with Juntlo down the drain.

When he was toweling off, the thoughts came back. *What do I do about the bones? Did I really see bones, or was that my imagination? If Juntlo thinks I saw the bones and he moved them, the police won't find them. People will think I'm a liar, and I'll be at old man Juntlo's mercy forever. It has to be my secret.*

⋏

Wednesday, October 28

Brent was relieved not to hear about his barn exploits from anyone during the following school day, except for his four friends who had been with him. *Good, so far my secret is safe*, he told himself. *Maybe I'm OK.* His worries about Elmer Juntlo began to fade. It was a short-lived feeling.

Brent was walking down the hallway to leave school after the final bell when he caught a glimpse of a red pickup truck parked on the street

134

outside of the school. His heart rate jumped two-fold in one second. *Good God. He must know I was in the barn. What will he do to me? Will I end up in one of his boxes?*

Brent abruptly changed course and scooted into the library. Sweat leeched onto his shirt collar. The librarian, Ms. Peach, suspected nothing and asked him if he was interested in anything specific.

Brent thought quickly, trying to push Juntlo out of his mind. "I'm looking for a book by Jack London. I don't remember the name."

"Sure, follow me." She led him to the shelf marked L.

"Great, Ms. Peach, I'll look here."

"OK, but I close in fifteen minutes."

Brent found *Call of the Wild* immediately but still took the full fifteen minutes to hang back in the shelves. When Ms. Peach called to him, he walked slowly to her desk and checked out the book. He left the library for the main entrance even more slowly, praying Juntlo was gone. To his relief, there was no sign of the truck. "Thank God," he mumbled.

At that moment, Brent fervently wished he hadn't been the one to break into Juntlo's barn. *I can't go back in time, but if I could …*

He took the alleys home, his head like an owl's, scanning in every direction for Elmer Juntlo.

Chapter 30

Wednesday, October 28

Barnes dutifully called the captain first thing after breakfast. Afterward, he made the scheduled mid-morning stop at the Hinton General Store. He first drove around the block and parked on a side street. He didn't want Chief Thompkins or other nosy people to see him at the store, so he entered through the side door for his appointment with Janice.

She met him at the door. "Detective Barnes?"

"Yes." He held out his ICC badge.

She motioned for him to follow her to the storeroom.

The woman's attractiveness, even in work clothes, was not lost on Barnes. She was tall and thin with straight dark hair that flowed down to just above her shoulders. He had expected a frumpy older woman. Instead, he guessed Janice was in her mid-thirties and could have been a model.

She called out to Bud, "Take care of the store for the next hour, please." She pointed to a chair. "Please sit, Mr. Barnes. Will you have a drink?"

Next to Barnes was a cart containing a variety of soft drinks. Barnes pulled out a Pepsi. "Thank you ... Mrs. Hinton?"

"Yes, I'm Janice Hinton. I'm the owner of this store. I took sole ownership after my husband passed away a couple years ago."

"Can I ask how he died?"

Janice eyed Barnes suspiciously. "Why?"

"I apologize, Mrs. Hinton, for being so forward. My wife, Clara, passed away from cancer around a year and a half ago. I'm sorry for your loss."

"My husband was killed in a hunting accident. They said it was an instantaneous death. I'm sorry for your loss as well. But we're not here to discuss our pasts." Janice's eyes softened.

"You want to talk about Gary Knowles and his death, correct, Mrs. Hinton?"

"Yes. Please call me Janice." Not wasting time, she asked, "What have you found out about the cause of his death?"

"The Reed County medical examiner conducted an autopsy and concluded he died of an overdose of a combination of sleeping pills, alcohol, and heroin. He also found marijuana residue."

"Do you believe that, Detective Barnes?"

"First, call me Fred. Yes, I believe the report. Do you know something that the medical examiner doesn't?"

"I certainly don't believe he killed himself. The Gary *I* knew wasn't taking all that stuff."

"Well, we know he smoked marijuana. Some people have linked marijuana use to future hard drug addiction. And we are aware of many soldiers who become addicted to hard drugs, like heroin. Some get treatment and quit, others, I'm sorry to say, don't." Barnes paused to give Janice time to understand what he was saying. He continued, "We also know Gary drank. Finally, a lot of veterans have difficulty sleeping from their war experiences. It makes sense."

"No, it doesn't. You're assuming too much," Janice said firmly. "You didn't know the man. He was troubled, yes. But he was coming out of it. He was going to dinner the night he died with folks who shared his feelings about the war. Gary was an honorable, decent man. He didn't kill himself."

All right, Barnes thought. *She has no evidence to support her claim. I can wrap this up shortly.*

"Did he have enemies in Brinson?"

"Yes, he did. There is a strong pro-war feeling throughout much of the town. One of our young men was just killed over there—Ward Jenkins. So, there were bound to be problems in the town with those who oppose the war, particularly a former soldier like Gary."

"Can you give me specific names?" Barnes pulled out a small notebook.

"You can start with Carl Dinkins and the other rabble that frequent the Thirsty Bull. Mayor Harry Templeton, Mable at the *Bee*, some farmers and the owner of the grain silos, too. There are others."

"What about the Jenkins?" Barnes inquired.

"At first, maybe, but their thinking evolved. They were trying to understand Gary's views. They weren't hostile to him. It was the same with the Frosts, Tim and Angela. They all were going to be at the dinner with Gary. He wanted to be there. You can call the Frosts and Jenkins. They'll confirm what I've told you."

"I'll speak to them." *Hmm, this may take a little longer than I thought,* Barnes surmised.

"Where do you stand on the war, Detective? I think it's wrong, and I've always felt that way. It's not a popular stance in Brinson."

"I'm a public servant, Janice. My private views are not important, and I keep them private."

Janice stared at Barnes and wrote the contact information for the Jenkins and Frosts on a piece of paper and gave it to Barnes. "Did you see Gary's body?"

"No, I didn't. I heard the medical examiner shipped it to Gary's cousin in California. His parents are dead."

"I was under the impression from Gary that his parents are alive," Janice countered.

"Did he say that explicitly?"

"No, but I know. I have pretty good intuition."

At that instant, Bud burst into the room shouting. "He didn't do what they say he did, Detective Barnes."

"Why do you say that, Bud?" Barnes remembered their previous brief conversation.

"A brother knows his brother, sir."

Janice intervened. "Bud and Gary both served in combat in Vietnam."

Bud calmed and Barnes slugged down his pop. "I have go now." He nodded to Janice and Bud. "I talked to my captain earlier. I need to go to Manlo and tie up some loose ends on a previous case. I'll be back Friday, and I'll follow up on what you've said."

Barnes left the store, returned to his car, and drove back to Carlson thinking, *The damned captain. He sends me here and tells me to wrap up the Knowles case, and then sends me without much notice to Manlo to do something a file clerk could do. Now I'll have to come back here for some extra days. Fluffy will not be happy.*

When Barnes opened the storm door to his motel room, he found a note attached to the bottom of the door that read, "Nov. 7, 1940."

Chapter 31

Thursday, October 29

Thursday proved similar to Wednesday for Brent, however, he sensed other classmates knew his secret. He braced for the inevitable. *Everyone is going to know soon. Which one of my friends blabbed—or was it all of them?*

At the end of the school day, the old red pickup truck was again parked outside of the school. The squeamish feeling Brent had about Elmer Juntlo mushroomed. Today, instead of wasting time in the library, he watched the debate team practice. He had no desire to join the team, but it allowed an extra hour in the day to advance. By that time, the truck was gone.

Friday, October 30

By Friday, word of Brent's encounter with Juntlo had spread among the freshman class. Even some of the sophomores were aware of it. Surprisingly to Brent, it wasn't all bad. Several kids in his classes had previous difficult encounters with Elmer. He was viewed as the town curmudgeon, and who knew what he kept in that onerous barn.

Kids Brent barely knew slapped him on the back and paid him compliments. He was even picked first in dodgeball during gym class, and did surprisingly well. By the end of the day, Brent felt good and his concerns had lessened.

Still, at the end of classes, and like a bad dream, the red truck waited outside the school. This time, though, Chief Thompkins' police car pulled up behind it and soon Juntlo disappeared. Brent felt less paranoid and walked by himself to Hinton's store to buy a snack. He spotted Juntlo's truck across the street by the Thirsty Bull, just like usual.

God, I hope old man Juntlo doesn't find out it was me in his barn, he thought inside the store as he watched men entering and leaving the bar, keeping an eye out for Juntlo. *I wish he would just die. Maybe he'll fall on one of his rusty pieces of junk.*

Feeling comfortable that Juntlo would stay in the bar and after a quick conversation with Bud, Brent took off for home. When he walked up to his house, he noticed an unfamiliar car in the driveway—a black Cadillac. When he went inside, he came face to face with someone who looked like a movie star.

The man reached for Brent's hand.

"Howdy, Brent. I'm Robert Franklin Frost."

Brent's face was creased with questions, like who is this guy? Before he could say anything, his father said, "Brent, Rob is visiting from Colorado."

"He called yesterday and said he was in town for a while. He's a Frost. We invited him to dinner tonight," Angela added.

"Please, call me Rob, son," Rob said in his deep voice as he adjusted the cowboy hat on top of his long silvery hair.

"We're long-lost relatives." Tim rubbed the side of his head. "I think Rob and I are third cousins, or something like that."

"Yeah, something like that." Rob laughed and Brent's parents joined in. Rob cleared his throat, "A long time ago, here in Brinson, there were two lines of Frosts. One line was under Orville and Elva Frost. They were farmers. One of their children had a boy, and that boy became the father of Richard Franklin Frost, who was my father. So that's four generations right there. My father, Richard, didn't like farming so he became an insurance broker.

"The second line was under Herman and Evaline Frost. They were town folk. The lineages of both families were related, but no one seemed to know for sure how. Anyway, your father is the great-grandson of Herman and Evaline. That makes you their great-great-grandson."

Brent couldn't take his eyes of this new man. He gave the appearance of a kind grandfather—from the west, the source of so many movies and television shows.

Rob pulled a bag off the chair next to him and handed it to Brent. "Here's a little something from Colorado, son. I was hoping to meet you and see your parents again. The last time I saw them they were kids, about seven or so. Now, you three are the last living Frosts in Brinson."

Brent opened the bag. Inside was a wide black leather belt. The belt buckle was silver and black with a golden "C" set in the center. The top and bottom edges of the belt were stitched. Brent hadn't seen anything like it before.

"This is the type of belt worn in Colorado." Rob smiled, his bushy white moustache curling down over the top of his lip. "I hope it fits."

"Brent, what do you say to Rob?" Angela prodded.

"Uh, thank you, Rob. Someday, I hope to get out to Colorado. What's the 'C' for?" Brent pointed to the belt buckle.

"Well, the 'C' could stand for corn or Carlson," Rob grinned with a soft chuckle. "But it stands for Colorado. When you come to Colorado, Brent, prepare to stay. I did. I was a policeman in Denver for twenty-five years. Never thought about leaving."

Angela announced dinner was ready and the four sat down.

"I fixed roast beef, potatoes, and carrots with a side of gravy and rolls. I hope you like it."

"I'm sure I will, Angela. Thank you." Rob beamed. "It smells and looks just like what my mother, Ethel, used to make. Please pass the meat."

"How does the beef in Colorado compare to Iowa's, Rob?" Tim held out his hand for the platter of roast beef.

"I gotta be honest, it's better here. That's about the only thing I miss about here."

"When did you leave Brinson?" Angela asked.

"Nineteen thirty-five, I went to college in Boulder, at the University of Colorado. I liked the University of Iowa, too. But the pull of the mountains was too much for me. So, I went west."

"You haven't come back to Brinson much since you moved out to Colorado, have you?" Tim reached for the gravy boat.

Rob paused between bites. Tim and Angela could tell he was savoring his meal.

"You'll have to excuse me, Angela. Your cooking is the best I've had in some time. May I please have more potatoes?"

"Sure." Angela smiled as she passed him the potatoes and carrots.

"Thank you, ma'am."

Rob finished chewing a mouthful of food and swallowed. He took a drink of cool water and smiled. Brent was in awe. He had never seen anyone in person like Rob Frost.

Rob looked at Angela, then Tim, and finally Brent. "I came back a couple times for quick visits when Mother was alive. I haven't been back here since she died in 1958."

"What about your dad?" Brent asked.

The smile left Rob's face. "My father disappeared in 1940, about this time of year."

Brent was intrigued. "Disappeared? Did they ever find out what happened to him?"

No one at the table was eating now. Tim and Angela knew the story, but Brent was unfamiliar with the details. He had heard a tale about the vanishing Richard Franklin Frost, but he had little interest in the matter; it had happened so long ago.

Rob cleared his throat. "No one knows if he was kidnapped or murdered, or whether he just walked out. The police made a half-hearted effort at solving the case, but they found no clues, no answers—nothing. I tried to get Mother to move to Colorado, but she liked it here. She had a lot of friends, but never remarried."

Brent did a quick calculation in his head. "Wow, that was thirty years ago."

"Yep, thirty years ago, son." Rob said. "That's a long time."

After several minutes of quiet eating, Angela announced, "We have pumpkin pie for dessert, in honor of our guest."

"Great, I love pumpkin pie, and it's not even Thanksgiving!" Brent piped in. His pleasure at the news of a special treat showed in his grin.

After Angela served the pie, Brent asked Rob, "Why did you come back?"

"I want to solve my father's case before I run out of time." Rob's smile returned. It was not a warm smile this time; it was forced, with a hint of grimness.

A thought that had been kept in the back of Brent's mind suddenly shifted to the front. That thought frightened him. *What if the bones I saw in Juntlo's barn are Richard Franklin Frost's?*

Brent sucked down his piece of pie and claimed he had homework to do. He said goodnight to Rob and took off for his room as his heart raced.

CHAPTER 32

Friday, October 30

The workday at the Hinton General Store drew to a close and October's end was at hand. Unlike most recent days, it had been a good day sales-wise. Yet, the day's profits did not make up for the decline in store earnings for September and October.

Janice sat in her office punching calculator keys with her right hand and holding a cigarette in her left. She gazed at the cigarette and put it out in the butt-filled metal ashtray shaped like a maple leaf.

God, I need to quit, she thought. *The surgeon general is right. My bad habit will kill me, but I don't know if that's such a bad thing, the way things are looking.*

Bud appeared in the office door. "Mrs. Hinton, we had a good day. I want to see my family tonight. Lily was chosen for the school play. You'll have to come see it. It's next month."

"Congratulations to Lily. Of course I'll go," she said peering through the residual cigarette haze. "I'll lock up tonight. See you tomorrow. Say hi to Alice and Lily for me."

"I will, Mrs. Hinton. But I can wait around and walk you home. It's dark outside." He paused for a moment. "You should quit smoking, you know. It's bad for you. That's why I keep reminding you."

"Thanks, but that's not necessary. I'll be OK. Go home to your family. And I promise to stop smoking."

"When?"

"Good night, Bud."

Bud left the store, locking it on the way out. Janice stared at her expense books for another hour and decided it was time to go home.

When she left, several cars lined Main Street. Some of the drivers were drinking at the Thirsty Bull. Others were attending the movie at Power's Theatre. Janice didn't look to see what movie was playing; she had other things on her mind.

She crossed Main Street and headed east on First Avenue. She became lost in her thoughts about the store's financial distress as she passed by two side streets. As she walked, she sensed that something was not right. It was dark and the few streetlights barely uncovered the night. She heard an odd sound back off to her left, but when she turned and looked, she did not see anything. She walked faster. She heard the same noise, now next to her. A shadow seemed to move from the sound. Behind her, she heard shoes slapping the pavement. She turned and saw a figure walking about half a block behind her.

She turned back and something flitted across the street in front of her. She froze. *God, what can I do? They're all around me.* A list of enemies entered her mind. *Carl Dinkins is the most likely. The mayor? Maybe Elmer Juntlo—he owes me money.* She muttered other names and concluded it was a long list.

The person behind her closed the gap. She grabbed her purse tightly, ready to swing it at her attacker. At least she would go down fighting.

"Mrs. Hinton," a familiar voice called out.

"Bud, is that you?" Janice said haltingly, silently ecstatic the voice was his.

"Yep, it's me."

"I thought you went home."

"Changed my mind. I got worried. Wanted to make sure you got home. Things aren't right in Brinson."

"Thank you. I'm glad you're here. I think someone was following me."

"Nope, just me." Bud walked Janice to her house. When she reached the door, she thanked him again and he left.

She entered the house and noticed a thin envelope had been slid under her door. She opened it with shaky hands, fearing what was inside. The typed note confirmed her fears.

YOU'RE NOT SAFE HERE

After finishing his assignment in Manlo, Barnes returned to his room at the Best Western–Carlson on Friday afternoon. He was still irked at the captain for summoning him to Manlo when he wanted to finish his work in Brinson before the weekend. *But orders are orders,* he thought. *Perhaps my efforts will mollify the captain.*

An hour later, Barnes knew that hope was wrong. He was sipping a brandy and Coke trying to relax while reliving the stern conversation he had just had with the captain.

"Where are you on the Brinson case?" the captain began. "Have you found anything that contradicts Knowles was a suicide?"

"No," Barnes answered. "I was in Manlo, finishing up the Washburn case, remember? But to answer your questions, the local police chief and the county medical examiner say it was suicide."

"How long to conclude your investigation?"

"I need to interview a few more people. The woman who owns the general store in Brinson is convinced he was murdered for his anti-war stance. She has been ostracized in the town for her views."

"Janice Hinton? She's the one who sent the note to the ICC, right? Anything else?"

"Yes, that's her. One thing that troubles me a little is that she employs a Vietnam veteran who swears adamantly that Knowles did not kill himself. The vet sustained a head injury in the war, so it's hard to tell about him."

"Jesus, Barnes. An anti-war woman and a mentally disabled man are what's holding you up? Get this wrapped up!"

"One more thing I'd like to pass by you—I saw a man fire a shotgun into a field at the Brinson town limits. I think he was firing at a person."

"What? Did you see the person? Did he injure anyone?"

"Not that I know of."

"Barnes, that's a Brinson police matter, not our concern. Report it to them and finish your case. Call me tomorrow. Then, I want you to take a vacation. Good-bye."

Barnes took a sip from his glass and the phone rang. *God, the captain again,* he thought. The voice was frantic, and female.

"Detective Barnes?" The voice shook.

"Yes, this is Detective Barnes." He paused, recognizing the voice. "Mrs. Hinton?"

"They're trying to silence me."

"Who is?"

"I don't know. They send me threatening notes and follow me home. They're serious. Boycotting my store is one thing. They killed Gary and I'm next. I know it."

"Breathe, Janice." Barnes glanced at his watch: eight-thirty. "Where are you?"

"I'm at home."

"I'll be right over and we can discuss this in person."

"Thank you, Fred," Janice said, and rattled off her address.

Barnes hung up and drained his glass of brandy. *It's going to be a long night,* he told himself. He put on his heavier jacket as it was cold. As he walked to his car in the motel parking lot, he looked for the black Cadillac. He did not see it.

As Barnes drove down Main Street past the Thirsty Bull, he noticed the Cadillac parked out front. *So, you are in town tonight, Mr. Frost,* he thought. He parked in front of Janice's house fifteen minutes after receiving her call.

Janice's house blazed brightly in the night like a jack-o-lantern. *She must have on every light in the house,* he thought as he went up the steps to the front door. Janice opened the door before he could ring the bell.

Her face was creased, and her eyes were puffy and red. She had a cigarette in her left hand. She looked differently to Barnes than she had at their previous meeting.

"Thanks for coming."

"Not a problem." Barnes stepped inside the house. Indeed, every light on the first floor had been turned on. She closed the door after Barnes and bolted it.

"Every day for the past four days I've found these notes at the store and in my mailbox." She handed Barnes several pieces of paper. They all read:

WE ARE WATCHING YOU

"Today," she continued, "this was underneath my door here." She pointed to the door that Barnes had just walked through.

YOU'RE NOT SAFE HERE

"And this is the note they left after killing and grotesquely displaying a poor raccoon outside my house a couple weeks ago."

THIS IS WHAT HAPPENS TO COWARDS AND TRAITORS
YOU'RE NEXT

Barnes frowned as he read the notes. "These are definitely threats."

Janice interrupted him. "Tonight, I know I was followed home by someone. I felt it. Thank God Bud came along when he did. Who knows what would've happened if he hadn't been keeping an eye out for me. In many ways, Bud has been my protector."

"Did you see who was following you?"

"No, they're good. First, they were behind me, then on my side, and finally in front of me," she said. Barnes noticed her hands were shaking. The lighted cigarette was about to extinguish itself at the filter.

"They mean to intimidate you," Barnes theorized as he reached for an ashtray. "There's a big difference between scaring someone and committing murder."

"I thought that, too, but they killed Gary, and they're capable of doing the same to me."

"Who do you think would do this to you?"

"The same bunch that killed Gary—just about anyone. You see, I'm not well liked by most of the town. I had an affair with a married man. It caused his divorce, and the family moved out of town. I've been to anti-war protests in Des Moines, Chicago, and Washington, D.C. People in town know where I stand on the war. I let Gary stay in my house, and I listened to him. I just know he didn't take his own life."

"First, it takes two to have an affair. I'll wager the married man carries as much of the blame as you, if not more. He was the one who was married. Second, your right to protest is protected by the constitution. Third, you gave shelter to a troubled veteran. I think you should be congratulated for helping Mr. Knowles."

"Thank you," she said as tiny tears formed in the corners of her eyes.

"Can you show me where Gary was staying?"

"Sure."

They entered the apartment through the inner door connecting the main house to the apartment. The lights were already on. It was a small space, with the main room serving as the living room, dining room, and bedroom with a pull-out bed. A small kitchen was at the back of the room. The bathroom was wedged into the space underneath the stairs. The apartment smelled like Pine-Sol.

"I cleaned the apartment the day after Gary died. He wasn't neat, but he didn't have a lot of things. I put them all in his duffle bag." She pointed to a bag underneath the kitchen table.

"Did the police take anything?" Barnes moved to the duffle bag. He noticed an army insignia stitched on the right side of the bag close to the zipper.

Janice shook her head. "I didn't see them take anything, except the needle Gary supposedly used to inject the heroin. They took his marijuana, too. The rest they left behind. But I wasn't here the entire time the police were."

Barnes sifted through Knowles' belongings. There were long and short sleeve shirts, three pairs of jeans, underwear and socks, tennis shoes and combat boots, a baseball cap, and an army jacket. He found a nail clipper, toothbrush, and other toiletries. "This is it?" Barnes asked without looking at Janice.

"Yes, I think so. I put everything back in the duffle bag, including his jacket. Why do you ask?"

"Where are his medals? Didn't he have medals and a photo of his unit? Soldiers always carry stuff like that."

She gasped. "He did show me his medals, more out of disgust than anything, and a photo of his platoon. He was really close to those guys. Ward was in the photo." Janice paused and put her hand to her mouth. "Gary carried a Bowie knife with him, too. He told me it was his best friend. I never saw the knife after they took his body away. The medals—or the photo, for that matter—either."

"Someone may have tampered with his belongings, so your story might have credibility. If so, you could be in danger."

"Oh my," Janice choked. "What do I do? I don't think I can trust our police chief."

Barnes felt a burst of protectiveness. "I'll stay here tonight, if you want." He nodded toward the pull-out bed. "Tomorrow, we can talk in more detail about our options. First, I need to move my car off the street, get it out of sight."

"There's room in my garage. I'll open it for you."

Barnes parked his car in the garage and returned to the apartment. He saw no signs of anyone outside.

"Here are some fresh linens and a towel." Janice handed them to Barnes. "Thank you, and good night, Fred."

"Have a safe night. Be sure to bolt the door at the top of the stairs. Someone may have a key to the apartment. You didn't find Gary's key, did you?

"No."

"We'll have the locks changed tomorrow. Is that telephone on a separate line from the one upstairs?" Barnes pointed to a phone placed on a small accent table in the apartment.

"Yes, it's a separate line. I'll call it if I need anything. And here's my number." Janice wrote it on a piece of paper and gave it to Barnes.

Janice walked up the stairs, and Barnes could hear the click of the bolt hitting home. He washed his face, checked his .38 Special, and placed it on the pull-out bed. *Just in case,* he thought. He turned off the lights and sat in the chair by the bed.

Chapter 33

Saturday, October 31

Barnes nodded off, hoping nothing would happen during the night while he was at Janice's. He was wrong. At four-thirty in the morning, Barnes jumped to the sound of glass shattering. It took a few seconds to get his bearings. He grabbed his firearm and raced through the outside door of the apartment and around to the front of the house, where he saw a broken window.

He ran up the stairs to the porch and stood by the front door. Janice, in her white nightgown, opened the door before Barnes had time to knock. She pointed to a large hole that had been punctured in the living room bay window. Barnes entered the house and saw a red brick on the floor surrounded by shards of glass.

"Stay back." Barnes held out his arm. He walked gingerly through the shards and retrieved the brick. Attached to it was a note in crude handwriting.

GET OUT OF TOWN, COMMIE BITCH WHORE

"What does it say?" Janice's voice shook.

Barnes debated whether to show it to her.

"Please, I want to see it," she said firmly as she reached out her hand.

Barnes hesitated and then pulled the note slowly from the brick and gave it to her.

"Things just got serious." Barnes walked to the phone and dialed.

After several rings, a groggy voice answered, "D'ya know what time it is?"

"Yes, I do, Chief. This is Barnes. One of your citizens is being threatened with bodily harm. I suggest you get over to Janice Hinton's house as soon as possible."

"What? Janice?" Thompkins was trying to process what was happening.

"She's fine, but you need to get over here." Barnes hung up.

Janice walked over to Barnes and gave him a brief hug. "Thank you for being here. I'm not one to be frightened easily, but I am now."

"Let's try and get some answers. First, get dressed. There will no more sleep tonight. Then, please make coffee—lots of it."

Janice left for her bedroom. Five minutes later, Chief Thompkins pulled up with his police lights throwing blue and red flashes through the broken window. He did not use the siren.

Barnes let Thompkins into the house where he, too, saw the glass fragments on the floor.

"What are ya doing here, anyway?" Thompkins asked Barnes, annoyed. "Are ya sure she's all right?"

"We'll explain everything when Janice is here."

Janice came back downstairs wearing jeans and a white sweater. She looked tired. "Give me a few moments and I'll make coffee."

"Are you ..." Thompkins started to ask Janice.

"I'm fine, Chief. It's been a tough night, though." Janice went to the kitchen.

Another set of police lights bounced around the living room, this time with a siren blaring as the police car parked in the driveway.

"Why is he here?" Thompkins asked dismissively.

"I called the sheriff's office to send someone," Barnes said.

Reed County Deputy Sheriff Wally Nelson stood in the doorway, and Barnes waved him inside. The three men sat at the dining room table.

"We're dealing with a serious matter, Chief, and I thought the more law enforcement officials we have, the better the outcome," Barnes explained.

"And ya don't think I can handle it?" Thompkins flashed angrily.

"No, I don't—and I can't, either. That's why I've involved the sheriff's office."

"This is a simple case of vandalism, Barnes."

"No, it is more than that." Barnes nodded to Janice as she brought in coffee and several cups on a silver tray. She set the tray down on the table and Barnes felt sympathy for her.

After the coffee was poured, Barnes turned to Janice, "Could you get those threatening notes you received?"

Janice nodded and left the table for a minute. She returned with several pieces of paper. She had dated each note for when she found them. "The notes say, 'We are watching you.' I received them on consecutive days here and at the store starting four days ago. And Ellis, you remember the note that was left on the dead raccoon.

"And this is the scribble I received yesterday at my house. It says, 'You're not safe here.' Somebody slid it under my door. And last night I was followed home from the store. Bud thankfully scared away whoever that was. Then someone just threw a brick with this note through my window."

Deputy Sheriff Nelson and Chief Thompkins took turns reading the notes.

"Someone obviously wants you out of Brinson," Nelson summarized. He blew on his steaming cup of coffee. "They're ramping up their efforts."

"The question is who's doing this?" Barnes said.

"And why?" Nelson added.

"There are a lot of 'suspects,' as you call them." Janice tugged at her hair. "I've found a lot of people here are kind, nice folks. They have been my neighbors, friends, and customers for years. But there are others I would not categorize that way."

The phone rang; it was five-thirty in the morning.

"I'll get that," Janice said. "I'm sure it's just a neighbor checking on me. Hello?"

The voice on the other end spoke in a low muffled tone. "I see you have invited the cops. It doesn't matter, they can't save you. Nothing can, bitch." The line went dead.

Janice stood holding the receiver in her hand, frozen. A look of fear spread over her face.

Barnes was watching her and noticed her mood shift. "Are you all right?" he asked.

"It was a man's voice," Janice said as the three men at the table gave her their full attention. "He said he knows you're involved and you can't help me. I'm frightened. Whoever this is has the upper hand."

"Did you recognize the voice?" Thompkins asked.

"No."

Barnes stood up and walked Janice back to the table. "He's lying. He doesn't have all the advantages, and he knows it. For one thing, you have three dedicated law enforcement officers on your side, and there's an army of good people behind us to help you."

Deputy Nelson added, "That's right. We'll start patrolling your house regularly. We'll coordinate with Chief Thompkins. We're also fortunate to have a detective with the Iowa Crimes Commission with us."

Barnes smiled at Deputy Nelson and looked at Janice. "Let's focus on the question of why." Barnes reached for the coffee pot and poured himself a second cup. He looked to see if anyone else needed a warmup. Everyone shook their head yes.

"This is the way I see it, and I must caution that my thoughts are based on the fact that I have been in Brinson for a very short time and have known Mrs. Hinton only a couple of days. Deputy Nelson—this gets you up to speed, too.

"The first possible reason—and I apologize, Janice—was her affair with Mr. Bridges. There are some folks who hold her responsible for breaking up his marriage and the Bridges leaving town."

Janice looked down, shaking her head in embarrassment at hearing of her affair—again.

"But from my conversations with people in Brinson, I don't think that's the reason for these threats." Barnes held up the brick.

"Second is Janice's involvement with the anti-war movement and her kindness toward Gary Knowles. Knowles was a decorated vet who had become disenchanted with the Vietnam War. You have Janice and Gary's anti-war views combined with the recent tragic death of Ward Jenkins, a favorite son of Brinson who was killed in the war. Those actions led to some harsh feelings in town toward Gary and Janice. I should add that Ward and Gary served together in Vietnam and were close friends.

"The third possibility involves Gary's apparent suicide." Barnes looked at Thompkins. "The chief here and the county medical examiner concluded that Gary committed suicide. Janice and others don't believe that, but rather that he was murdered. Someone may be trying to stop her from proving her allegations."

"He didn't kill himself! I told you all that." Bud stood in the doorway between the dining room and kitchen. His massive forearms hung at his sides, fists clenched, face scalding red.

"Good lord! How did you get in here?" Thompkins said in disbelief.

"He has a key," Janice said. "He's only to use it if I ask him to or in an emergency."

"I don't sleep well and was awake when I heard the sirens. I came running." Bud shook his head. "I thought something bad had happened to you," he said to Janice. "These sirens, they give me flashbacks."

Barnes held out a hand toward the empty chair. "Have a seat, Bud."

"Yes, sir," Bud sat down. "I'm right. I know I'm right."

The impromptu meeting lasted until the first shreds of light began to filter over the town. Several people had gathered outside of Janice's house, wondering what had happened.

Inside the house, the group agreed to keep everyone apprised should anything new develop. Chief Thompkins was the first to leave and spoke to those assembled. "Everything is fine, folks. There are vandals that need to be roped in, which is what I intend to do."

Thompkins stood by his police car smoking a cigarette as he waited for Barnes.

"Do you need to be here anymore, Barnes?" Thompkins asked between puffs. "Local law enforcement can provide security for Janice and catch the troublemakers."

"Why do you ask?" Barnes stared at Thompkins. "I believe Janice is still in real danger. And I have more work to do here, which is what I'll tell my superiors."

"We don't like Des Moines elitists coming up here and telling us what to do." Thompkins flicked his cigarette to the ground and crushed it hard with his boot. "We can take it from here."

Barnes didn't respond. Thompkins slid into his car and drove off. Deputy Nelson followed Thompkins. Barnes watched them leave and returned to the house.

"I'll drive you to work today."

"That's fine. I'll have Bud open the store. Then I have to call someone about replacing my window."

After Bud left for the store, Barnes helped Janice secure the hole in the window with a large blanket and duct tape. Once completed, Barnes dropped off Janice at the store. He had several visits he wanted to make. He told her that he would pick her up from the store after work. She readily accepted the offer.

His first stop was the Jenkins' house, where he wanted to get their views about Gary. Bert and Lola were distraught hearing about Janice's night.

"I can help," Bert said. "I'll make some calls and we'll replace her damaged window at no cost. Guys from my lumberyard will do the work."

"She's too good of a person to be treated like this," seconded Lola.

When Barnes brought up the issue of Gary's death, Bert and Lola were also convinced that he hadn't killed himself.

"He was coming to our house for dinner that night, and he was looking forward to it," Lola said firmly. "Dale, our son, told us so."

"The Frosts were coming as well, right?" Barnes asked.

"Yes, the Frosts: Tim, Angela, and their son, Brent. He's a friend of Dale's and knew Gary about as well as anyone in Brinson. They'll tell you the same thing, Detective."

Barnes' next stop was the *Brinson Bee.* The office was open on Saturday morning. He wanted to meet the owner, Max Sturgess. When he went in, he bumped into Rob, immaculate as always, wearing his black Stetson.

"Are you finding what you're looking for in Brinson, Fred?"

"Yes, I'm moving forward. How about you?"

"I'm doing fine, too. Just catching up on the goings on in town since I was last here. Have a nice day."

The two women stood at the *Brinson Bee* counter watching Rob leave.

"Hello, Detective. Isn't he the nicest man you've ever met?" Mabel purred like a kitten.

"I don't know, Mabel, Brenda. That's a question only you two can answer. I like his car, though—the black Cadillac."

"Hmmm …," Brenda sighed.

"Good morning, Detective Barnes." A man wearing a blue flannel shirt and tan slacks approached the counter from an office in the back. He had a slight paunch, but looked fit. He combed his hair over the top of his head in a deliberate attempt to mask the bald spot there. He had dark hair that looked dyed. Barnes surmised the man—under the dyed hair—was in his mid-sixties.

"I'm Max Sturgess, publisher, editor, and journalist here at the *Brinson Bee.*" He smiled and extended his hand to Barnes.

"Nice to meet you, Mr. Sturgess. How'd you know who I am?" Barnes' hand was enveloped in Sturgess' firm grip.

"Please, call me Max. Everyone in Brinson knows who you are and what you're doing here."

"And why is it I'm here?"

"You're here to verify that the troubled Knowles boy killed himself, right?"

"First, Gary Knowles was a man, a soldier, not a boy. He fought in a war that not many people want to fight in and won medals. So, yes, we want to confirm that a decorated veteran committed suicide."

"What have you found so far?"

"My investigation is ongoing and confidential. It should be wrapped up soon. You'll have access to my report when it's finished."

"So, you've got nothing to report yet?" Sturgess was fishing for information.

"I'm interested in what those familiar with his death think, such as yourself, Max. I'd like to interview you—say early next week? I have some questions that I think you can help me with."

"I need to check my schedule, but I think Tuesday morning works. I'm out of town Monday. How about ten o'clock? I didn't know the young man personally. I just report the facts, and all the facts point to him killing himself."

Barnes acknowledged Sturgess' opinion with a nod, then turned to leave. "See you Tuesday."

Outside the *Brinson Bee*'s office, Barnes was disappointed in himself. *I forgot to ask Sturgess if he knows anything about what occurred on November 7, 1940. Who put that note on my door? Later,* Barnes thought, *I've got another place to be.*

When Brent arrived home from running an errand, he was surprised to see a strange man sitting in the living room talking to his parents.

"Hi, Brent," Angela said as she poured water from a pitcher into Barnes' glass. "Everything OK, hon?"

"Fine," Brent answered as he looked at his mom, dad, and finally focused on the stranger.

"Brent," his father spoke, "This is Detective Barnes with the Iowa Crimes Commission. He's here asking us questions about Gary. He thought you might know something that we don't. You seemed to know Gary the best—besides maybe Janice and Bud."

Barnes sat in his chair and smiled to relax Brent. "Your folks have been very nice to me, and I appreciate that. I understand you showed kindness to Gary when other people in Brinson did not."

Brent glanced at his dad. "I saw Carl Dinkins and some other men throw him out of a bar."

"You're talking about the Thirsty Bull?"

"Yes, sir. I saw people yell at him, but Carl Dinkins hit him, hit him hard in the gut."

"Can you tell me the names of the other people?"

Brent added a couple names—Eddie Horst, Bert something—and became silent.

"Anyone else, Brent?" Tim prodded his son.

"He didn't kill himself, Detective Barnes. He was always friendly to me. We had good talks. He was a good football player. He was going to dinner at the Jenkins with Dad, Mom, and me the day he died." A tinge of defiance stirred in Brent's voice.

"It's all right, Brent," Barnes said soothingly. "There are people out there who share your opinion. I'm sorting things out."

The conversation lulled and Angela took the sign.

"Head upstairs, son," Angela said as she topped off everyone's water glasses. "Get some studying done before dinner. It's Halloween and I know you'll want to trick or treat, and maybe … maybe go to the dance."

"Yes, Mom. Good-bye, Detective Barnes." Brent headed upstairs to his room.

"He's a real good kid, Detective. He's sensitive with a good head. That's why I take his word regarding Gary." Tim nodded at Barnes and moved close to him. "Gary didn't commit suicide. Find who murdered him."

"I'm seeking the truth, Mr. and Mrs. Frost, wherever that leads. Thank you for your time."

Barnes left the Frosts' house in thought. *A lot of people believe Gary was murdered, not suicidal. Things are getting a bit more complicated. I need to ask Brent some follow-up questions.*

Chapter 34

Saturday, October 31

Barnes arrived at the Reed County Medical Examiner's office directly from the Frosts' house at three-thirty in the afternoon on Saturday, October 31, 1970. He knocked on a door with black lettering: Medical Examiner.

"Come on in," a cheerful voice called out from inside.

Barnes pushed the worn door handle down and entered. Deisman was sitting at his desk.

"Thanks for meeting me today—I know it's getting late on a Saturday. I'm Detective Fred Barnes with the Iowa Crimes Commission."

"Nice to meet you, Detective Barnes. I'm Dr. Henry Deisman, Medical Examiner for Reed County. I sometimes catch up on my work here on Saturday afternoons."

As the two men shook hands, Barnes hoped Deisman had washed his before their meeting. The doctor wore thick-lensed glasses. Barnes guessed he was in his late fifties to early sixties.

"You said on the telephone that you wanted to talk to me about Mr. Gary Knowles' death."

"Yes, that's correct, Doctor, and I'd like to read your detailed autopsy report." Barnes said as he scoped out the room. It was much smaller and messier than the medical examiner's office in Des Moines.

"That's no problem." Deisman walked over to his desk and reached for a file. He thumbed through it briefly and handed it to Barnes.

Barnes mumbled, "Thanks," and started to read the contents.

"I can save you some time, Detective. Gary Knowles overdosed on a stew of drugs and alcohol. I found heroin, marijuana, alcohol, and sleeping pills in his bloodstream. I can't tell you which was the most destructive, but they all contributed to some degree. Call it a synergistic effect. I heard he was an unhappy man who had little desire to live."

"The people I've talked to said he used alcohol and marijuana, but the sleeping pills, and the heroin in particular, are a surprise." Barnes tried to read the file as Deisman continued to talk.

"He's not the only vet who's succumbed to heroin. It's a nasty drug, Detective."

"How long have you been the county medical examiner?"

"It'll be fifteen years this coming December. I also have a busy private practice. Depending on the week, I'm generally here only a few hours a week, if that."

"In those fifteen years, have you ever seen a heroin overdose?"

"One." Deisman did not elaborate. "There's absolutely no doubt in my mind that drugs and alcohol were the cause of Knowles' death."

"Self-administered?" Barnes asked with a hint of skepticism.

"Oh yes. He killed himself. Whether by accident or on purpose, we'll never know. You may think, Detective, that I have little experience with such matters because I've had direct involvement with only one overdose death. I can assure you that I have much experience with drug addicted patients.

"I serve on the state board that oversees the control of illicit drugs and their effects on our population. I was appointed by the governor. I have attended numerous conferences and workshops on drug addictions.

"Did you know that the use of heroin by our soldiers in Vietnam is becoming rampant? Over there, the primary ways of using heroin are smoking, snorting, and ingesting. Mainlining—using a needle for injecting—is rarer but on the rise.

"Some of our boys leave heroin behind in Vietnam while others bring the habit home with them—they can't stop without help, and even with help it can be too difficult for them. In my opinion, Mr. Knowles was one of those soldiers."

Deisman eased back in his chair with a look that said the meeting was over.

Barnes took the clue. "I apologize, Doctor, if my remarks were misinterpreted. We both want to do what's right for Mr. Knowles. Thank you."

"We're good, Detective."

"May I get a copy of that report?"

"Not yet. That's a draft. I still need to review my notes and prepare a final report. Give me your card and I'll mail it to you when it's finished. Chief Thompkins said you'd be leaving for Des Moines soon."

"That'll be fine." Barnes handed the file back to Deisman along with his mailing address and prepared to leave.

Changing the subject, Deisman asked, "I've heard there are people in Brinson who don't believe Knowles killed himself and think he was murdered. Do you know why? Is that why you're here?"

"Yes, there are differing opinions on the matter—just like everything these days."

"I've heard that Janice Hinton is the leader of those who think he was murdered."

"She's not the only one. There are others."

"I hear she's a radical who doesn't believe in our government. She convinced the others to adopt her weird theories." Deisman removed his glasses and stared at Barnes.

"And what you just said is a theory as well. Good day." Barnes stared back at Deisman.

⅄

Thompkins picked up his phone. He was tired and not pleased with the caller.

"Chief Thompkins," the raspy voice began.

"Yes, Mayor Templeton, I'm here."

"Guess who just called me."

"I have no idea," Thompkins said with a hint of exasperation.

"Doc Deisman, that's who. From Carlson. He said that man from Des Moines is bothering him."

"Do ya mean Fred Barnes, with the ICC?"

"That's the one. He's thinking that hippie Knowles was murdered. Clearly, he's wrong. You need to turn him in the right direction. We don't need no city cop doing your job, Chief. And Elmer Juntlo has complained about him, too. You know I don't like talking to Juntlo."

"I have no control over what Barnes does, Mayor."

"I don't care, Chief. This is a local matter. Get Barnes back to Des Moines, for Christ's sake. Understand?"

"Yes, sir."

"Yeah, and I hear Barnes is living with that Hinton woman," the raspy voice continued. "She and that Knowles had a fling and now she's with a Des Moines cop. Get rid of her, too. We only like fine, solid citizens in Brinson, not floozies like her."

"Yes, sir." Thompkins hung up on him.

⚓

Barnes left Deisman and returned to the motel. He glanced at his watch. *Damn, I'm too late for the chocolate chip cookies,* he thought. As he took out his key to unlock his door, he felt a hand on his back. He reacted and turned abruptly to face the source, ready to counter whomever he found. He was relieved to see it was only the motel manager holding a plate of cookies.

Embarrassed that he had apparently scared the man, Barnes said a contrite "Sorry," then thrust his hands in his pockets.

"That's OK, sir," the motel manager muttered. "We, Mr. Frost and I, want you to have these cookies. A little something home cooked while you're away from Des Moines. You're a good guest and you seem to like them."

"Thank you, and sorry again for my abruptness. Long day." Barnes smiled as he took the plate, the aroma of chocolate and sugar lifting on the air, and opened his door. "Where is Mr. Frost? I didn't see his car in the lot."

"He took off just before you arrived. He comes and goes—I don't know where."

Barnes smiled. "The cookies look great. Thank you." He nodded to signal the conversation was at an end, went inside, and closed the door.

Barnes carefully set the plate of cookies on the small round table that served as a desk and dining table. He took out his notebook and began to write with one hand while he held a cookie in the other.

There is no evidence to indicate Gary Knowles was murdered. Brinson Police Chief Ellis Thompkins and the Reed County Medical Examiner Henry Deisman say all the evidence they have gathered confirms the conclusion of suicide.

The townspeople I have interviewed have good intentions to support Mr. Knowles, yet they have no evidence, only hunches. A belief is not evidence and without evidence, I cannot contradict the findings of Chief Thompkins and Dr. Deisman.

Will wrap up the investigation tomorrow.

At seven o'clock, Barnes realized his error. *God, I was supposed to pick up Janice at the store and stay a second night at her house. When will I learn.* He jumped from his chair at the little table, grabbed a change of clothes and drove fast to Brinson.

Janice was sitting at her kitchen table smoking a cigarette and drinking a glass of white wine. Barnes tapped at the door and she let him in.

"I'm sorry, Janice," he said with genuine remorse.

"That's fine," she answered coolly. "Bud walked me home after we closed the store. I thought you were coming, but you didn't show up. Trick or treat just started. I've had a bunch of kids already. The kids like me, at least. I'm quite generous." She pointed to the overflowing basket of candy by the door.

"Time got away from me. I was interviewing the Reed County Medical Examiner in Carlson, and afterward, I forgot about meeting you at the store. I'm sorry."

"What did the medical examiner tell you? Anything different than what I already know?" She put out the cigarette as the smoke dissipated above her head.

"He examined Knowles and has been the medical examiner for fifteen years. He has solid credentials. It would be awfully tough to dispute his findings, and add to that similar findings from the police chief. They're the experts with facts, and your side only has opinions. Knowles chose a difficult path."

"Then that's that." Janice hung her head. "Gary will not get justice. I suppose you'll leave tomorrow then?" She looked up into his eyes. The loneliness Barnes had kept inside began to melt.

"I don't know yet." Barnes avoided the truth and looked over at the damaged window. "I see Bert came through and did a solid job bracing your broken window until a new one can be installed."

"It should be a couple of days for the new window. It's nice when you can count on *someone*. And the Jenkins have been through enough hell." Janice's sad eyes made Barnes feel small.

"I'm still planning on spending the night in the apartment, like last night. I don't think they'll come back, but I want to be here."

"That's kind of you, but you won't be here tomorrow night or the night after that. I'm just going to continue being independent and weather this through. I've been doing it for some time, and I can continue doing it."

"Let's take one night at a time and see what happens," he said.

The two spent the rest of the evening drinking wine, answering the door for the goblins of the night, and talking about their lives, finding a shared pain in the loss of a spouse. Several times their eyes met in the soft glow of candles Janice had lit. She placed her hand lightly on his.

Barnes' first reaction was to withdraw his hand, but her touch and warm smile made him reconsider. He felt a bond forming between them, more than a platonic one. He knew she felt the same way.

At eleven o'clock, Barnes retired to the basement apartment. His feelings for Janice surprised him; he hadn't felt like this about anyone since Clara died. She made him feel warm, like Clara had. He flipped through a *National Geographic* magazine he had brought with him to Brinson, his mind full of Janice, so he paid little attention to the pages. He finally turned off the light and sat in the chair—this time without his revolver. A powerful feeling of loneliness and longing to be needed brushed over him.

A short time later, he heard the light patter of footsteps upstairs followed by the click of the lock on the door between the apartment and the rest of the house. The doorknob turned and a crack of light appeared. The sound of footsteps faded back into the house.

Barnes knew what that meant. *What would Clara think? Is what I'm thinking wrong? I so miss my wife, but I'm tired of the loneliness. My cat, Fluffy, has been my sole companion for a long time.*

Barnes had a dilemma to resolve.

Chapter 35

Saturday, October 31

Brent told himself this definitely would be his last year trick-or-treating. It was a Saturday night, which was perfect to end his Halloween career. When he was younger, Halloween was a holiday on par with Thanksgiving, but not quite Christmas. This year, his enthusiasm for costumes had waned, so he wore jeans, a plaid shirt, and a *Planet of the Apes* ape mask. People wouldn't know it was him and that would be fine.

He was going out with Dale and Ron. Jack had decided at the last minute that he was too old for trick-or-treating, and Tom had to help his mom set up for the Halloween dance at the high school that started at nine o'clock. Optimistically, Brent and his friends could do their candy grab between seven and nine o'clock, and still make the school dance—though Brent wasn't sure he wanted to go. He didn't have a date, and he didn't want to revisit the Juntlo barn incident *for the millionth time* with his schoolmates.

He walked to Dale's house, where Dale and Ron waited.

"Which neighborhoods are we going to hit tonight?" Dale asked.

"Why don't we start in the area around your house? We can go to my neighborhood after that," Ron said enthusiastically.

"Anywhere is fine with me, just as long as it's not down near Juntlo's barn," Brent declared.

"Who are you more afraid of, old man Juntlo or the vampire in the box?" Ron was kidding, but Brent didn't appreciate the joke.

"Not funny, Ron." Brent cringed at the thought of the box containing bones. *God, a vampire.*

"Too bad the vampire can't join us," Ron added, laughing. "He could help us get a better take. He'd scare all the little kids and they'd drop their bags of candy."

"We'll do fine without anyone's help. We'd better get going." Brent smiled but he was nervous. "Remember what my dad always says, 'maximum houses, minimum time.'"

"Yeah, and I've got the soap," Ron grinned. "If we know someone is home and they don't answer the door, they'll get a good window soaping."

"I'm for that," Brent said as his mind shifted from Juntlo and imaginary vampires to the night's real events.

The candy haul was fantastic in the boys' minds. Only two houses weren't handing out treats. The worst was old lady Garber. She had turned off all her lights and huddled in the back room watching Lawrence Welk. Her front windows received a thorough soaping.

One of the last houses the boys targeted was Janice's. Even though half the town had no use for her, the kids did. Because she owned the grocery store, it was well-known that she had tons of the best candy to hand out.

When Brent rang her doorbell, he was shocked when Barnes opened the door.

"Hi, kids," he said as he held out a basket full of candy.

The boys were mesmerized by the choice of treats being offered. "What's your trick?" Barnes added, bringing the boys back to reality.

"We don't have any tricks, sir," Brent replied. "We're the good guys."

"I see," Barnes said. "Is that why you have soap in your pocket?" He looked at Ron's pants pockets, where a bar of Ivory soap was about to fall out. "Are you guys also cleaning windows in the area?"

"No, sir, I mean yes, sir," Ron answered as he swayed nervously back and forth.

"Relax, boys. I was a kid once, too. Mrs. Hinton is on the phone, so I'm the substitute candy giver. Take three or four."

"Thanks, mister." The boys reached into the basket and eagerly pulled out four candies each.

Barnes winked at the trio, but aimed his gaze at Brent. The three boys took off down the street to the next house. As they ran off, Barnes watched them until they were out of sight. *Brent Frost,* he said to himself, *nice to see you again. What more can you tell me?*

⚓

Brent reluctantly decided to join his friends at the high school dance. He'd had a highly successful night securing candy. He left it unguarded at home, where he hoped his dad wouldn't eat most of it. Jack and Tom were already at the dance, and the five boys sat off to the side watching everyone else. None of them had a date.

Brent daydreamed as the music blared from the band. The ensemble was composed of local kids from Carlson. They weren't particularly good, but they were loud and energetic, and that was what the crowd wanted. They played songs by The Rolling Stones, Creedence Clearwater Revival, and Steppenwolf, among others, and a couple of slow dance numbers, including the always-popular *A Whiter Shade of Pale* by Procol Harum.

As Brent watched, his thoughts zigged-zagged between Detective Barnes, Gary, old man Juntlo, the bones in the box, and the possibility of a vampire hanging from the rafters in Juntlo's barn. *I know that's not real, I know that's not real,* he said to himself over and over.

"Brent, wake up!" Jack's voice shook Brent to the present.

He was startled to see Cindy Williams, the daughter of the Brinson banker, standing in front of him. She had dark brown curly hair that coiled down to her shoulders, pink skin, and a teasing smile. She was just a tad shorter than Brent and was a freshman. In Brent and his friends' vernacular, she was hot.

However, Cindy had little use for freshman boys; she thought they were naïve. She was already physically mature for her age, which caught the eyes of the older guys. Her father and mother were strict Methodists, though, and well aware of their daughter's attributes. They kept a sharp eye on whom she socialized with. Because tonight was an all-school social with plenty of chaperones, the event was fine for Cindy to attend.

"Hi, Brent," she said with a warm smile.

Brent melted. *Pull yourself together; don't be a fool.*

Brent said the first thing that popped into his head. "Oh, hi, Cindy. Are you enjoying the party?" His right knee bobbed up and down with nervousness.

"It's OK. It's the same people you see in school."

"The music is good. They're loud." Brent tried to be composed.

"Yes, they're loud. And that's fine. Do you want to dance? It's a good song."

The band was playing *Jumpin' Jack Flash* by The Rolling Stones. Brent's first reaction was disbelief. He had never asked a girl to dance, and now a girl was inviting him to dance. He had previously, begrudgingly, practiced dancing with his mom at home so he would be prepared if the possibility ever arose. Dancing with his mom would always be a secret between him and her. He smiled at Cindy while in his mind he thanked his mom.

"Sure," Brent agreed and the two ventured onto the gym floor. After Brent successfully maneuvered through several songs, Cindy suggested they go to the refreshment table for Hawaiian Punch.

Brent poured Cindy a glass and handed it to her before filling his own.

"Thanks." She took a sip and eyed him carefully. "You're not what I pictured."

Brent was surprised she had even pictured him at all. "How's that?"

"I always thought you were like your friends over there." Cindy glanced to the other four boys staring in disbelief at the exchange between Brent and her.

"You did the most courageous, crazy thing going into Juntlo's barn. They say he keeps dead bodies in there, and that it's haunted."

Brent gulped thinking of the bones in the metal box.

"I can't believe he shot at you. I'm so glad he missed."

"So am I." Brent tried his best to play it cool.

"What did you see in there?"

"Lots of old junk, cars, and stuff." He knew that was boring, so he spiced it up, "There was a dead deer I think he was going to skin. Oh, and there were several boxes that looked like caskets."

Cindy's eyes reflected fright. "Did you open any of them?" She touched his arm.

From the time he saw the bones, Brent had told himself that he would never, ever disclose that finding, and he wasn't going to do it now, even if it *was* Cindy who asked him. "Only one, it just had some dirt. Then old man Juntlo came in before I could open the others. I had to escape. I was lucky."

The dance ended and Cindy left to meet her parents. As they parted, she said, "Do you want to go to the drive-in Monday night? Tuesday is only a half-day."

"Sure," he answered, unsure how he would manage to take her to the drive-in.

"Great!" she smiled. "It's a date." She gave his hand a squeeze and left the gym.

Jack, Tom, Dale, and Ron dashed over to him. "We can't believe what we saw! Cindy Williams is out of our league!" they all shouted in various versions at once.

Brent smiled at his good fortune while his insides burned. *How can I keep up this front of impressing this super-hot girl when I'm just a run-of-the-mill freshman? And if most of the school knows of my run-in with old man Juntlo, then so does he.*

Brent was in big trouble.

Chapter 36

Sunday, November 1

Fred Barnes opened his eyes and for a second had no idea where he was. He wasn't at his home in Des Moines, the motel in Carlson, or the apartment at Janice's house. He closed his eyes and felt the warm form of a woman nestled against his back. The curtains were partially drawn, and rays of light streamed through the east-facing windows.

He was in Janice's bed. He gulped.

Since Clara's passing, he had never so much as looked at another woman. Marge, at the ICC headquarters, was a true friend; there was never a romantic spark between them. Plus, she was married. He had no interest in the other women at the ICC, or from his and Clara's circle of friends. Now, he was in bed with a woman he hardly knew. He sighed, wishing he were elsewhere.

The warmth of flannel sheets relaxed him. Janice's hand touched his shoulders.

"Good morning, Fred," she said in a soothing voice.

"Good morning." He hesitated before saying, "I think things went a little too far last night. I had too much wine."

"I don't think that was the case at all," she said and kissed his back. "It felt good to me that you were here, and I can tell it felt good to you."

"This was too fast. I feel like I betrayed my wife."

"I'm not competing with your deceased wife. I have no intention of doing so."

"I don't know. Things are confusing." He turned to face her. She looked pretty in the morning.

Janice's dark bangs were cut at her eyebrows, giving her the look of an Egyptian queen, at least from what Barnes could recall from a *National Geographic* magazine he read once.

"Your wife was the past. You live in the present. You need to do what makes you happy today. I don't believe my dead husband would object to me living my life the way I want. If the situation were reversed and I was dead, I would want my husband to be happy. I believe that's the same with Clara."

"I understand what you're saying, and it makes sense. I just don't know if I'm ready."

He left the bed and stretched. "It's Sunday, isn't it?"

"Yes, it is. I go to church on Sunday. I suppose you wouldn't be interested in going with me." She smiled knowing the answer.

"Nope, not today."

"The minister, Reverend McFadden, is a good man. You would like him. He gave a nice eulogy for Gary, and he barely knew him."

"I'll pass." Barnes paused and swallowed. "I'm headed to a park near the Des Moines River today for a break. Would you like to join me?"

"Yes, I would. I'll bring a picnic lunch." She sat up in the bed, her smile broad. "Bud's running the store today with Alice's help, so it's perfect timing for a trip. The weather shouldn't be an issue if you bring a coat."

"Good, we can go at noon." Barnes picked up his clothes and headed to the basement apartment to shower.

The water was comforting as he soaked his head. *Clara, I hope you can forgive me. Should I remain faithful to you, or is Janice right about living in the present? What would you do if you were me?*

A shot of cold water jolted him into reality. Janice had flushed the toilet upstairs. He heard her start the shower, and Barnes' water flow diminished. He grimaced. *Just like at home with Clara, time to get out.*

After drying off, he put on casual clothes and sat at the small table in the apartment. *I can review my notes while I wait for Janice to come back from church*, he thought. As he glanced at the thin file, he realized there wasn't much more information than when he took on the case. *The experts concluded that Gary Knowles committed suicide by drug overdose. Janice, Bud, and a few others are convinced Knowles wouldn't have done such a thing. It seems like a good number of townspeople didn't like Knowles because he was an anti-war, hippie drug user—the opposite of Ward Jenkins. At least, that's what they remember. I wonder what Jenkins' demons were? Every solider in combat has them. Now no one, not even his parents, will know what those demons were.*

The phone rang. Barnes thought it was Janice and answered after one ring.

"Good morning, Barnes." He recognized the captain's voice immediately.

"Good morning, sir," Barnes responded, in a bit of shock. *God, him again.*

"I got this number from the motel manager. How are things in Brinson?"

"It appears to be a typical little town …"

The captain cut him off sharply. "That's not what I meant, Barnes. How is your case proceeding—the dead soldier? You've been back there a couple of days now."

"I haven't found anything to dispute the conclusions of the Brinson Chief of Police and the Reed County Medical Examiner."

"Well, then, why isn't your report finished, and why aren't you on that vacation?"

"The town is really divided on the issue of the war and the suicide determination. The people who knew Knowles best don't think he killed himself. I'm still interviewing them. They are pretty adamant. One of them has received threats."

"You know as well as I do that opinions are not facts and lose substance when raised against facts. Find evidence that is contrary to the medical examiner's report or get back here by Thursday, Friday at the latest! I'll send Robinson there to help you. He misses you."

"Yes, Captain," Barnes said. He thought, *It's not a good idea to send a Black detective to rural Iowa—he would learn what a stone wall is—figuratively.* "I can manage here."

"Finish it. Got it?"

"Yes, sir."

Barnes' immediate thought after he hung up was of Janice. *Knowles committed suicide—the facts speak for themselves. But I need to figure out how to stay here longer,* he thought. *The menace Janice is experiencing isn't going to go away.* He heard Janice close the door and leave for church.

As he looked around the apartment, he focused on the small wooden bookcase squeezed into a tight space by the kitchen. He wandered over to see if there was anything interesting to read while he waited for Janice to return. He thumbed through the books on the first shelf and found westerns, old *Time* magazines, and a how-to-play-poker guide. Wedged in these publications was a worn copy of *Slaughterhouse-Five* by Kurt Vonnegut. Barnes pulled it from the shelf and looked at the cover.

"I've heard about you," he said to the book. As he opened it, a piece of paper fell out. He unfolded the sheet. The writing inside grabbed him by the throat.

▲

Janice returned from church and found Barnes sitting at her kitchen table. He had a cup of coffee in his right hand and a piece of paper in front of him.

"How was church?" he asked while fiddling with the paper.

"Fine. What have you got there?"

"I found this in a book on the bookcase downstairs—*Slaughterhouse-Five.* Do the book or note bring back any memories?"

She took the paper and read it. There were only seven words. She read them out loud. "'I want to come home for Thanksgiving.'"

"Do you know who wrote it?" Barnes sounded like a cop interviewing a suspect.

"No. Why?" Janice shook her head gently, puzzled at the note.

Barnes handed her the book where he found the note. "Is this your book?"

"No. I've never seen it before. I've read it, but I got the book from the library last year. I don't own a copy."

Barnes took the book back and opened it to the inside cover. The initials "GK" were lightly penciled on the upper right corner of the page.

"It's Knowles' book. This is big, Janice." Barnes placed the book down and clapped his hands. "This may be evidence indicating that Gary didn't commit suicide."

"Really? How so?"

"Do you have an example of his handwriting?"

"I don't know. There was no lease, and he didn't pay me anything." She sat down as her mind raced through her time with Gary. After a few minutes she frowned. "I can't think of anything I have. Lola may have something."

Barnes closed his eyes and said, "What about Bud? Did Gary ever write anything to Bud?"

"I don't know. Bud was drawn toward Gary, so it's possible." Janice picked up the phone and dialed Bud. After a quick exchange, she hung up, smiling.

Within five minutes, Bud stood at Janice's back door.

"Hi, Bud, please come in, and use the front door from now on."

"OK, Mrs. Hinton. Oh, hi, Detective Barnes," Bud said, breathing hard as he entered her house. "Alice is at the store alone. I can't stay long."

"Sure, Bud, did you bring the note Janice asked about?"

Bud nodded.

Bud, we are brothers, brothers who fought and survived Vietnam. Ward died, but we survived. We have our injuries, too. Even though we have burdens, it's up to us to carry on as Ward would have carried on and would want us to carry on.

It's up to us to live each day and try to do the best we can in memory of Ward and all those who died over there. We can do this.
Your brother, Gary

Barnes handed the note to Janice to read. When she finished, she put her hand to her mouth.

"I'll never let this note go, ever!" Bud said fiercely. "He was a good man and my friend. I like you, Detective Barnes, that's why I'm showing you the note, but I want it back."

"Sure. Now, what I want to do is compare Gary's writing here in the note to Bud to the writing I found in the book."

Barnes put Bud's note and the paper from the book that read "I want to come home for Thanksgiving" on the table. He was not a handwriting expert, but he knew enough to make general comparisons.

"Look here," he said. "The 'm's are the same in both notes. The 'a's and 'o's, as well. We'll need an expert to confirm, but I think they were written by the same person—Gary Knowles. Importantly, these words—'I want to come home for Thanksgiving'—show no indication that he intended to commit suicide. This is not a goodbye note. The question is, why did Gary write this note and to whom?"

After Bud left, Barnes and Janice did not have time to go on their picnic near the Des Moines River. Instead, they lunched at Westbrick Lake—Janice feeling vindicated that Gary had been murdered; Barnes wondering in what direction his case was going.

Chapter 37

Monday, November 2

Monday morning arrived like it always did—too early for Chief Ellis Thompkins. He took his time getting to work, puttering around the house and doing minor chores. On the way to work, he stopped at the D&R Drive-In for a cup of coffee and a jelly roll. When he pulled up to the police station, he was surprised to see a Lincoln with Minnesota plates in his usual spot. He was more surprised to see a woman and man sitting in his office.

"Hello?" Thompkins closed the door and removed his coat.

"Good morning, Chief Thompkins." The man stood and shook Thompkins' hand.

"Yes, it is." Thompkins sat down and took the lid off his coffee cup. "Who are ya and and how did ya get in here?"

"Oh, sorry, Chief," the man said. "I'm Herbert Waller, and this is my wife, Bea. One of the firemen next door let us in."

Thompkins quickly sized them up. Both were in their mid-fifties and short. The man was bald except on the lower sides and back of his head. The woman was homely with a mole on her right cheek. Whereas the man had a round chin, the woman's chin was pointed. *What the hell do these two bumpkins want?* he thought, annoyed that he had to wait to devour his jelly roll.

Thompkins sat back in his chair. "What can I do for ya, Mr. and Mrs. Waller?"

"We're here for our son," Bea spoke this time.

"Who's your son? I don't know anyone in town with the name Waller." Thompkins' irritation was notable.

"He hasn't gone by our name since he returned from the war, Chief," Bea continued.

"The war changed him," Herbert jumped in. "He was a good boy who got tangled up in something he had a hard time dealing with."

"OK, then. What has that got to do with me?" Thompkins kept staring at the bag containing the roll.

"He died in your town. We adopted Gary when his parents were killed in a car accident when he was two years old."

Thompkins no longer thought of his roll. "Your son was Gary Knowles?"

Bea stared into Thompkins' eyes. "Yes."

"We want to know what happened to him." Herbert's stare was as intense as his wife's.

"Ah, he committed suicide over two weeks ago. The medical examiner determined he died from an overdose of drugs and alcohol."

"We heard the official determination, but we don't agree with that," Herbert said derisively. "Most importantly, we want to claim his body."

"You want his body?"

"Yes. Where is his body?" Bea said firmly, raising her voice.

"He needs a proper military funeral, one fit for a decorated veteran. You do have his body or know where it is, don't you, Chief?" Herbert stood.

Thompkins realized he had underestimated the Wallers. They were not country bumpkins.

"Gary's body was shipped to his cousin in California a few days ago," Thompkins said. "I'm sure it's there by now."

"I'm sure his body is not there," Herbert snapped. "He doesn't have a cousin in California. They're all in Minnesota—we're from Minneapolis." He paused. "We're going to get to the bottom of this."

"How did ya find out about Gary's death?" Thompkins' mind raced to figure out how these people from Minneapolis learned about the death of a virtually unknown man in small-town Iowa.

"We have a guardian angel," was all Herbert said as he helped Bea stand.

She had tears in her eyes as she spoke. "We're staying at the Best Western in Carlson if you need to contact us. Otherwise, we'll be in touch with you. Good day, Chief Thompkins."

Chapter 38

Monday, November 2

Brent's thoughts swirled around Cindy Williams all day during school. He half-heartedly listened to his teachers and forgot to write down the algebra homework assignment. At lunch, he saw her in the hallway, and she smiled at him. *I can't believe Cindy is going with me to the drive-in tonight,* he thought.

At the end of the school day, Cindy headed to the yearbook club meeting. She caught Brent as he was leaving school.

Oh no! She's going to cancel our date tonight. His stomach churned as she approached him. *So much for thinking I could go out with someone like her.*

"Hi, Brent."

Here comes the letdown. Brent cringed. "Hi, Cindy."

"I want to talk to you about tonight."

Oh, boy. Brent could feel his body sweating. "Sure," he said, disappointment seeping into his voice.

"My parents won't let me go out solo yet. I can only go if it's in a group. I was going to invite some friends, and you can do the same."

Brent could not believe his ears. He'd thought the worst, and now it was the best. "That's fine with me. I'll talk to them." Brent was so relieved; he couldn't believe his luck.

"It's settled then." Cindy's eyes glistened as she talked.

Brent had never felt this way before. "Great!"

"My friends and I will meet you at seven o'clock at the D&R. Come hungry."

Brent tried to mask his exuberance, but failed to be cool. "Can't wait!"

Brent did not remember his walk home; he was thinking of Cindy and the D&R Drive-In.

"Hi, Mom," he said brightly as he entered the house.

"You're sure happy."

"Can I use the phone? And can you or Dad take me to the drive-in tonight?"

"Ah, isn't there school tomorrow?"

"Yeah, but it's just half a day, and we have an assembly. I can handle it. Please?"

"What's the occasion?"

"I'm meeting Cindy Williams and some of her friends. I need to call the guys and see if they can come, too." Brent beamed.

"Wow, Cindy Williams. I'm sure we can work something out."

Of course, Brent's friends eagerly agreed to go. A night out with Cindy and her friends was too good to pass up.

Tim said he would drive the boys. He gave Brent ten dollars and said, "Be sure and pay for Cindy." He then picked up Jack, Ron, and Tom. Dale canceled at the last minute—his parents wouldn't let him go out on a school night.

They arrived at the drive-in early. Brent started sweating when the time reached five after seven and there was no sign of the girls. *God, I'm going to get stood up*, he thought. *Oh, the ultimate embarrassment.*

Finally, Cindy and her friends arrived at ten after, driven by Mrs. Williams. Things started quietly at the drive-in, but once the food arrived, everyone loosened up, and giggling, loud talking, and laughter took over. Brent had a hard time believing that he was living this moment. *Not only is Cindy treating me nicely, but so are her friends. This has to be a dream.*

At a quarter of nine, Shirley, the ever-present waitress, reminded Brent's table that the drive-in closed at nine o'clock. Brent promptly paid for Cindy's dinner. The group decided to venture outside and wait for their rides home. Brent was enjoying the moment laughing with Cindy about something silly as they left the restaurant.

What they saw in the first parking space to the left of the entrance sucked the festivity out of the evening. In that spot sat Elmer Juntlo's red pickup truck. The drive-in was about to close and there were no other vehicles in the parking lot.

Juntlo stood by his truck holding a well-worn Louisville Slugger. He hadn't shaved in days, and the bill of his baseball cap almost covered his eyes. He kept hitting the bat into his left hand. The smacking sound could be heard by all the kids, producing the result Juntlo wanted—fear.

"I've been watchin' you boys. I know it was one of you little shits in my barn the other day. Sneakin' around, spyin' on me, and stealin' my stuff. I just want to talk to you." His bat suggested differently.

None of Brent's group said anything or moved.

"You girls get out of here. I know it wasn't you. It was one of you damned boys. Now, which one? Come on, out with it!"

Brent's heart pounded hard in his chest while his blood ran cold. Options flew through his mind. *I could run away, but that would look bad. Cindy would think I'm a coward. I could confess and see what happens. He wouldn't beat me in such a public place. I'd always have to look over my shoulder, though.*

He knew by the terrified reaction of his friends that he would be given up. Indeed, they glanced in his direction.

"Leave him alone, you crazy old man!" Cindy shouted.

Juntlo growled back, "Who?"

Brent knew his time was up. He started to step forward, ready to confess. But he stopped just as a vehicle pulled up to the right of Juntlo's truck. The driver emerged from the car, his badge strapped on his belt.

"What's going on here?" Barnes said as he stationed himself between the kids and Juntlo.

Barnes glanced at Brent's group. "Are you all right?" he asked.

They nodded hesitantly, thankful the cavalry had arrived.

"They're fine, cop. I've done nothing to 'em."

"I didn't ask you, Mr. Juntlo. I asked them."

"For the second time, you're interfering with me, you commie fed."

"How am I doing that, Mr. Juntlo? And as I said—I'm not a fed, I work for the state. And I'm certainly not a communist. You need to study up on your classifications."

"That don't matter none to me. I want to find the brat who snuck into my barn, see if he stole from me. I'm going to find him. You can't stop me, fed!"

"You shot at one of these boys!" Barnes closed in on Juntlo.

"He was trespassing. I've got a right to protect my property. You can't tell me what to do on *my* property."

"If you're shooting at someone, then it becomes a matter for law enforcement. Why didn't you report the incident to Chief Thompkins or the county sheriff?"

"They're peckers on a sow. They won't do nothin'. I'll take care of it myself. Just like I do with everything. Get your ass back to Des Moines. You're not wanted here."

"I would say the eight people behind me disagree with you. And I'll stay here as long as I see the need to, Mr. Juntlo. Now, *you* go on home."

Juntlo realized he wasn't going to get any further. He tossed the bat in the back of his truck and cursed loudly as he drove away, passing Tim Frost and Sam Williams as they drove up. The kids said quick goodnights and eagerly piled into their respective cars. Barnes gave Brent a sly wink.

"What was that all about?" Tim asked anyone who could hear him.

Barnes answered, "Mr. Juntlo has misconceptions about some matter. Don't worry about it, Mr. Frost. I'll talk to Chief Thompkins about this incident."

"Sure thing. Thanks, Detective Barnes." Tim drove away not thinking that his normally shy son was caught up in anything that involved crazy Elmer Juntlo.

After the vehicles left the parking lot, Shirley locked the doors signifying the drive-in was closed.

Damn, thought Barnes. *I just wanted to get take-out sundaes for me and Janice. I wanted to do something nice for her.* "Damned Juntlo," Barnes muttered.

Shirley noticed Barnes standing by the door and unlocked it.

"I saw what you did there. Elmer Juntlo is difficult to deal with. Thank you for arriving in time to avoid a problem. Whatever you want, it's on the house."

"You don't have to do that, ma'am," Barnes said and smiled.

"Yes, I do."

"OK then, two hot fudge sundaes to go, please. Thank you." As he waited, Barnes considered the connection between Brent and Elmer.

Chapter 39

Tuesday, November 3

The next morning arrived dark and brisk. Winter was beginning to flex its muscles, as cold November days tend to. Brent woke up at the end of the shortest night of sleep he could remember. He spent the night worrying as many thoughts crossed his mind—all bad. *When will Juntlo find out I'm the one he's looking for? Whose bones were in that box? What about the other two boxes? I should tell my mom and dad. What's worse, what my dad will do to me, or old man Juntlo? Crap!*

He managed to fall asleep just before it was time to get up.

"You look terrible," his mother said as he trudged down the stairs to the kitchen.

"I don't feel good, either."

"We shouldn't have let you go out last night. Even though you have a partial day at school today, it was still a school night. It's a good night to stay home and catch up on what you need to catch up on. Where do you feel bad, honey?"

"I'm fine, just tired. It's so dark in the morning." In the back of his mind, Brent wildly imagined that not attending school might somehow tip off Juntlo that he was the one who broke into the barn. *No, I've got to go to school,* he thought.

"Well then, why don't you go back upstairs, wash up, and dress. When you come down, I'll have pancakes and bacon ready for you. That's a good way to start the day. I have a few errands to run this morning, so I can drive you to school."

When Angela dropped Brent off at school, he was feeling better. The sugar rush from the pancakes and syrup had temporarily bolstered his energy and attitude.

Jack was the first to meet him in the hallway.

"Man, are you lucky, Brent. I think one of the guys would have ratted on you to that old turd Juntlo if that cop hadn't come along when he did."

Brent, consumed by worry again, stared straight ahead.

⚓

Barnes woke in Janice's warm embrace. After his confrontation with Juntlo, he went to Janice's house and they enjoyed the sundaes. After a night cap of cognac, they adjourned to her bedroom. Memories of Juntlo, the captain, and everything else were forgotten until morning.

"What can you tell me about Elmer Juntlo?" he asked, curling Janice's hair in his fingers.

"He's an odd man. He drinks a lot, but he's not a drunk. He's a World War II veteran. He used to dabble in the implement business when he wasn't helping his brother, Eldon, on the family farm. He gave that up, though, except for all the junk he stores in that barn of his." She laughed. "He's an occasional customer at the store. I've had to lend him credit sometimes, and he always pays with cash when he can."

"I can tell you from personal experience he does not like cops." Barnes got out of bed. "I have a list of things to get done today, so I'd better get going."

"Yes, and I need to go to the store. I feel bad that Bud has been opening so much lately. What are some of the things you need to do today?"

"Rob wants to meet this morning, and I agreed. I think he's the one who put the note on my door that read 'Nov. 7, 1940.'"

"That's an interesting story. His father, Richard, vanished about this time of year in 1940. There has been no trace of him since. His disappearance was the talk of the town for a while, then it fell into the shadows of World War II."

"What about Rob? Do you know him?"

"No, not personally. I heard he's returned to Brinson only once or twice since leaving for college. I never saw him then. It's kind of curious why he's here now."

"I've wondered the same thing."

On his way to Carlson, Barnes thought of Janice. *She's so pretty, and I like her company and generosity. She's not afraid to take a stand on hard issues. Yet, I miss Clara and I feel guilty sleeping with Janice. In a few days it won't matter anyway. I'll be leaving Brinson and won't see Janice again. Life will return to normal.*

Barnes arrived at the Best Western-Carlson at nine-thirty in the morning. Janice had given him a roll before he left so his stomach would remain calm until lunch. He parked next to the black Cadillac with Colorado plates. Beside the Cadillac was a Lincoln with Minnesota plates. He hadn't seen it before at the motel.

Barnes knocked on the motel room door and Rob answered dressed in his usual western wear, including the black Stetson. His bright belt buckle couldn't be missed.

"Mornin', Detective," Rob said, holding the door open so Barnes could enter the room. "Give me a second." He excused himself to make a call.

Barnes noticed four chairs had been placed in a circle. *Frost must have secured the other three chairs from the manager,* Barnes thought. *My room only has the one.*

"Have a seat. I have some coffee here."

A knock on the door interrupted Rob as he poured the coffee.

"Mornin', Bea and Herbert." Rob let the couple into the room. He pointed to the chairs. "Do you want some coffee, folks?"

Both nodded.

"Detective, I want to introduce you to Bea and Herbert Waller. Bea and Herbert, please meet Detective Fred Barnes from the Iowa Crimes Commission."

Barnes sat. *Who are they? What's Frost leading to?*

Rob continued, "The Wallers are Gary Knowles' parents. They adopted Gary when he was a toddler after his folks were killed in an auto accident."

Barnes almost dropped his empty coffee cup. He was instantly embarrassed. *I didn't know that. How did Rob find out this information? God, I should have looked harder into this case,* he thought. *I assumed too much.*

"I know what you're thinking, Detective," Rob spoke in his rich, almost mesmerizing voice. "How on earth did I come across this information, me being a retired cop and all, and from Colorado?"

Barnes nodded, not taking his eyes off Rob.

"Back in 1968," Rob continued, "I was sent to Minneapolis to cross-train with their police department on crowd control. There was a lot of interest in that topic since the wild affair at the Democratic National Convention in Chicago. Then there was all the campus unrest in the country. For me, it was an easy task. I think my boss was giving me an early retirement present. But I digress.

"I was in Minneapolis for a month and made a number of friends with the police there."

As he listened, Barnes wondered, *How does this man not make friends wherever he goes?*

"I've kept in contact with them and was talking to one the other day—the name is not important. This officer mentioned that he had received a missing persons inquiry from the Wallers about their son, Gary. The officer told the Wallers there wasn't much he could do because it wasn't certain Gary was actually missing. He may have gone to visit friends—the Wallers had mentioned that Gary had friends in Iowa and California.

"When I came to Iowa to follow up on my dad's disappearance, I heard about Gary's death. I put the pieces together, called Herbert and

Bea, and here we are. Once a cop, always a cop—you'll know what I mean someday, Fred."

Rob sat back in his chair, appearing relaxed, although Barnes could feel the man's tenseness.

The coffee was poured and Rob turned to the Wallers. "Tell Detective Barnes what you told me."

Bea and Herbert took turns detailing their life with their adopted son. "Gary was always a good kid. He graduated from high school with decent grades. He was a good athlete and got a college scholarship to play football, but he didn't want to go to college right away. So, he helped a local auto mechanic for a year to save money and figure out what he wanted to do with his life. Then the draft happened.

"Gary was a different person when he returned from the war. He was over in Vietnam for two one-year tours. He was honorably discharged six months ago, and disappeared last month.

"Before, he was an extrovert, loved hanging out with his friends and having fun. He became very introverted after. He stayed in his room for days at a time. He had nightmares and seemed lost. We tried to get him help, but he wouldn't listen. Then he disappeared for weeks. We now know he came to Brinson to attend the funeral for one of his fellow soldiers, Ward Jenkins.

"Gary called us out of the blue on Saturday, October 17. He told us he was tired, but fine, and wanted to come home for Thanksgiving. He didn't tell us where he was, though—I don't know why.

"Do you know what it's like, Detective, to hear that your son—your joy in life who you thought was lost—is coming home, only then to find out he died of an overdose? It rips your heart out." Bea was crying into a handkerchief; Herbert was exerting every effort not to cry.

"We found out from Mr. Frost that Gary's body was sent to a cousin in California for burial." Herbert's anger surfaced. "Only he doesn't *have* a cousin in California.

"And we know he didn't overdose on purpose. Yes, we know he smoked marijuana and drank, but he did not shoot up with heroin.

Good Lord. When you live with someone like Gary and love him like we do, you know him. He needed time to find himself. He did not kill himself!"

When the Wallers had finished, Rob nodded to them. He turned to Barnes, "Looks like you have a murder and cover-up on your hands. Time to put on your big-boy-detective pants."

Chapter 40

Tuesday, November 3

Rose Hancock stood at the sink in her farmhouse. Dawn was an hour away, but she could see snowflakes dancing across the outdoor porch light. Her husband of forty-three years, Gene, was already up and feeding the small herd of Hereford cattle they raised. The Hancock farm encompassed one hundred and sixty acres about four miles northeast of Brinson. One hundred and twenty acres were used to grow row crops, corn, and soybeans, which were rotated annually. Thirty-nine acres were left in pasture for the cattle and two horses. One acre housed the farm buildings, including the Hancock house and a huge garden where Rose grew prized tomatoes and pumpkins.

County Highway K ran north-south adjacent to the farm. The entrance to the farm was off the highway. The Hancocks had lived there for more than thirty years after they inherited it from Rose's parents. They raised two children there, both of whom fled to Des Moines as they had no interest in farming.

Gene dusted the snow off his jacket as he entered the house. "Boy, it's cold out there today."

"Yeah, I can see it snowing. Do you think it will amount to much?" she asked staring out the window.

"Nah, it's too early in the season. Maybe an inch or so is all." He took off his coat and hung it on the hand-carved walnut coat tree in the hall.

"Come here, will you? I can't get any water out of the faucet. I don't think the well pump is working," Rose said.

"The toilet didn't flush this morning, either, now that I think about it. Shit, I'll go take a look when it's lighter outside. In the meantime, gimme some of that breakfast you're fixing."

After breakfast, Gene took a quick visit to the wooden shed that housed the well and well pump. It was dark and cold, but he was used to it and knew how to repair things. Today, though, he was stumped. He returned to the house.

"I guess I gotta call the pump company. I think the pump burned out. Power's still good in here."

Two representatives of Burt's Well Pump Company from Carlson showed up four hours later. The older man was stocky; the other was lanky. Both had thick brown beards. They tried a few quick tests to no avail.

"We have to bring up the pump to check it, Mr. Hancock," the stocky man said. "We might have to bring up part of your well screen, too. Something is really stuck down there."

"Christ," Gene swore. "What the hell could that be? Sounds like you're telling me I may need a new well more than a pump. Are you two trying to sucker me?"

"No, sir," the stocky man replied. "We need to figure this out. The good news is the water table is pretty shallow here. We think your well depth is only thirty feet. The water table is at ten feet. Installing a new well may not be that expensive. We need to go back to the shop and review the records."

"Screw you!" Gene was convinced he was being gouged, and he didn't like it.

"Calm down, Gene." Rose had put on her coat and joined the three men. "Do you have any idea what's going on, boys?"

"We're going to pull your pump and find out. You'll probably need a pump and maybe a new well—and we're not making this up. Please know that we promise to be as economical as possible, Mr. and Mrs.

Hancock. We will get you water as soon as we can." The stocky man talked while the lanky man struggled with the equipment.

The two men worked for an hour and succeeded in bringing the pump and screen to the surface. They gasped as they began their inspection. They had never seen this before. The Hancocks joined them and were equally shocked.

"Mother of God," Rose cried, as she gazed at the pump, horrified. Gene was wide eyed and speechless.

The pump and screen were encased in pig bristles.

CHAPTER 41

Tuesday, November 3

Barnes left Rob's motel room stunned. *God, I'm a lousy detective. This was supposed to be an easy trip—simply verify that a man committed suicide. Now new information indicates that may not have been the case and instead I have a murder to solve. There's also that crazy old man harassing kids. And I have an unplanned relationship with a woman I hardly know. And what's the issue with Nov. 7, 1940?*

As Barnes drove into Brinson, he saw Thompkins and Janice standing by the south side of her store, away from Main Street. Thompkins had his hand on her shoulder. Their faces were close and looked friendly.

What the hell, Janice! He said to himself. *Is she playing me? What's Thompkins doing with her? Do they have something going on? What's up with this town? First thing's first.* He parked outside of the *Brinson Bee.*

He walked into the newspaper office at ten o'clock and was greeted by Mabel. "Hello, Detective Barnes."

"Hi, Mabel. I was wondering if you could help me with something."

"Sure, Detective," she said in a sultry voice. "I'm always ready to help a member of law enforcement."

Barnes couldn't tell if she was sincere.

"Good," he said. "What can you tell me about what happened on November 7, 1940 here in Brinson?"

"Oh, that's a big mystery."

Before Barnes could blink, Max Sturgess stood in front of him across the counter wearing a bright red plaid shirt.

"I was near thirty at the time. I can tell you all about the mysterious disappearance of Richard Franklin Frost," Sturgess proclaimed, ignoring Mabel. "Come back to my office. I'll fill you in."

Barnes followed Sturgess. It had been a spacious office at one time, but it was currently filled with newspapers, mementos, photographs, replicas of sculptures, and what seemed like trash. There were two deer heads and three taxidermized fish that looked like bass mounted on the walls.

"Sorry for the mess. I've been in the business since I was a young man. I started after college and took over when my dad passed. I love it."

"I can see that." Barnes continued to scan the office.

"You don't want to hear my old newspaper stories, though. You want to know about Richard Franklin Frost and 1940."

"It looks like I found the best source—you."

Sturgess motioned for Barnes to sit. Sturgess began talking, and Barnes was pleasantly surprised by the vast knowledge of the event conveyed by the newspaperman. Sturgess talked in detail about Richard Franklin Frost's life, his disappearance, and the follow-up investigations. The only thing Sturgess didn't know was what had happened to Richard. But in the end, no one knew.

When he finished, Sturgess called out, "Mabel, could you pull from archives all the editions from November and December 1940 for Detective Barnes? Add January and February 1941, too."

Sturgess turned to Barnes. "Those will be ready for you to review tomorrow morning. If you need anything else, please let me know. Perhaps you're the one who can finally solve the mystery. God knows, no one else could."

Sturgess excused himself for a meeting. After Sturgess had left, Barnes thought, *Damn it, I came to talk to Max about Gary and got completely sidetracked with this 1940 disappearance thing. I've got to focus and not think about Janice so much. I'll try again later with Max.*

Barnes decided to walk to the Hinton store to see how Janice would react to him. Janice was stocking a shelf on a step ladder when he entered.

"Hi, Fred," she said warmly.

"Hi," he responded, not looking at her.

"Is something wrong?" Janice asked, concerned, as she stepped down.

"It appears everything in Brinson is a potential problem." *Including you and Ellis Thompkins*, he thought. He paused and gave Janice a cold stare. He motioned for her to follow him back to her office.

"You were right. I'm now thinking Gary was murdered. Did you know that his parents are alive? I didn't. Gary was adopted at a young age by Herbert and Bea Waller, from Minnesota. They're currently staying in Carlson at the Best Western. And Gary's body is missing. I need to go."

Janice reached out and grabbed his arm. "What else?"

Barnes hesitated and said, "I saw you and Thompkins getting friendly by the store when I drove into town earlier. I didn't think you and he were like that."

She stared into his eyes. "We went out a couple of times after my husband died. Ellis isn't my type, so I ended it. He's under the false impression there is something between us. I can assure you, there was not and is not. But I can say that there is a spark between you and me. You need to let it happen. I'll leave the door unlocked tonight. It's your decision."

Barnes checked his watch. "I need to conduct another interview. I'll see you later."

Barnes arrived at the Frost house and watched Brent go in through the back door. At the front door, he was greeted by Angela, who was leaving.

"Good afternoon, Mrs. Frost. I see you're going somewhere."

"Yeah," she said. "Parent-teacher conferences are today at the school. I'm meeting Tim there. Did you need to talk to us?"

"Yes, and Brent, too. I want to follow-up on the incident at the drive-in last night."

"Tim told me about that." Angela stopped walking and gave Barnes a warm look. "You really came in the nick of time and saved the kids from something bad. Someone—Chief Thompkins—should put that crazy man, Juntlo, in jail. He is going to hurt someone. Hounding kids like that, terrible. He should stay in that building of his at the edge of town."

"I'll grant you, Elmer Juntlo is off center. I'm surprised he hasn't harmed anyone yet. I've already had two run-ins with him. He doesn't like law enforcement, particularly me."

"His older brother, Eldon, is worse, but he lives on a farm several miles outside of town, so we see very little of him, thank goodness. Elmer should move out there."

"Would you mind if I spoke to Brent about last night? Afterward, I'll pay Mr. Juntlo a visit."

"Go ahead, he's inside. I want to warn you that Brent is not feeling very well today. I think going out on a weeknight is to blame."

"Thank you, Mrs. Frost. I won't be long."

"You're welcome. And please, call me Angela."

Angela got in her car and drove off to the school. Barnes called upstairs, "Hello, Brent."

A dour-faced Brent answered. "Hi, Detective Barnes. My folks aren't here. They'll be at school. And thanks for being at the drive-in last night. Old man Juntlo is scary."

"No problem. Yes, he is scary, as you said. He needs to be stopped before he hurts someone. I intend to do that." Barnes paused. "Brent, I want to talk to you alone. Please have a seat."

"Sure." Brent nodded with his head down and took a seat opposite Barnes.

"I know it was you who Juntlo shot at the other day outside his barn."

Brent's eyes widened. *If Barnes knows, Juntlo must, too.*

"Relax, Brent," Barnes continued to smile. "I won't tell anyone about what I think happened. But it's true, isn't it?"

Brent paused and in a shaky voice mumbled a barely audible, "Yes."

"I'm not after you, Brent. Juntlo is my person of interest. A mildly rational man doesn't shoot at someone. My experience tells me Juntlo is hiding something in that barn. I believe you may have seen that something. I think it's more than trespassing that's causing Juntlo's behavior. What did you find?"

Brent froze. Detective Barnes knew his secret. *This is terrible,* he thought. *What do I do now? Do I tell him everything, nothing, or something to get him out of here?* Brent saw the ghoulish specter of Elmer Juntlo behind Barnes.

"You'll be my anonymous tipster." Barnes filled the conversation void. "I know he's after whoever he suspects trespassed in his building, and it's good he's still not sure who that was. I can protect you by putting pressure on him instead of him on you. I promise not to tell anyone. It'll be between you and me. Please, tell me what you know. It'll help."

Brent nodded and sighed. "Yeah, I was in old man Juntlo's barn. My friends and I wanted to see what he keeps in there. We thought there was gold or money. I wasn't going to steal anything, just look. I volunteered to go, which I know was wrong. We thought it would be safe since Juntlo goes to the bar every afternoon for a couple of hours. It was a big surprise when he returned early. I was still inside.

"He came in, and he knew someone was in the building. He started yelling and cursing. I was scared to death. I looked for a way out. I was lucky because there were a couple of broken boards at the bottom of one of the walls that I could squeeze under. I crawled under them and ran as fast as I could through the cornfield. I never looked back, even when he shot at me. Fortunately, he didn't hit me. I ran under the culvert and made it back to my friends. He would have killed me if he'd caught me. I know it. Now, he's after me."

"Juntlo's still not sure if it was you. That's why he's acting the way he is. He wants to scare you as a group, hoping someone will rat on you. Or he will notice your behavior is different than the others. I'm not going to let that happen." *But Juntlo knows it was you, Brent,* Barnes thought.

Barnes paused to see if Brent had anything else to say. He didn't.

"I don't think you're telling me the whole story, though. What did you find in the barn?"

Brent didn't think he could lie to a detective, but he tried. "I saw nothing really interesting. Juntlo's got a lot of junk in there—old cars, farm machinery, barrels of crap, some old boxes—just junk. Oh yeah, a dead deer hanging from a board. There was lots of blood underneath it and several knives."

"I see," Barnes brushed some lint off his slacks. "I still feel something is missing. If it was just junk, why did he react the way he did to an intruder?"

"That's the way he is. He's crazy," Brent said with a hint of desperation.

"I can see that," Barnes repeated and then let silence take over.

Barnes observed that the more time that went on, the more fidgety Brent became.

After a couple minutes of silence, Brent couldn't take it anymore. He'd spent several days with the heavy burden that kept weighing on his mind more and more. *I've got to think of something to get Detective Barnes off my back.*

Brent slid back in his chair; his eyes stared at the ceiling. "There were three boxes."

"You saw boxes?"

"Yeah, they were like caskets. I opened one. It just had dirt. Then he came in. I didn't have time to open the other two."

"Good, Brent. Anything else you want to add?"

"No. I just want this to all go away, along with Elmer Juntlo. I don't feel well."

"You have a nice group of friends, and your mom and dad are good parents. I want you to get back to enjoying life. Leave Juntlo to me. It's time he felt some heat."

Barnes smiled and stood up. His manner was so calm that Brent cracked a slight smile.

"I'll keep you updated on what I find, Brent. Remember, what we talked about is our secret—for now."

Barnes' detective instincts told him that there was more to the story. *I'll bet it has something to do with those three boxes.*

Brent was also thinking, *I can't keep it up much longer, not talking about the bones.*

Barnes left the Frost house for Juntlo's barn. Juntlo's red pickup was parked outside. He had just returned from his afternoon at the Thirsty Bull. Barnes guessed he would be in no mood to talk.

Barnes knocked on the door. He waited a minute and knocked again. The door opened about six inches. Barnes could see Juntlo's scraggly face through the crack.

"What the hell do you want, cop?" Juntlo's rough voice sounded like a scratched record.

"I want to follow-up on last night's problem at the D&R."

"One of those damned kids trespassed, and I'm going to find out who."

"And then what? Are you going to hurt him—or worse? I saw you fire your shotgun, Mr. Juntlo. Were you trying for a kill?

"Of course not! Just a warning. No one was harmed, was they?"

"I have no reports that anyone was injured or killed, no."

"If I wanted to, I wouldn't have missed. I was in the Army. I can do whatever I want, cop."

"No, you can't. Particularly, not shooting at a minor."

"But …" Juntlo started to speak.

"But nothing, Mr. Juntlo. Was anything taken from your building?"

"I don't know."

"You seem to be a man who guards his possessions tightly and knows when something is missing. So?"

"I found nothin' missing, cop, but that doesn't mean nothin' was stolen. And it's trespassin'."

"Then can I come in and take a look around to see whether something was stolen?"

"Get the hell off my property, you piece of shit. You gotta get a warrant, and I doubt you can. We don't like Des Moines cops here. Get the hell outta here!"

"One more thing, Mr. Juntlo. Where were you on the night of October 17?"

"Why do you give a shit, Barnes? That ain't none of your business." Juntlo's eyes narrowed.

"That's the night Gary Knowles died."

"Yeah, so? I heard it was suicide."

"Perhaps, but some people think his death was from something other than suicide."

"You think he was killed. And you think I had something to do with it." Juntlo stepped forward through the doorway and raised his fist in anger. "Jesus Christ, you shit face. You insult me!"

"Why is that?" Barnes tried hard to remain calm.

"I didn't know Gary Knowles personally. Some of my buddies at the bar didn't like him, but I told 'em to leave him alone. He's a vet, for God's sake, and us vets stick together. He got shit on by everybody. I would never hurt a vet—never! Particularly one who saw combat. That changes a man."

Barnes backed down and looked at the ground. *Is Juntlo telling the truth?*

"Did you serve, Barnes?" Juntlo lowered his fist.

"No."

"Figures. I'm not going to tell you again—get the hell off my property!" Juntlo stormed into his barn, reached back and slammed the door.

"I don't want to hear about you harassing any of the kids or anyone else in this town, Mr. Juntlo." Barnes regained his resolve and yelled through the door. "You'll find out that Des Moines has a long reach. I'm going to make sure Chief Thompkins and the Reed County sheriff keep an eye on you. Watch your step." Barnes turned and walked to his car.

Barnes drove to Carlson and parked outside the motel. He noticed that both the Colorado and Minnesota cars were gone. He sat in his room alone for an hour thinking about the day's events. His notebook lay on the desk in front of him, and he held a pen in his hand. A myriad of thoughts crossed his mind. *What's my next step with the Knowles case?*

What do I do about Juntlo? It seems Rob knows more than he's saying. And what about Janice? Even if she said there's nothing going on between Thompkins and her, is she believable? Brinson is a complicated mess.

Barnes decided to call the captain. He needed a warrant to search Juntlo's barn. After a surprisingly successful call, he traveled back to Brinson to talk with Janice. He sighed. *I'm worried that she still is the target of someone who wants to hurt her.*

When he rang her doorbell, this time it was Janice who was cool.

"I'm not going to apologize for today, for what you saw between Ellis and me. I told you there's nothing going on between us, and I meant it. You have to believe me."

She waved to Barnes to come inside. She sat down and opened her cigarette pack. She looked at Barnes and tossed them into a trash off to her side.

"I don't need these anymore."

"That's good. I quit the day Clara was diagnosed with cancer. It's not good for you."

"Bud agrees with you."

The phone rang and Janice answered. "It's Chief Thompkins, Fred."

Fred took the phone. "I knew ya would be there," Thompkins growled. "Got something for ya."

CHAPTER 42

Wednesday, November 4

Barnes lay awake most of the night in Janice's apartment, unsure about her relationship with Ellis Thompkins. *Is Janice like Charlotte Washburn?* he wondered. *Someone you don't suspect when she is up to her neck in it. In this case, with Knowles' murder. God, I hope not. It makes no sense, anyway. I'm tired.*

He finally fell asleep around four o'clock in the morning. When he opened his eyes, he heard Janice upstairs preparing breakfast. He closed his eyes again and went back through the conversation he had with Chief Thompkins hours earlier.

"We got him," Thompkins announced on the call.

"Who? Elmer Juntlo?"

"No, Carl Dinkins, for Gary Knowles' murder," the chief proudly said.

"What? Why?" Barnes was confused.

"He confessed, that's why."

"To the murder?"

"Not yet. But he admitted that he was trying to frighten your girlfriend."

Instantly annoyed, Barnes said, "I assume you mean Janice, and I don't think you can classify her as my girlfriend. She may object to that. What is your evidence that Dinkins murdered Knowles?"

"We'll get the evidence and the confession. It's just a matter of time. We know Dinkins hated Knowles and his anti-war antics. There was the fight outside the Thirsty Bull. If I hadn't intervened, Dinkins would have killed him right there."

"I heard Bud and Janice had a hand in stopping the fight." Barnes knew the story.

"They were there, but I'm the law enforcement in Brinson. It would have had a very different outcome if I hadn't stepped in. I also think Dinkins was responsible for the raccoon incident at Janice's. Ya weren't here when that happened."

"I heard about that, too. I would like to interview Dinkins."

"Ya can't—at least, not here. I transported him to the Carlson jail an hour ago. Our small cell is just for drunks to sleep it off. It's not for holding a murderer."

"He's an alleged murderer, Chief. In our system, he first needs to have his rights read to him. Then he can be formally charged, prosecuted, and convicted before he's called a murderer. You probably don't get many murder trials in Brinson, so you may be unaware of the process."

"Ya big-city cops think ya got all the answers. Well, ya don't. We'll get that confession. I think it's time for ya to return to Des Moines and manage yar big city cases. I'll keep ya updated when we receive new information."

"Thank you, I'm sure you will." Barnes tried to sound sincere to deescalate the tension between the two men.

Dinkins is a suspect for sure, Barnes thought after the call ended.

After replaying the conversation in his head, Barnes dressed and hustled upstairs. He intended to leave the house, but the smell of breakfast and the sound of Janice's sweet voice stopped him.

"Please join me for breakfast. I'm sorry about last night."

"I'm sorry too, Janice. I need to run into Carlson. We may have a break in the Knowles case."

Her eyes narrowed. "Can you tell me what that break is?"

"Not yet, but I will when things become clearer. It's all supposition at the moment." Barnes wolfed down the food. When finished, he thanked Janice and touched her hand. The next sound Janice heard was Barnes' Ford Ltd racing down the street.

Barnes arrived at the Reed County courthouse in record time. Deputy Sheriff Nelson met him at the door of the sheriff's office.

"Good morning, Deputy."

"Yes, it is Detective. We have the murder suspect in the Gary Knowles' case—Carl Dinkins. He was transferred to us earlier by Chief Thompkins," Nelson added. "Events have happened so fast. Just a day ago we believed Knowles committed suicide. Now, he appears to have been murdered."

"Has Dinkins confessed yet?"

"Not to the murder. He maintains his innocence on that one. He does admit to threatening Janice Hinton. He said he had no intention of hurting her—he just wanted to scare her out of supporting Knowles and into leaving Brinson."

"I guess he would assume throwing that brick through her window was a nonviolent act. She could have been badly hurt. Not to mention the mental trauma."

"He said Eddie Horst threw the brick. And the mayor, Templeton, has been putting thoughts in their heads about Knowles and Janice."

Barnes shook his head. "Can I interview Dinkins?"

"Not yet. We're going to file several charges against him, including harassment—whatever we can find. We'll see if that triggers a murder confession. We also want to talk in more detail to Chief Thompkins. Come back tomorrow morning at ten o'clock."

Disappointed, Barnes drove back to Brinson. He had an appointment at the *Brinson Bee* to review the articles from their archives regarding the 1940 disappearance of Richard Franklin Frost.

When Barnes arrived at the newspaper office, Mabel was waiting for him.

"I have the archives Max wanted you to look over. They're over there on that desk. Stay as long as you want," she purred.

Barnes looked around for Max. "Is Max here today?"

"Nope, we think he's at the hospital in Des Moines. He has cancer, and I overheard him talking to the doctor yesterday. It's lung cancer, but Max is very secretive about it—doesn't tell us anything. We don't even know whether he'll be in today. Don't tell him I told you.

"Does Max live in town or in Carlson?"

"Oh no. He lives on his farm out in the country, about four miles northwest of here. There's an abandoned church next to his land to the east. He's really not a farmer—anymore than us townies, Brenda and me." Mable nodded to Brenda.

"I remember seeing that church. It's in bad shape," Barnes acknowledged.

"Whatever, I'm in charge and I have a newspaper to get out today. This is just another day at the office for me and all the others," Mabel said sarcastically.

Barnes peered around the office again. He saw only Brenda. "That's a lot you have to do."

"I guess you could say Max is the brains and I, I mean we, are the brawn of this enterprise." She waved her hand in the air.

"How old were you when Richard Frost disappeared? Did you live in Brinson?"

"Are you fishing for information about me?" Mabel batted her eyes at Barnes.

"Uh, no." His face showed embarrassment.

"Too bad, but I've been married for twenty years now—to the same guy—and with two kids. Can you believe it? You missed your chance. You never know, though, what the future holds." Mabel laughed and Barnes didn't know what to say.

"Relax, Detective. I'm just having fun with you." She laughed again. "I was around ten years old at the time. I remember the disappearance was a big deal. Richard Frost was a prominent citizen of Brinson. Then all the commotion died down and life moved on. Say, hon, you have a nice physique."

"Huh, what?" He again was thrown off balance by Mabel.

"Do you work out?"

"Yeah, I jog a little and lift a few weights. Not as much as I should."

"Well, you look in fine shape to me, right Brenda? Now when Chief Thompkins came to town, he was a hunk. D'ya know he played football at a college in Illinois? Since he's been here, though, he's been enjoying those jelly rolls maybe a little too much, and now he's developing a roll of his own. You don't look like you enjoy those jelly rolls as much."

Mabel smiled, Brenda giggled, and Barnes cringed.

"I think I'll look at those articles now."

Barnes spent the next couple hours reading the materials he had been given. He read not only the stories pertaining to Richard Frost's disappearance, but the entirety of the newspapers. He took several pages of notes. When finished, he arranged all the papers into a neat pile.

"All done, Detective?" Mabel approached him.

"Yes." Barnes frowned.

"Are you stumped?"

"Yep."

"Don't feel bad, hon. Everyone else before you was just as stumped."

"I have a hard time believing that someone like Richard Frost could just vanish like that without leaving a clue."

"I've got another mystery for you, Detective."

Barnes looked up at Mabel with a wrinkled forehead. "What's that?"

"In November 1950, ten years to the date after Richard's disappearance, Constable Wilber Roberts was hit by a train and killed."

Mabel's comment piqued Barnes' interest. "And?"

"His police car was stopped on the railroad tracks. The bourbon bottles found inside and around the car suggest Constable Roberts was drunk and passed out when the train hit him."

"So?" Barnes squinted his left eye.

"Wilber Roberts never touched alcohol."

Chapter 43

Wednesday, November 4

The engines of several vehicles could be heard half a mile away on a crisp, dry November 4 early afternoon. The invasion of the Hancock farm had begun. Representatives from Burt's Well Pump Company, the Iowa Geological Survey, the Iowa Department of Environmental Quality, the Reed County Sheriff's office, and the State of Iowa Highway Patrol out of Carlson gathered at the site of the Hancock well. Even Max Sturgess surprisingly showed up. Rose made coffee from bottled water and heated up biscuits for the assemblage.

"I sure as hell don't know what caused this," Gene grouched as he gazed at the well screen encrusted with hog bristles.

"Ever raised hogs on your land, Mr. Hancock?" Deputy Nelson inquired.

"Nope, never touched 'em. I don't do livestock, except my Herefords, two horses, and a couple of chickens Rose keeps around. Then there's my dog, Pepper." A salt and pepper mutt sat at Gene's side.

"Ever seen dumping occur on your land?" Kevin Hogan, environmental scientist with the Iowa Department of Environmental Quality, asked.

"Nope." Gene looked at the ground.

"No farm dump, Mr. Hancock?" Hogan pried.

Gene hesitated and kicked leaves by the well shed.

"For goodness sakes, Gene," Rose said as she offered coffee. "Yes, we have a small dump over there where we've tossed an old refrigerator, stove, machinery parts, and stuff like that. It's pretty small. Gene, go and show 'em."

"Hmmm …" Gene glanced a hard look at Rose. "Follow me." They walked about a hundred feet to a hillside. Discarded, rusty debris crowded the downslope as Rose had described. The crew of men inspected the debris and found no organic matter.

"This dump is downgradient of the well," Hogan concluded. "Even if there were pig carcasses disposed of here, there's no way groundwater flowed upgradient and contaminated their well."

"I told you, no dead pigs here," Gene said, exasperated.

The group then trooped back to the well.

"How deep is your well, Mr. Hancock?" Cory Poleczyk, hydrogeologist from the Iowa Geological Survey, asked.

"Not very deep. I don't know the exact depth, if that's what you're asking. Them drilling guys know." Gene pointed to the workers from the well company.

"We checked our records—it's twenty-four feet deep, a little less than we thought. It's a sand point well," the short, stout man from the pump company said. "The water table depth is pretty shallow here, and it recharges fine. We set the well screen at ten to fifteen feet below ground. We can extend it to the full twenty-four feet, if needed."

"Do you remember when you installed this well, Mr. Hancock?" Poleczyk looked down into the well.

"We replaced the old well, what, about twelve years ago, right, Rose?"

"He's right. It was the summer of 1958, when I needed water for my garden," Rose confirmed.

"Do you have any enemies who might sabotage your well?" Vince Riggins with the Iowa Highway Patrol asked.

"Nobody we know would do anything like that. How could they?" Gene asserted, and Rose nodded in agreement.

Riggins looked to the two well men. "Is this possible?"

"Sure, anything is possible," the stout well man said. "I doubt it, though." He then discussed the steps someone would have to undertake to contaminate a well in the way the Hancocks' well had been impacted.

The group continued to kick the ground in an attempt to keep warm on the cold afternoon. Rose walked to the house to fetch more hot coffee.

As she was returning, she heard Hogan call out. He had walked a couple hundred feet along a slight upslope from the house. From that spot he gazed westward and looked as if he'd spied something in a grove of trees. He waved to the party to join him.

"Is this your land, Mr. Hancock?" Hogan asked, looking at the trees.

"No, that's Eldon Juntlo's land. It borders my property, but it's his land. Why?"

"You can't see the area within the trees from your house, can you?" Hogan pointed to the trees and then to the Hancocks' house.

"Nope. But I've seen lights coming from over there from time to time." Gene spit out the remnants of his tobacco chew and pointed to the west.

"Where are you going with this, Kevin?" Riggins asked.

"If you look closely, you can see a depressed area among the trees. That area has been covered recently. It could be a disposal site." Hogan squinted at the area.

"Whoa, that's a big assumption," Max Sturgess joined the conversation.

Hogan walked to the western edge of the Hancock property. Stubbles of corn from the latest harvest crunched under his feet. The other men followed.

"How have your crops done in this area recently, Mr. Hancock?" Hogan followed an imaginary line from Juntlo's grove to the Hancock wellhouse.

"Great." Gene nodded. "I've never had the corn grow taller or produce more full ears than it has this year."

"Do you know why?" Poleczyk asked.

"We had good moisture this spring. Maybe that was it." Gene smiled thinking of his bountiful corn crop.

Hogan motioned for Poleczyk, Riggins, and Deputy Nelson to join him. He spoke quietly to the group. "I believe dead hogs have been dumped illegally in that grove on Juntlo's property, and the residue has migrated onto the Hancocks' land and contaminated their well."

"That's a hell of a theory, Kevin." Riggins stared at the suspected dumping area. "What should we do about this?"

"Well, we could do a geophysical survey first and see if there's something unnatural. If so, then we could dig some soil test pits. But I know that's what happened here."

"Eldon won't like this," Sturgess said, looking at the Juntlo farm buildings in the distance. "And his brother, Elmer, won't either."

"I'll see what I can do," Nelson said. He huddled with Riggins.

Afterward, Riggins announced, "We'll get a court order. The state can take Juntlo's wrath. We're looking at a grave threat to public health."

"God, I hope you're right. The Juntlos will sue you if you're wrong," Sturgess said. "And make your life miserable."

"I'm not wrong." Hogan folded his arms across his chest. "You'll see."

"I just want my well working again, and for Rose and me to have clean water." Gene spit. "The Juntlos be damned! I'll take care of them myself."

"Stand back, Mr. Hancock," Riggins said. "We'll take it from here."

"When do you think you'll have the order?" Hogan asked.

"Soon. Be ready to go tomorrow. It may snow later in the week," Riggins said.

"And I'll be sure our department patrols this area frequently for the next twenty-four hours," added Deputy Nelson.

A judge granted the court order later that day. The order allowed the alleged dump on Juntlo's land to be accessed the following day, Thursday, November 5.

Chapter 44

Wednesday, November 4

Brent was confused when he returned to school the day after his talk with Detective Barnes. He felt terrible lying to Barnes about the human bones. *I should have told him.*

At lunch, he walked by the room where the yearbook club met. He glanced through the window in the door. Seated in the front was Cindy. Their eyes locked for a moment, and she smiled. Brent smiled back only to see the club advisor's back wedge up in the door frame, blocking his view.

Crap, Brent thought. *I'll go to the Hinton store and buy something she may like—Orange Crush or grape soda. Everyone likes those.*

At the store, his heart was so impassioned thinking about Cindy that he didn't notice the figure standing with his back to him at the meat counter. Brent wandered over to the tiny alcove where the candy was. He got a bag of M&Ms for Cindy in addition to the pop. When he turned around to check out, he was face to face with Elmer Juntlo.

"Hey, boy, I know you was in my barn." Juntlo spat.

"Ahh … no," Brent stammered.

"Come on, kid. Fess up and I'll let you be." Juntlo rested one hand on his hip as he pointed a dirty finger from his other hand to within inches of Brent's face.

"It wasn't me!"

"Then which of your brat friends was it? It was you or one of them. I think you!"

Brent couldn't move. "It wasn't any of us!"

"I don't sneak into your house and steal things. Maybe I should."

"Nothing was taken." Brent's brain tried to find any reason to get away from this grotesque being.

"Aha, it *was* you! I knew it! Now you'll pay!" Juntlo reached forward to grab Brent's shoulder. "We're going to my barn and you're going to get it." Juntlo gritted his teeth as he snarled.

Brent dropped the bottle of Orange Crush and it shattered against the floor. Juntlo reached for Brent, but Brent jerked away at the last second.

"Damn it," Juntlo growled.

A second later, Juntlo's body was being lifted off the ground.

"Leave the boy alone, you nasty man!" Bud grasped Juntlo's collar and jerked him up. Juntlo hung in the air flailing. "How could you, a vet, be such an ass!"

"Let go of me, you retard!" Juntlo shouted.

Bud dropped Juntlo, spun him around, and pulled him up several inches off the ground by his shirt collar. "What'd you call me?" The anger in Bud's voice resonated through the store.

"You heard me, you piece of shit. Put me down!"

Bud's right hand balled into a fist, which he intended to smash into Juntlo's weathered face. Juntlo closed his eyes, expecting the worst. He belatedly recalled that the one thing you did not want to do was anger Bud. And he had done that. "Sorry," he bleated softly.

"Bud, what's going on here?" Janice ran out from her office.

"He was going to hurt Brent. I'm not going to let that happen, Mrs. Hinton."

Brent stood by, dumbfounded. He had always viewed Bud as kind of a stooge. He and his friends made jokes about Bud, but never when he could hear. As he watched Bud become his defender, Brent vowed to never again say an unkind word about Bud.

Janice walked over to Juntlo as Bud held the man off the ground.

"Mr. Juntlo, is that true? Were you trying to hurt Brent?"

"Are you going to believe his word or mine?"

"I believe Bud. He doesn't lie. You, on the other hand, are one of the least trustworthy people I know." Janice glanced at Brent.

Brent didn't say anything. He was scared. He didn't want Juntlo to harm him or his family.

"Was Elmer trying to hurt you?" Janice bent down as she spoke to Brent.

Brent hesitated and nodded.

Janice stood erect and faced Juntlo. "I'm reporting you to Chief Thompkins and the Reed County Sheriff's office. You're a threat to children and you need to be dealt with."

"Careful, woman, no one is going to do nothin' to me. And see if I get back here again."

"Good. You're not allowed back here. Bud, show Mr. Juntlo out."

"Bitch, dumb ass," Juntlo shouted as Bud carried him out of the store, still not touching the floor. After they reached the door, Bud tossed him onto the sidewalk.

"Don't come back," Bud said firmly, "or I'll give you what you deserve."

Juntlo had enough sense to not say anything. He picked himself up off the pavement and walked down the street. He passed Barnes on the way, but neither was aware of the other. Juntlo plotted revenge, while Barnes pondered Wilber Roberts' death.

Barnes entered Janice's store and sensed instantly that something was wrong. Janice and Bud were huddled around a teary-eyed Brent.

"What happened?" Barnes asked the room.

Janice and Bud filled Barnes in. As they talked, Barnes reached out and patted Brent on the shoulder.

"It'll be all right. I'm going to take care of this. Juntlo is a bully, and he's going to be dealt with. I promise."

Brent felt a tiny bit of relief. *I've known Detective Barnes for only a short period, but I have trust in him*, he thought.

Barnes had had enough of Elmer Juntlo. Juntlo had done bad things and never seemed to be held accountable. *Why?* Barnes had his suspicions.

He asked Janice, "Can I use your office phone to make a long-distance call to my captain in Des Moines? I need to get into Juntlo's barn. It's urgent. I also need to contact the sheriff's office. We need a restraining order against Juntlo. That's urgent, too."

⚔

The captain sat in his office at ICC headquarters moving papers around. His second in command stood in front of him.

"I see you finally gave Barnes that search warrant, Captain."

"I did, what's your point?"

"Sounds like shaky grounds for a warrant."

"Sure it was." He leaned forward. "This is not to go outside of this office."

The second in command nodded.

The captain continued, "What will happen is that I will use it to get rid of Barnes once and for all. According to my sources, there's nothing illegal in that barn. It's a fool's hunt. They'll find nothing, and that'll be my excuse to show Barnes the door. He's no longer able to perform his duties as an ICC detective. All I ever hear about him are the problems he's causing."

CHAPTER 45

Thursday, November 5

Barnes reconsidered his life choices and spent the night with Janice. The previous day's problems had been washed away after the confrontation with Juntlo. Janice provided Barnes compelling reasons to stay with her, and he had come to terms with the fact that he had no reason not to. She was smart, pretty, and independent, and he now believed she had no romantic connection to Thompkins. And he thought she liked him, too. They enjoyed each other's company, as thoughts of their pasts became less paramount.

Before dawn arrived on that Thursday morning, Barnes reluctantly left Janice's warm bed for Carlson.

Rob left his motel room on the morning of November 5 and was surprised to see a note attached to his door. He opened the envelope and scanned the writing:

Sergeant Frost—please come to my room after you read this. Detective Fred Barnes

Intrigued, Rob walked to Barnes' room. Barnes opened the door before Rob could knock.

"Good morning, Rob—or should I say, Sergeant Robert Franklin Frost?" Barnes held out two cups of coffee.

Rob took one of the cups; it was hot. "Yes, good morning, Fred." The cup was so hot he had to switch hands to keep from getting burned. "I see you've done your homework." He adjusted his Stetson. "And by the way, you know it's *retired* Sergeant Frost."

"Please, tell me about yourself, Rob."

"You probably already know most of this."

"Some of it, but not all. Go ahead." Barnes took only a tiny sip of the coffee to avoid burning his tongue.

"I left Brinson in 1935 and attended the University of Colorado in Boulder. I graduated with a degree in social studies in 1939. I worked for a charitable program and then volunteered for duty in the war. After six months of training, my superiors noticed that I possessed a certain talent. I then served in security for General Omar Bradley throughout the war.

"When the war ended, I returned to Colorado to resume my career. However, doing the security detail during the war changed me. I no longer wanted to do social work. Instead, I chose to be a cop and joined the Denver Police Department. I worked cases for the department in vice, narcotics, and homicide, and ended up behind a desk as a sergeant. I worked there for twenty-five years and retired last month.

"I came back to Brinson to see what has changed because it's been over a decade since I was here. I want one last chance to solve my father's disappearance before I get too old and start losing my marbles." Rob pointed to his head.

"I'm pleased you located the Wallers." Barnes found the coffee had cooled enough to drink.

"I didn't know one way or the other whether Gary killed himself, but I was curious. When I found out Gary had been adopted by the Wallers, I invited them here to shake some rust off that lazy Chief Thompkins."

"The evidence has shifted, and I believe someone killed Gary. I just don't know who."

Rob sat down in the rickety motel chair. "Carl Dinkins seems the most obvious suspect from what I know. Start with him."

Barnes sat on the corner of the bed. "Yeah, I agree. I'm interviewing Dinkins later this morning. Do you have any idea where Knowles' body is?"

"No, although I believe it's still in the area."

"The medical examiner, Dr. Deisman, said they shipped it to a relative in California, but there seems to be no shipping paperwork and no relative."

"True, Knowles has no relatives in California. I will say that Dr. Deisman is a strange man, Fred. He's either incompetent or covering something up. I wouldn't want him as a medical examiner or as my doctor."

"I'll visit him again after I talk to Dinkins." Barnes put the cup down, indicating it was time for Rob to leave. "I have to go now. There are people I need to talk to."

⅄

Carl Dinkins sat in his small jail cell looking at the floor when Barnes appeared with a deputy.

"Thanks, Deputy, I'll need a few minutes alone with Mr. Dinkins. I just have some questions for him."

Barnes smiled and the deputy left the room.

"Hello, Mr. Dinkins. I'm Detective Fred Barnes with the Iowa Crimes Commission. Do you mind if I ask you a few questions?"

Dinkins shrugged and faced Barnes. "I didn't do it."

"Do what, Mr. Dinkins?"

"What they're going to charge me with. That's what."

"I'm still not sure what you're saying. What do you think you're being charged with?"

"Shit, you Des Moines cops are really slow—for murder, you asshole."

"I thought you meant for harassing Mrs. Hinton." Barnes kept a flat monotone, which irritated Dinkins.

"Yeah, like I told that other guy, I wrote her those notes and followed her home. But I didn't throw the brick through her window. Eddie Horst done that. I confessed to the other shit as well. Janice was helping that hippie commie, Gary Knowles. I couldn't stand it." Dinkins' face was red. "The mayor told us that Gary and Janice were traitors to our country and she broke up the Bridges."

"Do you realize that Gary was a war hero and a friend of Ward's? And that the Jenkins themselves had no animosity toward Gary? So why did you?"

"I don't know now. I'm confused. I drink too much a lot of the time. I say things and sometimes do things drunk that I regret when I'm sober."

"You did not kill Gary, did you, Mr. Dinkins?"

"No, I don't think so. I hope not. But I can't remember everything I do when I drink. Killing a man—that's bad."

"Do you know what heroin is?"

"Yes, it's what them addicts use in New York and California. They rob people for drug money and sleep on the streets."

"How do they use heroin? Do users swallow it, inhale it, inject it, or rub it on their skin?"

Dinkins closed his eyes. "All the above?"

"Yes. Sometimes addicts buy it in powder form, heat it until it's a liquid, and inject it into their veins. Heroin is very addictive."

"I know it's bad. God, I could never do that. I hate needles. I prefer beer."

"So, Mr. Dinkins, you never bought heroin, prepared it for Mr. Knowles, and injected it into his body?"

"No, sir! I had nothin' to do with that. I wouldn't even know where to get it!" Carl yelled. His loud voice brought the deputy back to the door.

"Do you need assistance, Detective Barnes?"

"No, thank you, Deputy. I got the information I need." Turning to Carl he said, "I believe you—about the heroin."

Barnes left the jail and paid a follow-up visit to Dr. Deisman at his medical clinic. The receptionist said he had an opening in half an hour if Barnes wanted to wait. Barnes nodded and sat in the waiting area.

After thirty minutes, Barnes looked at the receptionist, who avoided his eye. Ten long minutes later, after Barnes became agitated, the receptionist announced the doctor would see him.

"I would have preferred to see you at the medical examiner's office, Detective Barnes."

"Thank you for taking time to meet with me here, Doctor. I know you're a busy man."

"I am busy. So, what do you need?" Deisman looked at Barnes without emotion.

"Did you keep the pills, drugs, alcohol, and drug paraphernalia associated with Gary Knowles' death?"

"Good heavens, no. Why would I do that? Not for a suicide. Gary Knowles killed himself, whether by accident or on purpose. Those were my findings. It was an open and shut matter, Detective. Why? Have you found out something new?"

"I'm surprised you didn't hear. Knowles' parents, the Wallers, are here in town. They say Gary wouldn't have committed suicide and they want his body. Something else for you to consider. Carl Dinkins was arrested on suspicion of Knowles' murder."

"What, no, I didn't hear anything to that effect. Knowles has living parents? Who's Carl Dinkins?"

Barnes couldn't read Deisman's expression to tell whether he was lying. "Dinkins is a resident of Brinson. He was drunk the night of Knowles' death and doesn't remember anything. He's a suspect."

"Hmmm." Deisman rubbed the top of his balding head.

"If he did kill Knowles, Doctor, then your suicide determination is inaccurate."

"I do the best I can with what I've got in front of me. If Dinkins did kill Knowles, as you're implying, Dinkins did a masterful job of making it look like a suicide."

"Who sent Knowles' body to California?"

"The shipping service does all that. I think they said it went to a cousin. Why?" Deisman took out his handkerchief and wiped his forehead.

"The Wallers told me Gary doesn't have a cousin or any other relative in California."

"Good heavens. Ellis Thompkins informed me that Knowles' parents were dead." Deisman reached for a rubber squeeze ball on his desk.

"His biological parents are dead, true. However, the Wallers are his adopted parents and are here looking for answers. Can you give me the name of the shipping company your office uses to ship bodies?"

"Sure." Deisman called out to his receptionist. "Bonnie, call Linda at the medical examiner's office and see if she can find the shipping papers for Gary Knowles' body. Let me know what's found. Thanks."

Turning to Barnes, Deisman said, "We'll see what we find. Now, I've got to get back to work. You can see the waiting room is filling up."

Barnes saw several people sitting in the room outside the doctor's office.

"Thank you for your time, Doctor. I'll be in touch if I need anything more."

Afterward, Barnes stopped by the Best Western to pick up a notepad he needed to take to Brinson. He was startled to see a man sitting in the desk chair as he opened the door to his room.

▲

Ellis Thompkins answered the phone after one ring. "Hello?"

"What's going on there, Chief? I heard Knowles was murdered. I thought it was suicide. Who's putting all that together?"

"Myself, Barnes—the detective from the ICC—and I think Rob Frost. He's the son of Richard …"

"I know who he is." Templeton abruptly cut Thompkins off. "Well, this is a shit mess. Have they identified suspects? Do I need to cut my vacation short?"

"Carl Dinkins is the only one I'm aware of. By the way, where were you on the night of October 17, Mayor?"

"Go to hell!"

The phone slammed down hard on the other end, eliciting a satisfied grin from Thompkins.

Chapter 46

Thursday, November 5

The faded yellow backhoe rode piggyback on a flatbed truck parked on the side of the road. It was noon on a cold November 5 day. The sheriff and Iowa State troopers had already approached the Juntlo farmhouse and served Eldon the warrant to search his property for the suspected dump. Eldon was angry at first, but he noticed several government people carrying guns, so he relented and walked to the area in question with the group.

A man and woman conducted a series of transects using a magnetometer over the covered dump area. Afterward, they conducted a ground penetrating radar survey.

When they finished, the woman gave her preliminary report to the group, which consisted of personnel from the Highway Patrol, the sheriff's office, the Iowa Geological Survey, and the Iowa Department of Environmental Quality. The Hancocks were not on site, but Gene watched the action through binoculars from the loft of his barn.

"Something is down there," the woman holding the magnetometer said. "It's not a natural soil pattern, definitely a fill area. And there's buried metal there. See, the surface has been disturbed."

"Yeah, I put my old stove and broken water heater there. Shit I had no use for. So what?" Eldon explained gruffly. "Look around at these farms, they all got dumps. Old Hancock gots one over there. That ain't against the law."

"Mr. Juntlo, we are going to dig three test pits in this area using a backhoe. If what you say is true, we will be done here and gone," the woman added.

Reed County Deputy Yoder motioned to the flatbed truck driver. The driver left the cab and mounted the backhoe control seat. He fired up the backhoe, backed it off the truck ramp, and rumbled to the area of interest.

The first test pit revealed the old stove and water heater Eldon had mentioned. A fifty-five-gallon drum partially filled with an oily substance also was removed. Kevin Hogan, from the Iowa Department of Environmental Quality, shook his head upon seeing the drum.

Cory Poleczyk, the hydrogeologist, came walking fast from the eastern edge of the dump area.

"Take a look at this," he said excitedly.

The entire party moved as one, following Poleczyk.

"Look at these holes. They're running everywhere here." Poleczyk turned to Eldon. "Mr. Juntlo, do you know what caused these? They're about four inches in diameter and run throughout this part of the dump."

"How the hell should I know?" Eldon shrugged.

"I know," Hogan said. "I've seen this before. The holes were dug by rats. They're rat tunnels."

"What the hell. I ain't got no rat problem." Eldon flailed his arms in disgust.

Deputy Yoder motioned for the backhoe operator to press forward. He pointed to the area with the holes.

"I want an eight-foot-by-eight-foot pit dug here—ten feet deep."

The backhoe operator did as he was told. The first scoop dug up fill soil. A second, deeper scoop produced hog remains. The next scoops delivered partial carcasses of several hogs. They were in various stages of decomposition. The smell was gruesome.

"Mother of God!" Deputy Yoder cursed and turned his head away from the scene.

Other members of the group swore and stepped back.

Eldon didn't move from the sight or smell. "I don't know how the hell this got on my land. This ain't my doing."

The final test pit was dug and showed a combination of hog parts, soil, and farm debris.

Hogan walked from the edge of the test pit to the Juntlo/Hancock property line. He estimated the distance from the dump to the Hancocks' well was only one hundred fifty feet.

"I now know the source of the well malfunction." He pointed to the exhumed pile of rotting hog carcasses.

"This is a new one to me," exclaimed Highway Patrolman Riggins. "The hog bristles must have moved underground from here to there." He pointed to the test pits and then to the Hancocks' house. "Is that possible?"

"The water table is shallow here and with those rat tunnels, anything is possible," Poleczyk said. "I find this hard to believe, too."

"This is way above my pay grade," Hogan shook his head. "I need to call the director for guidance."

The group mulled the situation and their options in the cold as they took additional steps back from the odiferous pile.

"What the hell, Juntlo!" an irate Gene yelled as he approached the group, jabbing his finger toward Eldon. "I'm not paying a dime for my new well. It's a miracle Rose and me ain't sick or dead! You're going to pay, you ass!"

Deputy Yoder stepped between the two men.

"I swear I didn't do this, Hancock. I can't see this area from my house. Some son-of-a-bitch done this at night without me knowing."

"If you didn't do it, then who the hell did? You raise hogs on your land, don't you? I don't. What do you do with the dead ones?"

"I raise only fifty head or so. If one dies, I take it to the rendering works south of Carlson in my truck. I git a couple of dead hogs a year, if that."

"It would take two people to dump here," Deputy Yoder theorized. "One to drive the dump truck and another to operate the machinery."

"Or it could have been one guy," Hogan argued. "Has this always been a low area, Mr. Juntlo?"

"Yep, wet year-round." Eldon kept an eye on an angry Gene.

"Someone could have dug the pit, backed in and dumped the load of hog waste, and then come back with a truckload of soil to cover it," Hogan nodded. "A lot of work for not much savings. Maybe the hogs were sick. We'll need to do testing."

"How deep does the waste sit in this area?" Riggins asked the backhoe operator.

"Looks like there's about one foot of topsoil, six to eight feet of this shit, and then native soil." He pointed at the closest test pit.

The backhoe operator then moved the bucket out of the mass, spreading out some of the contents, along with the smell. A human skull emerged from the debris. The skull appeared tiny compared to the waste material that embedded it. The grotesque features of the skull leered at the group as they stared, trying to comprehend its meaning. *Who am I? How did I get here? Why?*

The smell was forgotten while they stared at the skull.

Chapter 47

Thursday, November 5

"Detective Robinson, I see you managed to find your way to Carlson and to my motel room. I hoped you wouldn't get lost." Barnes reached out and shook Robinson's hand.

"I got here as fast as I could. Got the search warrant from the captain, just as you requested. By the way, I've never seen so many white folks in one area. I feel a little lonely, man." Robinson smiled slyly.

"It's not Des Moines, that's for sure. Rural Iowa is a different animal than the cities, but I've grown to kind of like it here."

"I suppose a white man would. A Black man may not agree." Robinson was serious. "When the captain gave you this assignment, I thought you were going to have a nice vacation. You know, get away from Des Moines and him. Instead, it seems like you kicked up a nest of nasty old snakes."

"Yeah, there's an undercurrent in Brinson that's difficult to describe. There are nice people." Barnes thought of Bud, the Jenkins and Frosts, and especially Janice. "But something sinister is going on, too."

"I'll be honest with you, man, the captain wants to see you retire early from the force. He has a hornet up his ass about you."

"I think it's permanently wedged in there—at least with me. By the way, how are Marge and the gang doing?"

"Fine. Marge keeps asking about you. I think she has adopted you. You're like a wounded bird that she's taken under her wing."

Barnes laughed. "You realize she and I are the same age. I miss her homemade cookies and our talks. Let's get down to business. You've got the court order to enter Elmer Juntlo's barn?"

"Right here." Robinson pulled out the envelope and held it up. "I hope there's something worthwhile in there. The captain's filled me in—a bit."

"Elmer Juntlo has been harassing kids in town, trying to find out which one snuck into his barn. He's very threatening—that's why I think he's hiding something in there. We need to find out what. I want to shake him up, too, so he'll stop scaring kids after I leave here. I've asked the sheriff to issue Juntlo a restraining order."

"Any idea what he could be hiding?"

"Who knows? My guess is drugs. I've encountered him several times, and he's not a pleasant man."

"Do you know the kid who snuck into the barn?" Robinson tucked the envelope back in his coat pocket.

"Yes, I do. His name is Brent Frost, a fourteen-year-old boy from Brinson. But at this time, I want to keep his name between us. Juntlo is capable of anything."

"The name will have to be revealed at some time, man."

"Yeah, I know, just not now. But soon." Barnes sighed and pulled a piece of paper out of his pants pocket. He unfolded it and spread it out on the bed. "The kid drew this sketch for me. This is Elmer Juntlo's barn," Barnes said as his finger ran the edge of the barn. "Over here are various pieces of junk and old vehicles that Juntlo keeps inside. This is where a dead deer was hung." Barnes pointed to the northeast corner. "There were three boxes, like caskets, over here. We need to take a look inside them.

"Juntlo returned to his barn and surprised Brent. He was lucky to make it out alive. Juntlo took a shot at him after he escaped from the barn. I witnessed part of that. Like I said, Juntlo is capable of anything. He's guarding something in there."

"Damn." Robinson smiled. "Am I coming with you when you serve the warrant?"

"Yes. I've lined up Chief Thompkins, the town policeman, and someone from the Reed County Sheriffs' office. That way we can diffuse Juntlo's anger among several people. And let me tell you, Del, he doesn't like me—closer to hate." Barnes patted Robinson's shoulder and smiled.

"There's another item to discuss. I need your insight on the death of a veteran that recently occurred in Brinson. The medical examiner issued his report, which said it was suicide. It was murder, though, and I have several suspects in mind."

⚓

Barnes and Robinson arrived at Elmer Juntlo's barn at precisely two o'clock. Deputy Nelson followed behind. Chief Thompkins was supposed to be there as well, but he didn't show up. Juntlo's pickup was parked by the door. The men waited in their vehicles for the chief, and Barnes took the opportunity to introduce the deputy to Robinson.

"Where the hell is Thompkins?" An annoyed Barnes fidgeted with his keys. "He needs to be here when we serve the warrant. He's the local presence."

"Is he usually like this—undependable?" Robinson clasped the search warrant in his hand.

"He's someone you cannot count on. I haven't figured out yet whether it's incompetence or laziness, or if he's involved in hiding something."

"I just hope there's something in the barn that will confirm your source's story. The captain went through serious hoops to get this search warrant."

"Thanks. I know I'm on the captain's shit list. But part of me doesn't care. I've slipped up in the past, I know that. And I appreciate the people in my corner who've helped me." He smiled. "You're a good friend, Del."

"We're partners and we have each other's back."

At 2:15 p.m., the men watched Chief Thompkins' police car pull up slowly behind Deputy Nelson's white sheriff's sedan. Barnes exited the car first, followed by Robinson and Deputy Nelson. Thompkins remained seated in his car. Barnes tapped Thompkins' window and the chief rolled it down.

"He's not going to like this at all—invading his property." Thompkins gazed at the barn door. "He may take a shot at us."

"That's why you're here, Chief. So he'll be more agreeable. By the way, this is Detective Del Robinson, my partner at the ICC."

"Nice to meet ya, Robinson. I thought most of yar type had afros."

"No, not true. You're thinking of the *Mod Squad*. This isn't TV, and we don't have a type." Robinson patted his short-cropped hair and rolled his eyes.

Thompkins looked straight ahead. "Barnes, I hope ya have a proper search warrant. Ya know, that's pretty flimsy evidence to violate a person's rights." Thompkins glanced at the paper Robinson held. "Give me that warrant."

Robinson handed Thompkins the paper, who took a few minutes to read it before handing it back. Deputy Nelson walked up to the car carrying a shot gun.

"I know all about Elmer Juntlo. This may dissuade him from choosing the wrong course." Nelson patted the barrel of the shotgun.

"Let's go, then." Barnes opened the car door for Thompkins.

The four men carefully approached the building's entrance. Barnes nodded at Thompkins. "Please."

Thompkins placed three soft knocks on the door and stood back, expecting the worst. Nothing happened.

"For Pete's sake, Ellis," Nelson said and pounded several times on the door. "Elmer Juntlo," he shouted. "It's the police. We want to talk with you."

A minute passed, and finally the barn door opened a sliver.

"What the hell do you want? Shit, it's almost time to play cards," Elmer growled.

"Let us in, Elmer. They have a search warrant for the barn," Thompkins implored meekly.

"What the hell for? I ain't got nothing here but stuff I fiddle with. You're invading my property. Who got this search warrant?"

"I did, Mr. Juntlo."

Juntlo opened the door further and saw Barnes standing in front of him.

"Shit, I knew you're the bastard behind this." Juntlo pointed at Barnes. "You're a goddamned pain in my ass."

"Let us in, Elmer," said Thompkins. "We can be in and out. Then, you can go to your card game."

"Gimme that damned warrant." Juntlo opened the door a little more.

"Show it, but don't give it to him." Barnes looked over at Robinson. "Mr. Elmer Juntlo, this is Detective Del Robinson from the ICC."

Elmer eyed Robinson and the paper he held.

"We don't see your type here in Brinson," Elmer said as he squinted to read the warrant. He took a deep breath and exhaled. "You should stay in Des Moines."

Robinson expected the worst from this man, who he obviously thought was a racist. He was stunned at Juntlo's next words.

"When I served in World War II, my life was saved by a colored man, Isaiah Jones. We became friends. He died after the war. I missed his funeral. Oh hell."

With those words, all the fire exited Juntlo's body and he closed his eyes to remember his past. "Come on in and look around. Deputy, lower you gun. I won't give you no worry."

The four men entered warily. Barnes immediately looked to his left at the blood-stained floor. He started to say "What …" when Juntlo interrupted him.

"It's from a deer, you prick. I shot it properly and all, if you want to know. I got the permit and took it to the farm where Eldon lives. I dressed it and gave the meat away. Is that why you got this piece-of-shit warrant, Barnes?"

"Not quite," Barnes said.

Barnes and Robinson began looking around. While they searched, Thompkins and Juntlo chatted at the workbench. Nelson poked around out of boredom.

After about fifteen minutes, the search ended. They had even looked through the second floor. Robinson moved next to Barnes and spoke softly. "There's nothing here. I found a couple of questionable items, but no boxes, no caskets. We did a complete search. I'm sorry, man."

"Not as sorry as I am." Barnes sighed.

God, I'm in trouble now. Barnes thought. *I might as well resign and get it over with. The captain has no confidence in me, and Del will think I've lost it. I used to be a good detective; now I'm not fit for Thompkins' job.* Barnes' stomach churned. *What's going to happen to Brent? Was he telling the truth?*

Robinson walked and Barnes trudged back to the bench where Juntlo, Thompkins, and Nelson were standing.

"I told you that you would find nothin' here, right?" Juntlo said arrogantly. "Now get the hell out. I'm late for my card game."

"Thank you for your time, and we apologize for the inconvenience, Elmer," Thompkins said as the four men left the building.

"Asshole. I hope this is the last I see of you, Barnes," Juntlo spit. Looking at Robinson, Juntlo asked, "You a vet?"

Robinson nodded. "Korea."

Juntlo closed the door to his building. Barnes felt queasy.

"Any more wild goose chases ya want me to pursue, *Detective* Barnes of the ICC?" Thompkins piled on.

Robinson patted Barnes' back. "Let's go back to the motel and discuss where we are, man."

"Barnes doesn't stay at the motel, Robinson. He is at Janice Hinton's house enjoying the comforts of her hospitality," Thompkins sneered.

Barnes wanted to lash out, but he held his tongue.

Robinson waved off Thompkins. "Something's wrong with that man." He and Barnes got in the car.

Barnes felt shaky; his world was collapsing. He took a second to consider his situation when a motion to his right caught his eye. Deputy Nelson waved fervently at him.

Barnes rolled down his window.

"I just got a call from my counterpart, Deputy Yoder, at Eldon Juntlo's farm. They found a body—at least, part of a body!"

Chapter 48

Thursday, November 5

"Follow me!" Deputy Nelson shouted to Barnes and Robinson.

The two men trailed Nelson to the farm where Eldon Juntlo lived. Even in November, the dust on the gravel road hung in the air like a shroud. Barnes had to ease off on the speed to see ahead of him.

"Is it always this dusty driving on these gravel roads, man? This is shit," Robinson grumbled, annoyed. "I'll take the streets around Des Moines over this any day."

Within ten minutes, Deputy Nelson stopped his police cruiser and waited for Barnes and Robinson to catch up and park behind him. The cold north wind warned of frostbite. Barnes realized he was underdressed to be out in the countryside in this weather. He looked at Robinson and noticed he was wearing an even lighter layer of clothing.

"Things are freezing over here." Deputy Yoder motioned to the backhoe and a pile of something unrecognizable next to it.

That's not the only thing freezing, Barnes thought.

"Thanks, Deputy Yoder," Nelson said. The two deputies, Barnes, and Robinson walked over to the excavated mass.

"We suspected an illegal dumpsite here, so we dug three test pits. The excavation from this pit had this in it." Deputy Yoder pointed.

A human skull was held in place at the edge of a clump of rotting flesh. Barnes stared at the skull, and it stared back at him.

"Good God, what the hell." Barnes shook his head. "What's this?"

"A disposal for dead hogs and some other things." Yoder kept pointing at the skull.

"Are there any more remains?"

"What do you mean by remains?" Yoder answered.

"Human remains, Deputy, human remains. I don't care about hog carcasses or whatever else is in this pile." Barnes waved his hand in frustration.

"I sure as hell care!" Gene, who was standing nearby, stormed toward the group. "What I see sickens me to the very core of my being. I can't tell Rose about the skull. The hog shit is enough."

Barnes and Robinson gave Deputy Yoder puzzled looks.

Yoder explained. "What started the whole thing was the Hancocks' well," he looked at Gene, "stopped producing water. They live east of here." He pointed to Hancock's farmstead. "The well company inspected it and found the pump was clogged with pig bristles. We believe the bristles came from the pigs buried in this pit. When we dug the test pits, we found these hog remains and the skull."

"What the hell are you going to do, all you cops?" an agitated Gene asked.

Robinson politely ignored Gene. "Have you found any additional human remains?"

"No, but who knows what's in this mass?" Yoder knew what was coming as soon as he said it.

"Someone needs to separate this excavated material into smaller sections and look for human bones." Barnes gazed at the group. He could tell that his request was received with as much enthusiasm as cleaning out a poorly ventilated hog barn in August.

Someone muttered, "Some hog bones look similar to those of a human."

"I'll call the sheriff and he'll give the order. Deputy, can you get me the sheriff? I'll start with Dr. Deisman. We may have to get a forensics unit up here from Des Moines. I'll stay with you and assist where I can. And someone needs to help that farmer." Barnes pointed at Gene.

"Yeah, that'll take some doing," Yoder acknowledged.

"If we can get this waste to a manageable amount, perhaps Dr. Deisman can identify human bones from pig bones," Barnes continued.

Barnes waved for Robinson to join him in the car. Barnes wanted privacy and a chance to shake off the cold before facing round two with the outside elements.

"Del, the skull may be related to Richard Franklin Frost's disappearance. I doubt it's Gary Knowles based on the state of decomposition."

"Who's Richard Frost?" Robinson's confused face told Barnes to slow down.

"Frost was a businessman here who disappeared about this time in 1940. He was never seen again."

"That's a long time ago. Do you have a suspect?"

"Elmer may be a possible suspect. He's old enough to have been an adult at the time of the disappearance. He certainly has the aptitude for such a crime. We need to research his life in more detail, starting with his police record."

"I don't know, man." Robinson gently shook his head. "I know you've had bad experiences with that man, but from what I witnessed in the barn, Elmer is not a killer. And I guess he would have been in his early twenties when Frost vanished. He's not clever enough to pull off something like that."

A rapping on the car window disturbed their conversation. Barnes saw Max Sturgess looking anxious to talk. Barnes rolled down his window.

"Good afternoon, Detective," Sturgess said. He wore a coat with a hood and carried a small notebook in his hand. "What can you tell the press?"

"How do you know about what's going on here?"

"Police scanner. All good newspapermen have sources, and I have mine. Who is your friend here?" Sturgess alluded to Robinson without looking at him.

"This is Detective Del Robinson, my partner at the ICC. Del, Max Sturgess with the *Brinson Bee* newspaper."

Sturgess grunted acknowledgement and squinted toward the area of the backhoe. He started to move toward it.

"That's far enough, Mr. Sturgess. We're still investigating an illegal dumping operation," Deputy Nelson interceded as he walked over to Sturgess from the waste pile.

"We'll let you know when there's something to report, Max." Barnes nodded at Nelson.

"OK, then. Here's my card." Sturgess handed out his business card, distracted by the backhoe. Turning to Barnes he said, "Stop by the office sometime soon. Mabel has something to show you." Sturgess got in his car and drove away.

"I didn't realize small towns had newspapers and newspapermen," Robinson mused, watching Sturgess drive off. "And who is Mabel?"

"She works in Sturgess' office. I think she's the one who actually puts together the weekly paper. She can be a bit forward." Barnes chuckled recalling their previous encounters.

"Ah hmmm," Robinson grinned.

"Really! She's not my type. She's married. We can stop by the paper later. They have a lot of archived records on Frost's disappearance, and an odd accident in 1950 where the old town constable was killed by a train. Both occurred at this time of year. I want to see if there was a similar type of incident in November 1960."

"Why?"

"It's my detective curiosity."

The two detectives left Eldon Juntlo's farm. As they reached the outskirts of Brinson, Barnes anticipated Robinson's next question. "Yes, I'm staying in an apartment in Janice's house and not at the motel. She's been receiving threats. We have a suspect in custody, but we're not sure if she's safe. You can have my room at the motel."

"What did Janice do to receive these threats?"

"She took an unpopular stand on the war that some of the locals disagree with. I'll tell you the whole story and more about Richard Frost when we stop for a bite."

Chapter 49

Thursday, November 5

Brent stared out the window for the entire history class. They were discussing the collapse of the Roman Empire—at least, the Western Roman Empire. How the mighty empire of Julius Caesar, Augustus, and Constantine could have been trampled by barbarians baffled Brent. Normally, this subject would be of high interest to him. Today, though, his thoughts centered around the Hinton store, where Elmer Juntlo had confronted him.

The end-of-school bell rang and Cindy approached him.

"You feeling all right, Brent?" she asked, concern in her eyes.

"Not really. Old man Juntlo almost got me yesterday."

"Really?" she said, wide-eyed.

"In the candy section of the Hinton General Store at lunch. I was going to get you something, and when I turned around, he was blocking my way out. He knows I was the one in his barn. And now I'm going to get it."

"How did you escape? Did he hurt you?"

"No, Bud saved me. He pulled Juntlo up by the collar and just held him there. He's really strong. Then Janice—Mrs. Hinton—came out and had Bud throw Juntlo out of the store. I'll never make fun of Bud again."

"My God, Brent, what are you going to do?" Cindy felt Brent's fear.

"Detective Barnes knows what happened. He and old Juntlo don't get along. I'm hoping there's something he can do to Juntlo."

"I don't know. He's from out of town and who knows how long he'll be here. Elmer has lived here forever." She paused. "What about Chief Thompkins? Can't he help?"

"I doubt it. I think he's Juntlo's friend, or is scared of him."

"I'll talk to my folks. They'll know what to do."

"Please don't say anything to anyone—please," Brent pleaded. "Let me think some more. I need to talk to Detective Barnes again."

"OK, I won't say anything for now. But I'm worried about you." Cindy placed her hand on his shoulder. She moved close and kissed Brent on the cheek, then walked away.

Brent tingled with the kiss.

On the walk home from school, Jack, Ron, and Dale caught up to Brent.

"You were in the store with crazy Juntlo yesterday, weren't you?" Jack looked Brent in the eyes for confirmation.

Brent reluctantly told his friends the story and concluded, "Bud and Janice saved me."

Jack shook his head. "For now, but he *knows* it was you in his barn."

Dale added, "We shouldn't have done that, gone into his barn."

"I didn't think it would end like this, shit!" Ron seconded. "We just wanted to see if old Juntlo had gold in there."

"What are you guys worried about?" Brent squawked angrily. "He's after me!"

"What are you going to do?" Jack echoed Cindy's earlier question.

"You should tell your folks, that's what you should do," Dale nodded. "He's a bad man."

When Brent reached his house, his friends left for their homes, glad they weren't Brent. Darkness settled in for the day, mirroring Brent's mood. His parents were not at home. He grabbed his baseball bat from the garage, ready to use it against any intruder named Elmer Juntlo.

Brent wanted to tell his parents about what was going on in his life, but if he did, there would be all sorts of questions about why he broke into the barn. Thoughts of jail and the ominous shadow of Elmer Juntlo haunted him. Then there would be his parents' punishment. *Oh boy. If I could go back in time.* He thought about his favorite television show, "The Wild, Wild West." *I wish James West and Artemus Gordon would appear and take care of Juntlo for me. They were the good guys.*

With his mind tortured by these thoughts, he picked up the telephone, his hands shaking.

The voice on the other end answered matter-of-factly, "Good evening, Best Western-Carlson. May I help you?"

"Yes, sir." Brent spoke so quietly, the motel manager on the other end could barely hear him.

"One moment, sir. I'll see if he's in."

⟡

Elmer settled in at his older brother's kitchen at the farm. The scarred walnut table sat off to the side. Three well-worn wooden chairs surrounded the table. The kitchen cabinets were white and needed more than a fresh coat of paint. It was the same kitchen used by Elmer and Eldon's parents—except one of the chairs had broken and was never repaired or replaced. It was late afternoon and the police and environmental authorities had vacated the property for the day.

"I heard you've got problems." Elmer took a gulp from his can of Schlitz.

"Yep—them cops say I operated a dump against the law. It's my land, damn it. I can do what I want." Eldon finished his beer and reached for another.

"I got the same problem with my barn. They searched it today for something—which I don't know about. Seems OK for some punk kid to trespass—I try to defend *my* property, and the law comes after *me*. Shit!" Elmer opened his second beer. "That cop from Des Moines is really a pain in my ass. Name of Barnes."

"Yeah, he was out on my property today, too. I know he's the asshole who started this mess. If he hadn't come here, there would be no digging, and you'd have no barn problem."

"I'll drink to that, big brother."

"I hate cops—especially those smartasses from Des Moines—interfering with me, and that's what we got here." Eldon spat part of his tobacco chew into a cup. "They're all out to get me. They want my farm. I'm going to take care of this before that happens."

"Easy there, Eldon. I got in trouble for using my shotgun on the trespasser—even though I was in the right. I wasn't gonna hurt him, just scare him. Don't do nothin' stupid."

"No one tells me what to do—including you. I gotta defend my property! I don't trust cops."

"I'm curious, what'd you put in my barn?" Elmer took a full gulp of beer.

"You know I use your barn from time to time to store stuff. It's just temporary."

"What was in those boxes? I saw 'em. The cops seem to have their noses up their asses looking for something that may have been in 'em." Elmer put his beer down hard on the table.

"How the hell do I know? I get the shit from a guy in Des Moines. I hold it until he wants it back, then I give it to him. Easy money and I ask no questions. Let me remind you, little brother, that money saves our farm from the damned bank."

"You're getting more forgetful. Don't put your shit in my barn no more. You got plenty of room out here on the farm. I don't want that sheriff and Thompkins poking around with that asshole Barnes."

Eldon started to argue with his brother, but Elmer finished his beer and stood up. "You heard me—no more talk. And I don't know who's burying dead hogs on *our* farm, but that stops, too."

Elmer got in his red pickup and left.

Chapter 50

Thursday, November 5

At the D&R Drive-In, Barnes told Robinson about his time in Brinson. When he finished, he glanced at Robinson, who was grinning.

"You sly dog. A girlfriend in record time, and in Brinson."

"I never said anything about a girlfriend. We're just friends—I … I'm helping her out. She's going through tough times."

"Yes, sir. You're really good friends, man. You must have forgotten since you've been here that I'm a detective, a real good detective. I sense things others don't. And the way you talk about her tells me that she's more than a friend. I'm glad for you. You need this. There's no need to hide your feelings for her." Robinson gave Barnes a tap on the shoulder.

Barnes changed the subject. "The *Brinson Bee* closes soon. I want to stop there before it does."

They parked outside the *Bee*. Barnes pushed open the door and went in, followed by Robinson.

"Hi, Fred," Mabel's cheery voice echoed in the office. "Is this your sidekick?"

"Yeah, Mabel, this is Detective Robinson from the ICC. He thinks he's my boss, but …"

Robinson stepped in before Barnes could go further. "No, we're just partners, but I'm the smart one. Nice to meet you, Mabel."

"I know you're busy." Barnes paused. "Is Max in?"

"No, Max never came back from the Juntlo farm. What happened out there? You can tell me anything." Mabel's sultry voice hung in the air.

Barnes did not want to elaborate on the test pit findings. "I'm sure Max will fill you in when he returns to the office."

"I did hear about the Hancocks' well. That's the most disgusting thing since those wild dogs mauled Peter Hugh's prize hog." Mabel squinched her face.

Barnes moved on, "Mabel, was there a suspicious event in November 1960, around this time of year? Maybe someone died in a weird way or vanished? How about in November 1930?"

Mabel paused in thought. "No, I don't recall hearing about anything odd occurring in 1930. I was one year old then, but no. However, Suzi Thornton died in her house around this time in 1960. The authorities determined the cause was carbon monoxide poisoning from the furnace."

"Who's Suzi Thornton?" Robinson asked.

"She owned and operated Suzi's Diner across the street and up a couple of buildings," Mabel said. "She was an attractive woman, even when she was older. Lots of men tried to court her, but she preferred a solitary lifestyle. Nice woman."

"Was Suzi around when Richard Frost disappeared?"

"Oh yeah. There were rumors that she and Richard were carrying on, but I think that was just speculation. But who knows? There's no way to prove that now."

"Thanks," Barnes said. "Can you pull the newspapers regarding Suzi's death so we can look tomorrow?"

"Sure thing, Detective. Be sure and bring your sidekick back with you."

Barnes and Robinson returned to their car. Before getting in Barnes said, "I'm thirsty. Let's get a pop. I know a place."

"I hope it's less disparaging than in there." Robinson pointed at the Bee.

Barnes and Robinson entered the Hinton General Store and saw Janice and Bud standing at the cash register. No other customers were in the store. The worry on Janice's face tuned into a smile when she saw Barnes.

"Hi, Fred." She looked at Robinson.

"Hi, Janice, Bud—this is my partner, Detective Del Robinson. Del, Janice Hinton and Bud Nichols."

Robinson shook their hands and said, "My partner here is too formal. Please call me Del."

"I'm giving Del an experience in rural life here in Brinson."

"It's quiet, that's for sure." Robinson smiled. "I'm more of a big-city person. More action."

"Whatever you want, Del, it's on the house." Janice laughed.

"I'll take you up on that—although my partner said he would gladly pay. He's a generous man."

Bud, who hadn't said a word, asked, "Detective Robinson, did you serve?"

"Yes, in Korea. How did you know?"

"I didn't. I just had a feeling."

"Very intuitive of you. We should trade war stories sometime, man."

After Janice insisted, Barnes and Robinson accepted her generosity and each took a pop.

As they walked back to the car, Robinson said, "I like them. Bud's got the biggest arms I've ever seen. And Janice, she's a catch, man. Just sayin'." Robinson winked at Barnes.

◣

"What're you thinking? I know you've got thoughts rolling around up there, man." Robinson tapped the side of Barnes' head fondly as they drove to Carlson.

"There's a lot going on here. We have a suspect in custody who threatened Janice, a crude man who has threatened a boy, there's a skull of unknown origin in an illegal dump of hog remains, the unsolved murder of a Vietnam War veteran, and I believe a serial killer who strikes around November 7 in the first year of a decade.”

“You know what time of year it is?”

“That’s what I’m worried about, Del. We could have another murder in two days.”

“Do you think this alleged serial killer murdered Gary?”

“No, I don’t. I believe we have separate killers.”

Robinson followed up, “Whose skull do you think was dug up in that mess back there at the farm, Knowles’?”

“I doubt it. It could be Richard Frost’s, though.”

“Or just about anyone else’s. There’s a lot to untangle here, man. We should call the captain and fill him in.”

Barnes sighed. “I’ll let you do that. I’m on his bad side and I can’t seem to turn it around. And things here are getting more complicated. That’ll make him more unhappy with me.”

“We’re partners, and that’s what counts. We’ll get through this together.” Robinson gave Barnes a reassuring smile.

⅄

Rob picked up the telephone in his motel room. He expected the Wallers. Instead, the caller was a young man.

“Hello, Mr. Frost, sir?”

“Hello. Who’s this?”

“Brent Frost, sir. I was trying to reach Detective Barnes, but he’s not in. I know you’re staying at the same motel.”

“Are you OK, son?”

“I really need to speak to Detective Barnes. When you see him, can you have him call me? It’s real important, sir.”

“Yes, I will. Are your folks home?”

“No, they went to Des Moines for a meeting. They’ll be back by nine o’clock or so.”

"Let me see if I can find Detective Barnes." The two hung up.

Rob could hear the anxiety in Brent's voice. Rob's police instincts were flashing warning signs. He knew Barnes was staying at Janice's house, so he figured he'd have the best luck checking there.

When he left his motel room, he scanned the parking lot for Barnes' vehicle. *No Barnes.* He got in his Cadillac and drove to Brinson.

His first stop was Janice's house. He rang the doorbell three times followed by two sets of hard knocks. No one answered. His next stop was the Hinton General Store. Neither Janice nor Bud knew where Barnes was. Rob drove to Tim and Angela's house and knocked on the door. The shades moved slightly in a window near the front door.

After a pause, Brent opened the door and let Rob in. He was a welcome sight to Brent, wearing his ever-present black Stetson.

"Hi, Brent," Rob said in his western drawl as he scanned the part of the house he could see. He sat in the nearest chair and motioned for Brent to sit.

"I shouldn't have called you, sir," Brent said shyly. "But I remembered that you're a policeman in Denver."

"Was, but that's no problem, son. I'm glad you called. I'm still not sure how we're related, but I consider you family, and families stick together, don't you think?"

"Yes, sir, Mr. Frost."

Rob leaned forward in his chair. "Now, tell me what's going on in your life."

After initial prodding, Brent opened up to Rob like a kitchen faucet turned full on. Brent told him about breaking into Juntlo's barn and the aftermath.

At the conclusion of Brent's monologue, Rob asked, "Anything else? I feel like there's more to your story."

"Yes." Brent paused. "I saw them."

"What?" Rob scooted closer to Brent. "What did you see?"

"Three boxes, like caskets."

"Did you open any of them?"

Brent hesitated. He had never told anyone about the bones. "There were bones and a human skull in one of them. I didn't have time to open the other two."

"Just bones? Any clothes, or … flesh?"

"No, just bones and a skull—then Juntlo came in and I got outta there."

"And you've told no one else about the bones?"

"No, sir, not even Detective Barnes or my folks. I was too scared. Old man Juntlo is the devil. He would hurt me and Mom and Dad."

"It'll all be fine, Brent. Trust me. I'm going to stay right here until your folks come home. You need to tell your parents—that's what's best. Then, we can talk to Detective Barnes and Chief Thompkins. Mr. Juntlo won't bother you anymore. I promise that."

Brent was relieved and queasy at the same time: relieved that his secret was finally out; queasy that he was going to face unknown punishment. The phone rang in the nearby kitchen, and Brent jumped out of his chair, startled at the shrill disturbance.

He answered the phone hesitantly and then said, "Hi, Cindy."

"I've been worried about you. You're not in a good place."

"I'm fine. My 'Uncle' Rob is here—he used to be a cop."

"That's great to hear." The two talked for a couple minutes about school before saying good-bye.

Brent hung up the phone and walked back to Rob smiling, temporarily forgetting about Elmer Juntlo.

"I guess I'm your uncle now." Rob laughed. "Was that your girlfriend?"

"I wish."

Chapter 51

Thursday, November 5

"A couple more quick stops, Del?" Barnes looked at a tired Robinson.

"Sure, man, you're dealing with a hydra here. And I'm used to long hours."

Barnes and Robinson stopped at the medical examiner's office in Carlson. They were ushered back to Dr. Deisman's lab. A strong, oppressive scent of disinfectant hung in the air.

"You boys think I'm a miracle worker? I just received this disgusting pile of shit." An annoyed Deisman glanced up from a pile of bones and fleshy material. Set off to the side on a shelf was the skull.

"Sorry to interrupt your work, Doctor. Do you have any preliminary findings you can share with us?" Barnes edged closer to the examination table.

"Dr. Hill from Sioux County is helping me. Together, we'll get through it."

Barnes and Robinson surveyed the room and didn't see anyone but the three of them.

"He's at an early dinner," Deisman said by way of explanation. "Doc Hill has an iron stomach. After looking at this, I don't think I'll have an appetite for quite a while." Deisman turned away from the table to face Barnes and Robinson. He picked up the skull and held it out.

"This old boy has been around for some time. It does not belong to Gary Knowles—it's been exposed to the elements much longer than just a couple weeks."

"How about since 1940?" Robinson wondered.

"My partner is asking whether it could be Richard Franklin Frost," Barnes followed.

"I don't know, maybe. I'm not real familiar with that case," Deisman responded. "As you can see, the skull is badly damaged. There's not a shred of tissue on it, and most of the teeth on the lower right jaw are gone. I doubt if this skull can be tied to anyone."

"What about other bones? Have you found any other human bones?" Barnes stared at the table.

"The vast majority of bones are not human. We did find a possible human femur and ulna, however. A couple other bones may be, as well. Sometimes, a bone from a hog is similar to a human, but in this state of deterioration, it's tough to tell. The fleshy material is a different matter. There's no way to tell if any of that is human. We'll keep looking at the bones, though."

"Thanks, Doctor. We'll check in later." Barnes and Robinson left Dr. Deisman with his pile of bones and rotting flesh.

"God, I'm glad I'm not a medical examiner, man," Robinson said as he got in the car holding his nose. "Working with some of our living subjects is enough for me."

Barnes laughed. "I hear you."

"Where to next?" Robinson put a piece of gum in his mouth and offered Barnes a stick.

"Sure, thanks." Barnes took the gum. "I'd do about anything to get rid of that crappy disinfectant taste in my mouth. We're going to the Reed County Sheriff's headquarters. I want to check in to see if they have had any hiccups with obtaining the restraining order against Elmer Juntlo. I want him to leave Brent alone in no uncertain terms."

"Elmer won't be a problem. It's my gut feeling."

"I hope so. I would think that finding human remains on his brother's property would alter his thinking. That's my intuition. You seem to have made a connection with him."

Deputy Nelson met Barnes and Robinson at the sheriff's office.

"I've been expecting you," the deputy said. "There's paperwork to go over."

As they talked, Barnes and Robinson heard a shout from an adjacent room. "I'm telling you what I know, not what I *think* I know."

"Calm down, Mr. Reiss," a softer voice replied.

"I will not calm down until you listen to me and do something, Harold!" The voice became even louder. The man saw Nelson through the open door and waved him to come forward.

Nelson motioned to Barnes and Robinson, and the men moved quietly into the room where the voices were coming from. Inside were Sheriff Harold Larken and an older man. The man had short white hair topped with a black army beret with a red insignia, and he was frustrated.

Barnes had met Sheriff Larken on only one occasion, and was initially impressed with his professionalism. The sheriff was thin framed and wearing a hat—similar in style to Rob Frost's Stetson, except it was white.

"Wally, tell your boss that I'm not crazy." Donald Reiss stepped toward Nelson while pointing his finger at the sheriff.

"Donald, we have two detectives from the Iowa Crimes Commission with us—Detectives Fred Barnes and Del Robinson. Could you please explain your situation to us?" the deputy asked.

"Gladly," Reiss huffed before settling down a little.

"I've been telling the sheriff here what I saw and what I know. He doesn't want to listen to me, so maybe you will. Hopefully you will." Reiss paused and stared at the group to make sure they were listening. "I've been fishing on Westbrick Lake for decades—since I was a kid."

Larken interrupted. "Excuse me, Donald. Detectives, let me fill you in on some details. Westbrick Lake is an eighty-acre natural lake located about a mile and a half southwest of Carlson. It's marshy on the east and west ends. It's a quiet place except for kids partying at night. So we patrol the area after dark. You should also know Donald is a veteran and Carlson's former mayor. Go on, Donald."

Reiss stood like a statue as the sheriff talked. Hearing his name, Reiss resumed his story like a wind-up doll. "There's good fishing in the lake, if you know where to look." Reiss glanced at Larken with disdain. "The lake has smallmouth bass, bluegill, bullheads, and some other fish that I call rough fish. When I catch those scummy fish, I toss them on the bank for the raccoons."

Reiss paused, thinking about how many raccoons he had seen in the fall.

"Go ahead, Donald," Larken encouraged him.

"Yesterday, I took my boat out for one more fishing trip. I go as late in the season as I can. Anyway, the ice had started to form, but I could row right through it. I tossed one of my lines where I usually do. I was using live bait and dropped that fishing line about six inches from the bottom. I cast a Rapala lure with my other pole in an area of open water. See, I'm fishing with two lines." Reiss used his arms and hands to imitate his fishing methods.

"I wasn't getting a single bite from my deep line, which is unusual. So, I gave it a tug to bring it up and check the bait, but it was stuck. I tried everything to get it loose, but nothing worked. That's never happened before, never." Reiss again glanced at the sheriff. "Something is down there in the deep and I know it because I know this lake like the back of my hand. It has a mucky bottom."

"It's probably a log or a piece of junk someone recently tossed out there, Donald," Larken mused.

"Wrong, Sheriff," the older man's voice started rising again. "That stuff happens near the shore and swampy areas. I was fishing in the center of the lake, damn it. There's nothing like that out there—nothing."

"Well, what do you want us to do?"

"Isn't it obvious? Send a dive team down there and find out what snagged my line."

"I'm not going to do that. That would be a waste of county resources."

"So, you're going to ignore your responsibility as the sheriff? Remember who I am!"

Larken shook his head, searching for a way to get out of this situation. "Donald, we don't even know where to look, and there may be even more ice cover after tonight."

"No, sir. I marked the spot with my float. I cut the line right where it got stuck. You'll know exactly where to look."

Barnes' mind whirled. "Sheriff, this is not my jurisdiction, so I don't want to step on toes, but I think it may be worthwhile to see what snared Mr. Reiss' line. It's probably nothing, as you say, but you never know."

Robinson and Nelson nodded in concurrence with Barnes' request.

Sheriff Larken stared hard at Barnes and then at Reiss. "All right, I'll send a dive team out there tomorrow morning. When we find nothing, Donald, I don't want you to cry wolf anymore, got it? And Barnes, we already had your misadventure at Juntlo's barn. You're on thin ice."

Chapter 52

Thursday, November 5

Barnes dropped off Robinson at the motel. Before he left for Janice's house, the two went over their notes from the day. Barnes had been relieved to hear from Deputy Nelson that Carl Dinkins was still in the Carlson city jail. However, his release was imminent. Nelson added that he would be serving Elmer Juntlo with the restraining order against Brent Frost first thing in the morning.

"I heard you were out at the Juntlo farm today," Janice began as Barnes came into her house.

"Yeah—how did you hear about that?"

"Well, Brenda came into the store today, and sometimes she likes to talk. She's a little more accepting of me than Mabel. Max told Mabel and her that Eldon had a pit of dead pigs on his land, which likely contaminated the Hancocks' well."

"Brenda gets around, too, like Mabel." Barnes hoped Janice would offer him something to drink.

Janice read his mind and fetched a beer from the refrigerator. "Do you have any more evidence linking Carl to Gary's death?"

"Not yet. To the casual observer, it appears Carl is our man. You witnessed him beating Gary outside the Thirsty Bull. And he was involved in that raccoon stunt in your yard. So, he hated Gary. In my professional opinion, though, I don't think Carl did it. He isn't smart enough and doesn't know enough about drug use to inject Knowles with heroin. Something about Dr. Deisman is odd, too. And Mayor Templeton's name keeps coming up. I heard he also didn't care for Knowles."

Janice chuckled. "Yeah, the mayor—Lord knows I'm not in his good graces, either. He sees me as a cancer on Brinson's morality."

"I'm guessing here, but maybe he's played a part in your harassment and possibly in Gary's death, and—just saying—maybe Richard Frost's disappearance. He's old enough and, from what I hear, not a nice man."

"I doubt it, at least not directly. Indirectly, maybe. He's a manipulator of the gullible. He doesn't like to get his hands dirty."

"Do he and Chief Thompkins get along?"

"They tolerate each other, I'd say."

"Well, I guess I need to have a talk with Mayor Templeton."

"Ha!" Janice shook her head. "He's on vacation in Florida. He goes there from the first of November to the fifteenth. Been doing that trip for years. Everyone in town knows it."

"He's a suspect in something—just not sure what yet."

Barnes could tell Janice was itching for a cigarette. She told him that she had quit, but he knew how hard quitting was.

"Thank you for giving up smoking." He held her hand.

"I'm trying. Bud keeps after me." Janice offered a slight smile. "If not Carl, who do you think is the killer?"

"The killer is using Dinkins as a patsy. He knows drugs. He probably wanted Gary dead because of his anti-war views, maybe something else. I've got ideas, which I would like to keep to myself for the time being, if you don't mind. They're only theories."

The phone ringing broke into their conversation.

"Hello," Janice answered. "No … No. No." She hung up and stared at the receiver.

"What's wrong?" Barnes looked with concern. "Was that another threatening call?"

"No," she hesitated. "I'll be honest with you. That was Art Bridges."

"The man …"

"Yes, him," Janice interrupted. "The married man I had an affair with."

"I thought that was over." *What did I get into here?* Barnes thought.

"It is, and never should have happened. He wants me to come to Des Moines. I won't. What we did hurt too many people, including his wife and son. It's over. I'm not going back to him—ever."

Janice looked deep into Barnes' eyes with sincerity, pleading for acknowledgement.

"OK," he said, looking away. *Am I jealous? Does she really mean she and Bridges are through? Can I trust her?*

Barnes fell silent and Janice shrugged. "The past is in the *past*. I'm going to bed. The apartment door is open. Do as you wish."

Barnes finished his beer and joined her.

⬣

The last thing Brent wanted to do, besides see Elmer Juntlo again, was explain to his parents that he had trespassed on Juntlo's property and was shot at while escaping across the corn field. Brent's thoughts swirled around several questions. *My folks are going to be so mad at me and Juntlo. Is the whole town going to know what happened? What is going to be my punishment—grounding for life?*

Rob tried to put Brent at ease, but the later the clock on the wall read, the more apprehensive Brent became. Finally, the lights from the Frosts' car pulled in the driveway. They were surprised to see Rob's car out front.

Angela opened the front door and saw Rob standing next to Brent. "My goodness, Rob, I didn't expect you here." Her motherly instincts kicked in. "Brent, is everything all right?"

"Everything is fine, Angela," Rob interceded on Brent's behalf. "We do have issues to discuss, though."

"What's going on here?" Tim came abruptly in the back door after parking the car in the garage.

"I'm not going to cut corners, here," Rob said. "Your son needs to talk with you about an incident that occurred several days ago. Go ahead, Brent."

Angela's usually rosy complexion instantly became a frosty pale.

Brent spoke softly and mumbled so that no one could decipher what he was saying.

"Take your time and just tell us what happened out loud and clearly. That's all." Rob motioned for Tim to quit pacing and sit.

"Mom and Dad, I did something I shouldn't have. I'm really sorry." Brent's memories took over and he choked on his words. *My parents think I'm a good kid. Now, they won't think of me that way ever again.*

"It's fine. I promise I won't get mad. Just tell us." Tim's puzzled look focused on Brent.

"I went into Elmer Juntlo's barn without his permission."

"Tell them why." Rob encouraged.

"My friends and I thought he had stashed some gold or money in there. He's such a creep." Brent looked at Rob while he spoke, avoiding his parents.

"Did you find anything like that?" Rob asked.

"No, just junk."

"Except ..." Rob prodded.

"Except he had three big metal boxes. When I opened one, there were old bones in it."

"What?" Angela's voice registered disbelief.

"Human bones?" Tim immediately followed.

"I think so. There was a skull and some other bones."

Tim's and Angela's faces froze.

"Then what happened?" Rob glanced at Tim and Angela.

"Juntlo came back and surprised me. He knew someone was in his barn. I escaped under some rotten boards and, as I ran through the cornfield, he shot at me."

"What?" Tim shook his head.

"Mercy from God Almighty!" Angela placed her hand over her mouth. "He didn't hit you, did he?"

"No, Mom, I was too far away."

Tim and Angela sat in shock.

"Do other people know about this, Brent?" Rob turned back to Brent.

"Now they do, lots of people, including you and Detective Barnes and Cindy Williams and …"

"And Elmer Juntlo?" Tim interrupted his son.

"Yes, he knows." Brent shook his head.

"He threatened Brent a couple of times. I understand Detective Barnes is pursuing legal means to get him to leave Brent alone," Rob assured them. "Does Detective Barnes know about the bones?"

Brent stared at the floor. "No, I didn't tell him or anyone else about the bones—just that I was in the barn and saw dirt in the box I opened."

"I'm going straight over to Juntlo's right now to confront the bastard!" Tim shouted angrily. "No one threatens my son and shoots at him and gets away with it. This is crazy."

"No, you're not, Tim." Rob held out his hand. "It's late. Let's talk to Detective Barnes before doing anything rash. I'll get in touch with him first thing in the morning. The sheriff's office and Ellis Thompkins will also be part of the solution. The bones indicate foul play. Let the cops do their job."

"OK, Rob. I hear you. You're the cop." Tim backed off. "I'll wait until the morning before school, and then we'll see. No one, and I mean no one, shoots at my son!" Tim looked briefly at Angela and then his eyes focused like a laser beam on Brent. "There will be punishment for you, too. I thought we taught you better than to trespass. I'm disappointed, to say the very least."

Brent shared a sad glimpse with his mom and knew it would be a long time before things got back to normal in his household.

CHAPTER 53

Friday, November 6

First thing on the morning of November 6, Janice left early to open the store. Barnes had already traveled to the motel to meet Robinson. Instead, he found Rob waiting for him outside his room.

"You or someone needs to do something about that Elmer Juntlo character," Rob said forcefully. *"I mean today, now!"*

"I know. Juntlo keeps coming up on the bad side of things."

"Brent is scared to death of him, and I think for good reason. I spent the evening with him yesterday while his parents were out. Brent shouldn't have gone into Elmer's barn, but that is no excuse for Elmer's reaction. Did Brent tell you about the human bones he saw in the barn?"

"What? Bones?" Barnes paused in thought. "No. I knew he wasn't telling me the entire truth. We need to get back in that building right away. And I know how. The Reed County Sheriff's department is issuing Juntlo a restraining order this morning to keep him away from Brent. I want to be there when they issue it to him," Barnes said. "And I want another look in that barn."

"Good." Rob had calmed. "Now, how are you coming on the Knowles' case? I speak to the Wallers daily. Sometimes twice a day. I'll never say this to them, but it borders on pesty. I understand, though."

"I have a couple suspects in mind. I'll let you know if something substantive surfaces."

Robinson exited Barnes' motel room as Barnes and Rob were wrapping up their conversation.

"Morning, Fred. Who is this?" Robinson sauntered up to the two men.

"Del, this is Robert Frost. Rob, this is my partner, Detective Del Robinson. Del is up here to help me with Elmer Juntlo and the Knowles case. Del, Rob is a retired Denver policeman."

"Glad to meet you," Rob said, and the two men shook hands.

"I like your hat. Are you a cowboy?" Robinson stared at Rob's Stetson.

Rob laughed. "Only in appearance."

Turning his attention back to Barnes, Rob asked, "Is Del going to help you with my father's disappearance, too?"

"We haven't come to that point yet. We'll see. We gotta roll. I'll call you later."

"That would be great."

Barnes and Robinson left the motel for Brinson.

When they were on the road, Robinson asked, "Is there any reason you didn't tell Rob about the skull found in the dump?"

"Yes, two reasons. First, I don't want him in our investigation. He would assume the skull was his father's. Second, he may be a suspect."

Del shook his head in disbelief. "In his father's disappearance?"

"Yes. I heard Rob had a poor relationship with his father. Rob left for Colorado right after graduating from high school and very rarely came back to visit. Now he's back. That's odd, in my book. I'd like to know where he was on November 7, 1940."

"That's a big reach, man."

"Also, Rob just informed me that Brent saw a skeleton in a box in Juntlo's barn. When we give Juntlo the restraining order, I'm going to take another look around that barn."

"Good luck with that."

⁂

Elmer Juntlo sat at his workbench tinkering with a carburetor when he saw three cars pull up and park in front of the barn. One belonged to

Chief Thompkins, one to the sheriff's office, and the other was a Ford Ltd.

"Shit," Juntlo said to himself. "What now? That damned Barnes!"

Juntlo walked outside and growled, "What the hell are you assholes doing here again?"

Deputy Nelson stepped forward. "Easy, Mr. Juntlo."

"Don't tell me to get easy," Juntlo snapped back. "Why are they here?" He pointed at Barnes. After a quick moment, Juntlo nodded at Robinson. "I'll give Robinson a pass, but not him," he said, indicating Barnes.

"We're here to issue you this." Nelson extended a document to Juntlo.

"What's this, Nelson, summoning me to jury duty?" Juntlo laughed.

"No, sir, it's a restraining order. You are to leave Brent Frost alone. No contact, no threats, nothing. Neither Chief Thompkins nor I want to hear any more about this matter—nothing more. Are we clear?" Nelson placed the order in Juntlo's hands.

"What if he comes on my property? Can I shoot him?"

"Heavens, no, Mr. Juntlo. This is serious. Don't throw that order away." Nelson said.

"It's too late for that," Juntlo took the paper in his right hand and whacked his left forearm with the order.

The reaction to Juntlo's comment varied among the four law enforcement officers. Thompkins gently shook his head, while Nelson and Robinson stared at Juntlo. Barnes, though, clenched his fists and growled, "Why's that, Juntlo?"

"Because they've already been here, you fool," Elmer Juntlo hissed through yellow teeth.

"What? Who?" Barnes stared at Juntlo.

"The boy and his dad, that's who. They stopped by this morning, first thing well before school. The boy apologized for trespassin'. He said he didn't steal nothin', and I believe him. He couldn't have scooted out under the barn wall carrying somethin' anyway, and I don't have much of value to a kid in here.

"And I apologized for taking that pot shot. I shot in the air, not at him. In retrospect, I was wrong. If I wanted to, I could've hit him. After all, I was a soldier.

"There's more," Juntlo continued smugly. "The Frost kid is going to help me clean up my building, and I'm going to pay him one dollar an hour."

Barnes was dumbfounded. This was the last scenario he thought feasible when dealing with this mean, disgusting man.

"Don't worry, I promise not to harm the boy. You have my word as a soldier and patriot." Juntlo handed the paper back to Nelson. "This isn't necessary, Deputy." Juntlo pivoted toward Robinson. "Stop by sometime, Detective, please. I have a favor to ask of you. After all, we're brothers. I fought from Normandy to Germany. You fought in Korea. I want to know where. I knew people, good soldiers, over there."

"Yeah? When?" Robinson replied, unsure of what had just happened.

"How about in an hour? I've gotta do a couple things. You," Juntlo turned to Barnes, "I don't like you one damned bit. You're Des Moines trash. Do not come here again." Juntlo nodded and moved to vanish back inside the barn. As he did, he extended his middle finger at Barnes.

"Wait, Mr. Juntlo." Barnes raised his usually moderate voice. "I want to take a look inside for three boxes that look like caskets. They may contain something of interest to us."

"Think hard, Barnes," Juntlo spat. "I ain't got no casket boxes here. Jesus, you were just here. Did you see any boxes?"

"No," Barnes muttered, "but I heard they were here."

"Well, there ain't no boxes. And you ain't coming back in here again unless you get another warrant, which you ain't going to get. Screw yourself, Barnes."

Juntlo slammed shut the barn door, dashing Barnes' hopes.

CHAPTER 54

Friday, November 6

Ten o'clock in the morning on November 6, 1970, came as the overcast sky yielded to the sun. It was going to be a cold morning. A thin layer of ice covered the surface of Westbrick Lake just enough to support a fat vole. A pickup truck towing a trailer carrying a duck boat arrived at the south shore boat launch near the pavilion. Several cars followed and pulled up in the parking lot.

The driver turned the truck around and carefully backed the boat into the water. The crunch of breaking ice could be heard as the truck maneuvered the boat onto the boat landing and into the water.

"A little more," a man on the landing said and urged the truck driver to edge the trailer deeper into the water. "You've got another couple of feet."

When the boat was floating on the surface, a man wearing chest waders walked into the water and unhooked the boat from the trailer. He pulled the boat closer to shore.

The diving equipment was already on the boat. Two men clambered out of the truck in wet suits carrying their air tanks. Donald Reiss, wearing his beret, stood on shore by the boat watching the two scuba divers.

"Donald, get on board and the divers will follow you," the man wearing chest waders called out.

Reiss clambered onto the boat. One of the scuba divers followed and pushed past Reiss to the front of the boat. The other diver shoved the boat away from the shore and pulled himself on board.

"Nice day for a cruise," the second diver said smiling. "We stored this motor inside all night and it worked in our tank at the warehouse, so I hope it starts now."

He gave a tug on the ten-horse Johnson motor, and it started up. "Good," he said. "Now, let's find your marker, Mr. Reiss."

Reiss pointed in the direction where he had set the bobber, and the small aluminum boat puttered slowly to the area. Ice crunched as the boat advanced, like a tiny ice breaker in the arctic.

"What do you think they'll find out there?" Barnes asked the group of men standing with him.

"It's probably a tree branch." Chief Thompkins eyed the largely tree-lined lake. "Look at all the trees. What a waste of time and resources. Des Moines may have an unlimited budget for such things, but here we have to account for our spending."

"This is about the latest we could conduct this search without encountering more serious accessibility issues. Later in the winter, when there's thick ice cover, we'd have to cut a hole and go that route." Deputy Nelson ignored Thompkins and followed the boat as it maneuvered to the approximate center of the lake.

Thompkins added, "Ya'd never find the float then."

Barnes watched the boat crisscross the area searching for the float. When he looked to his side, he saw Rob and Max had joined him.

"How did you know about this?"

Rob just shrugged and Max said, "A good newspaperman knows where the stories are, Detective."

Barnes sighed. He wished he had worn more suitable clothes for the freezing weather. He thought of Janice's warm bed that he had slept in the night before.

The boat plied through the water, churning up thin ice chunks for an hour to no avail. The men on the boat could not locate the float. The cold was settling in, and Barnes' teeth began to chatter. He knew the men could not stay out on the water much longer.

Chief Thompkins shook his head. "Told you," he said to anyone listening. "What a damn waste, Barnes." He started to get back into his police car when Reiss yelled. A diver raised his hand and pointed down at the water.

Max squinted at the boat. "They found the marker!"

After a time of preparation, the two divers left the boat and descended into the cold Westbrick Lake. Ten minutes passed and both divers emerged, gesturing to Reiss.

"They have something. Don't know what yet," Max yelled.

The two-way radio crackled in Deputy Nelson's vehicle. Reiss' excitement was evident. "The guys said they found something down there. It's about fifteen feet down and it's murky. Something is wrapped in something held down by something. They're going down for another look to see if they can free the something."

"That's a whole lot of somethings," Max said, trying to be funny; no one laughed.

Nelson spoke into the radio, "What do they need, Donald?"

There was a pause as Reiss talked to the divers. "They're going to try and loosen whatever's holding it down and then insert floats to raise the object. It's not a log."

Reiss handed the men floats contained in a compartment on the boat and the divers re-submerged into the water.

"This is going to take a few minutes," Nelson announced to the assembly.

Barnes forgot about being cold, and thoughts of Janice vanished into the air like the breaths of the men standing on the shore.

"What do you think, Rob?" Barnes looked straight ahead.

"I wouldn't be surprised if it's a body. The question is, whose?"

Another ten minutes passed, and Nelson pointed, "They're going to run out of air soon."

At that moment, one float followed by a second, then a third and a fourth emerged from the water. Both divers' heads shot to the surface. One of the divers climbed into the boat, started the motor, and drove the boat slowly toward the landing. The second diver stayed in the water and kept the object secured to the boat.

"We're bringing in what they found." Reiss announced the obvious to those on shore.

The man in chest waders walked to the end of the boat landing. With water up to his belly, he grabbed the bow of the little boat and pulled it gently against the short dock, tying it securely. Another man wearing hip waders helped, reaching for the boat once it was in his range.

The men detached the object of attention from the floats and then the boat. They carried it up on shore. It was a tightly wrapped tarp. The men cut the chain bindings and pushed the tarp gently aside, exposing the contents. All the men in the group gathered around.

The face and body of a young man came into focus. His skin was as white as the snow that had started to dance around them.

"God in heaven." The man in hip waders shook his head.

"I knew it wasn't a log," said Reiss proudly.

"The cold water slowed decomposition," one of the divers said. "If this had been July …"

"I don't think he's been in the lake long." Barnes peered closely at the body. He turned to the group. "Does anyone know what Gary Knowles looks like?"

"That's Gary," Chief Thompkins said. "I talked to him on several occasions. How he got here, that's another mystery."

"Let's transport the body to Doc Deisman. I would like him to officially confirm the body is Gary Knowles'." Nelson pointed to the Carlson ambulance parked a few feet away.

Barnes walked over to Nelson and whispered in his ear, "Just so you know, Deisman may be a suspect in Knowles' death, and that's confidential, Deputy."

Nelson stared at Barnes in disbelief. "I don't know about that, but I want the doc to verify the identity."

"I hope it's quick," Rob joined in. "The Wallers want their son back. They've waited long enough."

"I agree with you, Mr. Frost," Nelson said. "We'll make this quick. The Wallers have been in touch with me daily for the past week. They want closure. I'll call and give them an update."

Barnes nodded to Rob. As he did, Barnes saw the divers beginning to remove their equipment. He hustled over to them.

"You men did great work today, but before you get out of your gear, I need you to go back and retrieve whatever was holding the body down in the water. It could provide clues about who disposed of the body so unceremoniously."

The divers grumbled, and one said, "This is not your jurisdiction."

"You heard the detective," Deputy Nelson intervened. "I'll buy beers tonight when you're done."

The divers walked back to the boat mumbling complaints.

"You'll buy that round and the next one, Detective Barnes," Nelson said with a hint of a smile. "You owe me."

⚲

Del Robinson was a man who defined timeliness. Promptly at ten o'clock in the morning on November 6, he knocked on Elmer's barn door. The door opened wide, and a smiling Juntlo appeared. He had shaved and put on jeans and a sweater. He also had removed his baseball cap and combed his graying hair. He looked ten years younger.

"Please, come in, Detective Robinson," Juntlo said.

"Thank you—call me Del. Can I call you Elmer?"

"Oh, yes, please," Juntlo said and waved for Robinson to enter.

Robinson did. He noticed the barn, at least what was viewable, had been cleaned up. A card table and two chairs had been set up to the right of the door. Two large coffee cups and cinnamon rolls were placed on the table. A standing lamp gave the area light.

"I got us something from the café downtown. I hope you like coffee and a roll." Juntlo motioned for Robinson to sit.

"I do." Robinson sat.

After a minute of small talk, Juntlo addressed what was on his mind. "You fought in Korea, right?"

"Yes."

"In combat?"

"Yes, I was a cop before Korea. Then I joined and fought. If I could do it over, I wouldn't have gone, man. Not my favorite memory. The Chosin Reservoir was absolutely brutal."

"Yep, I hear ya. I keep my wartime up here." Juntlo pointed to his head.

"Where were you stationed?"

"Europe, France, and Germany, mostly." Elmer took a bite of his roll. He sat forward in his chair and looked directly at Robinson. Seeing Robinson triggered strong emotions inside Juntlo that had been building for decades. He talked nonstop for an hour, forgetting about his roll and coffee.

"I fought in lots of battles, saw so many deaths on both sides, and worse casualties among innocent civilians. Here I am, a kid from Brinson, seeing the savagery of war and the worst of humans up close."

The high point of Juntlo's story was the Battle of the Bulge.

"We're outnumbered, out flanked. Men all around me dying or worse, wounded with no way out. Then a miracle happened. Isiah's unit rescued what was left of us. Imagine that, negroes coming to the aid of whites.

"I was hit—couldn't move. Isiah carried me on his back away from all the deaths through the shitstorm. He hummed a melody the entire time. The man was my guardian angel. I survived.

"We became instant friends, Isiah and me, and corresponded back and forth after the war until he died—car accident. It goes deeper. War carries scars you can't see. He had a wife and two young boys. We were supposed to get together, but time ran out.

"I've got two regrets in life. One, I survived the war when so many died. Two, I never went to Isiah's funeral, never got to meet his wife and sons. They'll be full grown by now, probably with kids of their own. I've got medals and nothin' to show for it. Damn it all to hell!"

Tears flowed from Elmer as he sobbed. "Why me? I should have done better with my life. All them dead would have done better than me. I'm a pathetic fool." The memories and bitterness he had kept inside all those years were released like an exorcist purging a demon.

Robinson reached across the table and put his hand on Juntlo's. Tears crept out of the corners of Robinson's eyes. "I feel the same way. I lost my best friend at the Chosin. I've got medals, too, but I would trade them all for just an hour with Darrell."

After a moment of silence, two hard men returned to the present. Robinson felt a strong longing to do something that needed to be done.

"Tell you what, Elmer," Robinson sipped his now cold coffee. "I'm retiring in a couple of years. How about you and me take a trip and meet Isiah's family. What do you say, man?"

Chapter 55

Friday, November 6

Barnes returned to Brinson at noon and joined Robinson in his car, which was parked on Main Street. Barnes churned with anger.

"We just pulled Gary Knowles' body from the lake. We now know the truth beyond question about what happened to him. He was murdered and his body disposed of worse than an animal's. He was a decorated veteran, for God's sake. There's obviously a coverup."

"Take a breath, man. Finding his body in the lake is evidence enough to show he was murdered. But you may be too close to identify a possible suspect."

"What does that mean?" Barnes stared hard at Robinson.

"Look," Robinson gazed at the windshield instead of at Barnes. "At one time, Janice was a suspect—those were your words. Also, it doesn't take a lot of imagination to know that you two are together. Perhaps she's clouding your judgment. Remember Charlotte Washburn?"

"Don't insult me—you of all people."

"I'm not, man," Robinson replied in his usual patient voice. "I'm considering everything. Let's take a break and stop at the café by the motel for a late lunch. We can go over our notes there."

A tapping at Robinson's car window disrupted the detectives' conversation. Rob stood outside the window wearing his usual cowboy hat, and today, an unzipped brown leather coat. He motioned for Barnes to roll down his window.

"Good day, detectives. I'm pleased Gary's body was found. The Wallers are exceptionally nice people who lost their son, but they can be nags." Rob smiled. He gave no sign that he was bothered by the cold weather. "We can now put the matter to rest."

"Not quite. We don't have his killer yet." Barnes stared at Rob wondering why the cold did not affect him.

"I've learned to live with cold." Frost read Barnes' thoughts. "How about an early dinner tonight? I'll be hungry."

"Sure, how about around four-thirty at Johnnie's Steak House? Let's meet at the motel first." Barnes said looking at Robinson, who nodded. "We can each provide our own theories about Gary's killer. In the meantime, we need to do a couple of things."

Rob gave the thumbs up and returned to his Cadillac.

"So much for lunch," Robinson sighed.

Barnes and Robinson drove by the Brinson police station. Barnes saw Thompkins' police car parked in front of the municipal building, and he told Robinson not to stop. Barnes then directed Robinson to a red brick ranch-style house on a quiet street on the north end of Brinson. Robinson parked, and the two went up to the front door of the house.

"Whose house is this?" Robinson was confused.

"Chief Ellis Thompkins'." Barnes knocked on the door. There was no answer.

"I don't understand," Robinson said. "We know he's at the police station, not here."

"I want to take a look around without him here."

"Why?"

"In my mind, Del, Thompkins is a suspect in Knowles' murder. He had the means to pull it off. He likely came across narcotics when he was a deputy in southern Illinois, so he's probably familiar with heroin. He's strong, too—almost Bud strong. His motive is not clear to me, though."

"A cop, a cold-blooded murderer. I don't know, man."

Barnes took a tour around the outside of the house and saw nothing out of the ordinary. He spotted a shed in the back with side-by-side doors locked with a chain that ran through the handles of each door. The chain and lock were new.

"See anything?" Robinson asked as Barnes returned to the car.

"Nope. You know, maybe I'm reaching for an answer. There's no evidence that points to Thompkins. I'm stumped for now."

"Where to next, man?" Robinson was anxious to move on. "We're going to need something substantive to tell the captain."

"Let's stop at the *Brinson Bee*. I want to know more about Suzi Thornton's death in 1960."

Barnes and Robinson expected Mabel at the front desk when they entered the newspaper office.

"Good afternoon, gents." A smiling Max stood behind the counter. "I gave Mabel the day off today. The weekly advertiser is out. It's slow and she's got something going on at her kids' school. What can I help you with?"

"That's all right, you're the person I wanted to talk with, anyway," Barnes said. "You seem to know the most of anyone about what goes on around here."

"At your service, sir." Sturgess bowed slightly.

Barnes pulled a small worn notebook from his coat pocket. "I'm interested in learning more about the death of a Suzi Thornton. Mabel told me she died this time of year in 1960."

"Yeah, that's correct. What else did Mabel tell you?"

Barnes summarized his conversation with Mabel: Suzi Thornton died by asphyxiation from a faulty furnace. The date of death was November 7, ten years ago.

"Suzi was sixty years old at the time of her passing." Sturgess folded his hands together in a prayer-like grip. "She worked really hard keeping her café open for as long as she did. She opened it in 1933 at the height of the Depression. Imagine that. She fed a lot of people who had no money at the time.

"Her husband left her in the late '30s. But she survived, and after the war had a thriving business. She never married again or had a boyfriend. She was a little odd that way.

"It was too difficult to tell the exact cause of her death as no autopsy was performed. She may have had a heart attack, and then the carbon monoxide finished her off. It was a terrible way to go for a fine lady and good citizen of Brinson."

Barnes took copious notes while Sturgess spoke. Robinson, too, jotted down a few details. "Do you have newspaper articles regarding the incident that we could take a look at?" Barnes glanced over at Robinson, who nodded.

"Sure, Mabel pulled the issue from the archive. I don't know what I'd do without her." Sturgess unfolded his hands. "Give me a minute." He moved down the counter to a small stack of newspapers. He found what he wanted and returned to Barnes and Robinson, handing Barnes a paper.

Barnes read the headline:

BRINSON WOMAN DIES OF AIR POISONING

The deck contained more useful information. "Suzi Thornton, beloved café owner, has died of carbon monoxide poisoning from a faulty furnace."

The rest of the article served little interest to Barnes, except the date of Thornton's death—November 7, 1960.

"Thanks, Max," Barnes said as he and Robinson finished reading the article. "I may want to refer to it again, and any other stories you wrote about her death. Right now, we have another appointment."

When Robinson and Barnes returned to their car, Barnes couldn't wait to speak. "Del, according to my notes, Richard Franklin Frost disappeared on November 7, 1940, Constable Wilber Roberts died by a train collision on November 7, 1950, and Suzi Thornton succumbed to carbon monoxide poisoning on November 7, 1960. What date is tomorrow?"

Robinson stared at Barnes. "November 7, 1970."

Chapter 56

Friday, November 6

Several thoughts pressed on Barnes' aching mind as he and Robinson made the short trip to the Best Western-Carlson from Brinson. *Someone killed Gary, but who? Dr. Deisman alone, or is there a conspiracy involving Deisman, Chief Thompkins, Elmer Juntlo, Carl Dinkins and his buddies, old Mayor Templeton, someone not on my radar? No one sticks out. Why?*

Shifting subjects, *I can't believe Juntlo is serious about his reconciliation with Brent. Del doesn't think he's a bad man, and Del is usually a good judge of character. God, I hope that turns out well.*

And tomorrow is November 7, the anniversary of the disappearance of Richard and the subsequent two deaths on the exact same date ten years apart. That's too coincidental. If there's a killer still out there, who will be targeted tomorrow? Who's the killer? Could it be Rob?

Barnes' final thought was the one he dreaded the most. *I know the captain can fire me at any moment. I've spent too much time here in Brinson and Carlson, and made plenty of enemies. I proved Knowles didn't commit suicide, but … to be drummed out of the ICC would be a disgrace. I'm in real trouble here.*

"Hey, Fred, I need to make a fast stop in the room before we go to dinner." Robinson interrupted Barnes' thoughts. "I need to pick up more of my notes. It'll only take a second. I also want to tell you about my conversation with Elmer. It's a real eye-opener, man."

God, I wish I could be more like Del. Nothing upsets the man, not even Elmer Juntlo. Barnes nodded to Robinson.

Rob met Barnes and Robinson at the motel. The time was four o'clock. Robinson left for his room, while Barnes walked to Rob's car.

As he approached the car, Barnes noticed that Rob's window was already down. *Does he drive like that all the time?* "Del is picking something up. He'll be out soon," Barnes said.

"I told you, Fred. I like the cold." Rob grinned as he saw Barnes eyeing the open window. "An open window provides fresh country air."

Five minutes passed and Barnes began to grow tired of waiting. The cold started playing with his mind. *I'd like the cold, too, if I could be in a warm car.*

"I'm going to check on Del," Barnes announced. "My gut tells me something's wrong."

"Give him five more minutes. Maybe he's using the bathroom. Get in the car."

Barnes waited the five minutes impatiently inside Rob's less-than-warm car. With no sign of Robinson, he told Rob, "I have an idea," and proceeded into the motel office where he expected to find the ever-present manager. This time, the man was nowhere to be seen. *That's odd,* he thought.

Rob quietly came up behind Barnes. "I think he sometimes takes a nap before cookie time, which is in about fifty minutes."

"Rob, it's been ten minutes since Del went to his room. I know him—something's not right about this. It should've only taken a minute at most for him to get his notes."

Barnes' thoughts swirled. *Is it possible Elmer Juntlo is waiting in the room for me but Del got in his way? Juntlo is crazy enough to do anything, and he hates me. Am I paranoid? Am I letting Juntlo get in my head? No, I must trust my instincts, and my instincts tell me Del is in trouble.*

"I know where the manager keeps an extra set of keys to the rooms." Rob came around to the back of the front desk and did a quick search. "Ah, here it is, the extra key to room 119. And here's the master key."

"Get the key to room 117 as well. I know there's no occupant in that room. Do you carry a gun?" Barnes' stern look showed he was serious.

Rob's brow wrinkled. "Yeah, in my car. Should I get it? Is it necessary?"

"Yes, Del should not have been in his room for this long. He's the most timely person I know, and he's hungry. Something's wrong. It's now been twelve minutes."

"What if he's calling your headquarters?"

Barnes was immediately upset with himself. He had not thought of that possibility. Yet, something inside him was screaming that Del was in trouble.

"Perhaps, but those calls go quick. If I'm wrong, there's no harm. Let's hurry."

"You'll give Del a fright."

Rob left and returned with a forty-five caliber Colt revolver that could have been used at the O.K. Corral.

Barnes glanced at the gun and sighed. "You're about a hundred years out of your time period. Where's the holster? Did Wyatt Earp take it?"

Rob laughed. "Perhaps, but if we have a shooting contest, my gun will beat yours."

"That thing might fall apart before you can shoot it." Barnes paused and became serious. "Here's the plan. Knock on the door of room 119 and say, 'Del?' I'll be in room 117—there's a side door that connects the two rooms. I'll have to unlock it from room 117. I need you to create a distraction outside the door to room 119. When you do that, I'll come into room 119 through the side door from 117. Be careful."

"OK, but I don't think this is necessary."

"I'll take the blame. I'm going to be fired, anyway. Have your firearm ready. Don't stand in front of the door—be off to the side."

"You've seen too many movies. OK, as you say." Rob smiled and took his position outside room 119. Barnes quietly opened the front door to room 117 and walked to the interior adjoining door. Without a sound, he tried opening it. The door was locked. *Thank God for the master key.* Before Barnes placed the key in the lock, he popped his head outside and gave the sign for Rob to count to ten. He walked quickly back to the adjoining door, thinking, *I'd better be right. Del will be really mad at me if I'm not.* Barnes removed his Smith & Wesson from its holster.

Rob knocked on the door. "Del," he said. "I'm hungry."

"Come in," said a voice from inside room 119.

Rob had only talked to Robinson on a couple of occasions, yet he knew the voice wasn't right. He removed his gun from his belt with his right hand and started to reach for the door handle. CRACK. A shotgun blast through the door stunned him.

Instantly, Barnes inserted the master key and turned it. The lock clicked, and he jumped into the room, shouting, "Police!"

He glimpsed a body on the floor before seeing a figure huddled near a chair. Barnes instantly recognized Del on the floor. The shooter was trying to use the chair for cover. Barnes glimpsed the image of a shotgun at the man's left side. The gun swung toward Barnes, and he instinctively aimed his gun at the chair. He fired one shot just as the man behind the chair fired his gun.

CRACK. The shotgun blast blew a hole in the wall to Barnes' right. "Ahhh …" He heard a groan from the shooter behind the chair. Barnes ducked and crawled over to the chair as Rob flew open the door and rushed in, ready to shoot.

"Hold your fire!" Barnes yelled to Rob.

Barnes peeked around the side of the chair and saw the shooter was sitting with his back up against the wall. The gun had fallen out of his hands. Barnes took it and moved it out of the way. Blood began to ooze from the shooter's shoulder.

"Call the police, Rob! We need two ambulances."

Barnes made his way over to Robinson's body lying on the floor. He was unconscious, but not dead. Barnes saw no evidence of blood coming from his body.

"Del! Del!" he shouted. Rotating to Rob, "Turn on the lights!"

Rob flipped on the lights and made the call. The light allowed Barnes to clearly see the identity of the shooter. It was a Juntlo. Only, to his shock, the man was not Elmer, but Eldon.

Robinson moaned and Barnes looked more closely at his friend. There was no sign of a gunshot or knife wound, but a dark ring was forming around Robinson's neck. Barnes quickly speculated, *Eldon surprised Del from behind when he entered the room, thinking Del was me. Eldon garroted Del until Del was unconscious. Eldon knew I would eventually come into the room, so he waited. Eldon's plan went awry when Rob distracted him at the front door and I entered through the side door.*

"Del, can you hear me?" Barnes grabbed a pillow from the bed and slid it under Robinson's head.

"Is that you, Fred?" Robinson croaked.

"Yes. Just rest. We called for help. You were being strangled."

A cry came from the corner of the room where Rob was attending to Eldon, putting pressure on his bullet wound.

"You hit him in the left shoulder, Fred," Rob said looking at the wound. "He'll live, too bad."

Eldon struggled to remain conscious. "Why are you here?" He groaned to Rob. "I wanted him, not you or the negro." Eldon glanced at Barnes with dazed eyes and pointed weakly. "I wanted to kill you, no one else."

"Why?" Rob asked. "What did Detective Barnes do to you?"

Eldon gulped air and swallowed. "He pissed off my brother, Elmer, and worse, he dug up my farm looking for shit that was none of his damned business. He's a bastard Des Moines cop. He was coming for me. I had to stop him first."

The pain became too much and Eldon passed out. Sirens filled the air. Within minutes, the emergency responders and a deputy sheriff made their way into the room.

Barnes nodded to the men and then Robinson. "He's an ICC detective, and my partner. He's got a badly bruised neck, and I don't know what else. That man over there is Eldon Juntlo. He's got a bullet wound in his shoulder. He may have lost a lot of blood. Put him under guard at the hospital and handcuff him to the bed. He tried to kill us. When he wakes up, for God's sake, read him his Miranda rights."

The responders quickly assessed the situation. Robinson and Eldon were prepped for transport and carried to the ambulances. One of the responders told Barnes they both would be taken to the Carlson Memorial Hospital, one mile northwest of the Best Western.

As the ambulances hurried to the hospital, Barnes left the room and watched Sheriff Larken and Deputy Nelson talk to the perspiring motel manager. Larken motioned Barnes and Rob over to him.

"What happened here, Detective?" Larken took off his sunglasses. His eyes bobbed from Barnes to Rob to room 119.

"We don't know yet, Sheriff. Eldon Juntlo thinks I had something to do with finding that illegal dump on his land. He's got that wrong. Looks like he planned to kill me, and Del got in the way."

"You've had run-ins with his brother, Elmer?"

"Yes. I was concerned Elmer Juntlo would harm a boy. He sure threatened him," Barnes said.

"Why?"

"The boy trespassed on his property. It's all been worked out between Elmer, the boy, and the boy's father."

"Are you sure about that?" Larken stared at Barnes. "Because, right now, I'm not sure about anything you do. My deputy has been keeping tabs on you, and I'm not impressed. You've brought a whole lot of problems with you, and have provided few answers.

"I've called your captain in Des Moines. He said you've been having trouble doing your job. Robinson saved your ass in Manlo, and now he was almost killed because of you. I glad I'm not you."

Sheriff Larken stuck his finger out at Barnes and strode briskly off to his car parked near the room 119 entrance.

"He's pretty mad at you." Deputy Nelson watched Larken drive out of sight. "I give him updates on what we do, he ordered me to. Just so you know, I've never complained about you or set you up to be ambushed. The sheriff likes the county to be nice and quiet, and you've upset that. I'll help you when I can."

"Thank you, Deputy." Barnes felt his life crumbling.

As Nelson turned to get into his car, Barnes asked, "Did the divers find what was holding down Knowles' body in the lake?"

Nelson picked up his radio and called his headquarters. Nelson listened and thanked the dispatcher.

"Yes, they did. They recovered it all."

"And?"

"There were two forty-five-pound plates, the type weightlifters use. Each weight plate was attached to an iron chain. Knowles' body was wrapped in a thick gray painter's tarp. One chain was strung tightly around his shoulders. The other was placed around his legs. I can assure you that Mr. Knowles was going to stay at the bottom of the lake for a very long time."

"That's what was intended. Thank you. One more thing—can I see the weights, chains, and tarp?"

"Sure, if you think it'll help. They're in our warehouse. Stop by at five-thirty and I'll show you."

"Why then?"

"Because the sheriff leaves for the day at five. I don't want him to know I'm helping you. If he knew, I could be terminated."

"I would like to go with you, Fred." Rob spoke for the first time since the ambulances arrived at the motel. "Any information I can give to the Wallers is good."

"OK, but please do not discuss our findings with them until we find the killer or killers, Rob."

"I won't, but I want to be kept in the loop."

⚚

At five-thirty, after Larken had left for home, Barnes, Rob, and Nelson met in the police storage room where the items found by the divers at Westbrick Lake had been placed on a heavy wooden table.

"We have the seven items the divers brought up." Nelson motioned to the table in front of him. "There's the tarp—basically, a painter's tarp. Note the holes that were cut around the upper and lower portions. That's where the killer ran the chains through to create a tight bond around the body.

"Here are the two chains. There's no rust on them, indicating they're new. They may have been purchased for this specific purpose.

"There are two forty-five-pound weightlifter plates. Also new—no evidence of rust. Whoever did this ran the chains through these center holes in the plates and through the holes in the tarp with the body inside. The chains were bound at the ends with these heavy-duty Master Locks. That's right, the locks are new, as well."

Nelson stood back waiting for Barnes' and Rob's reactions.

Barnes spoke first. "Whoever did this is a man, a strong man, and he planned his actions carefully. He would have had to prepare the body to transfer it—along with the weights and the chains—into a boat, take the boat out to the center of the lake, and dump the body overboard. All without being seen. The killer is a local, and he's good. Yet, I can't rule out that he had an accomplice. I just doubt it."

"Obviously, he or they never wanted the body to be found again, going through all that work. The problem for the killer is that Knowles' body and those items *were* found," Rob added.

"The man who disposed of Knowles in the lake is the same man who killed him," Barnes speculated. "Deputy Nelson, could you please write down the names of businesses in this area that sell exercise equipment? These forty-five-pound plates may be the clue we need to solve this."

"I know of one—Horace's Gym. It's here in Carlson, but closed now. They open at nine in the morning."

"Thanks, Wally." Barnes felt a growing trust in the man.

"I don't know if I understand Eldon Juntlo's motivation to kill you, Fred—by strangulation or shotgun. He was prepared for both, and the attack was premeditated. It's quite a step from disliking someone to trying to murder them," Rob said.

"Hopefully, we'll find out the reason. Right now, I'm going to drive to Brinson. I want to see how Brent is doing with his new-found friendship with Elmer. By the way, Eldon just included his name on my list of suspects for Knowles' murder and your father's disappearance. He is old enough for that."

Rob added, "Could be, Eldon's off his rocker. Tonight, though, I'm going to call the Wallers. I think we're almost there."

"Remember not to give them details, just that we made progress today. We *are* getting close." Barnes gave a slight smile.

"Remember what tomorrow is and what that means." Rob was dead serious.

"Yeah, I know. It sticks in my mind a lot—November 7."

Chapter 57

Friday, November 6

Dinnertime had ended at the Frost home when Barnes rang the doorbell.

"Hi, Detective Barnes." Tim opened the door. "Come inside. Angela is testing a new pecan pie recipe. She wants us as guinea pigs before she serves it to her church group. Have a piece and give her your honest opinion."

"Sounds delicious. I'm hungry. I'm sure it will be good."

Tim escorted Barnes to the dining room, and Angela greeted both men with two plates heaping with pie.

"Now, tell me the truth," Angela said squarely to Barnes. "Tim will only say it's good, and that's not the review I'm looking for." Angela looked with concern to the stairs. "Brent, pie is on the table, and Detective Barnes is here."

A muffled "OK" came from above, followed by Brent shuffling down the stairs, taking his time.

"Mom, I told you I don't want to try it. I don't like pies with nuts. How about that chocolate pie you made last week—any of that left?"

"No, your dad ate it all within a day or two. This is what you get tonight. Are you sure you don't want a piece?" Angela pointed to the pecan pie.

Brent shook his head.

Barnes looked at Brent. *Poor kid. He's been through the wringer the past few days. He's grown up faster because of it. The world can be cruel.*

Angela glanced to Tim and Barnes. "Do you two want coffee?"

"Sure," both men answered simultaneously. Angela disappeared into the kitchen and returned holding two cups of coffee and balancing a plate of pie on her forearm for herself.

Barnes took a bite of his slice of pie and savored it. "Mmmm," he said. He truly enjoyed the forkful. He took another sample of the pie and remembered why he was there.

"Brent, I just wanted to check on you after your time with Mr. Juntlo today." Barnes thought, *I have no intention of telling the Frosts about the incident at the motel this afternoon with Eldon. They'll find out soon enough.*

"It was good," Brent said as Barnes inhaled another bite of the scrumptious pie. "He wants me to come back on Monday. I said I would."

Barnes looked up, indicating he wanted more detail.

"He just talked about his time in the war. It was interesting. He showed me all his medals."

"I was there the entire time. That's not the Elmer I know—or knew, I should say." Tim took over the conversation. "He's made a one-eighty. He said he has sympathy for Gary and all the soldiers in Vietnam. Elmer fought two years in combat units during World War II. He said war makes brothers of men who normally would have nothing to do with each other. I can say he doesn't like you, though."

"I know," Barnes said without elaborating. He finished the pie.

"You've really helped my son, and for that I will always be grateful." Tim glanced at Angela. She nodded in agreement. "Brent has a new set of rules to follow—at least for a while."

"If I can take the burden off of Brent posed by Elmer Juntlo, then I'm all for that." Barnes smiled at the Frost family gathered around the table. For the first time in days, he had a positive feeling. *I'm not going to ask Brent about the bones anymore. He may have seen something, but that something is gone. It would be his word against Elmer's, and no one would win.*

"I need to call my captain," Barnes said as he waved off another helping of the heavenly pie. "I'll check in tomorrow to see if everything is still going well."

"Well, I'm going to wrap up a couple more pieces of pie. I know Janice would like one." Angela went to the kitchen and returned with a plate containing two mounds of pie wrapped in aluminum foil.

Barnes felt refreshed, thanked Angela, and bid the family good night.

When he walked into Janice's house, his good mood was dashed like a rowboat crashing on rocks.

"Hi, Honey." Janice tried to make light, knowing what she had to say next. "Your captain wants you to call him back as soon as you get here." She pointed to her phone. "Here's the number he wants you to call. He sounds like an unpleasant man."

"This isn't going to be good."

Barnes picked up the phone and slowly dialed the number. He recognized it as the captain's home number.

"Yes?" The phone was answered by the captain's deep voice.

"Good evening, Captain, it's Barnes."

"I figured it was you. Let me cut to the chase." The captain paused to let the seriousness of the matter set in. "Things are a mess in Brinson. I sent you there to verify a suicide—a simple case. Now I'll tell you where we are."

Barnes' frozen face told Janice what was transpiring on the other end of the phone.

"The suicide is now a murder and, as I understand it, there has been no arrest, but several theoretical suspects. Is that correct?"

"We have …" Barnes started to speak and was interrupted by the captain.

"You have nothing. Let me continue—worse, I have received complaints about your behavior and tactics from a number of people, including Mayor Templeton, Sheriff Larken, Chief Thompkins, Carl Dinkins, and not one but two Juntlos, and a couple others thrown in. No one in authority supports you.

"On top of that, Robinson—my top detective—is in the hospital because you wanted to dig on Eldon Juntlo's property for the bones of someone who went missing thirty years ago. That's a local matter, Barnes. Same as the trespassing issue between the boy and Elmer Juntlo. Have I got that right so far?"

Barnes gulped. *I know much of what the captain said is inaccurate and out of context. I'll wager Templeton, Larken, and Thompkins were responsible for the misinformation.* Once again, he began to speak and was cut off immediately.

"Now, here's the kicker. I called Max Sturgess. Sheriff Larken suggested I talk to him. He says you think there's a serial killer on the loose who strikes every ten years in November. Do you have any evidence of a serial killer? Do you know how crazy that sounds?" The captain's baritone voice was now a tenor.

"Your performance is not what I expect from a detective, but maybe a file room clerk. The ICC cannot suffer such performance. This was your chance to show me that you can redeem yourself. You failed.

"I'll give you a break tonight, but you're resigning—no if, ands, or buts. I'm only giving you this break because of your years of service with the ICC. I want you here in person by one o'clock tomorrow afternoon with your gun and badge to hand in your resignation, otherwise I'll have no choice but to fire you. Believe me, resigning is better. See you tomorrow, Barnes. Yeah, I know it's a Saturday." The captain slammed the phone down.

Barnes stood in shock with the phone still pressed against his ear. *Thinking you might be fired and actually being fired are very different. I can't believe my career with the ICC is over.* Barnes' initial concern was for his job and his reputation. Then, he got mad. *I'm being treated unfairly. I've done good work since I came to Brinson. I proved that Gary Knowles was murdered and didn't commit suicide. The captain can suck it.*

"How was your call?" Janice folded her arms over her chest, concern etched on her face. She had already surmised the answer to her question.

"Not good." Barnes stared at the floor. "I've just been canned. He gave me a choice: resign or be fired. The result is the same—I'm done with the ICC."

"Is there anything I can do?" Janice looked uncertain whether to hug Barnes or keep her distance.

He looked at her with a trembling bottom lip and moved to embrace her. He held her until he could control his urge to cry.

"I've worked almost my entire career with the ICC after five years as a beat cop. Fifteen, almost sixteen years are gone—and why? I did my job and did it well. I'm an asset to the ICC, not a liability, like the captain said. Screw him! *He* needs to retire. I've never seen anyone so set in his ways. Del should be the captain, but he's Black so that won't happen."

The more Barnes talked, the angrier he became. He let go of Janice, walked over to her liquor cabinet and pulled out a bottle of Jim Beam and a glass. He unscrewed the top of the bourbon whiskey and turned to Janice. Her sad look gave him pause. He put the top back on and returned the bottle to the cabinet.

"I won't turn to alcohol to make my problems go away. I won't do it."

"I'm proud of you. Dealing with problems clear headed is best. I haven't had a cigarette in days, and I don't miss it. It's just a crutch."

"What am I going to do now?" Barnes rubbed his forehead with both hands. "This is all I've known. I can't do anything else—I'm a cop." He sank into the sofa.

"Time will figure this out for you." Janice sat beside Barnes and rubbed his shoulder. She glimpsed at her watch—eight-thirty. She had a thought. "If you agree, I want you to talk to my pastor, Reverend McFadden. He burns the late-night oil, and he listens. You can tell him what you've been going through."

"Why would he talk to me? I don't know him and I'm not a Presbyterian."

"He's a good man. He spoke at Gary's service and did a fine job. He didn't know Gary, either."

Barnes shrugged, wishing Janice would keep massaging his shoulders.

"I'll make the call, and you can go visit him. He lives just five houses down. His wife, Beverly, works in Carlson, and she doesn't get home until ten tonight, so you won't have any interruptions."

Barnes was reluctant, but agreed. Janice arranged the meeting and Barnes trudged over to the reverend's house. He knocked quietly on the door, hoping there would be no answer. He wasn't surprised, though, to see the fiftyish-year-old man with flowing dark gray hair open the door.

"Good evening, Fred," the reverend said as he motioned for Barnes to enter.

"Sorry to disturb you this late, Reverend," Barnes reached to shake McFadden's hand and was surprised the pastor clasped both of his around Barnes'.

"There's no need to apologize. The Lord doesn't work on a set schedule." McFadden laughed. "Neither do I."

Barnes felt oddly at ease around this man he had never met.

"Would you like some tea? I've got a kettle steaming."

"Sure, that would be nice."

"I'll be back in a jiffy."

Barnes heard dishes clanging as he looked around the house to the extent he could see. Everything looked perfectly immaculate. *Someone knows how to maintain a very clean home,* Barnes thought.

"Here we are," McFadden announced as he brought all the elements of a good tea—the kettle, two cups, and a jar of sugar all placed on a silver tray.

McFadden poured the steaming tea into a cup and handed it to Barnes.

"Thank you for your hospitality, uh, Pastor ... Reverend."
"Please, call me Graham. Try just a touch of sugar. It'll cure what ails you." McFadden, smiling, poured his own cup of tea.

Barnes let the tea cool for a minute before taking a delicate sip. *This is delicious,* he thought, *and with a hint of mint.* The tea was soothing. For a moment, he relaxed and forgot about his problems.

McFadden's voice startled him. "Janice says you're in rough seas. Want to tell me what's going on?"

"Oh, I can handle it." Barnes took another sip of tea, this time a larger sample.

McFadden knew that wasn't true. "I'm here and you're here right now. I can't imagine the life of a detective. There must be so much stress. How do you cope?"

Barnes didn't know if it was the tea, the reverend's calm manner, the predicament he was in, or all three, but he opened up to Reverend McFadden like he had never done before. He discussed Gary, his interactions with Elmer, and getting fired from the ICC. Afterward, he was embarrassed about his openness and hoped he hadn't revealed any information about the cases he was working on.

The subject of Janice came up in their conversation. McFadden told Barnes, "Janice has had two traumatic events in her life. First was the tragic death of her husband. Second was her affair with Art Bridges, which wasn't good for anybody. There are those in Brinson who hold her accountable for the affair. But she's strong and has a good heart. She's helped the more unfortunate people of Brinson and the surrounding area, and is a valuable friend to Bud."

I need to appreciate Janice more, Barnes thought as McFadden talked.

To Barnes, it seemed like minutes since the two began talking when actually it had been almost an hour and a half. Beverly would be returning home any minute.

"Do you have any advice for *me?* Tomorrow will be a pivotal day."

"I can't tell you what to do. God can't either. But what I can tell you is that you have a strong moral compass, and you need to follow it. Do the right thing, and you cannot be wrong, no matter what. I believe you and Janice are good souls."

McFadden continued, "By the way, earlier today I talked with Elmer for the first time in many, many years. He's choosing a different path, a good path. I'm encouraged. You know, sometimes it's harder to forgive than to gain forgiveness."

"I'm not sure I know what you mean."

"That's between you and God, not me. You'll understand in time."

A car drew up outside, and Barnes knew his time with the reverend was over. He shook McFadden's hand, this time with his two hands, and said, "Thank you, Father."

"I'll pray for you, Fred, and for Del, Janice, Elmer, and even Eldon. We are all God's people."

Barnes left out the front door as Beverly came in through the back. He walked back to Janice's house and told her about his encouraging discussion with the reverend. She smiled and kissed him.

"I have a feeling your problems will vanish tomorrow," she said softly as she led him upstairs to bed.

Or crush me, Barnes thought as he followed her.

Chapter 58

Saturday, November 7

"Hello?" Rob awoke from a deep sleep to the irritating sound of the phone ringing beside his bed.

He was trying to regain his senses when a hushed voice whispered back. "Meet me at Hinton's house in fifteen minutes. I know who killed Gary."

Rob shook his head. "What?"

The phone went dead. Rob wasn't sure if the voice belonged to Barnes or someone else. *Who else could it be? No, it's got to be Fred. Why was he whispering? Is he in danger? Why did he call me at five o'clock in the morning? Who is the killer?*

The urge to solve the mystery was too strong, and Rob kicked off the covers and got out of bed. He stumbled to the sink and washed his face. He applied a stick of deodorant under his arms several times and gargled with Listerine. He put on a fresh set of clothes, grabbed his jacket, and headed out the door to his Cadillac. Within seconds, he returned to his room and put on his cowboy hat.

The drive from the motel to Brinson usually took just under ten minutes. Rob noticed that there was no one else on the road that early in the morning. It was dark in every direction.

I'll make good time. I'm happy Fred has solved the case—the poor guy needs a break. What's that flashing light up ahead? Need to slow down, maybe someone is in the ditch.

That was the last thought Rob Frost had before everything turned black.

Chapter 59

Saturday, November 7

Barnes rolled away from Janice. He had hardly slept as the events in Brinson and his looming termination from the ICC roiled in his mind. *November 7, God help us.* It was dark out, and he thought he heard a phone. It rang several times and showed no sign of ending. His watch read six-fifteen.

That's for me. He hurried downstairs and picked up the receiver.

"Barnes," he said gruffly.

"Fred, this is Wally. I'm at the hospital."

"Why? What's happened?"

"Rob is here. He was broadsided on Highway 40 just outside Brinson around five this morning,"

"Is he going to make it?"

"The doctors don't know yet. He has multiple broken bones, lacerations, and other injuries. He's slipping in and out of consciousness."

"Thank you, Wally. I'll be right there. Have they identified the other driver?"

"No, and I don't think they will. It was a hit and run. Maybe I've been around you too much, but this could be a hit job. Someone wanted Rob dead. Who that person is, I don't have a clue. Maybe it's the same person who killed Knowles."

"Is there snow or anything that could explain this incident as an accident?"

"No, nothing like that. We'll have to wait until there's better light and see what evidence there is. I doubt that will be useful, though."

"One more thought, Wally. If the accident didn't kill Rob, the perpetrator could have been counting on hypothermia. It's cold, and he could have been out there for a while before someone spotted him."

"Good point. Fortunately for Rob, a fellow deputy coming west on Highway 40 spotted his vehicle in the ditch by chance. The accident, or whatever you call it, had happened recently."

"And the deputy saw no sign of the other vehicle?" Barnes asked.

"None."

⋏

Barnes left for the hospital after dressing and explaining to Janice what had happened.

"I'll be at the store. Ring me when you can?" Janice said before he hurried away. "Remember, today is going to be a good day."

"Not the way it started, but we'll see."

Nelson met Barnes at the neon-lit emergency entrance to the hospital. "I don't want to make bad things worse, but Sheriff Larken is here, and he's looking for blood—your blood."

"I'm getting tired of that pain in the ass." Barnes glowered at the entrance. "Let's go see how Rob is doing. I want to check in on Del, too."

The two men walked together down the hospital corridor and stopped outside Rob's room. Larken waited for them at the door like a python ready to strike.

"Rob Frost said it was you who called and asked him to go to Brinson," Larken bellowed. "I have a theory that you lured him to the highway and ambushed him, hoping he'd die. Is that right?"

"When did Rob tell you this?" Barnes growled.

"He came to and answered some questions. I should arrest you, but I don't have enough evidence—yet," Larken spat.

Barnes' anger boiled over. "That is the most ridiculous thing I've ever heard. Rob is obviously delirious and on pain medication, so I don't know how much I'd trust what he's saying. Now, to the point: What's my motive, Sheriff? Rob played an important role in determining Gary Knowles was murdered and didn't commit suicide. Why would I try to kill an ally? Moreover, I was with someone this morning, not making phone calls and driving around, as you claim. And you can check my car for any damage because whoever hit Rob would have a pretty beat up front end."

"Who can vouch for your whereabouts?" Larken stepped back as his allegation began to lose credibility.

"I'd rather not say. That's private."

Larken folded his arms across his chest in a gesture suggesting he was right after all.

"But to get you off my back—I was with Janice Hinton in Brinson."

"I'll check on that. I heard she's a mixed-up woman, maybe a communist, so I don't know if I can trust what she says."

"Whatever, Sheriff. Now get out of my way. I want to see Rob."

Larken left in a huff, talking to himself.

"How that man got to be sheriff is a mystery to me," Barnes muttered to Nelson. "My initial impression of him was way off."

"He knows how to kiss ass. That's all I'll say."

"It sure wasn't because of his competency."

Barnes entered Rob's room. He saw the IV line running into Rob's left arm; presumably pain medication and, probably, an antibiotic. Rob's right arm was in a cast and his neck was in a brace. The rest of his body was covered by a white blanket.

Rob was asleep, so Barnes sat in the chair beside the bed.

"I'm going to sit here for a while, Wally. I want to be here when he wakes up, if even for a minute. I've got a lot of things to mull over."

"Yeah, I'm going to go home, say hi to my wife, take a shower, and put on fresh clothes. I'll be back in a couple hours. Don't let the sheriff get to you."

"I won't. Larken is just an impostor posing as a sheriff. I don't think he could solve the case of the missing coffee if the cup was leaning against his elbow. He's a politician with a badge. I've seen it before." *Like my captain.*

For the next two hours, Barnes sat still in the chair pondering two questions: Who is the primary suspect—or suspects—in Gary's murder? And who and why did someone try to kill Rob?

To Barnes, the most likely answer to the first question was Dr. Deisman. *He conducted the false autopsy, with his connections and background, he could have accessed the heroin, and was not a fan of anti-war people, like Knowles. The problem is that Deisman isn't strong enough to dispose of Knowles' body in the lake by himself. He had to have an accomplice. And what's Deisman's motive?*

Barnes had no idea, though, who had tried to hurt Rob. *Perhaps it was an accident and the driver just fled. Or was it on purpose, and if so, why? I don't know whether he has any enemies around here. Hopefully, Rob will wake up and tell me something to get me on the right track.* Then it hit Barnes. *It's November 7.*

Barnes grew restless and decided to take a walk to Robinson's room. He threw a quick glance back over his shoulder, still unsure he wanted to leave the man alone, when Rob opened his eyes.

"Hi, Fred," he mumbled.

"Geez Rob. I'm so sorry this happened to you."

"So am I." The slightest grin appeared on Rob's face, then he grimaced. "The doctors say I have some broken bones and internal stuff. Lots of cuts from glass, too. I … I may be here for a while."

Barnes sat on the edge of Rob's bed. "Do you remember what happened?"

Rob spoke in spurts. "I remember a call, five in the morning. The voice said to meet at Janice's house. I know that's where you're staying, so I assumed it was you. All I know is that the voice was male."

"It wasn't me. Why would he tell you to meet at Janice's?"

Rob coughed, winced, and coughed again. "There was a flashing light on the road. I thought there was an accident. I really don't feel good. The pain."

A nurse bustled into the room and Barnes hopped guiltily off the bed. "Mr. Frost, I'm going to adjust your medication to help you relax and ease the pain." She turned her hard, efficient stare to Barnes. "I'm going to ask you to leave now. You can come back this afternoon." She adjusted the IV flow to allow more of the bag's contents to enter Rob's blood stream.

As Barnes moved away from the bed, Rob weakly gestured to him. He muttered, "The voice said he knew Knowles' killer. Find the killer."

Rob's voice dropped off at his last word, and he fell asleep immediately.

Barnes had barely stepped through the doorway of Rob's room when he saw something in the hallway that made him freeze. *He's visiting his murderous brother, I'll wager.*

"Juntlo, Elmer Juntlo," Barnes shouted at the man walking halfway down the corridor.

Elmer turned around, and his expression surprised Barnes. There wasn't a hint of hatred or disgust on his face.

"Good morning, Detective Barnes," Juntlo said as he walked up the dull beige corridor toward Barnes.

"Why are you here?" Barnes blurted. "Your brother is down the other corridor."

"Oh, I didn't come here to see my sorry-ass brother, Barnes. I came to see how Del is doing. I want to talk to him—I need to talk to him more about *his* time in the Army. I did the talking before. It's important to me."

Barnes had a difficult time believing what he was hearing. He viewed Elmer as the very definition of a crude, racist redneck. Now it sounded like he and Del were friends. "What?" was all he could say.

"I'll give you the short version. Early in life, I was a naïve, mostly good kid. Then I was sent to Europe to fight in a war I had little understanding of. The other white soldiers teased me. I felt like an outcast. They called me a yokel—an Iowa potato head. I was in the Army more than two years and grew to be a good soldier. A man named Isiah Jones saved my life at the Battle of the Bulge, which got me through that damned war. He was the first Black man I knew personally. He and the other Black soldiers were heroes. Isiah was a good friend.

"When I got back to Brinson, I lost touch with Isiah. Time and distance can do that. I let Eldon's shit prejudices take over. I should've stood up for my beliefs, but I didn't. Seeing Del rekindled memories of Isiah and what he stood for—always having your brother's back. And I failed terribly. Del's a good man."

Barnes could only stand and stare dumbfounded.

Juntlo laughed. "Cat got yer tongue, Barnes? I had an epiphany after talking to Del and when young Frost and his father came to my building and apologized. You've heard about Dickens' *A Christmas Carol*, right? Well, that's me. I took stock of my situation and decided to change my life. So, here I am. There were no ghosts, though.

"I'm glad you took out my brother—he, on the other hand, is never going to change. He's a nasty man. He used my barn in town to store shit I didn't know about lots of times. He should've used the buildings on the farm. Why my barn?

"And using our land as his dump is plain wrong. I was supposed to be his partner on the farm, but I had nothing to do with it. No way was I going to work with him. I guess now it's my time on the farm. I don't know what got into him that he actually tried to kill you. Damn."

Barnes found himself asking, "How's Del doing?"

"He's doing good. He told me when his time with the ICC is over, me and him are going to search for Isiah's wife and kids so I can meet 'em and tell 'em about their father. Oh, and by the way, the Frost kid is doing good, too. In fact, I've hired a couple more of his friends to help me clean out my building. It's time. They're good kids, and they listen to an old man tell stories. Goodbye, Barnes."

Juntlo turned and walked down the corridor toward the exit. Barnes wavered. *I don't know if I trust that man. I've never known anyone who could change like that overnight. I've got to ask Del again about him. He has a good sense of a person's character.*

Robinson was sitting up in bed watching a morning television show when Barnes entered.

Barnes tried to sound cheery. "You're looking better today than yesterday."

"Yeah, thanks for saving my life. I guess we've each taken a turn at that."

"You know, I just saw the strangest thing—a reformed Elmer Juntlo. Is he for real?"

"I told you he has good inside, man. It just needed to come out. We're going to find his friend's family. I will say that sheriff is not to be trusted, though. He was here before you. He somehow has it in his tiny brain that you tried to kill Rob. He's right, isn't he, man?" Robinson winked.

"Yes, it's true." Barnes smiled and became serious. "Just so you know, the captain gave me a choice last night: quit or be fired. He thinks I've screwed everything up here in Brinson, including putting you in this hospital. And a number of people have complained to him about me. I'm finished with the ICC. First, though, I'm going to solve Knowles' murder—it's important to me. I'm so close I can feel it. The captain be damned."

"Well, you better get to it instead of jabbering with me." Robinson winked at Barnes again. "I'll be checking out after the doc comes by. I'll wager I can solve the case then. Just know that Elmer is not your man. He's changed, rediscovered his heart. How's Janice doing?"

"She's good." Barnes gave Robinson a weak salute and went to the nurses' station. Deputy Nelson was waiting for him, holding a piece of paper.

"Horace's Gym is open. Here's the number. Ask for Horace. By the way, Doc Deisman never showed up for work today."

"Is that strange?"

"As you know, he works Saturdays. What's more interesting is that he didn't go home last night, like he always does. His wife is beside herself. Something is off here. He never misses a day of work or a night at home."

"He's my prime suspect and I think he has an accomplice. Maybe he fled. We need to find him. And please give me that number for the gym. I want to check something out."

Nelson handed Barnes the number, nodded, and left the hospital.

Barnes asked a nearby nurse for a phone, and she took him to an unused office.

"You have to dial 9, then dial your number—it is local, isn't it?" she asked.

"Yep." Barnes dialed the number.

A gravelly voice answered. "Hello, Horace's Gym. Horace speaking."

Barnes explained the situation to him.

"Yeah, I sold two weight sets in the past six weeks to a couple of fathers whose sons are on the Carlson football team. I think the dads wanted the weights for their own use and just used their kids as a smoke-screen." Horace chuckled.

Barnes slumped in his seat. A thought flashed through his mind before he hung up. "What other businesses in this area sell equipment like you do?"

Horace was a fountain of information and rattled off seven names within a fifty-mile radius. Barnes thanked Horace, hung up the phone, and then dialed all seven numbers. No customer at any of the businesses fit the profile of the man Barnes was interested in. "Damn!" Barnes' discouragement peaked at a new high.

The seventh person on the list said that he had a cousin who worked at a sporting goods store north of Des Moines. The cousin's store was not on Horace's list. Barnes dialed that number with little hope. *This will turn out just like the other calls,* he thought.

At the end of the call, Barnes grinned. "Gotcha!"

Chapter 60

Saturday, November 7

"Did you bring the bolt cutters?" Barnes looked at Nelson.

"Yeah, they're in the trunk." Nelson got out of the car and opened the squeaky hatch. The tool was on top of a pile of other tools and clothing.

Barnes pointed at the trunk. "Does your house look like this?"

"The answer to your question is no. My wife is a neat freak. This is my storage locker. Where I put my man things."

Barnes shook his head. "Let's go."

The two men walked around the side of the brick house and stopped in front of a white wooden shed. Barnes motioned to the padlocked chain between the door handles. "Cut it, Wally."

Nelson hesitated. "You realize this is a law enforcement officer's property, don't you? If you're wrong, I'm in big trouble."

"You can join me in the unemployment line." Barnes flashed a grim smile. "No, don't worry. I'll take all the heat. It's my idea and you tried to stop me. After all, what more can they do to me?"

"Geez, Fred. You should still know better. How about breaking and entering, for starters? Then there's trespassing, damaging property— should I go on? You could get jail time."

"You can leave now if you want. But I'm not wrong. Evidence proving Knowles' murder is in this shed. And look at the lock and chain. Look familiar?"

Nelson stood his ground and shook his head.

Barnes placed his ear on the shed door. "I hear something in there. I'm going in. Give me the bolt cutters!"

This time Nelson relinquished the tool without protest. He stood back and watched Barnes cut the chain. The severed chain with the lock still attached fell to the ground with a dull thud.

Barnes tried to remain calm and confident while his insides swirled. He pulled the doors apart praying he would find something—anything—useful. Instead, what he saw left him gaping.

"What the hell!" Nelson attempted to see into the gloom of the shed beyond the reach of the overcast day.

"I didn't expect this." Barnes squinted at the man seated at the back of the shed. He pulled a flashlight from his pocket and shone it on the man, who was bound. He looked unconscious, or worse.

"Lord Jesus," Nelson exhaled. "That's Doc Deisman. What's he doing in here? I thought he was your suspect."

The shed was dark and cold as the two men rushed over to Deisman.

"He was, until I had that phone call with the manager of the fitness club near Des Moines. He told me he sold two pairs of forty-five weight plates to Ellis Thompkins around three weeks ago. He put them on hold and left his name. That was surprisingly careless."

Barnes reached out and put two fingers against Deisman's neck. There was a pulse, though it was weak.

"Is Doc alive?"

"Yes, alive, but he's in poor shape." Barnes shivered at the thought of what could have happened. "I believe Thompkins was going to kill him and dump his body in Westbrick Lake."

"Why would he do that?" Nelson didn't know what to think. "Why kidnap and hurt the doc?"

"Because the two collaborated in Knowles' murder. I think Thompkins killed him and Deisman covered up the cause of death by deliberately fudging the autopsy. Deisman was a loose end for Thompkins. At some point, he figured the doctor would tell someone what they did. If he lives, he'll be able to tell us everything. First, we need to get an ambulance here. I assume it has to come from Carlson?"

Nelson nodded and started backing out of the shed.

Barnes cut the duct tape bindings that tied Deisman to a heavy, wrought iron chair. The bindings were exceptionally tight, an unnecessary cruelty.

Deisman gasped as blood returned to his extremities. He moaned, "Water."

"I saw water in your car, Wally. Can you grab it while radioing the ambulance?"

Nelson left for his car in a rush while Barnes helped the doctor lie down on the floor of the shed.

"You'll be fine, Doctor," Barnes said. "Deputy Nelson is getting water for you and radioing for an ambulance."

Deisman was suffering from shock and hypothermia. Barnes looked around until he spotted a tarp shoved in a dark corner. He unfolded it and carefully placed as much as he could under Deisman to insulate him against the cold floor. Barnes then took off his coat and draped it around the doctor. *I'm glad he's not a large man*, Barnes thought.

When he glanced in front of him, Barnes saw two forty-five-pound weight plates leaning against the wall and several feet of chain hanging on hooks attached to the wall. *God have mercy.*

Nelson brought a thermos of water from his car and offered it to Deisman. He took a deep gulp and breathed heavily after Nelson took it from his lips. "The ambulance is on its way, Doc." Nelson moved next to Barnes.

Deisman's glazed eyes focused on Barnes, then Nelson, and finally back to Barnes. His body shook either from the cold or fright—probably both.

"He was going to kill me and drop me in that lake, just like Knowles." Deisman shivered.

"You're referring to Ellis Thompkins?" Barnes asked.

"Of course. Who else would I be referring to?" Deisman reached for another drink of water from Nelson's thermos and took several more deep gulps before he had his fill.

"How did you get here?" Barnes squatted by the doctor.

"Last night, he—Thompkins—told me to meet him here." Deisman pointed in the direction of Thompkins' house. "When I turned my back to him, he knocked me out. I came to in this shed, taped to this chair. Thompkins told me that I knew too much, so he had to get rid of me, like he did with Knowles. I would be the suspect who vanished, and people would think I was the killer."

"What would the end result be?" Barnes edged closer to Deisman.

"Out of spite, he would overdose me on heroin, wrap my body in the same tarp I'm lying on, and toss me in that damned cold lake with Knowles. Maybe I'd just die in this shed and he wouldn't have to use the heroin. You saved my life."

"Thompkins has heroin? Where did he get it?" Nelson asked this time.

"Check that cabinet," Deisman said, gesturing to the very back of the shed in the shadows. "It's all there. He's got connections in Illinois and Missouri. He hated Knowles. It made sense to Thompkins that because soldiers use heroin in Vietnam, Knowles became addicted over there and brought that addiction home, which caused his death."

Barnes walked to the cabinet and opened it. The light from his flashlight showed a package wrapped in newsprint on the second shelf.

"Damn," Barnes said as he unwrapped a bag of white powder, a candle, a spoon, and two syringes.

"Damn is right," seconded Nelson.

Barnes turned his attention back to Deisman. "You're correct about the drugs, and he wasn't playing games with you, either. The weights, tarp, and chain tell a similar story to Knowles' fate. Now, tell us why 'you knew too much,' as Thompkins put it."

"I didn't kill Knowles, if that's what you mean." Deisman retreated into his shivering.

"What was your involvement?" Barnes demanded. Nelson stood by, his hands resting on his hips.

"He made me do it," Deisman squeaked.

"Do what, Doctor? Falsify the autopsy report? Knowles didn't commit suicide, did he? Tell me in front of Deputy Nelson that Thompkins killed him, and you covered up the murder."

There are times when a decent person becomes involved in something totally out of character and then does not know what to do about the problem. In this case, it was Deisman, who became overwhelmed with guilt.

"Yes, yes, yes—you're right. Thompkins killed Knowles and I altered the autopsy report to make it look like suicide. I also destroyed any evidence that would prove otherwise. I fixed the shipping papers to make it look like Knowles' body was sent to California. Thompkins said if I did this for him, he wouldn't tell anyone about a lapse in judgment I had."

"What lapse?"

"Years ago, I had an affair with my office nurse. I ended it, but Thompkins somehow found out and was blackmailing me. My wife would be crushed. She has Parkinson's. I couldn't let her find out. My God, what's going to happen to me?"

"I believe you," Barnes said, and Nelson nodded in agreement. "You'll have to face the legal system, and I can't tell you what that result will be. Cooperating with us will help, though. First things first, we need to get you to the hospital. Deputy Nelson will accompany you." Barnes gazed at Deisman's pale, shuddering face.

"What are you going to do, Fred?" Nelson asked as the piercing screams of the approaching ambulance shattered the quiet. Barnes retrieved his overcoat and shrugged back into it.

"Take care of the doctor. Then I need you or a deputy you trust to come to Brinson. Don't tell Larken. If Thompkins is still here, I know where he'll be. Otherwise, he's gone."

"Where will he be?" Nelson asked as the ambulance pulled up.

"The Hinton store."

Chapter 61

Saturday, November 7

Early Saturday morning passed like usual for Brent. There were a few chores and television shows, and his mom made waffles unexpectedly for lunch. With his reconciliation with Elmer, Brent's parents relaxed some of the rules they had placed on him.

At two o'clock, he left to run a new weekly errand for Janice, which consisted of taking a grocery order to the widow Ericson at her home about four blocks east of the store. This was Brent's first time doing the task, which he hoped would result in repeats because Janice paid well.

Brent walked to the store breathing air influenced heavily by several people burning their annual harvest of fall leaves. About halfway there, he ran into Jack and Ron.

"Hey, Brent," Jack said. "Do you think Mrs. Hinton would have a part-time job for me? I'd like to do something for her for five dollars."

"How would I know? And this is only for an hour once a week."

"Sweet deal," Ron added. "While you're working, we'll be playing football."

"I'll be done in an hour. Get Tom and Dale. We'll still have some daylight."

"Ha," Jack laughed. "Tom's too busy sleeping, dreaming about Shirley."

"Outa here, guys." Brent finished walking the last block to the store by himself. As he did, he saw Cindy and thought, *She is more beautiful than ever.* She smiled at him and they had a short conversation. He waved goodbye to her as his heart fluttered.

Janice had asked Brent to enter the store through the side entrance. The bagged groceries would be placed on the table in the storeroom closest to the back door. He would pick up the bags, leave by the same door, and go straight to Mrs. Ericson's house. Today as he entered the storeroom, he froze in the doorway and stared in disbelief.

Barnes decided not to park directly in front of the Hinton store. It was a little before two-forty-five. He didn't want to draw attention to himself in case Tompkins was waiting for him, so he drove about fifty feet south and parked in front of the *Brinson Bee.*

He thought, *Not today, Mabel.* Barnes slid his handcuffs into his coat pocket; not the perfect place for them, but within easy reach. He had to be careful he didn't drop them. He checked his revolver and placed it in his shoulder holster. He made sure his overcoat covered it before he got out of his car and walked north. When he approached the Hinton General Store, he ducked and waddled close to the large window facing Main Street.

"You hurt yourself, Detective?" Barnes could hear Max Sturgess' voice from behind.

"I have a crick in my back."

"Need any help?"

"No, thank you. It's happened before. It'll work itself out. Give me a minute."

"You may want to make an appointment with Doc Deisman—he's in his office today." Sturgess turned to walk down to the newspaper building.

Whew, I lucked out there. Barnes exhaled deeply. *Max doesn't know about the Deisman kidnapping incident—yet.*

Barnes waited a minute for Sturgess to disappear inside before moving in front of the store window. He squinted through it, but couldn't see anything. As he squatted by the front door, he thought he could pick up parts of an angry man's words. "Traitor … you betrayed me … screwing Knowles … screwing worthless Barnes … bitch … could've had me … I'll fix this."

Thoughts of the debacle in Manlo returned to Barnes' mind. He pushed those thoughts aside. *It's not the same,* he told himself.

Barnes got back up on his feet, opened the door, and slowly made his way inside. He called out, "Janice, Bud?"

Janice appeared first. She had duct tape over her mouth, and more tape bound her hands behind her back. With his left arm pressed around her neck, Thompkins walked behind her carrying his gun in his right hand. He had a hulking appearance compared to Janice's thin body.

"Well, if it isn't Barney Fife coming to rescue his beloved," Thompkins snarled. "I knew ya'd come here."

"What are you doing, Ellis?" Barnes moved his hand to rest on the handle of his revolver.

"I see yar gun, Barnes. Drop it and we can talk about where we go from here." Thompkins stopped moving and put the gun to the right side of Janice's head, cocking it. "I'm not kidding. Drop the gun or I drop her."

Janice's eyes blazed with unspoken terror as she looked at Barnes. Barnes saw her fear and froze with indecision. *If I put my gun down, he'll shoot me and take Janice to who knows where. If I can get to my gun in time, I can try to hit him; I'm a good shot. But I don't have the advantage. I may hit Janice, or Thompkins will shoot her the moment I draw. I'm screwed anyway you look at it.* Barnes sighed and lifted his coat, further revealing his gun, and slid it slowly from the holster, keeping his finger away from the trigger. He moved to put it down on the shelf off to his side.

"NO! Put the gun on the floor and kick it over to me. Do ya think I'm stupid, letting ya keep that gun where ya can reach it?"

Barnes complied. He felt like he was watching himself in slow motion as he kicked his gun over to Thompkins.

"Where's Bud?" Barnes asked as the gun skidded to a stop at Thompkins' feet.

"Hanging around. He's not going to bother us. That's a smart move—kicking yar gun to me. Ya know, I read about yar fine work in Manlo. Ya had to be rescued by a negro, no less. Ya screwed up there, and ya screwed up here. How ya got to be a detective is beyond me. Now, it's time to end yar pitiful existence."

"Wait," Barnes pleaded. "First, tell me why you killed Knowles."

"Sure, why not, since Janice and I gotta get a move on and nobody else will know what I tell ya because ya'll be dead. Knowles was a traitor to our great country. He was whining about the war and why we shouldn't be in Nam. Hell yes we should. We've got to stop the commies from taking over the world. Ya know, like dominos.

"Knowles was brainwashed by the Viet Cong, and when he returned to the U.S., he started to spin those commie lies, like we killed Ward Jenkins. Shit! Maybe he was a spy for them. I'm a patriot, damn it, and no Cong sympathizer is going to turn me away from my country! I have buddies over there, real soldiers.

"Yeah, and ya know what else? Knowles was forcing himself on Janice. It makes me sick!"

Janice shook her head vigorously, her eyes wide with fright.

"The best part was that our self-serving, righteous mayor provided me with the perfect cover. He egged on Dinkins and his goons to harass Knowles and Janice, which provided ya with suspects and allowed me to take care of Knowles under the radar. I invited Knowles to my house for drinks to bridge over our differences. He accepted. When he wasn't looking, I spiked his drink and now here we are.

"And there's another reason for yar predicament, Barnes—ya stole my girl. She was coming back to me until ya came to town flashing that damned ICC badge. We're meant to be together. I don't know what spell ya put on her, but it's about to end. When I pull the trigger, it's good-bye, Barnes."

Grinning wickedly, Thompkins raised his revolver and pointed it at Barnes' head.

A scream like a war cry erupted behind Thompkins as Bud's large hand flashed through the air and slashed downward, knocking the gun out of Thompkins' hand. The gun discharged, but the bullet hit the floor harmlessly, then ricocheted out of the way into a wall. Bud's left hand pushed Janice aside while his right arm wrapped around the chief's mid-section. With a burst of brute strength, Bud's legs pushed off the floor, and the two men hurtled through the plate glass window at the front of the store. Glass exploded in all directions and crunched around them.

Bud landed hard on top of Thompkins, cushioning his landing, but both men began to bleed from glass cuts.

"You came to hurt my family and friends," Bud spit, the heavy landing not in any way abating his rage. "You failed, and now you're gonna deal with me." Bud's fist slammed into Thompkins cheek, knocking him out. He raised his fist again and stopped.

"At ease, soldier," Barnes ordered. "You've done your job. He isn't going anywhere."

Barnes still had to wrestle with Bud's muscular arm to prevent him from striking Thompkins again.

"I'll take it from here, Bud." Barnes whipped out his handcuffs from his coat pocket and snapped them around Thompkins' wrists. "You did good. You saved my life and Janice's. You did *real* good."

Thompkins gradually came to as a siren announced the arrival of the Reed County Sheriff's Department.

As he looked around to get his bearings, Thompkins' eyes settled on Bud. "How the hell are ya here, dummy?"

Bud looked at Thompkins with disgust and pointed back to the store. Brent stood in the doorway, not moving.

"He's the real hero, *dummy*! You're a bad man, Ellis Thompkins, and a terrible cop. Goodbye to you!"

"What do you mean, Bud?" Barnes was confused. "Brent was involved?"

"Thompkins jumped me in the store. Janice had gone out on some errands, so I was alone. He pretended to be my friend and asked for something in the storeroom. I went back to get it. When I turned my back, he had his gun to my head. He told me if I didn't do what he said, he'd shoot me and then kill Alice and Lily. I can't let nothin' happen to them, so I didn't move or say nothin'. He tied my hands behind my back and taped my mouth shut. He put a noose around my neck and slung the rope over a ceiling pipe. He told me to stand on a chair and pulled the rope tight and tied it to the hook on the wall where we hang coats. He taped my legs together so I couldn't move. If I did, I would hang myself. I was in a bad spot.

"I never wanted to hurt somebody more than him, but I didn't want my family killed. I'd do anything to protect them. Thompkins said all would be OK if I didn't move because someone would find me and untie me. Then he jostled the chair with his foot and laughed."

People from the nearby stores and Main Street began to surround Thompkins, Bud, and Barnes. Janice stood by Brent, dazed, her hand resting on his shoulder. He had cut the tape that bound her hands.

Bud continued, "My body stretched as much as I could take. I felt wobbly. I couldn't yell or anything. I knew I couldn't keep my balance very long. I felt lightheaded. He was gonna let me hang.

"Janice had returned, and I could hear Thompkins yellin' at her, and he wasn't being kind. He said he would take her out into the country and kill her. Then he would kill himself. If he couldn't have Janice, no one would, especially you, Detective Barnes. He didn't like me working so close with her, either. I was so mad and couldn't do nothing.

"Then off to my right I saw him, Brent. He was coming in for his Saturday grocery pickup for Mrs. Ericson. Tell 'em, Brent."

Brent shuffled his feet and spoke softly, his voice shaking. "When I came in the storeroom, Bud shook his head at me—warning me. He was tied up and standing on a chair with a rope around his neck. I knew something was wrong, really wrong. I heard Mrs. Hinton and Chief Thompkins arguing in the front of the store. I was afraid.

"Bud kept turning his head to the left, and I saw the box cutters on a shelf. I used them to cut him loose. When he got down, he whispered to me there was a reckoning coming, and for me to run for help, but I couldn't move. Bud went out to where Mrs. Hinton and Chief Thompkins were, and I heard Detective Barnes' voice. Bud saved the day."

Brent looked at Bud as if he were a superhero from one of his comic books.

The crowd had grown larger. One new arrival was Carl Dinkins, released from custody, who was running an errand at the café.

"What's this?" Dinkins shouted as he rushed to the front of the crowd.

More deputies from Reed County pulled up as Barnes shouted to the crowd. "Back off and let the deputies do their job. Ellis Thompkins is going to be arrested for the murder of Gary Knowles and for the kidnapping and attempted murder of Dr. Deisman."

The crowd gasped. Their chief of police's involvement in such crimes was shocking.

"You asshole, Thompkins. You tried to blame me for murdering Knowles." Dinkins continued to push forward, but was stopped by a deputy.

Things quieted down and Barnes waved to Deputy Nelson. "Read Ellis Thompkins his rights and make sure he understands them. Then take him to the Carlson jail."

Nelson acknowledged and placed a shaken Thompkins in the squad car. "Good work, Fred." Nelson tipped his hat.

Afterward, Barnes said, "Everyone, go home. I'm sure the *Bee* will have the story soon." Barnes nodded to Max in the crowd.

"Let's go inside for a minute," Barnes said to Janice, Bud, and Brent. "Where it's quiet and we can talk."

Inside, Bud had finally cooled down and the fear in Janice's eyes had been replaced with a look of gratefulness. Brent still appeared in shock. Barnes went to the cooler and returned with several pops. "My treat," Barnes said and offered an Orange Crush to Brent. "You're a hero, son."

Brent forced a tiny smile.

Barnes continued, "I imagine the county attorney will take your statements, which will be used in Thompkins' trial. Janice, it would be best if you closed the store for the rest of the day. I can call Bert Jenkins and see if he can block the broken window with plywood. I'll drive all of you home once that's done. You were all incredibly brave today. Because of your courage, a criminal is going to be put away, hopefully for as long as he lives." Barnes gave the group a reassuring smile, thinking, *I am a good cop.*

Chapter 62

Saturday, November 7

Barnes underestimated the time it would take to do his drop offs after the altercation at the Hinton store. The town was abuzz about the happenings there, which prevented Barnes from sticking to the schedule he had set for himself.

First, when he could get away, Barnes drove Bud to his house. Bud's serious face had been replaced by a wide smile when he saw Alice and Lily. He was a proud man, and his wife and daughter were in awe of his courage. Never again would he be referred to as a man with a "damaged" mind, or in worse, even more derogatory terms. Bud was being hailed as a hero.

Barnes' next stop was Brent's house. Angela was home, and Tim drove in at the same time as Barnes. Tim slammed on his brakes and jumped out of his car.

"Your father was just coming downtown to pick you up," Angela cried as Brent climbed out of the car. "Are you all right?" She enveloped him in a tight embrace. "That had to be so scary."

Brent hugged her back.

"What happened? The town's in an uproar." Tim went over to Barnes and Janice.

"Thank God you're all safe. Janice, we were so worried." Angela left Brent and hugged the other woman.

They all turned to Barnes. "It was a team effort," he said. "Without Brent, Bud, and Janice's courage, people would have been badly hurt or killed. And we wouldn't have captured Gary's killer—alleged killer, I mean."

"I can't believe Ellis could have done that." Angela shook her head. Tim murmured an agreement.

"We don't fully understand Thompkins' motive." Barnes tapped his head. "He also kidnapped Dr. Deisman and was going to kill him, as well. He tried kidnapping Janice. We need to look into his past as a police officer. I wonder if anyone in Brinson ever checked out his record. Mayor Templeton needs to answer questions about Thompkins' hiring and several other things when he gets back from Florida."

"But Thompkins seemed to be doing a good job. He's about the last man I can think of who would do such a thing. He had us fooled." Tim placed an arm around his son.

"Janice told me he was too aggressive when he asked her out. And then Knowles moved into her apartment. Perhaps Thompkins thought Janice and Knowles were involved romantically. That and their anti-war views may have been the spark that drove him to murder. Janice and me being together may have turned that spark into a fire." Barnes shared a brief smile with Janice.

"Why did he kidnap Doc Deisman?" Angela asked. "He's well respected in the county."

"We're investigating his role. The doctor had a hand in covering up Knowles' death, and Thompkins wanted him gone. My guess is the doctor will readily confess and testify against Thompkins."

"We heard about the incident at the Best Western in Carlson yesterday—Eldon Juntlo injuring your partner and you shooting him," Tim said. "What a day!"

Brent looked at Barnes with surprise and then relief. "That's Mr. Juntlo's crazy brother. I'm glad he missed you."

"So am I."

"What's this world coming to?" added Angela.

"It could've been worse at the motel," Barnes said. "Fortunately, Detective Robinson and Mr. Juntlo will survive—they'll just spend their futures in different places."

Tim added, "It's well-known around here that Eldon's paranoia has gotten worse over the past few years. Something you said or did must have set him off."

"That's possible, though I'm not sure what."

"How's Rob doing?" Brent asked.

Angela's face was marked with concern. "Yes, we heard about the accident this morning. He's such a nice man."

"They don't know yet. They're pretty sure he'll recover, but say your prayers." Barnes thought of Reverent McFadden.

Angela looked lovingly at her son. "I want to tell you that the phone has been ringing off the hook during the past half-hour. There were the Jenkins, Jack, Ron, and Cindy—she called first. Lots of people are concerned about you. I can't tell you enough how thrilled your father and I are that you're safe and with us. My brave son."

Brent was happiest to hear Cindy's name. *She really likes me*, he thought.

"God, I hope the divisions in this town can heal a bit now," Tim said as he shook Barnes' hand. "It's been a rough couple of months here. Thank you."

Barnes glanced at Janice. She looked pale and restless. "Excuse me, everyone. I need to take Janice home. It's been a tough day for her.

Tim and Angela nodded, and Barnes and Janice left for her house. When they arrived, Barnes started to take Janice upstairs to rest.

"No, I'm not tired. Please stay with me."

"I need to go to Carlson. The day's not over yet. I'll be back in two shakes of a squirrel's tail." He smiled as he kissed her.

"It's a lamb's tail, silly." She laughed. "Honey, my brave detective, you took no credit for how things worked out. You deserve so much of our gratitude. If you hadn't been here, a lot of bad things would have happened. And Gary's death would have been ruled a suicide. Now he has justice."

"Oh, I give much of the credit to you and Bud. You two initiated Gary's need for justice when no one else did, and you didn't back down in the face of adversity. Rob deserves our thanks, too. He kept us on the right path. God, I hope he'll be OK."

Janice moved close to Barnes, staring into his eyes. "I don't know if I should say this, Fred, but … I'm falling hard for you. You're the bravest, most decent man I've ever met. It doesn't matter what happens at the ICC."

Barnes was taken off guard by her remarks and was at a loss for words, or words that made sense.

She put her finger on his lips. "You don't have to say anything. I know this has been fast, our relationship. But it feels right between us. You may not agree now, or ever. I just want you to know how I feel. I really care for you."

Barnes pulled Janice tight to his body and kissed her as thoughts jumbled in his mind. *I really like Janice and spending time with her. She's in Brinson, though, and I'm in Des Moines. How can that work out? Now, I have no job. Will that make a difference to her? What would Clara think?*

The doorbell rang, breaking the moment between the two. Barnes looked through the window to see who was there. He smiled, relieved. "You have visitors, Janice."

"Who?"

"The Jenkins—Lola and Bert."

"Please let them in."

"We'll talk later." Barnes kissed Janice, then opened the door.

Lola rushed in, hugging Janice. "We almost lost you!"

Barnes shook Bert's hand. "Thanks for coming, Bert, and for taking care of the store window. I gotta go."

Barnes slipped out of the house and motored his way back to Carlson. It was just after five o'clock in the late afternoon, and the sun was at the end of making its dreary descent into the November night.

Barnes' mind immediately shifted to thoughts of Janice. *Do Janice and I have a future together? What would that future be? Will it be love? What is my future after today? God, I need to focus on Rob.*

His first stop was the Reed County Sheriff's building. Neither Sheriff Larken nor Deputy Nelson was there, so he drove to the single-story county hospital.

Larken and Nelson stood outside Thompkins' room. Barnes glanced in and saw Thompkins wearing several bandages. He was handcuffed to his bed railing.

"We had to move him here," Nelson said. "His injuries are pretty severe. That Bud sure is strong. He would have killed Thompkins if you hadn't stopped him."

"I suppose you'll want a medal for your performance, Barnes," Larken scoffed.

"Well, you certainly don't deserve one," Barnes argued.

Barnes and Larken moved within a foot of each other, glaring.

"Easy, you two." Deputy Nelson pushed his way between them. "We're on the same side."

"I'm not sure about that, Deputy." Barnes continued to stare at Larken.

"I heard from your captain that today is your last day at the ICC. At least you finished with a bang. Time for you to go. It's after one o'clock in Des Moines, Barnes. Your captain is looking for you."

"We solved a murder, Sheriff." Barnes took two steps back and relaxed.

"I'll give you a little credit for that one. I also know that the hospital is full of people you've been involved with—Ellis Thompkins, Eldon Juntlo, your partner, and Doc Deisman. What does that say?"

"That your county isn't as clean as you think it is."

Larken frowned and stalked down the corridor without looking back.

Barnes turned to Nelson. "Wally, you'll want to keep an eye on Thompkins. He's shifty, and if he escapes, I bet he'll disappear."

"I understand. I'm planning on spending the night right here. In a couple of days, when he's better, we will transfer him to jail. Oh, and you should know we found a fishing boat stored in a Carlson warehouse—it's registered to Ellis Thompkins."

Barnes smiled. "Thanks, that's good to know."

Barnes walked to Robinson's room, who was preparing to check out of the hospital.

"Well, if it isn't the hero." Robinson laughed as Barnes entered his room. "Deputy Nelson stopped by and told me about you and Thompkins. What a nasty dude."

"It was teamwork that brought Thompkins down." Barnes patted Del on the back.

"You were the leader of the team. I think you should ask the captain for your position back—and a big raise. You have leverage, man."

"No, I'm going to resign. I can't work for that man anymore. I'll just have to find another job. One thing's for sure, you won't find another partner as handsome and wonderful as me!"

Both men laughed and Robinson added, "Yeah, I can retire in a couple years, and I will. Then Elmer and I are going to find the relatives of someone he fought with in the war. It'll be a spiritual vacation."

"Del, I'm having a hard time. Do you really think Elmer has changed that dramatically?"

"You have to be in a war to understand a warrior. To answer your question, yes, I believe in Elmer."

"What about your wife?"

"She'll want me to go. She says she needs a vacation from me. I must not be the teddy bear I think I am! Now, tell me about you and Janice. Any more details to reveal?"

"I haven't given any real thought to where we're going. I like her, but I live in Des Moines and she's here in Brinson. Long-distance relationships don't work. And I'm still not sure that I'm her type."

"What type is that?"

"I don't know if I'm ready for another commitment."

"Listen, partner. I've only known her for a few minutes. She's the way out of your loneliness. I promise, Clara wouldn't mind."

"We'll see." Barnes smiled.

Robinson smiled back. "That's all I need to know, man."

Robinson picked up a small bag of personal items from his stay at the hospital. He paused. "Tell me, do you have any more thoughts about the serial killer?"

"No, but I haven't forgotten. Three events have occurred on November 7: The disappearance of Richard Franklin Frost in 1940, the death of Constable Wilber Roberts by a train in 1950, and the death of Suzi Thornton by asphyxiation in 1960."

"You'll be hard pressed to convince anyone that those events are the work of one person. None of them have the word 'murder' written in red letters. We don't know and we may never know whether the bones found at Eldon's farm are Richard Frost's. Same with the bones Brent reportedly saw. Today is November 7 and no one has died or disappeared." Robinson scratched his cheek.

"Yet," Barnes intimated. "Any number of people could have died today. Rob, in particular, and the incident at the Hinton store could have claimed Janice, Bud, Thompkins, or me."

"That's true, but what's the motive for the serial killer that you've conjured up?"

"Today's incidents don't have anything to do with what has historically occurred on November 7. If you go back to 1940, Thompkins wasn't here then. The perpetrator is someone who has infinite patience and a deep hatred for Richard Franklin Frost. Wilber and Suzi seem connected to him. The mayor, perhaps? Eldon Juntlo? Whoever it is, he's a male at least fifty years old and from Brinson. But you seem convinced it's not Elmer."

"That's right, it's not Elmer. Sounds like you don't have any real suspects." Robinson raised his eyebrows. "Thirty years, 1940 to 1970, is a long time, man. He could be dead by now."

"Yeah, I know. The person I suspected as of last night was broadsided early this morning on his way to Brinson," Barnes said.

"You mean Rob?"

"Yeah, wrong theory. He fit the age profile. He was in his early twenties when his father went missing. From what I could find out, he and his father fought a lot. I also found a record that he may have been in Brinson the night Wilber Roberts died. But he's no longer a suspect. In fact, I believe he's the target."

"Let's ask him directly and get his thoughts."

"Good idea," responded Barnes. "His room is right down the corridor."

Rob was awake and watching television when the detectives entered his room. A nurse was taking his blood pressure. Also in the room was Max Sturgess.

"How did you get in here?" Barnes asked Sturgess, irritated.

"The deputies let me in. I'm doing a story on Ellis Thompkins' capture, and I want to hear Mr. Frost's insight and involvement in the case." Sturgess folded a sheet of paper and inserted it into his notebook.

"The story is going to have to wait, Max," Barnes said. "Rob is not in good shape."

Sturgess was disappointed. Barnes felt pity and said, "I promise to stop by your office at the *Bee* on Monday and give you as many details as I can, if that's good for you."

"Great. Say, nine o'clock?"

Barnes nodded.

Sturgess walked over to the window, which faced the parking lot. He gazed out the window for over a minute, prompting Barnes to ask, "What's so fascinating out there?"

"Nothing really." Sturgess kept staring. "I like looking at the night sky when daylight has ended. It has a calming presence, don't you agree?"

"Sure, but now you have to leave. I'll see you Monday."

"Good." Sturgess waved goodbye and left.

Barnes turned to Rob. "How are you feeling?"

Rob ignored the question and mumbled, "Besides this," he pointed at the hospital bed, "it's been a good day."

"Yes, it has." Barnes' smile lasted no more than a second. "We caught Knowles' killer, and Thompkins will hopefully be sent to prison for the rest of his life. No one died. But I know it's been a bad day for you."

"I'm just glad you got Thompkins. That was good detective work. The Wallers will be relieved." Rob tried a smile, but the pain was too much.

To Barnes, it looked like Rob had aged ten years in one day. He had the appearance of an old man, not the rugged, handsome Coloradoan.

"Can we discuss with you a little more, if you can take it, a November 7 suspect?" Robinson glanced at Barnes and said, "We think this person is going to strike again today, and you may be the target. We can't take that chance, so we'll request the sheriff's office provide security for you tonight."

"I have no idea who he is," Rob said, coughing, "but I'm convinced he tried to kill me and almost succeeded. I doubt he'll try again, considering there are less than six hours left in the day, and the police are here. Did anyone retrieve my Stetson from the accident scene?"

Barnes grinned. "We'll check. First, can we go over the events involving your father again? He disappeared on November 7, 1940. Did he have any enemies that would want to harm him?"

"No." Rob shook his head. "He lent money to several people, but I don't ever recall anyone threatening him. He wasn't a very nice man, though, especially to my mother and me."

"What about Wilber Roberts' death on November 7, 1950?" Robinson asked.

"Wilber was suspected of having an affair with my mother, but I know that's not true. He did have a crush on her, though. It bothers me that Wilber, a known teetotaler, would get so drunk that he would pass out on train tracks. That never made sense to me."

"Stranger things have happened, man." Robinson sat back in his chair.

"What about Suzi Thornton?" Barnes asked.

"Rumor had it that Dad and Suzi were also having an affair. I don't know about that one—perhaps yes, perhaps no. No one ever caught them, but I know they liked each other."

"Finally, why would anyone want to harm you?" Barnes sat on the edge of the bed. "You're not well-known here."

"I think it comes full circle. It all goes back to my dad and someone he pissed off. The other two, and me, are all spokes coming from Dad."

"The killer likely would be a least fifty to fifty-five years old with lots of patience," Barnes told him. "Ten years between events is a long time to wait. He's making a statement—'I'm so in control, I can do what I want.'"

"That's why this person doesn't fit any profile I have ever seen," Robinson added.

Rob fell asleep. Barnes and Robinson sat in silence thinking of possible suspects.

CRACK! An explosion of broken glass burst across the room.

Chapter 63

Saturday, November 7

Pandemonium broke out in Rob's room and spread into the hospital corridor. Barnes' mind darted for the cause of the shattered window. *Was it from a random blast? A rock? A bird?*

A nurse burst through the doorway. "What the—" she stammered.

Robinson shouted, "Look at the wall!"

Barnes' head spun to his left. In the wall just to the right of Rob's bed was a large black hole.

"Shit, that's from a bullet!"

Barnes threw himself under the window frame and yanked the blinds shut. "Turn off the lights!" he shouted.

The nurse flipped off the lights, then dropped to a crouch on the floor.

"Del, help me!" Barnes yelled. The two men pushed Rob's bed away from the window and next to a wall. Barnes, on his hands and knees, grabbed Rob's IV pole and wheeled it next to the bed. "He's OK."

Rob groaned, "What happened?"

Robinson and Barnes looked at the bullet hole in the wall. It didn't take long for both men to picture for whom it had been intended.

"Someone tried to kill you again, Rob—this time with a high-powered rifle," Barnes explained. "You're safe now."

"Someone really wants you dead," seconded Robinson.

"That's twice today. Who could be doing this?" Barnes asked no one in particular as his mind thought of the short list of possible suspects.

"Don't know," Rob murmured. "Not a clue. It could be people from my past … my past … in Denver. But why would they come here? And I don't know anyone here well enough to … to be their target."

"It totally fits the pattern we just discussed," Robinson said. "It's the completion of the circle, man."

Barnes moved into the corridor still crouching and stood up once he was alongside the wall. He waved for Robinson and the nurse to follow him.

"I know who the killer is, Del. At least, I think I do."

"Who?" Robinson squinted at Barnes.

Barnes whispered a name into Robinson's ear. Robinson's eyebrows shot up in surprise.

"I'm going to play out my hunch. I'll radio you when I know something. I need you to stay here and guard Rob. We can't afford a third attempt on his life if I'm wrong."

Deputy Nelson ran up to Barnes and Robinson. "I heard the hospital took fire. I only have two deputies here."

"I don't have time to explain. Follow what Del says. And for God's sake, keep eyes on Thompkins and Juntlo. They may take this opportunity to escape. Call for assistance."

Barnes grabbed his overcoat and ran hell bent to his car in the parking lot. As he climbed into the car, a thought ran through his mind. *That was reckless. What if the gunman was lying in wait for me or anyone else to leave the hospital?* Barnes took a deep breath. To his relief, there were no follow-up gunshots. He looked toward the road and in the distance saw the taillights of a pickup truck moving fast away from the hospital on the highway going north. *That's him. That's the shooter.*

Barnes followed the truck for about half a mile. *If my hunch is right, I know where you're going, so I'm going to take another way. I'm glad I took the time to get to know these roads.* Barnes took a left onto a gravel road at the next intersection. Barnes didn't know it, but the decision saved his life.

The pickup truck stopped and pulled over at the downslope of a hill. The driver left the truck with his rifle and waited for Barnes to drive over the hill and down to him.

The gunman cursed after waiting for two minutes, realizing Barnes had turned back, or was going somewhere else. The man glanced at his watch. It showed six-thirty. *There are still at least five hours to get Rob Frost,* he thought. *I'll return home and regroup. It's dark, and the night is just beginning. Maybe I can substitute that interfering Barnes for Frost as my final kill. He's become a real pain in my ass.*

The gunman got back into his car and drove to his farm. The farmstead consisted of a residence and several outbuildings, including a typical barn, a pole barn, and three thirty-foot silos. The buildings were surrounded by one hundred and fifteen acres of prime farmland.

Barnes reached the farm ahead of the gunman and parked out of sight from the road and behind an outbuilding. He did not have a rifle, so his reliable Smith & Wesson .38 Special would have to do. Using the outbuilding for cover, Barnes watched as the gunman drove his vehicle up to the farmhouse, left the truck, and crossed to the house carrying his rifle. *He's got a big bore rifle,* Barnes thought. *Getting into a gunfight with him will not be good—he could easily blow me away.*

The gunman and his rifle vanished into the house only to return a minute later. He stepped out onto the porch stretching his arms over his head and staring into the dark night at Barnes' location. He turned and went back inside, closing the door.

Barnes had little time to think about what he was going to do. He radioed Deputy Nelson with his location. He stared at the gunman's house, thinking about Manlo. *He knows I'm out here. This time, I don't have Del to back me up. It's just me against him. To hell with procedures. This may be stupid, but I don't intend to lose this time. I must act now.*

He reached into his glove compartment and pulled out his backup firearm. It was older than the .38 Special, but it would have to do. He checked the gun's ammunition and when satisfied, tucked the gun in his belt behind his back. *Good to go,* he thought.

Barnes inhaled deeply and smelled the country air on a cold night. He sneaked quietly onto the porch and turned the doorknob—it was unlocked. He knew the gunman was waiting for him. With his revolver at the ready, Barnes walked cautiously into the house.

The front door opened into an empty foyer with a mirror hanging on the wall facing the door. Barnes moved silently into the living room, his gun leading the way. There was a small lamp on an end table that provided dim light to the room. *No sign of the gunman here.* The living room adjoined the kitchen. Other than some light provided by a night light by the stove, the kitchen was dark. Barnes was sweating even though the house was chilly. He used his coat sleeve to dry off his forehead.

Side-by-side wooden doorframes ahead showed Barnes two ways out of the kitchen. One room was dark, and the other had a soft light coming from a lamp with a stained-glass shade. Barnes trod quietly into the room with the lamp. He froze when he saw the dark outline of a figure sitting on a leather sofa facing him.

"Good evening, Detective Barnes—or, should I say, good evening, Fred." The figure spoke in a steely monotone. "Welcome to my home."

"You don't believe in using lighting much, do you, Max."

"There are times I don't care to be seen." Sturgess' figure blended in with the shadows. Sturgess sat forward and Barnes saw Sturgess' rifle pointed at his chest.

"Please put your gun on the floor and step over to me. This rifle can blow a hole in you as big as a softball."

Barnes sighed and did as he was told. "How did you know I was here?"

"I could say it was because of my highly skilled hunting instincts, or I could say I saw the reflection off one of your taillights—you pick."

"Why do all this?"

"We all have times when evil takes over our minds, and this is one of those times." Sturgess patted his rifle.

"Is that why you killed Richard Frost, Wilber Roberts, and Suzi Thornton, and tried to kill Rob Frost?"

"Are you theorizing, or do you have evidence? Pardon me, I'm not showing you any hospitality. Would you care for a drink?"

Barnes ignored Sturgess' questions, although he was thirsty. "I know it was you who shot at Rob in the hospital. I saw the taillights of your pickup drive off, and they're the same lights I watched come to the farm a few minutes ago. You've been a suspect of mine for a couple days now."

"Good for you, but that's just your word against mine. I have a wonderful reputation in town," Sturgess said smugly. "No one would believe you—an outsider—over me. I can tell you Sheriff Larken sure wouldn't."

"Let's go back to the beginning, Max. Why Richard? What did he do to you?"

"Technically, Richard didn't do anything to me—at least, not directly. It was my father. You see, Richard was greedy—one of the worst. My father needed money to keep the paper going, so Richard lent him what he needed. The amount isn't important, but it was substantial. Dad was struggling to get out of the Great Depression—his advertisers were hurting and subscriptions had decreased. So, Richard's loan kept the paper afloat. That's the good, don't you think?

"However, the time came to repay the loan. Dad begged Richard for a break in the repayments—just a year's grace period, that was all—but Richard would have none of it. He demanded full payment on the loan's due date or he would take ownership of the paper and sell it to an interested party in Carlson. That may have been Richard's plan all along. It tore my dad up and he suffered. That's the bad.

"You see, when you have newspapering in your blood, you just can't cast it aside. It runs too deep. My father suffered a mental breakdown and then a stroke when he was about to lose the paper. He was a vegetable after that. Can you imagine, a vital, caring man reduced to nothing better than a piece of wood because of *him*?

"Richard cared nothing about the paper, except to harass my mother about the loan. Two days before the foreclosure, he simply disappeared. It was perfect and no evidence ever came forward regarding what happened to the son of a bitch. His ledger book of debtors disappeared with him—never found.

"I got a kick out of what people said, that he was murdered, took off with a mistress, and, my favorite, that he was abducted by aliens."

"What did you do with the body?"

"Look around you—Richard Frost is everywhere."

"Is it the partial skeleton we found in Eldon's dump site? Or the bones in Elmer's barn?"

"I don't have the answer to those questions. You should know that back then, a lot of people in town owed that predator money. I did them all a favor."

"What about Wilber Roberts and Suzi Thornton? Why did you kill them?"

"There you go again, Fred. You assume I killed them." Sturgess cocked his head to the left and grinned.

"Did you?"

"I may have had a hand in their demise. It was actually a train that killed Wilber and a furnace that finished Suzi. Wilber was a friend of Richard's and an admirer of Ethel. He also collected debts from people who owed Richard, like my father. Suzi was pretty, no doubt about that. She was also a friend of Richard's and, in my mind, too friendly for a friend. I liked Ethel. She was too good for her parasitic husband."

"Then we have Rob. Why him?"

"Rob is Richard's scion. I know they didn't get along and, at first, I had no intention of involving Rob. But he came back snooping around, and he's the seed from the rotten fruit. That reminds me, the time today to get him grows shorter." Sturgess winked.

"I don't understand how you missed Rob in the hospital. I thought you were a crack shot."

"Actually, you should know, that was my second option," Sturgess said matter-of-factly. "My first option was to adjust his medication just enough to kill him—painlessly, I might add. In fact, Wilber and Suzi had merciful deaths. But, that nurse and one of those cops were always in Rob's room, and I never had a chance to fix that.

"So, I decided to shoot him. It's always good to have a plan B," Sturgess said as he patted his rifle again. "I parked my truck in the lot outside his room. A single-story hospital allows for a dead-on shot. I was checking out my shot line from inside the room when you showed up.

"I went back out to my truck and set the shot. It was dark and no one was around. I stood on the truck bed and used the top of the cab to steady my aim. But that damned cancer and those treatments caused my arms to shake, and I missed him by a hair! Those worthless doctors screwing me around." Sturgess' calm demeanor changed to frustration.

"In my younger days, it would have been an easy shot, but now I get the shakes. Rob is like a cat—he has more than one life.

"By the way, just so you know, my shaking is under control now. There is some good to modern medicine," Sturgess said, shrugging.

Barnes cringed. Stalling, he asked, "Why does this all occur on November 7?" Trying not to be obvious, Barnes felt the butt of his gun on his backside.

"If you would have done your homework like a good detective, you would have learned that date was my dad's birthday. He turned fifty-five the day that asshole Richard was about to steal the paper from him. He had the stroke then. I was thirty at the time. I was the mild, meek man who sat off to the side. I was a ghost in the office."

Barnes started to reach for his weapon, only to be halted by Sturgess' gaze. It was a chilling look of absolute calm.

"I'm not really a serial killer, Fred. I do have great patience, though. Ten years is a long time to wait between events. The paper kept me busy. Except, I have one last task to accomplish, and then I can rest in peace. You, sir, are in my way. Come to think of it, you've added yourself to my list of prey. You can take Rob's place."

Barnes wanted one more piece of information. "I'll bet there's a truck in one of your buildings with a smashed front end."

"What makes you think it was the front end? Once again, you assume too much. I knew traffic coming from Carlson to Brinson would be light that early in the morning, and it was. I put up a barrel with a flashing light and a couple of cones in the road when I saw headlights about half a mile away.

"I waited and when the car slowed down and I saw it was the black Cadillac, I rammed the back end of my truck hard into the driver's side of his car. There was quite an impact. I pushed Rob's car into the deep ditch at that spot. I figured if the crash didn't kill him, the cold would. I never thought another car would come by so quickly. I picked up my barricade and cones and returned here, unseen.

"Now, where is that pickup?" Sturgess continued icily. "You'll never know." Then he laughed.

In an instant, Sturgess lifted the rifle and fired at the sole light in the room. The explosion from the gun and the bursting glass from the lamp were simultaneous.

Barnes belly flopped on the floor and crawled like a snake with its tail on fire to the open door leading into a dark room.

"You know I like to hunt, and I've honed my hunting skills, so I sense things in the dark," Sturgess' voice called out. "Your backup peashooter won't help you against my rifle. I know where you are. I only need one shot."

In the dimly lit house, Barnes saw a door leading outside. He raced to it on his hands and knees, jumped back up on his feet, and, still ducking, flung it open and ran outside. *I have a better chance out here,* he thought. The cold night air brushed against his face. The air was still. He wasn't concerned about the weather, though, only the man inside. He pulled the revolver from behind his back. "Thank God, I made it outside with this gun," he muttered.

Barnes noticed a small white structure to his left and dashed for it, rolling onto the ground as he reached the building. An undersized yard light fought to illuminate the area between the house and the building, providing shadow cover for Barnes.

A voice came from outside the house to Barnes' right. "You need to be a little stealthier, Fred. I know where you are."

Barnes shook his head. *I don't think he can see me.* He knew he had to be silent as a mouse with a fox nearby. The door to the building was partially open. Barnes peered into the dark and saw what looked like the outline of a pickup truck. The rear was smashed in.

He knew he had to make a choice: barricade himself inside the building or stay outside. Both choices carried risks. *If I stay inside, Sturgess will have to come to me. On the other hand, I could be trapped and maybe that's what he wants. If I stay outside, I'll have the freedom to move about and can't be pinned down. Yet, he has the advantage outside. He knows his farm, and I don't. Shit.*

Barnes thought of the trap in the basement in Manlo. *I know what to do.*

He moved away from the door and crept along the edge of the building. The small clearing with the muted yard light lay in front of him. He remained there, not moving. The farm was completely silent. There was no wind, no animals, no Sturgess, nothing. Barnes knew Sturgess was not playing anymore.

Barnes was alarmed to see his breath crystallizing in front of his face. *God, Sturgess will see that and shoot me in the head.* Barnes slowed his breathing and took shallow breaths. Seconds passed that felt like hours. The cold penetrated his body, but he didn't care. *Sturgess wants me to move from this position, and when I do, I'm finished.*

Barnes was shocked to hear a voice that seemed to come from above him.

"I know where you are, Fred. It's only a matter of time. You'll get cold, start shaking, and make an error. Then you're mine. Oh, and when the police come after I call them, I'll tell them I shot an armed intruder who I thought was going to rob me or do even worse. I was scared for my life. They'll believe me, a life-long resident with an impeccable reputation, while you're an interloper with a checkered past who's made enemies in your short time here. And, you'll be dead, so you won't have a say."

Barnes knew the standoff was coming to an end. *Sturgess is trying to trick me into revealing my position by getting me to talk. I won't do that. I'm not going to screw this up. I'm down to one play before I either freeze or Sturgess picks me off.*

Barnes calculated the likely spot where Sturgess was. It was near the top of the silo on Barnes' left. He felt along the edge of the outbuilding where he was crouched and found a loose fist-sized rock. *First break I've had tonight,* he thought.

As quietly as possible, Barnes tossed the rock off to his left into the shadows where it hit something hard. The blast from the silo shattered the rock as it hit the object. Barnes saw the flash of Sturgess' gun. Barnes stood and unloaded five shots at the flash. He then flung himself behind the safety of the building, hugging the wall.

After a moment, Barnes heard a thud, like a bag of grain falling from the sky, followed by a moan. He counted to ten and heard nothing further. He reversed his way back around the building that had been his shelter. In the faint light, he saw a body on the ground, unmoving. He heard another groan. Barnes walked in a wide arc and approached the body from behind. As he got closer, he saw Sturgess lying on his back.

Off in the distance, Barnes could hear the wailing of sirens coming his way.

"You didn't get me," Sturgess gasped. "It was my lousy balance. Damned cancer. I should have finished you off in my study. I tried to be too clever and that did me in."

"You would have been discovered anyway, Max. I told the deputy and my partner that I suspected you, and I radioed into them that I was at your farm. Even if you had killed me, it was over. Hear them coming?"

Sturgess gurgled up blood. "Rob was to be my last. I'm dying of cancer, so if you didn't get me, the cancer would have. I'll never spend a minute in jail. Too bad, huh?" Sturgess' words came in gasps, and he grew quieter. "I don't regret anything. Make … make sure Mabel keeps the paper going. I'm a newspaperman."

Sturgess turned his head and exhaled a final breath.

Deputy Nelson was the first to arrive at Sturgess' farm. Robinson rode with the deputy. Next was the Reed County sheriff. A host of emergency vehicles followed close behind, including ambulances, a fire truck, and an Iowa State Trooper sedan. The lights from the vehicles focused on Barnes as he squatted by Sturgess.

"Drop your weapon, Barnes, and put your hands behind your back." Sheriff Larken jumped from his vehicle and pointed his gun at Barnes.

"Wait," Barnes yelled back. "I didn't try to kill Rob—it was Max Sturgess, and he just tried to kill me."

"We'll see about that, Barnes. Looks to me like you're mixed up in this in a bad way. Max was a friend of mine, and a prominent Brinson citizen. And you're armed and trespassing on his property. God, you're involved in a lot of shit around here. Now, do as I say!"

Barnes gently placed his gun on the ground and put his hands up.

"Arrest him, Deputy." Larken nodded at Nelson.

"The truck Sturgess used to ram Rob's car is in this building. Check the back end." Barnes pointed to the small outbuilding.

Several men with flashlights hustled into the shed. Deputy Nelson emerged and shouted, "Detective Barnes is telling the truth. The truck is in here. It has a damaged back end."

"Sturgess didn't die from a bullet. It looks like a fall from up there killed him," Robinson said as he swept his flashlight over Sturgess' body and then up to the top of a silo at a walkway without a railing. Robinson also saw Sturgess lying on his rifle. The end of the barrel pointed out from under Sturgess' left shoulder. "Detective Barnes is telling the truth."

"And," Barnes added, "Sturgess is behind three murders and two attempted murders."

"Back off, Sheriff." Nelson walked over and stood between Larken and Barnes. "It's over."

Larken slid his gun into its holster. Without looking at Barnes or anyone else, he swore, got in his car, and drove away.

Robinson came up to Barnes. "That's pretty impressive detective work, man. Solving two cases in one day, and the cherry on top is getting that pompous ass of a sheriff to drive away with his tail between his legs."

"That's a real compliment coming from you, Detective Robinson."

The two men embraced awkwardly before Barnes said, "I'm so glad this is over. I feel like a weight has been thrown off me."

"Nice work, Fred." Nelson patted Barnes on the back. "We'll close off the farm tonight and search for evidence in the morning."

"When you search the house, I think you'll find all the evidence you need. I'll bet he kept souvenirs of his deeds."

Barnes stayed on the scene for another hour. When he had accomplished all he needed to for the night, he drove to Janice's house. She anxiously awaited him.

"It's all over now. We have Gary's killer in custody, and we know who tried to kill Rob—it was Max Sturgess."

"I just heard from Bert. Wow!" She closed her eyes and gently shook her head. "Never would I have thought that he was capable of such violence. Just like Ellis—who would have known? Angela has said many times, 'What's this world coming to.' Now I know what she means."

"Sturgess was also the perpetrator behind three murders," Barnes explained. "Wilber Roberts, Suzi Thornton, and Richard Franklin Frost, and almost two others—Rob and me."

"Brinson owes you big time." For the first time in a while, her voice was light and relaxed. "I want to be the first to reward you."

They kissed, and Janice started to unbutton his shirt.

"I think I'll favor this reward over all the others." Barnes smiled. "First, let me make us a couple of Old Fashioneds."

Des Moines, Iowa

2020

Chapter 64

Tuesday, September 22

They say that in the eyes of a child, a year is an eon. To an older person, a year seems like the blink of eye. George Harrison sang All Things Must Pass, *and so do the years. In some ways, Brinson, Iowa, did not change in the fifty years since 1970. The town continued to exist with its Main Street and commercial and residential buildings. New houses were constructed on the east side of town. The population remained around two thousand souls.*

Yet, the people and businesses in those buildings changed between 1970 and 2020. After changing hands several times, the Thirsty Bull became Down-the-Hole. The theater closed and was turned into a museum. The drive-in restaurant and bowling alley managed to stay open. Most people who lived in Brinson in 1970 died or left town during those intervening years.

Eldon Juntlo was found guilty of the attempted murder of two police officers and operating an illegal dump. He was sentenced to twenty years in prison. He was later diagnosed with paranoid-schizophrenia and dementia, and was moved to a mental facility in north central Iowa. He lasted less than six months before he was found dead of natural causes in the facility's laundry room.

Ellis Thompkins was convicted of murdering Gary Knowles and kidnapping Dr. Henry Deisman with the intent to murder, among other serious crimes. He was sentenced to life in prison at the Iowa State Penitentiary. He did not have Eldon's luck and survived more than twenty years there.

Elmer Juntlo took over his brother's farm and operated it far better than Eldon had. All dumping on the property ceased. Elmer's transformation continued, and within five years, he was voted to the Brinson Town Council. He married late in life.

Because of his value as a doctor to the community and no previous criminal history, Dr. Henry Deisman was sentenced to five years' probation for his involvement in covering up Knowles' murder. He never stepped outside the law again.

Harry "Civil War" Templeton died in Florida one day after Ellis Thompkins' arrest and Max Sturgess' death. Foul play was not suspected and because of his age, no autopsy was conducted. He was succeeded by Bert Jenkins, who proved to be a good, effective mayor.

Even though Max Sturgess was an alleged serial killer, the matter did not attain much prominence in the media. His attempt to kill Rob Frost and Fred Barnes was without question; however, his role in Richard Franklin Frost's disappearance and the deaths of Wilber Roberts and Suzi Thornton proved to be murky. Barnes, Robinson, and other law enforcement officials knew Sturgess was the killer. Yet, Sturgess was dead, as were his victims. No law enforcement department cared to spend much time or money pursuing the cases further, so they were dropped.

Max Sturgess had no family, so he bequeathed the Brinson Bee *to Mabel Knuth upon his death. She was to be the owner and publisher. The bequest stated she had to wait ten years before selling it. Mabel did what was required. On the first week after ten years had passed, she sold the paper to a Carlson interest and moved to Reno, Nevada, with her husband.*

The Reed County supervisors grew dissatisfied with Sheriff Larken and his management of Sturgess' and Knowles' deaths. Barnes', Robinson's, and Deputy Wally Nelson's testimonies before the supervisors hastened their decision. Larken was given the choice to resign or be fired. He retired and moved to the Sand Hills of Nebraska. Nelson replaced him as sheriff.

Bud Nichols was given a well-deserved award for his bravery in capturing Thompkins. He eventually purchased the Hinton General Store from Janice at a reduced price, and he and Alice operated it successfully for fifteen years before selling it and retiring. Lily attended the University of Iowa and became a certified public accountant.

Del Robinson retired from the ICC two years after his time in Brinson. He kept his promise to Elmer and the two found Isiah Jones' family, who were living in

Texas. Upon returning to Des Moines, Del and his wife moved to Iowa City where he volunteered at the Veteran's Administration Hospital.

After he recovered from his injuries, Rob Frost returned to Colorado. This time, he drove back in a white Cadillac wearing his usual black Stetson, which was a little worse for wear. He died of a massive heart attack seven years after his return. He told Fred he felt great relief after Max was identified as the man who kidnapped and killed his father. Rob and Brent corresponded occasionally before Rob's death. In his last correspondence, Rob sent Brent a plaque with the following words:

Take all the things life gives you.
Take the bad, embrace it and learn from it, then push it aside.
Take the good, embrace it and learn from it, then hold it
dearly.
Choose the path that will take you
To where the corn grows tallest.

Tim and Angela Frost were born, lived, and died in Brinson. In their later years, they traveled around the country a little including to Washington, D.C. They even took a Caribbean cruise. They were good parents to Brent and taught him how to do the right things and live life to the fullest. When they passed, there were no more Frosts residing in Brinson.

Fred Barnes was given several commendations for his key role in solving Gary Knowles' murder, as well as the crimes committed by Max Sturgess. The ICC captain offered Fred his job back. He declined the offer. The Brinson town council instead appointed him as the Chief of Police in place of Ellis Thompkins. Fred accepted the appointment and chose Bud as an adjunct deputy. Fred and Elmer reconciled. They weren't friends, but they respected each other.

Fred and Janice did fall in love. They were married in late summer of 1971, and Fred moved with Fluffy to Brinson. Fred and Janice found true happiness together. Janice continued to own and run the Hinton Store until she sold it to Bud.

After four terms in office, Fred retired. He and Janice moved to Santa Fe, New Mexico and opened a studio for local artists. They had a daughter in Brinson and named her Claire. She is currently a pediatrician in Albuquerque, New Mexico.

The Wallers returned to Carlson to bring Gary's body back to Minnesota for burial. A year later, the folks in Brinson had a 'moral correction' and held a memorial service for Gary at the cemetery. The lieutenant governor and other dignitaries attended. The Veterans of Foreign Wars saluted Gary's memory, and the Wallers were presented with a perfectly folded American flag. Carl Dinkins attended the ceremony sober and in clean clothes. The sun shone that day.

Brent's friends all chose different paths that led them away from Brinson. Jack became a high school science teacher in northeast Iowa, which was a surprise to his friends. Ron went into government as an IRS agent. Tom moved to the West Coast and was a mountain guide for a time. He returned to Iowa up by Lake Okoboji in later years and became a successful farmer. Shy Dale became a fighter pilot.

Cindy was accepted into the Northwestern University Medical School and became a doctor specializing in endocrinology at a hospital in Illinois. She and Brent remained good friends throughout high school. They went to prom together during their junior and senior years. It was years later that he learned she had married another doctor.

As for Brent, I am here to tell you that I'm doing fine. I graduated from Brinson High School in 1974. During 1970-1974, I worked for Elmer in his barn and on the farm. In all my years and travels, I never met a more interesting person than Elmer.

I never settled down or lived anywhere very long. I worked in the Forest Service in the Black Hills of South Dakota, as a game warden in Minnesota, and as a policeman in Kansas City and Sacramento. I also write mystery novels in my spare time. The fall of 1970 and my travels since have given me a lot of material about which to write, including for this book.

I never married. I came close on two occasions, but the truth is, no one measured up to Cindy in my own stubborn mind. I guess you could say she was my first crush and my only true love.

You may wonder what became of the casket-like boxes (including the one with the bones) I saw in Elmer's barn that went missing. An investigation was launched, but unfortunately the only person with knowledge about them was Eldon, and he never divulged any information. Perhaps he never knew anything as he was strictly a middleman, or he just forgot with his dementia. He kept no records. The matter was dropped after Eldon died.

You also may wonder what became of the bones found in the dump site on Eldon's farm. The identity of the skull and bones was never determined. The forensic tools of today, including DNA analysis, could be used to help identify them, but the skull and bones were lost over time. Whether they were Richard Franklin Frost's remains a mystery—some mysteries are never solved. I believe the bones were his, though.

I'd like to add that for the first time in my writing career, I have written a non-fiction book—this book. The story in this book is true and is a biography of sorts. I collaborated with my good friend, Fred Barnes, to write this account, while both of our memories are still intact. Fred also kept copious notes, which proved invaluable.

To my readers, I want to thank you for following an aging man's recollections of the most influential time of his life. The fall of 1970 was a time of change for the country, the state, the local folks, and me. For some people, the changes were for the better; for others, they were not so good. But that's what life is—a time of inevitable and constant change. Those who do well adapt to the changes and move forward. That's what I've tried to do with my own life—go where the corn grows tallest.

A final note: The Vietnam War came to its ugly, convulsive, and predictable end in the spring of 1975. I'll let you, my readers, decide whether the sacrifices made by our servicemen—such as Bud Nichols, Ward Jenkins, and Gary Knowles—were worth it. I do know this: We owe them our deepest gratitude and appreciation.

Chapter 65

Tuesday, September 22

Brent Frost circled the title "Epilogue" at the top of the last chapter of the book. He carefully shuffled the pages together and placed them in a folder. He smiled a smile of complete satisfaction.

"It's done," he said to Barkley. "Now it's off to the publisher."

The dog wagged her tail, hoping for a treat. "You need to go outside?"

The dog jumped up on her hind legs with her front paws resting on Brent's blue jeans.

"OK, girl, OK." Brent opened the door of his Des Moines home and Barkley sprinted outside.

A minute later the dog returned. "Here's your treat." Brent tossed it to the dog.

Brent walked over and pulled a putter out of his golf bag and lined up a shot. He putted the golf ball into the electric horizontal cup that returned the ball to him. *Nice*, he thought.

Two more times he putted directly into the hole with the same positive results. He felt his stomach growl and looked at his watch. *Wow, where did the time go? It's five forty-five and I'm hungry.*

"Barkley, what do you say, let's celebrate. I'll order a pizza from Roselli's."

Brent dialed the number from memory and placed the order.

"Thirty minutes," he announced to the dog. "You can have some crust."

While Brent waited for the pizza, he walked back over to the table and opened his laptop. After he clicked a couple of buttons, he read the email message. He had reread it multiple times, but he enjoyed reading it again.

Hi Brent,

I'm so pleased we've reconnected after all these years. See, there are some good things about social media!

I want to let you know that I'll be visiting Des Moines in three weeks and hope to arrive at my sister's house on Wednesday, October 15. You remember my sister, Cheryl? She lives in West Des Moines.

My divorce from Rick has been finalized, and I have retired from my medical practice—it was time for both. I'm considering moving to Des Moines to be closer to my family and old friends, and to start over.

If I'm not intruding, I'd like to see you when I'm back. I think often about our days in Brinson with my family, your family, Elmer Juntlo, and the rest.

I'd like us to be reacquainted again. Below is my cell phone number.
Warmest Regards,
Cindy

Brent still could not believe what he was reading. Fifty years had vanished in a flash. He remembered that first kiss she placed on his cheek. He knew Cindy was the only girl he could love. He felt warm inside.

Memories from Brent's past flooded into his mind as he rubbed Barkley. *I've been fortunate to have had a good life,* he thought. *I have a few regrets. One is the Billy Bridges matter. Dale told me Billy is an Episcopalian priest in Virginia. Good for Billy. I hope he's doing well.*

Brent flashed a brief scowl. *My biggest regret is not trying harder with Cindy. We should have ended up together, like in the fairy tales, but I let her get away. I should have done something—anything—but I didn't. I was too immature. She was always my one true love and I believe I was hers.*

Now we have come full circle as we will both be in Des Moines and who knows, maybe we can finally be together.

In the end, we can't control time—it controls us. How we manage our lives within the margins of that time is what counts. I value that time and accept nothing less.

The End

ACKNOWLEDGEMENTS

I would not be where I am with *Where the Corn Grows Tallest* without several talented people's contributions to the book.

Lindsay Pietenpol was the primary person who I depended on during my work on the book. Lindsay patiently incorporated multiple rounds of revisions to the manuscript. She also provided advice and was my copy editor and chief proofreader. She wore many important "hats."

Ann Howard Creel was my developmental editor and reader. Having never written a murder mystery novel, I found her comments to be thought provoking and they made the book better.

Nicky Galliers was my editor for the second editions of *Into the Realm of Time* and *From the Realm of Time*. For these Roman-based books, she guided me to add greater authenticity and improved writing. For *Where the Corn Grows Tallest*, Nicky again was an editor and her recommendations to improve the book were invaluable.

Jim Tasse provided insight to characters in the book who were veterans. Jim served in the U.S. Navy from 1971 to 1975 and achieved the rank of HM2. He served part of that time off the coast of Vietnam on an aircraft carrier. Today, Jim is a lecturer in the theatre department at the University of Wisconsin-Milwaukee. He is a co-founder of Feast of Crispian, a veteran's support group.

Kimmy Tran prepared the cover for the book. She is a graphic designer who loves combining her passion for books with her artistic talents. With 10 years of design experience under her belt, she's discovered that book covers are her favorite projects to work on.

Ashley Eklund, Jason Hattery, and **Shanna McLain** were my primary contacts in document production. I am "old school" and like to read the page in front of me rather than on a computer screen. They provided those printed pages to me and other reviewers.

My family, including my wife, **Marcie**, son, **Jeff**, and daughters, **Emily** and **Christy**, provided opinions, comments, and encouragement to me during the completion of the book. I truly value their contributions.